THE WOLF HUNT

ALSO BY TIM HODKINSON

Odin's Game
The Raven Banner
The Wolf Hunt

THE WOLF HUNT

Book Three of The Whale Road Chronicles

Tim Hodkinson

An Aries Book

First published in the the United Kingdom in 2020 by Aries,
an imprint of Head of Zeus Ltd

This paperback edition first published in 2021 by Aries

9 7 5 3 2 4 6 8

A CIP catalogue record for this book is available from the
British Library.

ISBN (PB): 9781800246409
ISBN (E): 9781788549974

Typeset by Siliconchips Services Ltd UK

Cover design © Chris Shamwana

Printed and bound in Great Britain by
CPI Group (UK) Ltd, Croydon CRO 4YY

Aries
c/o Head of Zeus
First Floor East
5–8 Hardwick Street
London EC1R 4RG

www.headofzeus.com

For Trudy and my three valkyries: Emily,
Clara and Alice.

One

Gandvik, Norway
ad 935 – Early Summer

The dead horse's eyes, black and shiny as a pool in a bog, gazed upwards as though fixed on something high in the sky. Its jaw was slack and the big purple tongue, dry and rough, lolled from the open mouth. There were flecks of dried blood along the muzzle. Its thick neck stopped short, severed about a hand's breadth beneath the animal's ears. It sat, skewered, on the top end of a wooden pole that was about the height of a man. The bottom end of the pole was driven deep into the earth of a little island. The pole was black with the dried blood of the creature. There was no sign of a body.

Surt ran a finger down the long, cold cheek of the beast, disturbing a cloud of flies that buzzed around it. The skin of his hand was almost as black as the horse's eyes.

'Why would someone do this to such a beautiful creature?' he said, shaking his head in disbelief. His words were in the tongue of the Norse but his accent spoke of the blazing hot lands far to the south beyond Serkland.

'It's a *níðstang*,' Einar Thorfinnsson, who stood beside Surt, said. 'A cursing pole.'

The whites of Surt's eyes flashed as he glanced right and left.

'This is witchcraft?' he said, his voice reduced to a hoarse whisper.

They had spotted the cursing pole as they sailed along the fjord. The little island it sat on was in the middle of the water that stretched between mountainous shores whose summits were still snow-capped despite the approaching summer. Ulrich, the leader of the crew, had ordered Roan the skipper to guide the ship in so they could take a closer look. The skipper had grounded his *knarr* on the rocky beach and the little company aboard clambered ashore. Now they stood in a semicircle around the cursing pole. The sea that filled the fjord was as smooth and flat as if it were frozen. A soft wind rolled down from the surrounding mountains to tug at the hair of the ten men and one woman with fingers chilled by the snow. The same breeze ruffled the fur of the wolf pelts that seven of the men wore around their shoulders, the cloaks of the *úlfhéðnar*, Odin's own wolf warriors.

'Witchcraft?' Einar said. 'Yes. This is *seiðr*.'

Ulrich, his upper lip curled, looked up at the dark, forbidding cliffs that glowered around them.

'Gandvik is a wild, witch-haunted country,' he said. 'The folk here have strange beliefs and odd notions about the gods.'

'Who would want to curse travellers sailing up the fjord?' Surt said.

Skarphedin Harsson – Skar to his friends – grunted. The big man was squatting on his haunches as he examined the pole from a closer distance.

'This is just for us, Surt. There are runes here,' he said, running his finger along the grooves that were cut into the pole. Blood from the horse's head had been smeared into the carvings so now the letters stood out, black against the brown of the wood. 'That's my name cut here. You're here too, Einar. Ulrich as well. See these runes here?'

Surt nodded, looking at the angular lines carved in the wood that Skar's finger pointed to.

'That says *Blámaðr, thrall of King Eirik*,' Skar said. 'That's you. I don't know of any other black men around here.'

Surt's eyes widened further. His breathing was fast. Einar was surprised that so big and powerful a man as Surt should appear so frightened at something so intangible.

Despite his clear apprehension, Surt gnashed his teeth together.

'My days as a slave are over,' he said, his voice harsh and guttural. 'I'm nothing of no one.'

Ulrich, the small, wiry leader of the úlfhéðnar pack turned away and spat. He touched the iron of his belt buckle. The others did the same, pressing fingers to buckles, rings, the head of the broken spear Einar held, anything made from the metal which could give protection against evil.

'What about me?' Affreca said. She ran her fingers through the auburn stubble that covered her head in a self-conscious gesture that had recently become a habit. It was many weeks now since the nuns in Britain had forcibly shaved her head. Her hair was growing but it was still very short. Her dark, eye makeup was heavily applied, as if to emphasise her femininity in place of her former long mane.

'*The bitch-whelp of Guthfrith*?' Skar said over his shoulder, pointing at some runes further down the pole. 'I assume that means you.'

Affreca shrugged. 'Nice to be included, I suppose.'

'Everyone is named, except Roan,' Skar said, standing up and turning to face the others.

The Frisian skipper, impassive as ever, folded his arms and turned the corners of his mouth down.

'The runes call down curses on us all,' Skar went on. 'They call on the *Norns* who rule our fates to bring ill luck, calamity and death to us. They summon the *dísir* spirits of the land here and command them to give us no succour. They warn the folk who live around here that anyone who helps us will feel the wrath of the king.'

For a few moments they all fell into silence. The only sound was that of the small waves lapping on the rocks of the island and the lonely cry of a single seabird as it swooped low over the water.

'Gunnhild,' Bodvar said. 'This is her work. I saw her make one of these once before.'

Einar felt a shiver scurry down his backbone as he thought of the beautiful but deadly wife of King Eirik Bloody Axe of Norway. The others had told him tales of her and the thought that such a woman was now an enemy was daunting.

'What do we do now, Ulrich?' Skar said to his leader.

Ulrich sighed and shook his head. He did not reply.

'You're not taking this seriously, are you?' Einar said. 'Only the gullible believe in such things.'

Ulrich looked at him, an expression on his face that suggested disappointment mixed with disdain. Then the little Wolf Coat turned away and waded into the shallows back towards the grounded longship.

'What?' Einar made a questioning shrug to Skar as the others all began to follow Ulrich back to Roan's knarr.

'Think about it lad,' Skar said. 'The blood is dry but the horse's head is quite fresh. If Gunnhild raised that cursing pole what does it tell you?'

Einar's jaw dropped open. Now he got it.

'She knows we're not dead,' he said. His face reddened in shame that he had not caught on faster. 'But how?'

Then his jaw dropped further.

'If they know we're not dead then Eirik will be searching for us?' he said.

Skar nodded.

'The hunters become the hunted,' he said. 'Best we get moving again, eh?'

The others clambered onto the ship as Skar, Einar and Bodvar put their shoulders to the prow and shoved it back off the rocks to float it. Then they hauled themselves over the strakes and joined the others in the boat.

Ulrich looked around at the mountainous sides of the fjord that towered over them.

'Norway was once our home,' he said. 'But now it's a hostile land and the king himself and all his men are hunting us. We have no war gear but a couple of old swords and a broken spear. The first thing we need to do is change that.'

'Something else may be more important,' Roan said. The skipper was pointing up the fjord. 'There are ships coming.'

All eyes turned to look at where he was pointing. They were still some way off but close enough to be able to make out the dragons on their prows and the large red axe painted on their sails.

'We need to get under sail,' Ulrich said. 'Those are ships of King Eirik.'

Two

The longships were coming at them from the direction the Wolf Coats had been sailing towards, so once off the shale of the island Roan had to turn his ship around. The ropes creaked as the sail filled, driving the wide-bodied knarr onwards, back in the direction they had originally come from.

Einar stood near the steering oar at the back of the ship. Despite the wind he could see that they were not getting any further away from the other ships. In fact they were getting steadily closer.

'They're *snekkjas*,' Skar said, one hand held across his brow to shade his eyes so he could see better. 'Just like our old ship. And they're full of men by the look of it. We won't be able to outrun them in this tub.'

Roan scowled but Einar knew Skar was right. The skipper's vessel was a merchant ship, wide bodied and designed for bearing cargo rather than speed. The snekkjas were small, light warships, fast and agile and made for hit-and-run raiding, either over sea or penetrating up rivers. As well as being propelled by the wind, their crews were rowing.

Einar rolled his shoulders, anticipating the exertion to come.

'Should we take to the oars?' he said.

Ulrich shook his head.

'There aren't enough of us to make a difference,' he said. 'They'll catch us before we get halfway back up the fjord.'

'We can't fight them,' Skar said. 'If those are Eirik's ships then the men onboard will be armed to the teeth. Unlike us.'

'Do you think they're looking for us?' Einar said.

'We'll soon find out,' Ulrich said. He turned to Roan.

'Head for the shore,' he said. The skipper pushed the steering oar over to the side.

The knarr turned, its prow moving to point towards the steep, forest-swathed side of the fjord. It was not long before the other ships also changed course in the same direction.

'They're after us all right,' Skar said. 'What do we do?'

'We can't outsail them,' Ulrich said. 'So we'll beach the ship and see if we can lose them in that forest.'

As they drew closer to the shore, the pursuing ships got ever nearer. Soon Einar could make out the flash of sunlight on metal as the spring sun glinted on the helmets and mail of the men who crewed the snekkjas. The sails were full of wind and the oars rippled up and down like the wings of the dragons that decorated their prows.

Roan spotted a short rocky shore and guided the ship as close as he could. When the sound of rock bumping against the keel came from below he dropped the anchor stone.

'Grab the weapons. Everyone get ashore,' Ulrich said and the crew clambered over the side into the water. Einar grabbed the broken-shafted spear that was one of their few weapons and followed the others. He sucked in breath through his teeth as the freezing water ran in through his breeches and down into his boots, then he sloshed through the shallows and across the short, rocky shore up onto a grassy bank and joined the other ten.

They now stood at the edge of a thick pine forest.

Taking a look around, Einar saw that the snekkjas were not far behind them.

'Into the trees,' Ulrich barked.

The crew scrambled through the bushes at the edge of the shore and into the forest. The carpet of pine needles beneath their feet had smothered all other vegetation so there was no undergrowth to impede them as they ran. The ground sloped uphill however and the trees were tightly packed, making them have to dodge left and right. It was heavy going and in no time they were out of breath and starting to sweat. The strange quiet of the forest stifled sound so all Einar could hear was the dull thumps of their running feet and his own heavy breathing.

Then behind them came shouting.

Einar stopped and looked back. Through the trees he could see the two dragon prows of the pursuing longships rammed into the shale of the shore beside Roan's knarr. Warriors in helmets and mail were pouring over the sides and onto the shore.

'Keep going!' Ulrich said. 'Up! Up!'

They began running up the slope once more. Einar's thighs were already burning from the effort. From behind the shouting of the warriors continued but was joined by a strange popping and crackling noise and a sound like heavy hammering on wood.

Up ahead the gloom of the forest lightened and Einar

could see a linear break in the trees overhead was letting in sunlight. A few strides higher and he saw that it was a road that cut through the forest.

They burst from the treeline onto a muddy trackway. It was well used by the look of it and pitted by horse hooves and ruts made by cartwheels. Einar reasoned that this must be the main thoroughfare along the shore of the fjord. On the opposite side of the road the forest began again and the slope continued upwards.

Standing at the roadside was a runestone. These tall standing stones carved with runes were a common memorial raised by bereaved relatives beside roads all over the northern world to commemorate the lives of illustrious relatives. Einar could not but help notice that this particular runestone had been daubed with an extra painted symbol. This desecration made him pause, even in the situation he was in, to take it all in.

In contrast to the carefully chiselled and coloured runes that recounted the exploits of the departed, this stone was also painted with what looked like a large *Odal* rune. The rune, which resembled a large X-shape with the bottom half of another X on top of it, had been slapped over the face of the rock in red paint in either a careless or hasty manner. The paint had run in places.

Everyone stopped and turned around to look back down the slope. Through the trees, about thirty or forty paces below, he could see warriors clambering up after them.

Affreca dropped to a squat and picked a couple of small round stones out of the mud of the track.

'What are you doing?' Einar said, then understood as

she stood up and undid the knot that held the leather sling wrapped around her wrist like an armband.

Loading the sling with the pebbles she had picked up, Affreca let two stones fly in quick succession. She had little time to aim and the warriors below them were moving in and out of the trees. Her first stone zoomed over their heads. Then there was a resounding clack as the second one hit a tree trunk. It was followed almost immediately by a metallic clang and cursing that told Einar the rebounding missile had struck one of their pursuers either on the helmet or shield boss. His companions dropped to the forest floor to avoid any further stones.

'Good work,' Ulrich said. 'Come on. We need to keep moving. Back into the trees and keep climbing.'

They turned around again and crossed the road. Running past the painted runestone, they jumped over the ditch that ran along the side of the track and scrambled into the forest beyond. Then they were climbing again as fast as they could manage given the incline of the slope. Behind them came shouting as the warriors below began the chase again. Einar fervently hoped they were now doing so in a more cautious, and therefore slower, manner.

The slope kept rising and Einar felt that they must be climbing a mountainside. The forest showed no sign of thinning and the slope was so steep he was almost on hands and knees. His thigh muscles burned with the exertion and sweat ran free down his face and neck. The others were pushing on and Einar knew he was dropping behind them.

'Odin's Blood!' he heard Ulrich curse from ahead.

Looking up, Einar saw a vast wall of rock rising sheer

out of the forest floor and travelling straight upwards above the trees. It was a cliff. He looked left and right. It stretched as far as he could see through the trees on either side like a vast wall.

Thinking of their options now, Einar spotted a tall pine tree that had fallen at the base of the cliff. That could give him a start in scaling the cliff if he wanted to try. He had climbed higher as a boy in Iceland but he knew his progress would be too slow. Before he got far the warriors chasing them would be up the slope and lobbing spears at him. Hanging off the side of the rock face he would be a simple target. The others could not climb like him anyway.

They had nowhere to go. They were trapped.

Three

Back down the slope, the warriors from the snekkja had reached the road. Looking through the trees, Einar saw them fan out along the road then advance across it. They moved in step in a way that it was clear was well practised. These were full-time warriors, not men pulled from their farmsteads and pushed into service in the *Here*, the kings' army. Most snekkjas had twenty rowing benches. With two men per bench and two ships that meant there could be anything up to eighty men chasing them. There were seven of the Wolf Coats plus himself, Affreca, Surt and Roan. They were hopelessly outnumbered.

'Lord Rognvald!' he heard one of the men on the road shouting. He was pointing at the paint splattered runestone. 'There's another one!'

A broad-shouldered warrior in a shining silvered helmet, his wide chest encased in a *brynja* mail shirt and his shoulders swathed in an expensive, fur-trimmed cloak, strode over to join his companion in front of the runestone. A black beard spilled from beneath the visor of his helmet and his long black hair hung in a braid down his back over his cloak. After a moment he let out a snarl of pure rage audible even at the top of the slope where Einar watched from. From his bearing, his fine equipment and the deference the warriors around him showed him, this man was clearly in charge of this warband. He levelled his drawn sword at the Odal rune daubed on the stone.

'When I get my hands on the rebel bastards doing this,' he said, speaking in a loud voice meant not just for his own men but anyone else who might be listening from the forest. 'I'll see they suffer the blood eagle. You hear that? Your Odal rights are gone. My grandfather took them and you'll never get them back. Your King Frodi is dead. He's not coming back. Odin I swear this to you: You will have the blood of these fools as a sacrifice!'

'Well, well,' Einar heard Ulrich say. The little Wolf Coat leader was speaking in a quiet voice, half to himself. 'Rognvald Eiriksson.'

'You know him?' Einar said. 'Eiriksson? Is he—'

'The king's son?' Ulrich said. 'Yes. Not a legitimate one though. Eirik sired him on a jarl's wife. Gunnhild hates him as much as she hates us. Maybe more. She doesn't like to be reminded of Eirik's disloyalties, of which there have been a few. Gunnhild is supposed to be on her way to Orkney with the rest of Eirik's brats. So with her out of the way it looks like Eirik has had the balls to bring Rognvald back into his household.'

'If she made that pole then she must be still around,' Einar said.

'Then I wouldn't want to be in Eirik's boots when she finds out about this,' Ulrich said, smirking. 'Men: that fallen tree. Let's give it a shave.'

The Wolf Coats swarmed around the pine tree that lay at the base of the cliff. Bodvar and Skar, who had the two old swords, began hacking branches from the tree. The others used their bare hands to twist and break branches off the trunk.

'King's daughter,' Ulrich said to Affreca. 'A few more of your stones if you please. Try to slow them down.'

The warriors below were now all across the track and moving into the forest. Affreca shot another couple of stones down through the trees. The missiles buzzed through the air, cracking as they bounced off tree trunks, scattering their pursuers once again as they sought cover from the deadly missiles. Einar could see this would not hold them for long, though. There were too many of them.

Affreca was soon out of stones and crouched to the forest floor, running her fingers through the carpet of brown pine needles, scouring for more pebbles beneath.

'Now we lift this,' Ulrich said, referring to the fallen tree. 'We'll send it down on them as a present. That should slow them down more.'

Bodvar handed his sword to Ulrich then he and the rest of the Wolf Coats ceased trying to strip the branches and took up positions around the tree trunk. Einar joined them, sliding his hands under the trunk and preparing to push. As one, they bent their knees, straightened their backs and heaved. The trunk shifted a bit but did not move free of the loam that had gathered around it since it fell.

'You Norsemen are pathetic,' Surt said. He went to the bottom end of the tree where the roots, torn from the ground when the tree fell, splayed out in a wooden web. He grasped several big roots and braced his legs, the sinews and muscles of his thighs standing out like the knotted wood of the tree.

'Push,' he roared.

The others added their own strength to the effort. With a damp tearing sound the tree came free of the earth it was half buried in. Once free, it moved faster. Roaring and screaming like madmen the Wolf Coats shoved the fallen tree down the slope. In moments it had gained so much speed they had to let go or be dragged down the hill with it. Einar now saw why Ulrich wanted them to strip the branches. Without them the tree rolled better. With a crash the trunk bounced off a standing tree and flipped around, now falling straight down the slope.

At the tremendous crashing sound from above, the warriors in the trees below looked up. Even at the distance they were at, Einar could see mouths dropping open and hear cries of consternation. Then they were scattering, their orderly line disintegrating in panic as they tried to escape the falling tree.

The trunk crashed into another tree as it fell faster, the impact making it change direction again. The warriors below did the same. Then the tree bounced off a couple more trees, changing direction and getting faster with each one. Einar saw one man just standing, rooted to the spot, paralysed by indecision, not knowing which way to run. Then the tree smashed into him, pulverising him into a tangled mess of smashed limbs.

From the anguished screams that rose up the slope Einar could tell the tree had taken out several of the other warriors as well before it bounced out onto the roadway and came to a halt.

'That should give them something to think about,' Ulrich said, his face split in a vicious grin.

'What now, Ulrich?' Atli said. 'We're stuck at the bottom of this cliff. Rognvald and his men won't stay down there for long.'

Ulrich stood for a moment, lost in thought.

'Psst!'

Einar stopped and looked at Affreca. She was looking back at him. It was obvious that it was not her who had made the sound.

'Psst!'

It came again. For the first time Einar noticed another man a little way off through the trees, crouching near where the tangled roots of the fallen tree had been. He was old, going by his very long white hair and beard, both of which were combed straight and smooth and flowed like an avalanche over his shoulders. On his head he wore a wide-brimmed hat, the sort some wore to keep the sun and rain off their faces and shoulders. His tunic was dark and plain and his feet and shins were clad in long deerskin boots. He had a long walking staff grasped in one hand.

Einar blinked, wondering why he had not spotted the man before. The forest had seemed deserted last time he looked in that direction.

'Who in Hel's name are you?' Ulrich said.

The old man did not reply, but instead waved his staff in a gesture that could only mean they should come closer. Einar looked at Ulrich. Ulrich shrugged as if to say what other choice do we have?

They traversed the slope to gather round the stranger. As they reached him he pointed his staff downhill towards the pursuing warriors.

'Can I suggest another stone or two, lady?' the stranger

said to Affreca. He spoke with the heavy accent of the wilder parts of Norway.

Affreca, who by now had found some pebbles under the pine needles, nodded and shot another couple of stones down through the trees, sending their pursuers ducking for cover once again.

While their heads were still down the old man said, 'Follow me. It will be a bit cramped I'm afraid.'

He turned with surprising agility for one his age, seemed to slide down into the ground. In a moment he was gone.

Four

Einar blinked. It seemed like the old man had just vanished.

'Is this an elf?' he said, his eyes wide and mouth open.

A loud tut came from beside him. Affreca had caught his look of astonishment.

'There's a hole in the ground, idiot,' she said. 'What did you think? That he just disappeared? Come on.'

She went to where the old man had disappeared. There was indeed a ragged hole in the forest floor near where the end of the fallen tree had been. Affreca slid herself into the hole and then too was gone. The others followed her in quick succession and Einar found himself standing alone in the forest. The shouts of the warriors down the slope told him they were restarting their pursuit.

Realising he could not afford to wait, Einar slid down after the others. The ground fell away and Einar felt a brief moment of panic as he felt himself sliding fast down a very steep slope, scattering dead pine needles and earth in every direction as he went. He did not go far though as the ground levelled again and he skidded into a packed crush of bodies.

Looking around in the gloom, Einar now realised

what was going on. They were in a shallow bowl-shaped depression in the ground. It had been made by the fallen tree, whose roots had rent the earth as it toppled, tearing up the soil that had once held it firm in the ground. Einar guessed that if he had stood up again, his head and shoulders would have been protruding above ground level. The angry shouts of the warriors coming up the slope told them they were getting near. However the hole left by the roots now had a roof. Someone, presumably the old man, had covered the space with dead pine branches, sticks and fallen leaves so it looked just like any other part of the forest floor.

The old man was not the only one there, either. Huddled in the dark were three young men about the same age as Einar. Their eyes were wide and even in the gloom Einar could see splatters of red paint on their faces and hands.

'You painted that runestone,' he said.

The white-haired old man raised a finger to his lips and Einar fell silent. The old man then moved passed him, lifted a branch and pushed it into the hole they had entered by, closing it off. Then they all waited, huddled tightly together in the cool, semi-darkness, their nostrils filled with the musty smell of damp earth and old pine needles. The only sound was their breathing.

Outside, the raised voices came closer. Einar fought to control his breathing, knowing that the noise could give away their hiding place. His heart drummed in his chest so hard he feared that too might give them away. He felt a finger on his chin. Looking up he saw it belonged to Skar who was crushed into the hole beside him. The big man pushed Einar's mouth closed and then pointed to his own nose. Einar saw Skar was taking long, deep breaths via his nose instead of his mouth. A quick glance around told him the other Wolf Coats were doing the same, controlling their breathing so they were not making heavy panting noises. Einar did the same, though with the rising anxiety in his chest it was difficult to keep his breath steady.

'Where are those bastards?' The voice of Rognvald rang through the trees outside.

'There's a cliff here, lord,' another voice responded. 'They can't have climbed it. Unless they're spiders they'd still be halfway up.'

'They must have gone along the bottom,' Rognvald said. 'They can't have got far.'

'Which way, lord?' the other voice said.

'Split up,' Rognvald said. 'Send half the men right and go with them. I'll take the others left. I'll give a silver arm ring to the man who brings me Ulrich's head.'

Crouching in the half-darkness, Einar heard the dull thumps of many boots tramping on the soft forest floor. Einar held his breath completely as he saw through the matted branches and leaves above the outlines of several men passing by just outside. His knuckles whitened as he gripped the broken shaft of the spear. Then they moved on across the slope. The sound of footsteps and chatter of voices moved away and after a short time the strange quiet of the pine forest returned.

'I don't know who you are or why you did it,' Ulrich said to the old man in the broad-brimmed hat, 'but thank you.'

The old man made a face.

'You were running from the king's men,' he said. 'The enemy of an enemy should be our friend.'

'This is a nice hiding place you've built here,' Einar said in a whisper.

'We have several in these forests,' the old man said. 'They are at different points along the road. We built them in case Eirik's men come and we have to hide. We were painting that runestone on the road when your ship hit the shore. We thought it was them so we ran to this hide.'

'Why are you painting the runestones?' Einar said, remembering one of Rognvald's men had mentioned 'another one'. 'And why does it annoy Rognvald so much?'

The old man waved his hand in the air as if to dispel all conversation.

'It won't be long before they realise you didn't go along the bottom of the cliff,' he said. 'You should get back to your ship. There's not much time.'

Ulrich and Skar nodded.

Bodvar poked a branch up and took a quick look around to see if there was anyone outside. Then he looked back and nodded.

'Let's go,' Ulrich said.

One by one they scrambled up the side of the hole and out into the forest once more. Einar could hear the crashing of branches and sound of voices through the trees on either side, but they were far enough away to mean his company could get back to the ship before getting caught. If they moved fast.

They set off down the slope, moving at a dangerous speed through the trees. Einar had seen them do it many times, but was still amazed at how silently the Wolf Coats were able to move, even when going fast through rough terrain like this. His own heart was in his mouth. He felt like each of his footfalls made a noise like thunder that would alert the king's men while at the same time praying to the Norns who ruled his luck that he did not miss his step. At the speed they travelled on the steep slope, one wrong footfall into a deadfall or unseen hole would result in his leg snapping like one of the dead branches that littered the forest floor.

They made it to the road and crossed it, passing the mangled remains of the warriors smeared across the track by the falling tree trunk, then set off down the slope on the other side. Einar noticed that the chopping sound he had heard before had stopped. There was still the crackling and popping, now even louder, and the unmistakable smell of burning reached his nose. There was grey smoke hanging in the forest canopy above.

'My ship!' Roan cried out, in a voice that sounded like he was calling out about his wife or child.

At the same time the noise of voices rose again from behind them at the top of the slope. The king's men were returning.

Roan's knarr had been shoved out into the fjord to refloat in the deeper water. It was listing badly though and from the vantage point of being up the slope Einar could see water pouring into the hull from a large hole hacked in its side. A fire blazed across the deck and the sail, though filled with wind that pulled the ship further out into the fjord, was also alight.

Four warriors stood on the shore, admiring their handiwork. Three of them had the long-handled axes they had used to chop the hole in the side of Roan's ship, either slung over their shoulders or held against their legs. The fourth had a burning torch in one hand. A barrel of whatever they had used to set the ship alight, sat beside them on the shore.

Ulrich, still running, pointed at the man furthest right, then to himself. Then he pointed to the next man and pointed to Skar. The third man he delegated to Einar.

Einar grabbed the broken spear in both hands, picking the spot on the back of the man before him where Skar had taught him would do most damage.

Then Roan let out a howl like a rabid dog.

'You sank my ship you bastards!' he screamed.

Einar could not believe such emotion was pouring from the normally placid skipper. Roan leapt into the air and landed on the back of one of the startled axemen, wrapping his thighs round the man and grabbing at his face with his hands. The other warriors on the shore spun around. Ulrich struck. His blade slashed through the neck of the man with the torch, unleashing a sheet of bright blood that gushed down the chest of his mail shirt. The warrior dropped the torch and grasped at the wound as if he were choking as his strength and life poured out of him with his blood. His knees sagged and he dropped to the ground.

Skar charged into another warrior before he had time to lift his axe. The man went sprawling onto his back on the stones. Skar stepped over him and drove his own blade up under the man's chin. His body thrashed for a moment then he was dead.

The man Roan had jumped on stumbled forward and managed to throw the skipper off his back. Roan landed in the water with a splash.

The warrior before Einar had time to swing his axe up into both hands. As he came forward the fighting movements

Skar had been drilling into them for weeks came to Einar without thought. He sidestepped, moving aside as his would-be attacker's axe swooped harmlessly through thin air instead of into Einar's head.

Einar swept his rear leg forward, taking his attacker's feet from beneath him and sending him sprawling face first to the ground. Holding the broken spear shaft in both hands, Einar drove the spear under the back of the man's helmet. He heard the crunch of shattering bone as the blade went into the man's head.

The last axeman was raising his weapon to kill Roan when Skar and Ulrich both drove their swords through his body as one.

'Get up you mad old fool and get that snekkja under sail,' Ulrich said to Roan, holding his hand out for the skipper to use to pull himself to his feet. 'The rest of you get the other one afloat.'

The others swarmed into the water and shoved the vessel off the shore. As they did so Ulrich lifted the barrel and tossed it into the ship. It landed, tipped over and the whale oil inside spilled out over the deck. Ulrich then grabbed the torch and threw it in as well. With a whoosh and a blast of hot air the oil ignited and soon the deck was blazing. When the Wolf Coats and Surt were waist deep in the fjord they gave one final shove then waded back to the shore again. The snekkja kept drifting away from the land, its deck and sail wrapped in flame.

To Einar's surprise, the old man had managed to keep up with them. He and the paint-splattered young lads clambered into the other snekkja. The Wolf Coats, Surt, Einar and Affreca jumped in after them.

'Row!' Ulrich shouted.

They all scrambled into places on the rowing benches. The oars went over the side and soon they were pulling away from the shore. The sail filled with wind and they began to move even faster.

Behind them Rognvald and his warriors burst from the trees and onto the shore. Einar glanced over his shoulder and smiled as he saw the big black-haired son of Eirik tear the helmet from his head and throw it to the ground, roaring in inarticulate frustration.

'If you could leave us off on the other side of the fjord,' the old man said. 'With their ship on fire we'll be safe enough from Rognvald and his men there.'

'They're after us, not you,' Ulrich said.

'They are not here just for you,' the old man said. 'Rognvald brought the war arrow here to Gandvik. The bidding stick that summons all fighting men to the king's army.'

'Eirik is going to war?' Skar said.

The old man nodded.

'His half-brothers, Olaf and Sigrod, have risen against him,' he said. 'They've declared themselves kings and are gathering their own army at Tunsberg in Viken.'

Ulrich looked at Skar.

'Then that is where we should go next,' he said. His Prow Man nodded.

The old man smiled.

'Very good,' he said. 'And I shall meet you there before long.'

Five

Hamnavoe, Orkney

The grey stallion reared up on its hind legs, front hooves thrashing. The brown stallion did the same, rearing against the grey and thrashing its head against the other horse's neck. It twisted and bit the other animal, its teeth drawing a semicircle of blood on the grey stallion's neck. The grey whinnied in pain and pulled away, stepping backwards and away from the other horse.

Half of the men watching cheered. The other half groaned.

The horses were fighting in a ring of standing stones that had been placed there when the world was young. It was on the top of a *ness* that stretched out into the sea. The landscape was flat as far as the eye could see until it ended in distant hills. A warm, early summer sun shone from a bright, blue sky that was mirrored by the colour of the flat sea. The spaces between the stones had been fenced off so the horses could not follow their natural instinct and run away from each other. Enclosed within the stone circle, they had no choice but to fight. Both were harnessed and each had a long pole attached to the harness that trailed behind them. The fence was lined with men engrossed in watching the contest. A mare, whose affections the two stallions were competing for, was tied up close to the ring of stones.

The horses went for each other again, both clashing heads together as they reared up on their back legs, each one trying to be taller than the other. The crowd watching started shouting again, each one yelling encouragement for one or other of the stallions in a jumbled cacophony of noise. Those watching were a mixture of the inhabitants of the isles, from hardy farmers to richly dressed landowners, all jammed in side by side behind the fence in the gaps between the stones.

One man, however, was not crowded. He had his own space between two of the tall stones and no one stood beside him. He was very tall and though his iron-grey hair showed he was in his later middle years the bunched muscles of his shoulders, upper arms and the bare forearms he leaned on the fence were like those of a warrior. His wool tunic was dyed green and embroidered with many colours, showing how wealthy he was. He was Thorfinn, also known as *Hausakljúfr*, the 'Skull Cleaver', and he was Jarl of Orkney.

The grey stallion snickered and pulled away from the brown. He ducked his head, turned tail and ran away from the other animal. The brown horse recognised the grey's submission and reared aloft again, this time in triumph.

The scowl on Thorfinn's face betrayed that he was not pleased with what he was watching. It was not due to any scruples about making two such magnificent animals fight for the entertainment of the crowd.

'I thought you said the grey was a fighter, Aulvir,' he said. 'By the look of it that mare has more fight in it.'

Aulvir, who was in charge of the jarl's horses, looked a little hurt but also awkward.

'He is, lord,' he said. 'But I did not know Bjarni was bringing that big brown today. He's one vicious brute.'

'In the name of Thor!' the jarl said. 'Now this is embarrassing!'

The brown stallion was now chasing his horse around the ring of stones.

'Get in there and make the cowardly bastard fight,' Thorfinn said.

Aulvir gathered another of the jarl's men and then signalled to Bjarni, the *hersir* from Burray who owned the brown stallion, that they were going to enter the ring. Bjarni gestured to a couple of his own men. One of the fences was pulled aside to allow them into the ring and the four men all ran in. Careful to avoid falling under the hooves of the running horses, they gathered the long poles that trailed behind the stallions, each pair grabbing the pole of his master's horse.

With much shouting and a lot of effort Aulvir and his companion managed to use the pole to turn the grey horse around to face the brown again. Bjarni's men did the same with the brown, though as it was already keen to fight they did not have as big a struggle.

Then both sets of men shoved the horses at each other, forcing them to fight whether they wanted to or not. The grey whinnied in terror as the brown reared up once more, teeth and hooves flashing. The grey reared up as well, but more in an effort to get away than attack. It twisted in its harness, managing to half turn, wrenching the pole from the hands of Aulvir and the other man and throwing them to the ground. The brown stallion barged into the grey, driving its big chest into the other. The blow shoved the grey horse backwards. Unable to move properly with the harness and pole, the beast toppled over, falling at the feet of its opponent.

The brown stallion reared once again then brought its forelegs down on the grey's head. Its hooves landed on the side of the grey's muzzle with a crack of bone that sent shivers down the backbones of all watching.

Thorfinn winced and cursed.

Bjarni's men pulled the brown horse aside, whispering calming words and stroking its flanks. The grey horse was in a bad way. It tried to rise but flopped back down again. Its shattered face was caved in and one of its eyes was gone, crushed by the falling hooves.

'Kill it, Aulvir,' Thorfinn said. 'I won't let it live maimed like that. Its wounds disgust me.'

Aulvir, who was just picking himself up from the ground, scurried out of the ring to find a weapon with which to put the creature out of its misery.

Bjarni the hersir approached his jarl, a sheepish expression on his face. He took off the felt hat he wore and fiddled with its brim with nervous fingers.

'Lord Thorfinn,' he said. 'I can only guess my horse got lucky to be able to beat yours. Please, let me split my winnings with you.'

Thorfinn grunted.

'Don't be silly, Bjarni,' he said. 'What sport would a *Hestavíg* be if no one paid their due when they lost?'

The jarl held out his hand. Bjarni held his under it and Thorfinn dropped eight roughly hacked pieces of silver into it.

'It's decent of you to be so understanding, lord,' Bjarni said, a relieved smile spreading across his face. 'It was bad enough when I found my horse was up against yours. Then when it beat yours as well I started to wonder, can things get any worse?'

'Bjarni. What do you take me for?' Thorfinn said. 'A bad loser?'

Bjarni turned to go.

'One thing though,' the jarl said.

Bjarni stopped and turned around again.

'Yes, lord?'

'I don't think it was bad luck that made my horse fall,' Thorfinn said. 'I think it was because your men shoved your horse too hard forwards.'

Bjarni opened his mouth to speak, then closed it again without saying anything.

'If you agree then I believe I am due compensation,' the jarl continued. 'Of course you are within your legal rights to disagree. If so we can settle it at the next Law meeting.'

Bjarni began fiddling with his hat again.

'Lord, it would be folly for someone like me to challenge such a powerful man as you in Law,' he said. 'What sort of compensation price would you find acceptable?'

Thorfinn scratched his chin for a moment.

'Let's say nine pieces of silver,' Thorfinn said. 'Do you think that's fair?'

'Yes Lord,' Bjarni said, looking at the ground. He handed the jarl's silver back to him, then added another from his own purse.

An unpleasant wet chop sound came from the ring of stones. They looked around and saw Aulvir had just beheaded Thorfinn's grey stallion with a large axe.

'One more thing,' the jarl said. 'I am now also short of a horse.'

Bjarni's eyes blinked. Thorfinn wondered if the sparkle in them was tears. Whether of anger or humiliation he neither knew nor cared.

'Can I offer you my brown stallion?' Bjarni said in a small voice.

'That's very generous of you, Bjarni,' Thorfinn said, grinning. 'I accept. It was a pleasure competing with you.'

As he watched Bjarni walk away, head bowed, a new voice spoke up.

'Really Lord Thorfinn, I would have expected more generosity of spirit from a jarl.'

Thorfinn turned around and saw that a new group of people had arrived at the stone circle. They had clearly arrived on horseback as their steeds now sat cropping grass at the edge of the track that lead to the stones. Their arrival had not been noticed as everyone's attention was focused on the Hestavíg, the horse fight.

There were several warriors, armed with shields and spears. Beside them walked a tall, very thin man in a long white robe. He bore a staff in one hand. The top of his head was bald but a ring of long, lank white hair hung from the edges of his crown.

Thorfinn felt an involuntary shudder at the sight of the

man. It was Vakir, his worker of spellcraft. With Vakir were two strangers. One was very tall with a brown fur cloak and hair shorn so short Thorfinn at first thought he was bald. The other was not old, but his long, straight hair was completely white and he had no beard.

Beside these men were three children and a woman of arresting beauty. The eldest boy was perhaps twelve winters old. Another boy of perhaps two stood holding the woman's right hand as she cradled the third child, no more than a baby swathed in furs, in the crook of her left arm.

The woman was dressed in furs and her long black hair was tied in a braid that hung down her back. Her skin was white as milk and her eyes were a blue as pale as the sea that covered the white sand on the beach beside the ness. There was a playful smile on her lips and it was she who had spoken.

Thorfinn swallowed.

Queen Gunnhild had arrived.

Six

'Vakir,' Thorfinn said. 'Welcome back my *Galdr maðr*. And you bring such welcome, important guests. My lady.'

Thorfinn dipped his head in respect.

'We were expecting you but I did not know you had landed already. I'm very sorry that I was not there to meet you.'

The queen waved a hand as if batting away his concerns.

'It's me who should thank you, Lord Thorfinn,' she said, 'for giving us a safe haven here while my husband deals with the rebels in Norway.'

'I have sacrificed to Odin and had many *galdr* sung for his victory,' Thorfinn said. 'It's my honour to look after my king's family while he fights.'

'We landed near your hall at Jarls Gard,' Gunnhild said. 'They told us there that you had travelled here for the Hestavíg. I left the rest of my men there and we borrowed horses to ride here. Vakir showed us the way.'

Thorfinn ran his eyes over the warriors with the queen, counting them in his head.

'Have you many more warriors with you, lady?' he said, running his tongue over his lips.

Gunnhild smiled.

'We came with three ships full of warriors,' she said. 'Almost two hundred men. Eirik wanted to make sure there was a strong enough company with me to deter anyone who might think I would make a very valuable hostage.'

For a moment they locked eyes.

'Very clever of him,' Thorfinn said after a moment.

'That's why he's the king,' Gunnhild said. 'For added insurance I am also under the personal protection of Sigtryggr *snarfari* and Hallvard *harðfari*, here.'

She gestured with her free arm to the two strangers beside Vakir.

Thorfinn straightened his shoulders.

'So these two are the famous Hising brothers?' he said. 'Sigtryggr and Hallvard, your fame is known throughout the northern lands.'

The two men just nodded.

'I see you did not have much luck today?' Gunnhild said, cocking her head towards the beheaded horse lying in the stone circle.

'I'm sorry you had to witness that unpleasantness, lady,' the jarl said.

'I've been to many Hestavígs in my life, Jarl Thorfinn,' Gunnhild said. 'My father was obsessed with horse fighting. I also decapitated several horses before we left Norway.'

Thorfinn raised his right eyebrow.

'There were spells to cast,' she said. 'I was lucky I had your Vakir to help me. It was necessary, unfortunately.'

'Lord Thorfinn,' Vakir spoke for the first time. 'There is something I must tell you.'

'Before we discuss that,' Thorfinn held up his hand. 'Did

you request King Eirik do the favour I asked of him? Is Einar dead?'

'That is what I wish to tell you, lord,' Vakir said. 'King Eirik granted your request and sent Einar to die by fighting the Blámaðr. Somehow Einar managed to get the Blámaðr to conspire with him to escape.'

Thorfinn did not say anything for a moment. He stood as if frozen. Then he blinked and said, 'What about Ulrich and his Wolf Coats?'

'They escaped too,' Vakir said.

Thorfinn threw his head back and glared up into the sky. The muscles at the top of his jaw were bunched like marbles and all around could hear the grinding noise from his teeth. Aulvir, who had been approaching saw his jarl's demeanour and recognised the portents the way a seasoned sailor can spot the signs of an imminent storm. He turned and hurried away again.

The queen laid a hand on Thorfinn's forearm.

'Jarl Thorfinn,' she said. 'Let us walk off a little way. We have much to talk about just between ourselves.'

The Skull Cleaver glared at her, his lips working but no sound coming out as rage strangled them within his throat. Then it seemed like gazing on her beauty made the clouds of anger clear from before his eyes.

'Yes. Of course,' he said. His voice was thick and gravelling.

The queen passed her sleeping baby to the man with long white hair who took it with surprising carefulness, then she and the jarl set off, walking far enough from the others that their words could not be heard.

'You look surprised about something, Lord Thorfinn?' Gunnhild said.

'Just that you trust your child to one of old King Harald's most notorious killers,' Thorfinn said, glancing again towards the white-haired man holding the baby. He was now jiggling the crooked arm he held the child in to comfort it.

'Sigtryggr may have killed many, many men,' the queen said. 'But he was devoted to King Harald, and Harald Fairhair's blood flows in that child. The child is named Harald after his grandfather. Sigtryggr will guard my son with his life.'

'They're brothers, aren't they?' Thorfinn said, glancing once again at Sigtryggr and Hallvard. 'They don't look related.'

'Come, let us talk of your son and his companions instead,' Gunnhild said. 'I know it must be frustrating that Ulrich and Einar still live, Jarl Thorfinn. King Eirik is just as angry about it. He has made sure the people know that anyone who gives them support or shelter will be punished in the most severe way. Don't worry, when he deals with his brothers in Viken he will hunt Ulrich and his band down. I've cursed them with powerful runes and cursing poles. I called on the dísir, the *landvættir* and all the other spirits of the land to turn on them, destroy their luck and bring them to disaster.'

'I appreciate your efforts, lady,' Thorfinn said, 'But I'd rather there was hard, sharp iron descending on Einar's neck as well as the spirits.'

'Why do you hate him so much?' the queen said. 'Vakir tells me you've only met him once.'

Thorfinn looked at her, surprise on his face. For a few moments he thought about it, then said, 'He killed my son.'

'But he is your son too?' Gunnhild said.

'My *bastard* son,' Thorfinn said. 'He's the son of my bed-slave. I treated her well but she ran away. She humiliated me. She made me look weak.'

'So you hate him because of her?' the queen said.

Thorfinn scowled.

'She was a haughty Irish bitch,' he said. 'Beautiful and too clever for her own good.'

'That's what they say about me,' Gunnhild smiled.

'But she was a slave, not a queen,' Thorfinn said. 'She brought Einar up. She'll have filled his ears with venom against me. There will be too much of her in him for me to ever trust him.'

'I'm told she is in Iceland?' Gunnhild said.

'Aye,' Thorfinn said. 'I only found out recently. She'd been hiding from me there for eighteen years.'

'This Einar must be very resourceful,' the queen said. 'He has managed to survive so far.'

'Luck,' Thorfinn spat. 'That and innate craftiness. That comes from his mother's Irish blood. But I was stupid to ask King Eirik to kill him. I should have done it myself.'

He looked the queen in the eyes.

'As soon as I can I will set sail, hunt the bastard down and take his head,' he said, speaking through clenched teeth.

'But right now you're stuck here, child-minding a queen and her children?' Gunnhild said, raising one of her dark eyebrows.

'I mean no offence to you, lady,' Thorfinn said. 'But you must understand my frustration? I want Einar dead but my obligations to Eirik mean I must stay here in Orkney and make sure both you and the royal children are safe.'

'Perhaps you need to think about your problems in a different way,' Gunnhild said. 'If you can't go to get him, perhaps you should make him come to you?'

Thorfinn grunted.

'Good idea. If I was waiting for him to come to me it would be easier to kill him,' he said.

'Have you tried provoking him?' Gunnhild said. 'Men tend to act very predictably when incensed.'

'I've tried to kill him twice!' the jarl said. 'That would be enough provocation for most men. But like I said, he's too clever to sail straight here for revenge. Or too cowardly.'

'Perhaps you need to do something even more provocative, then,' the queen said. 'I have more to ask of you, I'm afraid, Jarl Thorfinn. My husband requests you send someone to Norway to let him know we have arrived safely.'

'Of course, lady,' Thorfinn said. 'I will send Vakir.'

'Your Galdr maðr?' the queen said. 'But he has just returned with me? Don't you need him? I'm skilled in seiðr myself and can see that he's a powerful spell crafter.'

'Aye,' the jarl said. 'But if Olaf, Sigrod, Hakon or Aethelstan send ships to get you I need warriors; men who can stand in a shield wall, not magic workers. Vakir is better suited for scurrying around in the dark where he isn't supposed to be, finding out things he's not supposed to or doing secret harm. Also, between you and me, he's a good man, reliable and effective, but there's something about his presence that makes my skin crawl.'

Gunnhild nodded.

'I know what you mean,' she said.

'Mother!'

The eldest boy came running towards Gunnhild. He threw his arms around her and she tousled his hair with her free hand; it was thick and black like his father's.

'Can we go yet?' the boy said. 'We missed the horse fight. This is boring now. There's nothing to do.'

'We will go soon, Gamle, I promise,' Gunnhild said. 'Now run along and wait with the others.'

Scowling, the boy ran off again.

'We all have our problems with bastards, Jarl Thorfinn,' Gunnhild said as she watched him go. 'My husband is far too fond of one of his, Rognvald. I'm sure now I'm out of the country he'll be back on his father's knee. But I'm very protective of my children's future. I will let nothing stand in the way of my boy Gamle being King of Norway after his father.'

'If, lady,' Thorfinn looked at the ground, 'you ever have need of some help to make sure Rognvald does not impede Gamle's path to kingship, please do not hesitate to ask me.'

'That's very kind of you, Jarl Thorfinn,' Gunnhild said. 'I will bear that in mind.'

The boy looked around again and waved at Gunnhild.

'He certainly loves his mother,' Thorfinn said. 'You can see that.'

'What boy doesn't?' Gunnhild said. 'A boy's best friend is his mother and she is always in his mind. I know Gamle will always look after me too.'

She looked sideways at Thorfinn.

'It must be hard on Einar,' she said. 'Stuck in Norway, knowing his mother is all alone in Iceland. Knowing that there's nothing he can do to protect her if anything were to happen to her. He must be constantly worrying.'

Thorfinn caught her eye again. A smile now was spreading across his lips.

'And if something was to happen to her,' Gunnhild continued, 'I'm sure he would be very upset. Very upset indeed. It would be very... provoking for him.'

Thorfinn laughed.

'Perhaps, lady, if your husband can abide a short delay in knowing you are safe,' he said, 'I will get Vakir to make his journey to Norway by way of Iceland.'

'I think Eirik will be fine with that,' Gunnhild said. 'And Vakir can take Sigtryggr snarfari and Hallvard harðfari to help him on his voyage.'

Seven

An army sprawled across the hillside above the town of Tunsberg.

The wooden jetties that jutted into the sea from the town were jammed with ships. Behind them the thatched roofs of the many longhouses of the town nestled, the air above them smeared grey with the smoke of their cooking fires. Beyond them a steep hillside rose, its slopes thronged with the tents of the army, which got larger and more expensive the closer to the summit they were. The banners of jarls, lords and hersirs fluttered in the breeze while on the hilltop two flagpoles of twin height rose above all others: The red dragon banner of Olaf Haraldsson and the black wolf of his brother, Sigrod Haraldsson danced in the wind.

With no room in the town harbour, Roan beached the longship on the sickle-shaped shore that ran from the town around the base of the hill. Einar was first to leap off the prow onto the shale of the beach, his knees bending to a crouch as he crunched onto the stones. He straightened up, his nose wrinkling as the fug of the army camp reached his nostrils; an uncanny mixture of woodsmoke, fresh baking bread, piss and shit, the odour of so many men gathered together in tents in one small area.

Despite the stench, he was glad to be off the ship. The sailing of the previous days had been hard. After escaping from Rognvald they had voyaged south on a course for Tunsberg. As Eirik had betrayed them, Ulrich's plan now was that his úlfhéðnar should join the forces of the king's enemies. Einar wondered if Ulrich had perhaps taken Eirik's betrayal too much to heart. The little Wolf Coat leader had barely said a word on the journey. Instead he had stood at the curved prow of the ship, staring out at the waves and brooding who knew what dark thoughts.

The snekkja was a fast ship, but they had also been driven southward by a gale. Though it meant fast progress, it also meant enduring constant discomfort as the ship bucked and fell on the waves it rode on. The rolling of the deck, along with the howling of the wind and the freezing spray of the sea had all conspired to make sleep hard to find and sent Einar's stomach surging like the waves they sailed over.

All the while Skar had been relentless in drilling them in how to fight. They had practised how to stand in a shield wall and how to battle both as a pack and alone. To the Wolf Coats it had just been more practice. Surt had once been a warrior, so found it easy to adapt his own knowledge but to Einar and Affreca it was new. Skar had taught use of the sword, the axe and spear, though having no real weapons they had to improvise with sticks and oars. Some of his wrestling knowledge had helped, but Einar had been surprised that most of the learning had been about how to stand and move rather than how to strike with a weapon. Over and over again, Skar had made them practise where to place their feet, what stance to adopt and how to move into the right position to deliver a fatal blow. Day after day they had moved up and down the deck, sometimes together, moving as one, sometimes alone, looking like folk engaged in some strange ritual dance.

Then came a time of real danger. King Eirik's war fleet was sailing in the same direction and two days before they had rounded a headland and almost sailed right into it as it rode at anchor in a bay, sheltering from the weather. Roan's sailing skills had taken them back round the headland then out to sea. They had made it without being spotted, but all the same, for the last day they had travelled with the feeling crawling down their necks that Eirik's ships were coming after them.

The others – Bodvar, Sigurd, Atli, Kari, Starkad, Skar, Affreca, Surt and finally Ulrich –followed Einar onto the shore then they set off up the hill while Roan waited with the ship. It was late afternoon and the early summer sun was already sinking towards the horizon. The stiff wind that had propelled their journey drummed on the leather of the countless tents, whipping their guide ropes and making the many war banners and pennants dance on their poles. It also had the benefit of driving away the clouds of midges that were already starting to rise from the meres and bogs further inland. Men of all ages sat on stools or reclined on the ground, gathered around their cooking fires. Every hersir was obliged to bring one hundred men to fight for his lord, so the camp was filled with every rank of man able to hold a weapon. There were weapons and mail everywhere.

Shining brynjas, coats made of countless interlinked metal rings, stood like scarecrows on T-shaped poles outside the tents of the more wealthy men. Thralls and younger boys cleaned weapons, sharpened blades or painted shields. Outside less grand tents, more humble protection made of thick, toughened leather was being washed and prepared by freemen farmers.

War was coming and the thought occurred to Einar that many of these men may soon be dead. He and his companions would have to kill or be killed. Then he remembered that only a few days before he had himself killed a man. How many was it now? The first had caused him sleepless nights but the ones that had followed had troubled him less and less. Was he becoming like the Wolf Coats: Just another heartless killer wandering the whale roads? A Viking? What would his mother think of him now?

This was also the second time in a few short months that he had been in the midst of an army preparing for war. A year before, such adventure as this would have been only a dream to him. Growing up in Iceland there were large gatherings of people for the Thing but not for a war. Fights broke out and sometimes men died but this was on a different scale altogether. At home feuds between families could lead to a skirmish where a couple of men got killed. Then there would be the interminable, inextricable lawsuits as the families tried to work out the original problem along with whatever compensation was now required.

This was different. This was war. There would be no compensation paid to the families of those who died in the coming battle.

The air of excited tension in the camp was inescapable.

As the Wolf Coats moved through the forest of tents, some men looked up and hailed Ulrich and Skar as old friends, their faces lit up by smiles of recognition. An equal number of men scowled as they passed, regarding the Wolf Coats with eyes that held both surprise and suspicion. Most gawped in astonishment or quickly averted their eyes and touched iron as Surt walked by. The black-skinned man just glared back at them, his upper lip curled in a sneer.

'Are you sure this is a good idea, Ulrich?' Skar said as they climbed higher up the hill towards the largest tents at the summit where the flags of the most important noblemen flew. 'We haven't exactly been allies of the other Haraldssons over the years. I recall fighting against Sigrod's men at least once.'

'Have you got a better idea?' Ulrich said. 'Besides, if Olaf and Sigrod accept our service then we'll get weapons and the chance to pay Eirik back for his treachery.'

'We could always just run,' Bodvar said. 'Leave this land to the dogs who want to fight over it.'

'That would all have been fine if Eirik still thought we were dead,' Ulrich said. His voice was tetchy. 'But he doesn't. That horse's head means he knows we're still alive. You know him as well as I do. He won't rest until we *are* dead. It's us or him now. Our only choice is to try to bring him down before he brings us down and so we must help his enemies. Would you really prefer to run away and skulk like beaten, whipped curs? No.'

The last word was snarled through clenched teeth.

'Eirik might take us back into his service?' Atli said.

Ulrich just glared at him. Atli looked away and the company settled back into silence. When they reached the summit of the hill they found it was sealed off by a ring of warriors. Unlike the others they had passed in the camp these men were armed for fighting. Their torsos and legs were clad in thick leather jerkins and breeches. Over these the countless bright rings of their mail shirts gleamed in the sunlight. They had newly painted shields slung across their backs and hands rested on the pommels of their sheathed swords. Eyes that were both watchful and alert glared out from the shadows of their helmet visors. They formed an iron circle around the big tents on the hilltop where Olaf, Sigrod and their most trusted men were camped.

Seeing the Wolf Coats approaching, the warriors closed together, narrowing the gap between them to create a solid barrier.

'Ulrich Rognisson? You have some nerve showing your face here.'

These words were spoken by a tall, broad-shouldered man who stood a little behind the ring of warriors but was armed just like them. He pulled off his helmet, unleashing a torrent of long brown hair that cascaded around his shoulders. The expression on his handsome face was half amused, half suspicious.

'Skarphedin Harsson too,' he said. 'Is this the whole of Eirik Bloody Axe's wolf pack I see here before me?'

Ulrich straightened up and pushed his shoulders back, though he was still a head and shoulders smaller than the big man who confronted them.

'Gorm Njalsson,' Ulrich said. 'The last time we stood face to face was across a shield wall.'

'Indeed it was,' Gorm said. 'And what brings Eirik's most loyal killers to our camp? Has Eirik decided to surrender?'

47

Ulrich shook his head.

'We're no longer Eirik's men,' he said. His voice was hoarse as if his throat was tight and it was hard for him to get the words out. 'He betrayed our loyalty. We are here to swear oaths to fight for Sigrod and Olaf's cause.'

For a moment Gorm did not reply. Then he nodded, his eyebrows raised and the corners of his mouth turned down.

'Very well,' he said. 'Wait here.'

He turned on his heel and entered the flap of the largest tent.

As the Wolf Coats waited, Einar shook his head. He and Affreca stood a little way away from the others.

'What's the matter with you?' Affreca said, catching the expression on Einar's face.

Einar sighed. 'I was just wondering what I'm doing here.'

She gave him a quizzical look.

'Everyone on the way up here looked like they wanted to kill us,' Einar said. 'I've been thinking–'

'Well you should stop that,' Affreca cut him off. 'You think too much.'

Einar snorted and stuck out his lower lip. He folded his arms and for a time there was silence between them.

A smile played on Affreca's lips and she reached out to run her fingers through the bushy straggles that were sprouting from his beard. They had been on the run for some time now and all of them were in need of a good bath and some personal grooming.

'This could do with a trim,' she said.

'Unlike your hair,' Einar said. The words were out of his mouth before he could stop them. With an expression on her face like she had just tasted soured milk she turned away.

Einar felt his face flushing and he bit his lip. He had been trying to be funny, to lighten the moment but he could not have picked more wrong words. How could he be so stupid?

At that moment, Gorm re-emerged from the tent.

'Let them in,' he said to the warriors on guard. Two of them stood aside to make an opening in their ring of steel. 'But you must surrender all weapons before entering.'

'That's easily done,' Ulrich said, handing over Einar's broken spear. The others also passed over the couple of notched and rusty swords that made up their entire weapon horde.

Gorm shook his head.

'Come on Ulrich,' he said, nodding to the two warriors who had made the gap. 'You must take us for fools.'

The warriors stepped in and ran practised hands up and down Ulrich's body, feeling for concealed knives or anything else that could cause harm. When they found nothing they moved on to the other Wolf Coats who subjected themselves to the search with unconcealed surly displeasure. Surt, Einar and Affreca were searched too. The warriors turned back to Gorm and shrugged.

'Nothing else,' one of them said.

A look of genuine surprise crossed Gorm's face, then he flicked his head in the direction of the tent entrance.

'All right. In you go.'

Ulrich smiled at Skar.

'See?' he said. 'I knew Olaf and Sigrod wouldn't resist the offer of our help.'

He turned and strutted ahead into the tent.

'Let's hope that's true,' Skar muttered from the side of his mouth to Einar as they followed behind. 'And they haven't just decided to decorate their tent with our severed heads.'

Eight

The scene that greeted them inside did not bode well. All eyes in the tent glared at the newcomers. Their looks were hostile and suspicious.

Einar had never seen a tent so huge. It was about as big as his mother's farmhouse back in Iceland. The leather it was made from must have come from fifty or more cows. The interior was as comfortable as any jarl's hall. The ground was covered by fresh, sweet smelling rushes. A very long, narrow tapestry, embroidered with warriors, dragons, *jǫtnar* and battles was hung high up on three sides of the walls. Whale oil lamps burned on tall metal stands, providing light. There were about twenty men gathered around a table in the centre of the floor. Their clothing showed all of them were wealthy. Their tunics were dyed in bright colours and embellished with embroidery. Their cloaks were fur or of the finest wool, clasped at their shoulders by big, round, gold or silver brooches that glittered in the lamplight.

The steel of their drawn knives and swords also gleamed in the flames of the lamps.

Which ones were the sons of Harald Fairhair was obvious. Two men stood right beside the table. Their resemblance to Hakon and Eirik was clear; the same long nose, piercing blue eyes and handsome features. Both were taller than most men and had shoulders like the crossbeam of a longship. The only nod to the fact they had different mothers was that while Hakon's hair was blond and Eirik's was black, the hair of the younger of the two in the tent was brown, and the other's was white. Einar mused that the blood that had flowed through Harald Fairhair's veins was indeed strong, indomitable stuff.

Ulrich made a pained expression.

'You greet me with a drawn sword, my Lord Olaf?' he said to the elder of the two half-brothers.

Olaf made a sardonic grunt. His white hair showed he was old, but age had neither made him fat nor feeble. His body was lean and the sinewy muscles of his arms were like mistletoe-wrapped branches of an ancient oak tree.

'When the chief killer of my brother Eirik comes before me,' he said, 'I will greet him the way I would greet any dangerous dog.'

Ulrich turned the corners of his mouth down. He held out both hands, palm upward.

'I'm unarmed, Olaf,' he said. 'We were Eirik's wolves, not his dogs, true, but he betrayed us. We no longer serve Bloody Axe.'

'How do we know that, Ulrich?' Olaf said. 'You're no stranger to treachery yourself. How do we know you're not here to murder? Or to spy on our battle plans?'

As he spoke he moved in front of the table, coming between Ulrich and what lay upon it. Einar leaned sideways and saw that the surface of the table was covered with what looked like gaming pieces. It was like the Wolf Coats had interrupted a giant game of *tafl*, though somehow he doubted that these important men had gathered here for fun. Then he realised that they were indeed engaged in a game, albeit a very real, very deadly one. The tabletop represented the field on which the armies of Eirik, Olaf and Sigrod would meet, and the playing pieces were their warriors. The brother kings and their most powerful allies were planning how the clash would unfold in the same way the Gods must be above the real battlefield outside.

'You will have to take me at my word,' Ulrich said. 'But look how I come before you. We have no weapons, no helmets, no mail or shields. We throw ourselves on your mercy.'

Olaf shook his head and lifted his sword. 'No weapons? You've not much to offer us then, do you?'

'Lord Olaf,' Ulrich said. 'You know what my crew can do in a fight. If you arm us and place us in a crucial spot on the field we can swing the battle for you.'

King Olaf of Viken ran his eyes over the people standing before him. He lowered his sword, reversed it then slid it into its sheath that hung from his belt. With the gesture, Einar sensed the tension in the tent drop a little. Others around the table also lowered their weapons.

'Your crew indeed has a fearsome reputation, Ulrich,' he said. 'But what do I see before me today? An Úlfhéðnar company always has twelve in it. You come here with only seven warriors and two young lads. No, wait.'

Olaf narrowed his eyes as he took a second look at Affreca.

'A young lad and a *woman*,' he continued. 'And great Thor's mighty hammer! Is that Eirik's Blámaðr?'

Olaf raised a finger towards Surt, whose face broke into

a wide grin at the clear discomfort his presence seemed to invoke on the faces of the men gathered around the table.

'True, Lord Olaf, we have lost some of our number,' Ulrich said, 'but the lad here is Einar Thorfinnsson. His father is the Skull Cleaver, Jarl of Orkney. The "girl" is Affreca, daughter of King Guthfrith of Dublin. As for Surt here? Well, I'm sure you're well aware of his prowess. You must have seen him fight a few times.'

'I've seen him beat men to death with his bare hands,' Olaf said. 'But I need men who can hold a position in a shield wall, not brawlers. I don't see much to impress me here, Ulrich.'

Einar could sense the Wolf Coats around him stiffen. Some twitched fingers, others folded their arms, some clenched fists.

'They are all worthy members of my company,' Ulrich said.

As the Wolf Coat leader spoke Einar noticed Affreca's back straighten and saw her chin raise.

Olaf looked nonplussed.

'Have they all been through the Úlfhéðnar initiation?' he said, waggling his finger in the direction of Surt.

'With respect, what do you know of the Úlfhéðnar initiation, lord?' Ulrich said.

'I am a king, Ulrich,' Olaf said. 'And the son of a king. My father had companies of berserkers and wolf coats who fought for him. I know all about your secret rituals and weird customs.'

Einar could see that Ulrich was disconcerted by Olaf's words. He wondered at the nature of these hidden practices, if the fact that someone outside the pack knew about them could cause such clear discomfort in the Wolf Coat leader.

'Father, who are these men?'

A new voice made everyone look around. A young, tow-haired boy pushed his way through the crowd to stand beside Olaf. He was a tall lad but Einar judged he was probably only about eight or nine winters old. His precocious tone, expensive clothes and the self-assured manner in which he bore himself spoke of the confidence and entitlement brought by wealth and privilege.

The boy reminded Einar of a younger version of Audun, the arrogant son of Hrapp, the chieftain of his district back home in Iceland. Einar felt a feeling of satisfaction as he recalled the startled expression on Audun's face as Einar had smashed his fist into it. It was hard to believe that their fight during a game of *knattleikr* on the ice back home was only about half a year ago now. To Einar, it seemed like a lifetime before. His pleasure was quickly replaced by sadness at the thought that it was his anger on that day that had led to him being outlawed from Iceland, separated from his home and his mother. Was she all right?

'These men want to fight for me, my son,' Olaf said, ruffling the hair of the boy and smiling down at him in evident pleasure. Einar had heard that old men treasure sons born to them late in their years and clearly Olaf was no exception. 'What do you think?'

'They don't look like much father,' the boy said, his face turning to a sneer as he surveyed the ragged crew standing before his father. As he spoke another boy, younger, dark haired and slightly less well dressed came to stand beside him. This child's eyes flicked around the crowd in a nervous fashion. It was obvious he lacked the confidence of his companion.

Ulrich tutted in annoyance and turned to Olaf's brother, the brown-haired Sigrod Haraldsson who stood beside the King of Viken with his arms folded.

'I thought this war was a joint adventure,' Ulrich said. 'Do you share Olaf's opinion, Lord Sigrod?'

Sigrod looked annoyed just to be addressed. He shook his head, his expression angry. Einar judged that this was perhaps less of a joint venture, and Sigrod was probably more of a sidekick.

'Lords, what can I say or do to convince you?' Ulrich said, spreading his hands wide. 'We are here to help your rebellion.'

Einar sensed the atmosphere in the tent change in a moment. It felt as if the flap had opened to let the cold wind blow in. Olaf, Sigrod and their men all glared at Ulrich. For a few moments there was silence.

'*Rebellion*?' Olaf finally spoke. His voice grated as if he had a throatful of gravel. 'This is not a *rebellion*, Ulrich. Our father split the Kingdom of Norway between his sons. We were each to have our own kingdom. I was given Viken, Sigrod was given Trondheim and Eirik was supposed to have the Uplands and the west. Our brother seems to have forgotten that. He claims all of Norway as his own.'

'Perhaps there is too much of your father in him,' Skar said. 'Harald would allow no king but himself.'

'So the other dogs have tongues too?' Olaf said, his lip curling into a snarl. 'Skarphedin, isn't it? I must say neither of you are doing much to convince me you aren't still Eirik's men.'

Skar just raised an eyebrow and pursed his lips.

'What do you want me to do, lord?' Ulrich said, his frustration evident in the wide-eyed expression on his face. 'Bring you Eirik's head on a trencher? I would if I could but it will be hard without any weapons.'

Olaf looked at Ulrich for a long moment. Then the King of Viken dropped his hand to the hilt of his sword. With a scrape of metal Olaf drew the long, wide-bladed weapon once again.

Everyone in the tent tensed.

'Outside,' Olaf said, flicking his head in the direction of a back entrance of the tent.

Nine

For a moment there was nervous silence.

Einar looked around. The Wolf Coats were outnumbered just by the noblemen in the tent, and most of them were armed. Behind him at the tent entrance was Gorm and ten of the warriors from outside. They were not just armed but were clad in war gear; mail, shields and helmets. If there was a fight, dangerous as they were, the úlfhéðnar would not stand a chance. There was little they could do right now except do what they were told.

Ulrich nodded to his men, signalling that they should comply, then he led the way outside, exiting through another flap that was in the back end of the tent. The brother kings and all their noblemen and their warriors all filed in behind them.

Outside, Einar blinked for a moment as his eyes readjusted to the sunshine. Olaf walked over to Ulrich and the two men faced each other once more.

Then Olaf tossed his sword into the air so it flipped around. He caught it by the end of the blade and proffered the weapon hilt first to Ulrich.

Ulrich's eyebrows shot upwards in surprise but he took

the sword. He held it up, watching how the sun danced across the patterns in the metal.

Then Einar saw the prisoner.

The man was squatting on the ground. His hands were bound behind his back in shackles attached to a long, heavy chain anchored into the ground by a spike. He was stripped to his waist, wearing only a pair of leather breeches. He looked familiar to Einar but he could not quite place where he had seen him before. The task of recognition was made harder by the fact that his face and torso were a mess of bruises and cuts. His right eye was swollen and closed over and his short grey hair was matted with blood. He had clearly taken quite a beating after his capture.

'You know who this is?' Olaf said.

Ulrich nodded, looking down at the prisoner.

'It's Grettir,' he said. 'The leader of King Eirik's household warriors. Hello Grettir. You've had a haircut since we last met.'

The prisoner looked up, peering with his good eye.

'Ulrich,' Grettir said with a sneer, revealing broken teeth and bloody gums. 'So it's true. You did escape death at the witches' skerry.'

'No thanks to you, Grettir,' Ulrich said. 'You left us there to drown like cats in a sack, you bastard.'

'You always were lucky, Ulrich,' Grettir said, his head dipped as he struggled to deal with the pain that wracked his beaten body.

Ulrich snorted and swept his hand around his bedraggled crew.

'The Norns who rule our luck don't seem to be watching

us at the moment,' he said. 'Yours seem distracted by something more interesting too.'

'We caught him trying to spy on us,' Olaf said. 'The arrogant idiot thought by cutting his hair short no one would recognise him and he could just walk into our camp. Now, Ulrich: Here is one of Eirik's right-hand men. If you're serious about joining our cause you can kill him for us.'

'Well, Grettir,' Ulrich said with a smile. 'I have to admit I'm actually pleased to see you again. It looks like it's you or me.'

To Einar's surprise, Grettir chuckled.

'Those Norns are still watching us, Ulrich,' he said, snorting through the blood that clotted his broken nose. 'And they're laughing. A week or so ago we were in exactly the opposite situation. This is quite a game they play.'

His face became serious. Then he took a deep breath and squared his shoulders. He glanced at Olaf.

'I don't suppose I can hold a sword?' he said. 'Even a blunted one? I'd like to die with a weapon in my hand.'

Olaf shook his head.

Grettir turned back to Ulrich, meeting his gaze with his one open eye.

'Very well,' he said. 'Make it quick, you bastard. Don't make a mess of it.'

Ulrich grasped the hilt of Olaf's sword with both hands and readied himself to strike. Then Sigrod stepped forward and laid a hand on Ulrich's forearm. He looked at his brother Olaf.

'Wait,' he said, nodding towards Olaf's son and his companion. 'What about the children?'

'My son needs to see this,' Olaf said, puffing out his chest. He gently pulled the tow-haired boy before him and laid his hands on his shoulders. 'Watch this and take heed, Trygve. This is how a king deals with his enemies. One day you will have to do the same, my boy. Where's the other lad? He should see this too.'

There was a moment of disturbance as everyone looked for the younger boy then he was pushed forward by the surrounding nobles so he was beside Olaf as well. The dark-haired boy looked as reluctant as his friend Trygve to have such a close-up view of proceedings.

'Gudrod,' Olaf addressed the boy in a voice all could hear. 'Eirik Bloody Axe killed your father. This man is one of Eirik's men. Here you will now see part of the vengeance that is your right delivered by me.'

Olaf nodded to Ulrich.

Ulrich placed his feet apart and twisted his body, cocking the sword back above his right shoulder. He took a moment to aim, then struck.

It was a perfect blow. The blade hit Grettir's neck a few fingers' breadth below his ear. Grettir had no time to cry out. In an instant the sword sheared through skin, flesh and parted the bones in his neck. Grettir's head rolled backwards off his decapitated torso and fell behind him to the earth with a dull thump.

Trygve flinched at the sight. Olaf tightened his grip on the boy's shoulders, ensuring he could not turn away. Gudrod's eyes were screwed shut.

The momentum of Ulrich's blow made him stagger a little. Two strong jets of blood erupted from the purple flesh of Grettir's severed neck. All the men gathered around took a hasty step backwards so their expensive clothes were not splattered.

Ulrich's nostrils were flared, his eyes glittered and there was a fierce grin on his face. As Grettir's body collapsed sideways to the ground Ulrich straightened up, taking a couple of deep breaths as he fought to regain composure. He wiped the bloodied sword on the grass then offered it to Olaf.

The King of Viken, now smiling, took back his weapon. He stooped and picked up Grettir's severed head by grabbing a handful of its grey hair and held it up so all could see. Einar saw Grettir's dead face, now white as snow, fixed in an expression of disappointed rage.

'Today we killed Grettir,' Olaf said in a loud voice. 'Soon it will be Eirik himself!'

Those around him on the hilltop cheered. The blustering wind carried off the sound so it was not as loud as would have been expected and almost sounded half-hearted.

Olaf dropped Grettir's head. Noticing his right hand was splashed with blood, he turned to his son and wiped his bloody fingers across both the boy's cheeks. Einar noticed that the previous haughty expression on the face of Trygve had been replaced with a gaze of stunned horror.

As the cheering died away, the sound of someone clapping with enthusiasm came from a group of men standing among the other nobles. Einar turned to see a blond-haired young man in rich clothes. He had a clean-shaven chin but long, combed moustache. It was he who was doing the clapping. He was surrounded by eight men in fabulous, glittering war gear. Every man wore a conspicuous, gleaming silver cross around their neck.

'Well done, Lord Olaf,' the blond man said. 'Very well done. A king should act with such resolve.'

Einar frowned. This man spoke in the Norse tongue, but with the accent of the West Saxons of Britain.

Olaf did not acknowledge the comment but instead turned to Ulrich.

'Nice work,' Olaf said. 'The reputation of you and your men is indeed fearsome. I'm glad you will be fighting with us not against us. Welcome aboard. Now go and get yourselves armed. Battle is coming.'

He gestured to Gorm who inclined his head, indicating that Ulrich and the others should follow him. As they filed in behind Gorm and four other warriors who led them away from the tent, Einar turned to Skar.

'Our revenge is off to a good start, eh?' he said, grinning. 'One enemy has fallen already!'

Skar did not look so pleased.

'If Grettir was here,' the big man said. 'Eirik won't be too far away.'

Ten

'There's an old tale about long ago, in the youth of the world,' Skar said. 'It tells how the God Ríg came to this Middle Earth and walked on green roads.'

'Ríg?' Einar screwed up his face. 'I've never heard of that god.'

'He's one of the ancient ones, the *Vanir*,' Skar said. 'The old Gods people worshipped before they knew of the *Aesir*.'

'They still do in some places,' Ulrich said, running his fingers along the blade of a sword laid on a table before him. 'Out in the backwoods. In the wild forests. In places like the Uplands, Telemark or Lundr.'

They stood within another tent that was filled with weapons and war gear. The tent housed the kings' weapon horde, used by their personal hearth men, bodyguards and other esteemed warriors. Gorm had led them there from Olaf and Sigrod's command tent. Olaf had said they could take whatever they needed.

'Those folk are strange,' Ulrich went on. 'Some say, though, that Ríg was just Heimdall in disguise. Others say it was Odin.'

'Some? Others?' Einar screwed up his face.

Ulrich made an enigmatic smile and moved his hand to another sword. 'Those who know better,' he said.

Einar sighed. He was in no mood for Ulrich's religious mysteries.

'Anyway,' he turned back to Skar, 'What's so special about this Ríg?'

'The tale goes that he came to earth and created the orders that mankind must be ranked by,' Skar said. 'There is the race of *thralls* – the slaves. Then there are the freeholder farmers and at the top there are kings, jarls and nobles.'

'In the original tale it was just kings,' Ulrich said, running his eye across the wicked-sharp blade of a seax knife. 'It was Eirik's father, King Harald, who put the jarls above the freemen.'

'The point is, each one is separate,' Skar said, looking annoyed at Ulrich's interruption. 'They were set in their place by the Gods, the one above the other. And there they should stay. Thralls do not become freeholders and freeholders do not become kings. How have you not heard this? Every child is taught it.'

'Perhaps in Norway but not in Iceland,' Einar said. 'Is there a point to this tale?'

'I was just thinking,' Skar said, placing a hand on Einar's shoulder. There was an earnest look on his face. 'This time last year you were just a farm boy in Iceland. Now you move among the company of kings. I hope this has not offended the Gods.'

Ulrich looked round, his eyes narrowed.

'Something has made our luck desert us,' he said. 'And we have enough bad luck as it is with Gunnhild's curse on us.'

'And you're all sons of lords then are you? The Gods will be happy with you mixing with kings and jarls?' Einar said. His tone was deriding but as he looked around he realised from the expressions on the faces of the others that this was indeed true. It made sense when he thought about it. The days of farmers' sons were filled with working the land and tending the beasts. It took money and slaves to have enough spare time to spend practising weaponcraft.

Einar's cheeks flushed.

'Well I am an Icelander and all Icelanders are free men,' he said, aware that his voice was rising. 'Our forefathers left this land to start a new life in a new world. Away from kings and jarls and old stories that tell men they have to stay in their place.'

'Anyway: He may have grown up on a farm in Iceland but he's the son of the Jarl of Orkney,' Affreca said. 'The bastard son, true, but blood is blood.'

'Can you lot get on with the task in hand?' Gorm said. He sounded bored. 'The kings are hosting a feast tonight and I would like to get washed before it.'

The Wolf Coats – Ulrich, Skar, Bodvar, Atli, Sigurd, Starkad and Kari – as well as Einar, Surt and Affreca returned to picking over the weapons and war gear laid out before them. Roan stood apart. He was a sailor and would take no part in any fighting.

'This is all old,' Bodvar said. 'Is there nothing better?'

'The best has all been taken,' Gorm said. 'Many men have come to fight behind Olaf and Sigrod's banners. Olaf has already granted arms to lots of them. You're arriving late to this feast.'

Skar curled his lip as he turned a rusted, dented helmet over in his hands. He set it down again and picked up a long-handled axe.

'Can you fight with weapons, Surt?' he said over his shoulder. 'I've only ever seen you wrestle.'

Surt stepped closer to the table and took his hood down. He had grown tired of the staring eyes of the people in the camp he passed by and had pulled the hood up on the walk to this tent. The black man ran his hands over the swords, axes, spears and other implements of destruction on the table.

'When I was younger, before I was enslaved,' he said, 'I was a warrior. I fought in the army of the Emir of Córdoba. I can fight with many different weapons and have killed men with each one. I've used Greek Fire and other implements of death you haven't even dreamed of. *These*, though—'

He lifted a sword and cast a disparaging eye over it.

'The weapons of you northern peoples are like farm tools,' he said. 'They're barbaric, uncouth. There is no sophistication to them. What are you looking at?'

Surt had caught sight of Gorm who was gaping open-mouthed at him.

'I think he has never seen a *blámaðr* up close before,' Skar said.

Gorm's mouth moved soundlessly for a few moments, then he said, 'I've heard of King Eirik's Blámaðr but I did not think you could speak our tongue? Your skin: It's black. Are you a troll?'

'Your skin is white,' Surt said. 'Are you a ghost?'

'Surt here is a man, just like you and I,' Ulrich said. 'All you need to know is that he is one of my crew.'

Gorm looked unsure. His hand crept towards the hilt of his sheathed sword. Surt bared his teeth at him and growled, then gave out a hearty laugh as Gorm flinched backwards.

Skar lifted a very long spear with a cross pole. He looked delighted.

'I can't be a *merkismaðr* if I don't have a standard to bear,' he said.

'We have a banner?' Einar said.

'We have the Raven Banner, lad!' Skar said. 'Have you forgotten already?'

'But it's a fake,' Einar said. 'It has no magic.'

'Magic is what men believe in their minds,' Ulrich said.

Einar, still puzzled, shook his head. He picked up a sword and held it up, examining it in a manner that he hoped looked like he knew what he was looking for. Out of the corner of his eye he saw Skar looking at him. Einar sighed.

'I suppose you're going to tell me to put the sword down and get an axe?' he said. 'I've been practising, Skar. You've been *making* me practice. I'm not as useless with a sword as I used to be.'

'No, not at all,' Skar said, shaking his head. 'In battle you'll need as many weapons as you can carry.'

Einar felt a cold feeling in his guts at the thought that soon he would be in a battle. He remembered the terror and the fury of the skirmishes he had fought in over the last year. What would a full-scale war be like?

'I wouldn't take that particular sword though,' Skar said, taking it out of Einar's hand and laying it back on the table. 'It has no ring.'

The big man sifted through the other blades on the table then lifted another and handed it to Einar. Einar saw that there was a ring attached to the bottom of the hilt.

'You can tie a leather thong through that,' Skar said. 'And tie the other around the wrist of your sword arm. Let the sword hang from it. When the time comes that you need it, you might be so crushed against the men around you there is no room to draw it from a scabbard. If it's hanging from your hand all you need to do is grab the hilt. Keep that broken spear as well. The short shaft makes it perfect for close-in fighting.'

'Are there any smaller shields?' Affreca said to no one in particular.

'What for?' Skar replied.

Affreca made a half-amused frown. 'There is a battle coming? I'll need one same as rest of you. How will I take my place in the shield wall without one?'

Skar just looked at her. Affreca's shoulders sagged.

'Don't you dare,' she said, her face flushing. She held up a forefinger. 'I'm as much a part of this crew as the rest of you. Don't you try and say I can't stand in the shield wall alongside you.'

'Have you ever stood in a shield wall, my lady, the king's daughter?' Skar said, folding his arms across his chest. 'Have you ever been crushed against your enemy, face to face with him with nothing between you but your shield and his? Your nose is full of his stinking, ale-soaked bad breath. His spit is flying in your face as he screams curses at you and drives into you while you both try to shove your blade into each other's guts. Or face. Then, if you manage to do it, you watch the light die from his eyes right before you. Have you ever cowered, bracing yourself with all your might, trying to get every morsel of protection the slim wood of the shield can give you while some huge bastard, mad with battle rage, tries to batter his way through it to get to you?'

'Very poetic. Einar will be jealous he didn't say that,' Affreca said. 'You think I can't do that because I'm a woman?'

'It's not about being a woman—' Skar said.

'Oh *really*?' Affreca cut him off. She now stood with arms folded, her voice dripping with sarcasm. She looked at Ulrich.

'Do you agree with this?' she said.

Ulrich shrugged.

'Skarphedin is both *stafnbúi* and merkismaðr of this company. He is my Prow Man and our Standard Bearer,' he said. 'I'm the leader but if we are in an open battle then Skar commands. He's fought many battles all over this Middle Earth and he knows what he is doing. So whatever my merkismaðr says, goes.'

'I'm as good as the rest of you,' Affreca said. She pointed at Einar. 'I'm certainly as much use as him. He'll be so busy daydreaming or thinking about what's the right thing to do that he'll forget there's a battle to be fought.'

Einar opened his mouth to speak but could not find the words. He felt as if she had stabbed him with the sword she held in one hand, right through the middle of his chest.

Skar sighed.

'All right. I'll show you what I mean,' he said. 'Grab a shield.'

Affreca picked up a round wooden shield from the table and grasped its handle with her left hand.

Skar picked up a visored helmet and plonked it on her head.

'You'll need that too,' he said. 'Bodvar, Atli, grab a shield and stand either side of the king's daughter here.'

The two burly Wolf Coats lifted shields and took up position in line.

'*Skjaldborg*!' Skar barked the order and all three dropped to a half crouch, shields overlapping and locked together with a loud clack of wood on wood.

Skar lifted a sword, still in its scabbard, from the table. He grabbed it by the hilt, then picked up a shield and slung it on his other arm. He threw his head back and took in a sharp breath through his nose. Dropping his head again, the big man let out a roar that made everyone in the tent jump. He crouched, dipped his left shoulder behind his shield and charged straight into the others.

Bodvar, Affreca and Atli just had time to brace themselves before Skar smashed into them. There was a loud bang as his shield clattered against Affreca's. The weight of his impact knocked her reeling backwards, away from the other two. She toppled over, falling flat on her back. Skar stepped into the gap where she had stood. With exaggerated slowness, he swiped the sheathed sword to the right tapping Bodvar across his exposed back.

'That's him dead,' Skar said.

Then he swiped left, tapping Atli in a similar way.

'He's now dead too,' Skar said, then he stepped forward, straddling the prone Affreca. He levelled the point of the scabbard at the point just under her chin.

'Now you're dead too,' he said.

Affreca, panting, looked up along the length of the sheathed sword.

'It's not about whether you're a man or a woman,' Skar said. 'It's about weight.'

'There will be boys in the shield wall smaller than me,' Affreca said. 'I saw them in the camp.'

'They have no choice but to take their place and they will be the first to die,' Skar said. 'If we hit their shield wall it will be the boys I'll be looking for so I can smash a way through. You may want to stand in the shield wall, lady, but do any of you others want to stand at her side?'

Affreca looked around. All she saw were the others shaking their heads, amused grins and smirks on their faces.

'Fuck you, Skarphedin,' she said.

'This is quite the dangerous crew you have, Ulrich,' Gorm said, trying to regain some of his air of bravado. 'Seven warriors, an old skipper, an Icelandic farmer, a black-skinned *jǫtunn* and a girl.'

Ulrich offered his hand to Affreca. She hesitated, then grasped it and pulled herself back to her feet. Ulrich held out a bow to her.

'Lady Affreca,' Ulrich said. 'With this you're more dangerous than all the rest of us put together. I'll feel safer knowing you're protecting us with that.'

'Fuck you too, Ulrich,' Affreca said, brushing herself down and rubbing her left elbow where it had hit the ground hard.

'Ulrich won't join us in the shield wall either,' Skar said. 'He's far too small as well. This lad on the other hand,'

He clapped a hand on Einar's shoulder.

'Maybe a daydreamer but he's a big heavy brute,' Skar continued. 'And that's all we need.'

Gorm gave a chuckle.

'Well they'll all need to be good,' he said. 'King Olaf has a special place in mind for you in the battle against King Eirik. Right in the front of the battle ranks.'

Eleven

Iceland

Unn woke with a start. Her heart was racing and her breath came in pants. The dream had come again.

Dream? It was more nightmare than dream.

She had not had any dreams for years. In her young days in Ireland, the daughter of a king, many had said that Unn Ni Muirchertach had been touched by the magic of the *sidhe*, the people who lived under the hills. She had dreamed often, and many times her dreams had contained messages, visions or portents that proved true in the real world. Sometimes they were warnings.

Her life had changed forever when the Norsemen had come, bringing fire and death. She had been ripped from her home and carried off in their dragon ships to become bed-slave of Thorfinn the Skull Cleaver. No dream had warned her of that. In fact her dreams had come less and less after that. Perhaps it was being away from those hills of Ireland and the influence of whatever magic the little people had left in them. There had been the occasional dream but when one did come they were always more vague, their meaning more obscure than they had been in her young days.

Unn was now an old woman. Her life had certainly not turned out the way she had expected when she was a girl. She should have been married to an Irish prince and ruled a kingdom beside him, surrounded by her own clan and cousins, speaking their own tongue and worshipping the one, true God. Instead, as she went into her twilight years, she was in Iceland, a God-forsaken island at the very edge of the world, surrounded by pagans. She was not even known by her real name any more. Here she was Unn Kjartinssdottir.

It had been an eventful life, however. She had escaped from Thorfinn's lair in Orkney and hidden in Iceland. It was the very remoteness of the place that had kept her safe from the jarl's rage. To the other settlers of that bleak land she was just another fugitive. Most others were running from the tyranny of Harald Fairhair, King of Norway. She had been accepted and built up her own farmstead. That was gone now. Thorfinn had finally found where she was hiding and sent his son Hrolf to kill her. Her farm was a burned-out ruin. Thorfinn had paid for trying that. Hrolf now lay under a mound beside where her house had stood.

Despite all this, she would not change the path she had walked. It had brought her the one thing she was proud of more than anything: The son Thorfinn had sired on her. Einar. He was tall, strong like his father but without the cruel streak in his nature. And he was a poet, the best singer to come out of Iceland in at least a generation. That was what he had got from her side and it was not just motherly pride, she knew. Many had said it. One day he would be a great man.

She had not done too badly anyway. Now she was the wife of Hrapp, the *Goði* of the district. He was a rich man; the Chieftain, the Law Keeper and religious superior of the whole area. It was the heathen religion but still, in Unn's eyes that meant he had some form of morality. He was not godless. Now as his wife she ran his household and, when he was away from the territory as he was now, she ran the district in his stead. In a way she had ended up a sort of queen after all. The district Hrapp was Goði of was certainly larger than the average Irish kingdom.

Now the dreams had come again to trouble her sleep.

She had had the same dream two nights before while in bed. The details were dark and most fled her mind when she awoke but she recalled it had entailed being in a forest at night. She was wandering among tall trees. There was snow on the ground and a baleful full moon shone down from above bare branches that looked like the long bony fingers of skeletons. Her breath rose in clouds into the cold air. Einar was there too. She could not see him but she could sense him somewhere. She felt he was in danger. She pushed through the undergrowth and came on a clearing, in the centre of which stood a mighty ash tree. Every branch bore a horrific fruit. The corpses of every sort of creature from dogs to men swung in the wind, hung by their necks. The darkness hid the horrors of their putrefaction but their outlines were bloated and the ropes that suspended them creaked as the bodies swayed back and forth.

Movement caught her eye and she spotted a figure standing beside the trunk of the tree, half hidden in the shadow thrown by the moonbeams. It was a man wrapped in a long, grey cloak. He carried a walking staff and wore a wide-brimmed hat that cast his face into shadow. There was a silver glitter deep within the shadow where his right eye should be. It looked like a lone star twinkling in the night sky. There was no similar glitter from the other side of his face where the left eye should be. As she watched he crooked a finger towards her, then he turned and walked away, disappearing from view behind the wide tree trunk.

Then a crashing of undergrowth made her turn. Einar ran into the clearing. He was pale in the moonlight and out of breath. Something was chasing him, she somehow knew this. She sensed an evil presence, somewhere deep in the dark of the forest. It was coming closer.

A pack of wolves burst from the trees behind Einar. Was this what pursued him? Then she realised he was not running from them. He was running with them. As he ran past her, out of breath and desperate, he cast a glance in her direction. She saw sorrow on his face. Regret. Shame perhaps?

Then the thing came. A huge, dark, rushing presence. Immense and evil, invisible yet somehow familiar. It was in the trees and coming closer. It was on the edge of the clearing—.

It was then she woke. When the dream had come two nights before she had woken panting in her bed. She reached out for her new husband, Hrapp, forgetting he was away from home travelling. All she felt was the cold furs of the empty space in the bed beside her.

This time she woke to find herself in her chair in the workroom of the house. She had been working on embroidering a tapestry and the heat of the fire must have made her doze off.

With a sigh Unn set her work down. It was an embroidery of a large black hare but it was getting too dark to work anyway. Unn left the workroom and entered the main, long room of Hrapp's house.

She stopped, spotting the stranger straight away.

Servants, farmhands and others of the household all lined the long table, eating their evening meal. There were a lot less than would usually be there. Hrapp had many of his men with him which left a lot of gaps at the table. Sitting near one end was a man she had not seen before, hunched over a bowl of goat stew. He had lived many winters but was not stooped or bent by age. He was painfully thin, the bones of his shoulders visible even through the grey wool jerkin he wore. The top of his head was bald but a ring of long, lank, white hair hung from the edges of his crown.

Unn caught the arm of a servant girl who was hurrying past with a trencher of bread for the table.

'Who's that?' she hissed to the girl, indicating the newcomer with her eyes.

'He is a wanderer, lady,' the girl said. 'He says he can tell fortunes and is travelling around Iceland looking for work. He came to the door a little while ago and asked for shelter for the night.'

'And you let him in?' Unn said. Her misgiving was evident in her tone. 'The Lord Hrapp is away. Did you think it was wise to let strangers into our house?'

'Lady, you were asleep,' the girl said. 'And...'

Her voice trailed off. Her cheeks reddened.

'And what?' Unn demanded.

'Lady, they say Odin himself wanders the world on winter nights,' the girl's voice dropped to a hushed whisper. 'It's unwise to turn wanderers away. Who's to say it's not the God himself?'

Unn was about to chide the girl's idle superstition when the words of her father's priest, quoting Jesus, surfaced in her mind from somewhere in her childhood.

Behold, I stand at the door and knock. If anyone hears my voice and opens the door, I will come in to him and eat with him, and he with me.

'Very well,' Unn said. She dismissed the girl and walked to the end of the table where the stranger sat. As if aware of her gaze he turned towards her and stood up as she approached.

'My lady,' he said. 'I humbly thank you for your kind hospitality. My name is Vakir Solmundarsson. I am travelling through these parts and will not trouble you for more than one night. I believe your husband is away?'

Unn nodded. 'He has business in the Westmann Islands. I understand you are a fortune teller? Perhaps you will do that for the household after supper? The dark nights are still long and Lord knows we need something to pass the time.'

The old man made a pained face.

'Sadly, my gift cannot be called on at will,' he said, an obsequious grin revealing long, yellow teeth. 'I could perhaps do some tricks however that distract folk for a time.'

Unn felt a sudden shiver run down her spine. What had caused it she had no idea. Perhaps there was something in this strange man's eyes?

'Well I bid you welcome,' she said, nevertheless. 'While you are here please treat this house as your home.'

'I am grateful, lady,' Vakir said with a small bow. He still smiled but Unn felt it was more like a leer.

Deciding that she was being foolish – the strange dream had unnerved her – she left and went to get her own evening meal.

After supper, when the tables had been cleared and the household chores completed, the old stranger made good his promise and performed some magic for those gathered around the dying embers of the fire. His tricks were paltry, however, mere sleight of hand such as producing an egg from the ear of a servant girl or making coins belonging to household members disappear. He was not too good at making them reappear either. Unimpressed, Unn retired to her bed early and fell into a deep, this time untroubled sleep.

Later still, in the dead of night, when all the household was asleep, Vakir sat up in the straw bed he had been given at the edge of the hall. They had offered him a place closer to the hearth where residual heat from the fire could help his old bones but he had refused, saying he was happy near the door.

In the darkness, Vakir got out of bed and crept across the hall, trying to be as quiet as possible. He reached the door and opened it.

Outside, Sigtryggr snarfari and Hallvard harðfari stood.

The moonlight glittered on the blades of their drawn knives.

'As we were told, the Goði and his men are away,' Vakir whispered. 'Only the servants and the woman are here.'

He stood aside as the other two rushed past him into the house.

Twelve

Tunsberg, Norway

'I'm surprised we were invited to this feast,' Skar said.

They were walking through the camp down the hill towards the town of Tunsberg. It was later and the sun was on the horizon, just on the verge of sliding behind the mountains. Darkness was leaking across the sky. The wind, still strong and chilled with the final breath of winter, roared in from the sea, drumming against the leather of the tents and whipping and snapping the banners of the army. Braziers and campfires crackled and spat.

'Odin says you should keep your enemies where you can see them,' Ulrich said. 'Olaf probably wants us in sight so he knows we're not sneaking back to King Eirik. Everyone keep their wits about them. Don't drink too much. Be careful what you say.'

'I thought we were on their side now,' Bodvar said.

'Let's not rush into trust,' Ulrich said.

'Who will be there apart from us?' Einar asked.

'I would guess that most of the people you saw in that

tent earlier will be there,' Ulrich said. 'Olaf and Sigrod have a lot of noblemen and allies they need to keep happy.'

'Did you notice the Saxons outside Olaf's tent earlier?' Skar said. 'What do you think they're doing here?'

'I don't know,' Ulrich said. 'But I don't like it.'

Einar glanced down at his shabby wool jerkin and breeches. It was not exactly the fine clothes that should be worn when mixing with kings and jarls.

Olaf and Sigrod were hosting a feast in a great mead hall in the town. Ulrich and his crew had to walk from the camp to a gate in the ramparts that guarded Tunsberg. It seemed as though most of the other people on the track were leaving the town in the opposite direction.

The gate was guarded by twenty warriors. They were well armed, carried shields and spears and did not look like the bored sentries often found at town gates.

'No one from the army is allowed in the town after sunset, lads,' a big, broad-shouldered guard said as they approached.

When Ulrich explained who they were and that they were on the way to the king's feast, they were allowed through and given directions to where they would find the mead hall.

'Why does Olaf keep his warriors out of the town?' Einar said as they made their way along a wooden-planked street lined on either side by thatched longhouses. The stink of the army outside was intensified inside the town ramparts and Einar was glad of the gale that gusted fresh air in from the sea.

'Warriors, ale taverns and women are a bad combination, lad,' Skar said. 'Everyone in an army is excited and impatient for the coming fight. You must have sensed the atmosphere in the camp? It's like dry grassland in the height of summer. A woman is like a careless flame tossed into that grass. Before you know it the whole lot is up in flames. Drunk warriors will fight with anyone; each other, town people, their own shadows. Olaf doesn't need the main town in his kingdom wrecked when a tavern brawl turns to outright war.'

'Many rich men will have houses in town and Olaf needs their support,' Ulrich said. 'They won't want to have to lock up their daughters the whole time the army is camped outside.'

'They should probably do that anyway,' Bodvar said, casting a hungry, wolf-like glare at a pretty young woman passing on the other way in the street. 'Thor's mighty hammer but we've been on that ship for an age! Some female company would be very welcome.'

'You've got female company,' Ulrich said, nodding towards Affreca.

Bodvar grunted. 'I mean the sort of female who won't cut my balls off if I put my hand on her thigh.'

'Forget about that Bodvar,' Ulrich said. 'We're here to fight.'

'And tonight we're here to feast,' Skar said with a grin. 'I can't wait. I'm starving.'

The great feasting hall stood in the centre of the town. Like most jarl's halls, it was tall and narrow but very long, with a curved shingled roof that made it look like a ship placed upside down in the middle of Tunsberg. It was not as grand as the hall of Guthfrith of Dublin, Affreca's father, or that of Einar's own father, Jarl Thorfinn of Orkney, but then Tunsberg was not as large a town as Dublin.

Another line of warriors guarded the double doors of the hall. They allowed Ulrich and his crew through into the warmth and noise within.

Heat radiated from long fire pits in the floor. Einar took a deep breath, savouring the aroma of ale, fresh bread, roasting meat and the greasy smell of whale oil from the lamps that provided light. Long, narrow tapestries woven in many colours decorated the walls. Happy chatter bubbled up from the crowd of feasters lined on the benches and tables that ran the length of the floor. After the cold, wet discomfort of weeks spent on the ship this place seemed like Odin's own Valour Hall.

Olaf and Sigrod, the brother kings, greeted their guests at the entrance. Both were splendidly dressed in tunics embroidered in bright coloured threads that made Einar even more self-conscious of his own shabby attire. Olaf's white hair was now swept back and braided in a ponytail. Several other noblemen and women stood beside them, drinking horns brimming with white-frothed ale in their hands.

'Ulrich! Welcome!' Olaf said. Then to a nearby thrall he added, 'Get these men a drink!'

He stood with his arms wide. All his former hostility gone. It seemed as though he were welcoming home a brother thought to have been lost at sea.

'I am sorry for my harsh words earlier,' he said in a very loud voice. Einar noticed how the attention of the others around them was caught by it. 'My brother and I are glad to welcome some of Eirik's most dangerous warriors into our ranks. When even Eirik's own Wolf Coats turn against him, what hope does he have, eh?'

Olaf's face held a slight flush and beads of sweat glistened beneath his white hairline. He grabbed a nearby horn from a passing serving slave and chugged a long draft of ale from it.

Ulrich and Skar exchanged glances.

'Isn't it a bit early to be celebrating?' Ulrich asked, the smile on his face looking a bit forced. 'We haven't beaten Eirik yet.'

'We're celebrating this alliance of great men!' Olaf said, sweeping his hand around to indicate the noblemen gathered around him. 'This bonding will break the over-proud tyrant Eirik and bring him to his death.'

Sigrod, who stood beside Olaf, looked away for a moment.

'I would say we are simply marking this occasion,' Sigrod said, his voice a half-mutter and a blush on his cheeks. 'Rather than celebrating anything.'

'When Eirik arrives we'll be ready for him,' Olaf said, cuffing ale froth from his moustache with the back of his hand.

'What news of Hakon, Lord King?' Ulrich said.

A sad expression fell across Sigrod's face.

'These are dark days,' Sigrod said, the expression on his face suggesting he actually felt that emotion. 'These are the wolf times, the axe times. Norway is torn in three. Eirik is in the west. We have the east. Hakon landed from Britain in the north.'

'Has he any support?' Ulrich said.

'Jarl Sigurd of Hlader has sworn his support for him,' Sigrod said. 'Many of the free folk are following him.'

'But why?' Ulrich looked genuinely surprised. 'He's a Christian.'

'He's making all sorts of mad promises,' Olaf said, scowling. 'He says he'll return them their Odal rights. But our little brother will rue the day he left the knee of Aethelstan. After we've crushed Eirik we'll march north and smash that whelp. That will leave...'

Olaf hesitated for a moment as if catching his words before they left his mouth. His eyes slid sideways towards his half-brother.

'... *us*, as joint kings of Norway,' Olaf continued. 'I think that's worth celebrating. And we've even more men coming. The Jarls Vega and Guthorm will join us within days.'

'Days, lord?' Ulrich said. 'We passed Eirik's fleet the day before yesterday, somewhere near Lundr. It was at anchor just along the coast.'

Olaf's mouth dropped open for a moment but he made no sound. Then he and Sigrod exchanged glances.

'He's closer than we were told,' Sigrod said to his brother.

'We were driven here by a gale,' Ulrich said. 'The same wind probably brought Eirik faster than you were expecting.'

Olaf waved his hand again.

'No matter,' he said. 'When he comes we will be ready and we will beat him.'

He took another swig of ale and his face brightened.

'Besides,' the king went on, clapping a big hand on Ulrich's shoulder. 'We have Eirik's Wolf Coats on our side.'

Ulrich's tight-lipped smile widened. He did not reply.

'That was good sword work earlier. A good clean kill.'

A new voice made them all turn. The blond-haired Saxon

lord who had applauded Ulrich's execution of Grettir walked over. His long hair was combed straight and he held his clean shaven chin high as if looking down his nose at all those around him. One of his warriors stood beside him. Both were now dressed in elegant, embroidered wool tunics and breeches of dark red and green. The silver crosses at their throats caught the gleams of the torchlight in the hall. These were rich men.

'Ulrich, let me introduce another of our great allies,' Olaf said. 'This is Lord Edwin, *Aetheling* of Wessex. Hakon is not the only one with allies in Britain.'

'It's an honour to meet a prince of the – what is it you like to call yourselves these days? Aenglish isn't it?' Ulrich said.

Edwin's expression soured. 'My half-brother Aethelstan likes to use that term, yes. I am a West Saxon like my father and forefather.'

'I fought in Aethelstan's army,' Ulrich said. 'We raided Scotland for him.'

The expression on Edwin's face darkened further, his eyes narrowing in undisguised suspicion.

'Don't worry,' Ulrich said with a smile. 'We didn't fight for Aethelstan by choice. We were prisoners and had to fight or be hung.'

Olaf planted a meaty hand on the Saxon's shoulder.

'Edwin has the same problems with his brother Aethelstan that Sigrod and I have with Eirik,' he said. 'We share a common bond.'

'At least Eirik is legitimate,' Edwin said. 'My brother is a bastard born of a whore. Our father sired him on a milkmaid. He has no right to the throne.'

At that moment the sound of raised voices made them all turn back towards the doors of the hall. Einar could see the warriors there had bunched together to block entrance to a couple of people outside.

'What's going on?' Olaf shouted to his men.

Gorm, who as usual was in charge of the guarding warriors, half turned.

'These two poor folk, Lord King,' he said. 'They say they want to speak to you.'

Olaf narrowed his eyes, straining to see who stood outside.

'Grimnir!' he said, a smile of recognition spreading across his face. 'This man is welcome here, Gorm. Let him in.'

With a shrug the warrior stood aside. Einar saw standing beyond him an old man. His very long white hair and beard were combed straight and smooth and flowed like an avalanche over his shoulders and chest. On his head he wore a wide-brimmed hat, the sort some wore to keep the sun and rain off their faces and shoulders. He wore a dark, plain tunic and long deerskin boots, simple clothes unlike the finery of the rich feasters in the hall. In his right hand he bore a long walking staff.

'Well, well,' Ulrich said. 'If it isn't our old friend from the forest.'

Einar recognised the man who had helped them escape from Rognvald's men a few days before, but it was the sight of the person now standing beside the old man that made his jaw drop.

Thirteen

The young woman was beautiful. She was around the same age as Einar with long, straight, golden hair, worn unbound which showed she was not yet married. Her features were fine and her skin pale. The two warriors who moved aside to grant her and the old man entrance both looked down in appreciation at her lithe body beneath her tight-fitting dress. Einar could see they had deliberately only moved far enough apart so the girl would still have to brush against them as she passed. Fleet footed, she moved like she was dancing to hop between them without touching either.

The old man, Grimnir, removed his hat as he and the young woman approached Olaf, both nodding at each of those gathered there in a way that conveyed respectful deference, though Einar could not help think there was a glance of mischief in the woman's eyes. As she passed by him those same eyes flickered over him and for a delicious moment they locked together. He saw a smile twitch on her face and felt a surge of joy in his chest, accompanied by a blaze of something else much lower down.

When she was passed him, Einar blinked, realising he had been gaping like a fish at her. He glanced around, hoping no one had noticed, but then saw Affreca was looking at him, an expression of withering contempt on her face.

'Lord King,' the old man said, dipping his head towards Olaf. 'I'm sorry for coming to this grand feast where I have no right to be, but we've travelled a long way to beg your favour.'

'Grimnir, Grimnir,' Olaf consoled, 'you are a loyal subject of mine, as are all the folk of Gandvik. You are always welcome in my hall.'

The old man caught sight of Olaf's son.

'Trygve? Is that you lad?' Grimnir said, smiling. 'How you've grown!'

'He's getting to be a big fellow,' Olaf said, his chest visibly puffing out. 'How's Vifil, that hersir of yours, Grimnir? What's that old goat up to?'

Grimnir's expression became sombre.

'Vifil is dead, my lord,' the old man said.

Einar could tell by the look on Olaf's face that this news brought genuine dismay to the king.

'I'm sorry to hear that,' Olaf said. 'We were fostered together. He remained a faithful friend to me ever since.'

Einar had always wondered what it must have been like to be fostered. It was common for folk to send their children to be brought up among another family, often a distant relation, but his mother had no relatives in Iceland and she needed him on the farm so he had never been through it. He often pondered what would it have been like to grow up among other children, instead of just his mother and him.

'That is why we are here,' Grimnir said.

'We?' Olaf said, frowning.

All attention turned to the beautiful young woman. Grimnir laid a hand on her shoulder.

'This is Halgerd Vifilsdottir,' he said. 'Surely you remember her?'

Olaf's eyes widened.

'Halgerd?' he said, looking at the woman as if seeing her for the first time. 'Last time I saw you, you were a little girl. I see those days are over.'

The king licked his lips in a way that Einar did not like.

'I've brought her here because she is Vifil's eldest child,' Grimnir said.

Olaf looked confused.

'Lord King,' Grimnir said. 'Now her father is dead his farm should be hers. It is her birth right. Her *Odal* right.'

Olaf still looked mystified, then Einar spotted realisation showing in the king's eyes.

'And?' Olaf's tone of voice was suddenly curt.

'The jarl, Onund, has laid claim to Vifil's land, lord,' Grimnir said. 'He says he wants to buy it. The jarl is a powerful man. There is little poor freemen like us can do to stop him. If the jarl buys their farm what will become of Vifil's children? Your old friend's family will be homeless.'

Olaf sighed. His brows knitted as he mulled over something in his head. An awkward silence descended on the gathering as everyone waited the king's response.

'I see the Jarl Onund sits at the top table,' the girl said. She was now looking down the hall towards the far end where a long table sat on a raised dais. This was where Olaf and Sigrod's most favoured guests were seated for the feast. Her teeth were bared in a grin that was all bitterness and no humour. 'It seems our journey here has been a wasted one, Grimnir.'

The king opened his mouth as if to say something, then he stopped. Einar could see he was looking sideways at his son, Trygve. Then his eyes slid towards Ulrich. Einar could almost see his mind working. Then Olaf moved between Grimnir and Halgerd and put an arm around the shoulders of each. Einar noted that in doing so Olaf also steered them both away from looking at who sat on the dais.

'Come, come,' Olaf said. 'Let's not argue. Perhaps we can help each other out. I'll tell you what I'll do. I'll have a word with Jarl Onund about the farm. And there is something you can do for me.'

'Whatever you ask, Lord King,' Grimnir said. Halgerd nodded.

Olaf cast a glance at those who stood around them.

'Not now. Go and take a seat. Enjoy the feast,' Olaf said. 'I'll send for you later and tell you what I need done. Ulrich?'

The leader of the Wolf Coats raised his eyebrows.

'Grimnir and Halgerd shall sit beside your men,' Olaf said. He gestured to a nearby servant. 'Show these people to their places, thrall. Edwin's Saxons are sitting beside you Ulrich so make sure this young lady is not offended by any coarse talk, all right?'

'Hello again, old man,' Ulrich said. 'Still out painting rocks?'

Grimnir smiled. 'So you took my advice and joined Olaf's army, then? It looks like tonight you'll look after us the way I looked after you in the forest.'

Ulrich nodded but looked less than pleased at the task he had been given. Einar could understand. Protecting a woman's sensitivities among a bunch of drunken warriors was not what the Wolf Coats did best.

On the other hand, as the thrall led the way down the hall and he fell in behind Halgerd, his gaze wandering up and down her figure, Einar was delighted.

Fourteen

Fire pits ran up the middle of the floor from the front of the hall to the back. On either side were long tables lined with benches thronged with feasters. Like in Guthfrith and Thorfinn's halls, there was a raised platform at the far end with a table set facing up the hall where all the most important guests sat. Instead of the usual one high seat in the centre of the table, there were two, one each for the brother kings.

Ulrich's crew were ushered to seats at a table beside the wall, almost beside the front doors. It was about as far from the dais as it was possible to get.

'Olaf mustn't want to keep that close an eye on us,' Skar said. The expression on his face showed his displeasure at the lack of esteem their position in the hall denoted.

'I'm happy to be away from that drunk,' Ulrich said.

Slaves approached with brimming horns of ale but Ulrich waved them away with an angry gesture. Einar ran his tongue over lips that all of a sudden felt very dry.

'I told you we need to keep our wits about us,' Ulrich said, seeing the looks of dismay on the faces around him.

'If Olaf's commanding this army then we're all dead men,' Kari said. 'I don't like this, Ulrich. I'm not happy being at the front of his battle line. We hit and run. We don't stand in shield walls and wait to be attacked like peasants.'

'You won't win glory skulking at the back,' Skar said.

'This isn't our fight,' Atli spoke up. 'Why should we die for these fools? They don't even realise how near Eirik is! We should leave this shambolic lot and meet him. We should fall on our knees and plead with him to let us back into his service.'

'I'll never kneel to that treacherous bastard again,' Ulrich said, glowering at Atli like a dog facing an intruder. 'You think Eirik will welcome us with open arms? Don't be an idiot. He'll have our heads off while you're still grovelling for his forgiveness.'

As they took their seats, Einar stuck right behind Halgerd so that when they sat down on the bench he would be beside her. He took a deep breath, sure he could smell a sweet fragrance from her. Her very presence seemed intoxicating. Grimnir sat opposite and the others filled out the rest of the table to the end.

'What's this talk of dying anyway?' said Ulrich. 'I only intend to kill.'

'I thought you Danes could drink,' a voice from down the table said.

They all turned and saw they shared the table with the Saxon warriors of Edwin. Each man had a large horn full of frothing ale grasped in his fist. Einar's eyes widened at the finery of their clothes and he felt even more aware of his own plain attire. Their tunics were of the finest wool and dyed red or green. They were embroidered with bright coloured threads that outlined twisting beasts and swirling patterns, some of which glittered and could have been gold.

A silver cross amulet gleamed at the neck of every one of them. Their long hair was combed straight, as were their long moustaches that hung down to their clean-shaven chins. Affreca's words about Einar's scruffy appearance came back to him and he realised what a contrast he would be to these handsome young men in the eyes of Halgerd.

'We're Norwegians, not Danes,' Ulrich, who now sat beside Grimnir, said.

'I'm an Icelander,' Einar added.

A blond-haired Saxon shrugged and made a face.

'We call you all Danes,' he said. 'And I was told you liked a drink but you're not drinking! I hope you're not going to be boring company tonight. I'm sure you young ladies won't be.'

He shot a wink across the table at Halgerd and Affreca. Einar felt the hairs on the back of his neck rise.

'What's with those fur cloaks you all wear?' the Saxon said. 'Is this a trend here?'

'We are Úlfhéðnar,' Ulrich said, straightening his back. 'We are warriors of Odin.'

'Úlfhéðnar means Wolf Coats in our tongue,' Einar said. 'Those fur cloaks are wolfskins.'

The Saxon narrowed his eyes. 'I've heard of you. We call you Werewolves in Britain. The men-wolves.'

Ulrich looked pleased.

'You've a lot in common with them, then,' a dark-haired companion of the Saxon, a big man sitting on his left with a face like a shovel blade, nudged him with his elbow. 'Eh, Wulfhelm? They're the wolf's coat and you're the wolf's helmet. Among you you're the whole wolf's clothes!'

The blond-haired Saxon made a pained smile.

'You all speak our tongue?' Einar said.

Wulfhelm shrugged.

'It's not that different from our own,' he said. 'And we've been here for months now. It was learn the language or starve. Anyway, how else would we chat to the local women? Know what I mean?'

'Just what *are* you doing here?' Ulrich said.

'We're housecarls of Lord Edwin's *Gedriht*,' Wulfhelm said. 'His oathsworn warriors. He came here so we came with him. He wants to stop Hakon gaining the throne of Norway and he thinks Olaf and Sigrod have the best chance of doing that.'

'They have to beat Eirik first,' Ulrich said. 'But I'd have thought Christians would want a Christian king? Hakon believes in your Christ God.'

'Ah!' Wulfhelm held up a finger. 'But Hakon is Aethelstan's puppet, and Lord Edwin is obsessed with thwarting his half-brother any way he can.'

His big companion nudged him again and touched his big finger to his lips. His face was cast in a reproachful expression.

'What? It's common knowledge!' Wulfhelm said, then took a long swig of ale. Einar licked his lips again. His throat felt as dry as a salted cod. 'Aethelstan made sure it was known across the world.'

Wulfhelm turned back to Ulrich and the others.

'Edwin tried to usurp his brother,' he said. 'Unlike Olaf and Sigrod, he did not have enough men to challenge him in battle, so he brewed up a plot to have him murdered. But Aethelstan has eyes and ears everywhere. His network of spies is like the web of a spider.'

Einar remembered the army of priests and clerics in Britain. The men who could move between kingdoms, always listening, writing everything down, and their Church favoured Aethelstan.

'Needless to say he found out about the plan,' Ulrich said.

Wulfhelm nodded.

'We had to flee for our lives,' he said. 'We were very lucky to get away.'

'And you came here?' Einar asked.

'Aethelstan is now Emperor of Britain,' the Saxon replied. 'Since his war against the Scots there's now no one left there who we could take shelter with. They're all too scared of him and would betray us. Lord Edwin knows Aethelstan wants Hakon on the throne of Norway so we came here to help in the fight against him.'

'No doubt your Lord Edwin also believes,' Ulrich said, stroking his chin in the way he did while thinking, 'that if you help Olaf beat Eirik, then Hakon, Olaf will give him men in recompense. Then he can sail back home to take the throne from Aethelstan.'

Wulfhelm raised his eyebrows.

'You're more cunning than you look,' he said.

'Underestimating me is a mistake many now dead men have made,' Ulrich said.

'But enough of statecraft!' Wulfhelm said, banging his fist on the table. 'I'm sure we're boring these lovely women here.'

Affreca and Halgerd exchanged glances.

'I am daughter of the King of Dublin,' Affreca said. 'We talked of nothing but statecraft when I was young. Perhaps in Britain things are different for women?'

A look of surprise crossed Wulfhelm's face but he managed to hide it quickly.

'So are none of you drinking?' he said. 'Come on! It's supposed to be a celebration.'

'Eirik is coming,' Ulrich said. 'If he arrives, the party will be over. I don't want my men having to fight Bloody Axe's warriors and a hangover at the same time.'

'The lads could do with a drink, Ulrich,' Skar said from across the table. 'We've been through a lot lately. In the words of Odin himself, *Foolish is he who lies awake at night worrying about what will come tomorrow. In the morning all his cares are still there, except now he is tired as well.*'

Ulrich rolled his eyes.

'You quote holy sayings to me?' he said. 'Very well. But don't overdo it.'

The Wolf Coats cheered and beckoned to passing thralls for ale. The Saxons cheered too and Einar caught Wulfhelm sending another wink towards Halgerd and Affreca.

As he lifted a horn of ale and took a greedy swig, relishing the malty, honey sweetened taste as it filled his dry throat, he recalled Skar's words from earlier about warriors, women and ale and hoped this night would not end in any grass fires.

Fifteen

'How did you get here so fast, old man?' Ulrich tipped his ale horn in Grimnir's direction. 'We only got here ourselves this morning.'

'We sailed fast,' Grimnir said. 'The gales pushed us along. There's a short land route through the forest and over the mountains but the snow still lies up there. It would be too hard.'

'You saw Eirik's ships?' Ulrich said.

'Aye,' Grimnir replied.

'With luck and the blessings of the Norns you won't have to worry about Eirik much longer,' Ulrich said.

'So you are the famous Ulrich Rognisson and this is your wolf pack?' Grimnir said. 'I had no idea I was in such company back in the forest.'

'You've heard of us?' Ulrich said.

'We found four or five cursing poles around the shores of our fjord, all with your names on them,' the old man said. 'Queen Gunnhild really doesn't like you.'

'I thought the queen was supposed to be going to Orkney,' Einar said.

'Oh, she's gone all right,' Grimnir said. 'But she left

those níðstang on her way. The queen is a powerful magic-woman. I would not like to be under her curse.'

'The way our luck has been going lately it certainly seems like we're cursed,' Ulrich said.

'The curse of a witch is a grave and dangerous thing,' Grimnir said. 'But I know the ways it can be broken.'

A loud banging came from the other end of the feasting hall and all conversation died away. Everyone looked around and saw that the brother kings, Olaf and Sigrod and their wives had taken their places with the other nobles at the top table on the raised dais at the far end of the hall. Olaf's herald was thumping his staff against a table for silence. Once enough of a respectful hush had fallen in the hall to satisfy him, the herald began proclaiming something in a loud, booming voice.

'What's he saying?' Skar said, screwing his eyes up as if that would improve his hearing.

'I can't hear,' Affreca said. 'He's too far away.'

'Olaf's drinking something from a huge silver cup,' Einar said, relaying what he saw going on at the dais.

'That would be the *bragrfull*,' Ulrich said. 'It symbolises his claim to the kingship as his by right. Sigrod will drink it next, I expect.'

Halgerd made a loud tut.

'Kings and jarls talk of their rights,' she said. 'But what about the ordinary free folk? What about *our* rights?'

Ulrich shot a glance in her direction.

'Kings and jarls have swords, axes and warriors,' he said. 'Rights belong to those who can take them. Those who are strong enough to hold and defend them.'

'There was a time when it wasn't so,' the old man,

Grimnir said. His eyes were wide and he prodded the table with a forefinger. 'There was a time when all free men had rights. Not just the rich. We had our Odal rights. King Frodi granted them in ancient times. If a family had lived on land for six generations then it was theirs by Odal right. A rich man could not come along and buy it unless the family permitted it.'

'Frodi?' Einar said. 'Rognvald was shouting about him in the forest when we last saw you. He said Frodi was dead.'

'He is not dead,' Halgerd said. 'He is only sleeping. When our land needs him most he and his warriors will come back to help us.'

'It's a legend in Gandvik, our district,' Grimnir said. 'He was a just and noble king in the time of our forefathers. In his day Halgerd here would not be in the position she is now, where Jarl Onund can just pass silver to the king and her farm becomes his.'

'Careful old man,' Ulrich said. 'If the kings overhear such talk they'll think you a rebel.'

'The Odal rune: You painted it on that wayside runestone,' Einar said.

'Aye, lad,' Grimnir said, grabbing two drinking horns from a passing thrall. He passed one to Halgerd and took one himself. 'And not just on that one. We painted it on every runestone we came across along that road. And on walls. Anywhere the king's men might see it.'

'But why?' Einar said.

'To show our defiance,' Grimnir said. 'To show we still remember that things were not always this way. That it was not the way the world was set in place by the Gods. Our rights were taken from us by Harald Fairhair who took all the land for himself and set jarls above us to extort taxes. We do this to show that once the free folk were really free and we have not forgotten that.'

Ulrich smirked.

'A fine speech, old man,' he said. 'But Olaf and Sigrod, like their brother king Eirik, are also sons of Harald Fairhair. And Olaf needs Jarl Onund's support. Do you really think you can change anything by painting a few stones?'

The fierce glitter in the old man's eyes died away and he fell silent. Halgerd sighed and took a drink of ale. She looked so sad Einar longed to throw his arm around her shoulders.

'Hakon has told the people in the north he will give them their Odal rights back if they make him king,' Halgerd said. She spoke in a quiet voice. 'Many flock to his banner...'

All eyes looked at Halgerd. Ulrich's jaw dropped open slightly.

'... and if Olaf and Sigrod think that there are those in their own lands who want their rights back,' she said, as if speaking to herself, 'who might support Hakon, then they might consider it themselves? Is that what you're up to?'

'But what would make them think that?' Einar said.

'Perhaps a few painted stones?' Grimnir smiled and winked.

'Hakon is also a Christian,' Ulrich said with a sneer. 'He'll give you your rights back but take away your Gods. Are folk really so stupid? So faithless?'

'My family has owned our farm for nine generations,' Halgerd said. Her eyes blazed with a fire that sent a thrill of excitement through Einar. 'By the rights of the Odal law that means we have the first right to it. When my grandfather died the jarl's father tried to take it then but because of my father's Odal right he inherited it instead.'

'Now those rights are gone,' Grimnir said, shaking his head. 'Now the land belongs to the king: Be it Eirik, Olaf or whoever. If Onund wants it, all he has to do is buy it from the king. The family of the ordinary people have no say. I had thought if we talked to Olaf he might grant us favour, for the sake of his old friendship with Halgerd's father.'

Grimnir took a drink and he and Halgerd sent annoyed glances towards the dais.

There was a brief interruption as thralls plonked wide clay bowls heaped with steaming, boiled crayfish onto the tables. Einar almost drooled at the sight and smell. They all dug in, pulling the shellfish apart and sucking the delicious juice from inside.

'Jarls are rich men,' Einar said. He spoke with difficulty as he had the leg of a crayfish clamped between his teeth. 'Why not take Onund's silver and live a comfortable life?'

The look Halgerd sent in his direction made Einar regret his words straight away.

'Live where?' she said, her beautiful face twisted with anger. 'Forsake the land my family has farmed for generations? Become a landless wanderer in the world? We'd be worse than Vikings. Like you all.'

Einar frowned. He held the crayfish leg towards Halgerd like a stick.

'Actually,' he said, 'I'm not one of them. I'm a skald.'

He heard a loud tut from Affreca sitting on his left.

'Don't be fooled by his talk of being a poet,' she said. 'He killed a man a few days ago. He's as savage a Viking as any one of this crew.'

Halgerd raised her eyebrows.

'So you're a warrior poet?' she said. 'How interesting.'

'Aren't they all?' Affreca said. 'At least when they're on a *strandhögg* raid for your heart. Or your virtue. Men are sheep or wolves. Einar here is a wolf but just doesn't want to accept the fact.'

'I prefer to see myself more as a sheep dog,' Einar said. 'I protect the sheep from the wolves.'

'And yet,' Affreca said, pointing at the úlfhéðnar seated beside them with a crayfish claw, 'you run with a pack of wolves.'

'What's this about poetry?' Wulfhelm said, interrupting. His words were a little slurred.

'Einar here is a skald,' Halgerd said.

'I'm a bit of a *scop* myself,' the Saxon said, grinning.

'What did I tell you?' Affreca said, arching one eyebrow towards Halgerd.

'No, listen, what do you think of this?' Wulfhelm said, leaning forward across the table.

'I'm a great help to women,
The hope of something to come. I harm
No one but the one who slays me.
Rooted I stand high on a bed.
I am hairy down below. Sometimes a lovely
Peasant's daughter, the eager-armed,
Proud woman grabs my body,
Rushes my red skin, holds me hard,
And claims my head. The curly-haired
Woman who catches me fast will feel
Our meeting. Her eye will be wet
What am I?'

For a few moments there was an awkward silence. Einar felt his cheeks redden.

Ulrich leaned across the table and stabbed his knife into the wood.

'I'll ask you to mind your tongue, Saxon,' he said. 'Olaf commanded my men and I ensure that the conversation at this table is one suitable for the lady present.'

'You mean ladies?' Affreca said.

'What's the problem?' Wulfhelm said, holding up both hands. 'The poem is about an onion!'

His face broke into a grin.

'I cannot help what your filthy minds thought it was,' he said. He smiled at Halgerd. 'I see you seem to have come up with a different answer, lady.'

Halgerd threw back her head and laughed. Einar frowned.

'Grimnir, a word please.'

The new voice interrupted the table and they all looked around to see Olaf's man, Gorm standing over them. He beckoned with his head and the old man got up and walked a little way off. For a few moments they stood in intense discussion, then Gorm left again and Grimnir came back to the table.

'Halgerd, we must go,' he said.

Halgerd's face fell.

'Now? The feast is just starting,' she said.

'We must go,' Grimnir repeated, his voice louder, his tone insistent. 'King Olaf is sending someone to meet us at the tavern. He wants us to leave tonight.'

Halgerd sighed but stood up nonetheless.

'You leave a kings' feast for a tavern?' Ulrich said.

'It's where we're staying in the town,' Grimnir said. 'And we must go there. Goodnight everyone. Thank you all for your company this evening. I hope we will meet again.'

He held out a hand and ushered Halgerd out of the hall.

The seated warriors watched them go, then they all turned back to the pile of food before them. Then another voice interrupted them.

'Wulfhelm!'

Einar looked up to see Edwin the Aetheling of Wessex a little way away, beckoning to his warrior seated at the table. Wulfhelm made a face but got up and walked over to his Lord. The two talked for a few moments like Grimnir and Gorm had, then, shaking his head, Wulfhelm also left the hall.

'I wonder where he's going?' Einar said.

'If Edwin has any sense,' Ulrich said, 'He's asked his man to do the same thing I'm going to ask you to do. Affreca, Einar: a word please.'

He got up and walked off to a short distance from the table, far enough away that anyone seated could not overhear what they said.

'Follow the old man and the girl,' Ulrich said. 'Find out what's going on. Olaf is up to something.'

'What interest is it to us?' Einar said.

'*Everything* is of interest to us, lad,' Ulrich said. 'If we're going to fight on this side I need to know everything that's going on.'

Einar cast a rueful gaze at the pile of steaming shellfish on the table.

'But we've just started eating,' he said. 'I'm starving! Why us? If you want to know what's going on why don't you and Skar go?'

'We're all well known here,' Ulrich said. 'You two aren't. You won't draw suspicion. Now do you want to be part of this crew or not?'

Einar opened his mouth to speak then felt a sharp pinch on his arm. He looked down and saw Affreca digging her nails into his forearm.

'We'll do it,' she said. 'Let's go.'

Einar rolled his eyes and sighed, but still followed her out into the night.

Sixteen

Einar and Affreca trudged down the wooden walkway that lined the street. Darkness had fallen and the town was now lit by burning torches set in high brackets here and there along the walkways. They walked slower than normal, trying not to get too close to Grimnir and Halgerd while still not getting too far away that they lost sight of them.

There was no sign of Wulfhelm.

'Ulrich orders us around like we're one of his wolf pack,' Einar said. 'It's not right.'

'Most men would sacrifice their firstborn child to be an *Úlfhéðinn*,' Affreca said. 'Yet the son of Thorfinn the Skull Cleaver complains when he's treated like one of the crew? Something's not right.'

'You still have your heart set on joining Ulrich's band of killers, then?' Einar said.

'I told you before, Einar,' Affreca said, 'what choices do I have in life? I can go home to Dublin to be married off to some Irish king to seal an alliance. I'll spend the rest of my life living in one of their round mud huts, counting how many head of cattle he owns.'

'You'd be a rich woman,' Einar said.

'I'd be no more than a slave,' Affreca said. She turned her head and spat into the mud. 'Ulrich's crew sails the whale roads across the world. They live a life of adventure. Men fear them and admire them. Sigurd the dragon slayer wore the Helm of Awe that terrified his enemies, but these men have no need for such magic. The sight of their wolf cloaks is enough to send men running.'

'And yet these great, invincible warriors still need us to help them out,' Einar said.

Affreca stopped and laid a hand on Einar's arm. He stopped as well.

'That must be the tavern they are staying in,' she said. 'Hide! Quick!'

They both moved sideways into the shadows at the side of the street. Further down the street Einar saw that Grimnir and Halgerd had stopped outside a longhouse that was bigger than all those around it. A large wooden sign above the door was painted with a picture of three hammers. The door was open and light spilled from it. Even at a distance Einar and Affreca could hear the noise of lively conversation from inside.

Grimnir looked all around, checking there was no one watching them from the street, then he and Halgerd entered the tavern.

'What do you think?' Affreca said.

'Well we won't find out much from back here,' Einar said. 'We need to get closer.'

Moving swiftly but looking all around as they went, Einar and Affreca hurried down the street until they were outside the tavern. They looked up and down the street then, hovering outside still in the shadows, peeked around the door.

Inside was a sort of small entrance hallway leading to the main tavern room beyond another door. One side of the hallway was full of big wooden barrels stacked three rows high. Einar knew they would be filled with ale and food and felt a brief moment of regret at the thought of the feast going on without them. Past the far door in the main tavern the guests were lined at tables, eating platters of food, drinking horns of ale or both. The noise of chatter flowed out from in there.

'Come on,' Affreca said, stepping inside the door.

Einar followed her. Then they saw Halgerd standing at the other side of the tavern floor. She was looking the other way so did not see them. Grimnir was coming down a set of stairs that led to an upper room. He had two bags in his hands. Both Einar and Affreca stepped sideways so they could not be seen from inside the tavern.

'They're coming back out,' Affreca said.

'In here,' Einar said. 'Behind the barrels.'

There was just enough space between the stack of barrels and the wall for Einar and Affreca to squeeze behind. It was cramped and smelled of stale beer and mice but there were a few gaps that allowed them to look out and see what was going on. Conscious of his heavy breathing, Einar used the nose breathing trick Skar had shown him in the forest a few days before to reduce the noise he made.

Peeking through a gap in the barrels, Einar saw Halgerd and Grimnir enter the entrance hall. For a few moments they waited, unaware they were being watched. Then someone else arrived. At first Einar could not see who it was, then he saw that Gorm, Olaf's trusted *hirðmaðr*, had entered from the outer door to the street.

'Close that door,' he said. Halgerd pulled shut the inner door into the tavern.

Gorm was not alone.

He ushered two small figures wrapped in dark cloaks before him. Their hoods were up but Einar could tell who they were even before they pulled them down. They were Olaf's son, Trygve, and his companion Gudrod.

'King Olaf orders you to leave straight away,' Gorm said.

'I don't want to go!' Trygve said. 'There will be a battle here. I want to see it. We'll miss all the excitement.'

'You will have excitement enough, lad,' Grimnir said. 'We will have a great adventure travelling to Gandvik in secret.'

'Make sure you do that,' Gorm said. Then he turned to the boy. 'Your father will come for you when he defeats King Eirik and all is safe.'

'But—' Trygve began.

'Go,' Gorm said. His commanding tone ensured no further argument.

Grimnir, Halgerd and the two boys hurried past him. Grimnir peered out the door, looked up and down the street, then led the others out into the night. Gorm remained in the hallway.

Behind the barrels, Einar and Affreca exchanged looks. How long was he going to stand there?

Then the sound of scuffling came from outside. Gorm stiffened.

'Get in there,' a man's voice from outside shouted.

Wulfhelm came stumbling through the door. He was out of control and Einar surmised he had been propelled by a shove or boot. Behind him two armed warriors, knives drawn, entered the hallway. They slammed the door behind them.

Wulfhelm crashed into Gorm who caught him in both hands, then shoved him backwards so he slammed into the now-closed door to the street.

'We found him skulking outside,' one of the warriors said. 'He was lurking in the shadows at the side of the inn, watching what's going on.'

'What have you seen, Saxon?' Gorm said.

'I saw you come in here with two boys,' Wulfhelm said. He wiped his mouth with the back of his hand. It was smeared with blood from a split in his bottom lip. 'Then I saw that old man and the pretty girl leave with the same boys.'

'Do you know who they were?' Gorm demanded.

'If I was a betting man,' Wulfhelm said, straightening himself up, 'Which I am, by the way, I'd say they were Olaf's son and his mate Gudrod.'

'Good guess,' Gorm said. 'But more the pity for you. No one is to know that the king has sent his son away. Men, take him out and cut his throat. Do it quietly. Dump the body in the sea.'

'Wait—' Wulfhelm began.

Without thinking, Einar flattened his hands against the middle row of stacked barrels and shoved. Two of them toppled forwards, bringing the barrels on top of them down as well. In a moment all the rest were falling too. Gorm let out a surprisingly high-pitched cry at the sight of the wooden avalanche tumbling down on him. Then the tremendous crashing of the barrels clattering into the ground drowned out all else. Gorm and his two warriors disappeared under the torrent. Some of the barrels burst open and in an instant the hallway was awash with frothing ale and chunks of salted meat and butter.

The wall of barrels gone, Affreca shoved Einar towards the door. Wulfhelm was standing there, untouched by the falling barrels but now soaked with beer and splattered with what looked like butter. He was staring in disbelief at the jumble of shattered wood from which protruded the arms and legs of the men who had just been preparing to kill him. Whether they were unconscious or dead it was impossible to tell.

Seeing Affreca and Einar, he realised what had happened. Without waiting to be told he pulled open the outer door and ran outside. Einar and Affreca followed him. As they left, Einar heard shouts from behind the inner door as people from the tavern, alerted by the mighty crash of the falling barrels, tried to push the door open and found it was jammed by the debris outside.

Once in the street they looked left and right. It was dark and the street was deserted.

'Thanks,' Wulfhelm said. 'You saved my life.'

'I suggest you get out of here,' Affreca said.

The Saxon nodded and loped off into the night.

'We'd better make ourselves scarce too,' Einar said.

'Why did you do that?' Affreca said. 'The last thing Ulrich said was to not draw attention to ourselves.'

Einar shrugged. 'I don't know. He seemed like a decent man. I liked his onion poem.'

Affreca sighed.

'Come on,' she said. 'Let's get back to the feasting hall and see if there's any food left.'

Trying to stick to the shadows, they made their way back along the street. The feast was still in full swing when they got back.

'So Olaf is perhaps not as confident of victory as he pretends to be,' Ulrich said after they had told their tale. 'Otherwise why send his son away to safety? Perhaps our news of how close Eirik is made him think. Go ahead and join the others. Tell no one else about this. It's probably a waste of time me saying this, but try not to drink too much.'

Einar and Affreca sat down and tucked into the roasted pork now heaped on the trenchers. Wulfhelm never returned to join his Saxon companions. Despite Ulrich's words, Einar took full advantage of the free-flowing ale and his mind was in a haze when he eventually collapsed into a leather sleeping bag in the tent back in the camp that Olaf had loaned Ulrich for his crew to use.

The next thing he knew horns were blowing.

He opened his eyes, wincing at the pain in his head provoked by the sunlight now poking in through the open tent flap. The horns were sounding the alarm. He could hear voices outside shouting.

'Get your weapons. Get your shields. Eirik Bloody Axe has come!'

Seventeen

Einar scrambled out of the sleeping bag and stumbled outside. The sky was overcast and the brisk wind that had been blowing for days had still not let up.

There was chaos all around. The camp was alive with men running this way and that, pulling on mail shirts, grabbing swords and spears and slinging shields over their backs. Like many streams converging to a mighty river, warriors were flooding from all over the camp towards the battlefield which was marked out by hazel poles on the slope between the camp and the beach. Once there, standard bearers and hersirs marshalled each warband to the position that had been assigned to them.

'I'll say this for Olaf and Sigrod,' said Ulrich, who stood, already dressed in his war gear, outside the tent, 'They've prepared well for this. They really have it all planned out.'

'Have you seen Atli?' Skar said to Einar.

Einar looked around and realised the Wolf Coat company was one short.

'Not since last night,' he said.

Skar frowned. 'Where has he got to? If he doesn't hurry up Eirik Bloody Axe will be here.'

He pointed down the slope and Einar felt his stomach

lurch as he saw the fleet of ships that now filled the bay. The ships of Olaf and Sigrod's army already crammed the beaches but now another army of ships approached from the open sea. There was perhaps a hundred, maybe more, which meant Eirik had come with perhaps a thousand men or more.

Some had already hit the shallows and warriors from them were wading ashore. Their weapons, helmets and mail gleamed in the morning light.

'Shouldn't we stop them before they even get ashore?'

'No,' Ulrich shook his head. 'It's too uncertain. Some might get through and then there would be chaos.'

'Chaos, when men are running this way and that, when no one knows who is who,' Skar said, 'is the most dangerous time in battle. That's when most men die. Chaos will come. It cannot be avoided, but it's best to keep things controlled as long as possible. If possible until you are sure of victory.'

'Olaf will let them get ashore,' Ulrich said, 'then Eirik will have to attack us uphill. It'll be very hard for him.'

'This should be a piece of piss, lads,' Skar said. 'Get ready.'

Looking at the warriors streaming ashore, Einar found Skar's confidence hard to share.

He hurried off to empty his bowels into the loathsome pits dug at the edge of the camp for that purpose, then returned and, like the others, began arming himself for battle with the war gear he had borrowed from Olaf's arming tent.

Einar pulled on a thick leather jerkin over his head. His head was sore and his throat dry because of the ale he had drunk the night before, but the trembling in his fingers that made it hard to lace up the jerkin was due to more than a hangover. He had raided a town in Scotland and fought his brother's war party in Iceland but there was something about the coming fight that sent an icy chill through his guts. Standing shoulder to shoulder, shield to shield with other men as another horde of warriors charged into them, intent on killing, seemed to go against every instinct he had.

He pulled on leather breeches then shrugged the brynja over his head, pulling it down so it covered his body. The mail rings of the brynja were dull and rusted in places. Just beneath his left ribs and at the right shoulder were two large holes that he could imagine one of the enemy sliding a blade into, which was probably what had happened to the previous owner of the mail coat. He fastened his belt around his middle to keep the brynja tight to his body.

As Skar had instructed, Einar fastened a leather thong through the ring on his sword pommel. With his left hand and the help of his teeth he managed to tie the other end of the thong to his right arm, just below where the sleeve of the brynja ended.

He put the visored helmet on and fastened its strap under his chin. Then slung his shield over his shoulder, lifted the rest of his war gear and he was ready for battle.

Warbands with their flags filed past on their way to the battlefield. Einar watched the faces of the men as they went by. Some were grizzled old warriors, but as many were mere boys, several winters younger than himself. Their expressions went from bright-eyed excitement to grim, set-jaw determination to pale terror. Some looked like fighting was their everyday job while others looked more like they were marching out for a day's work on the farm. The thought occurred to Einar that by midday many of these men could be dead. These were the last moments of their lives. Maybe the same fate awaited him. It seemed so unreal, almost like a dream. The air was alive with a strange mix of excitement and fear. Somewhere, unseen, the Norns who governed the destiny of men were working with feverous fingers at the vast tapestry they wove, each thread on it the life of one person. Many of those threads would converge today. Many would end.

'I'm a sailor, not a warrior,' Roan said. 'I'll leave you men to it and wait in the town. I know we'll meet again and I will see you afterwards.'

The others said their goodbyes.

'If you see Atli on your way,' Skar said, 'tell him to get his arse up here before he misses the whole battle.'

The wizened old man nodded then said his farewells and headed off towards the town.

'Let's go,' Skar said.

They slung their shields over their shoulders and set off down the hill, joining the lines of others streaming to their positions on the battlefield. The feet of many men had already churned the ground to mire and the going became heavy at the point where everyone converged to leave the camp.

Standing a little way onto the field were the brother kings and their battle leaders. Olaf looked rough from the amount he had drunk the night before. Still, he was an impressive sight in his shining brynja, his gilded battle helmet and fur cloak. A huge sword, its blade incised with runes, hung by a strap at his side. Beside him stood Sigrod whose war gear was less impressive but was still much better than the old equipment Einar was clad in. Several jarls who had been at the feast the night before, including Onund and the Saxon

Aetheling, Edwin, stood beside them. Einar noted there was no sign of Gorm or Wulfhelm.

'So you were right, Ulrich,' Olaf said. 'Eirik was a lot closer than we thought. The bastard must have sailed night and day to get here. No matter. We were ready to fight anyway.'

'Lord King,' Ulrich said. 'Gorm said something about you wanting us in the shield wall at the front of the battle ranks? With respect, we could be more effective if we can range across the field, attacking where the most need is or where we spot points of weakness in the enemy. It's the way we train.'

Olaf smiled but the expression looked forced.

'Ulrich, where else would I want my most fearsome warriors?' he said, spreading his hands wide. 'Eirik is down there. My army will be drawn up on the heights of this ridge above the town. Eirik has to land his ships and attack uphill. We'll slaughter him and his men before they even get near us. Your men will be key to that. What army has ever won attacking uphill? And I want Eirik to see his own men now stand against him when he comes up that slope. Go. The standard bearers will direct you to where I want you to fight. Odin watches us now. He will bring us victory.'

The ground chosen for the battle was indeed steep. It was a wide, sweeping pasture that covered the slopes of a large hill rising behind the town to a ridge that ensured no one could attack from behind. On the left side the camp and the town ran along the boundary and the far right side was marked by a thick forest that covered the slopes from shore to the ridge. Below was the bay, the beach and the grounding ships of Eirik's army. The field sloped at such an angle Einar took some comfort in the thought that in places the men standing behind their front ranks could also strike down on the oncoming enemy. For Eirik's warriors, already struggling to fight up the hill, it would be like fighting two men at once.

He took a deep breath through his nose. Perhaps Skar was right and the battle was a foregone conclusion. Men would still die though.

With Skar in the lead, they walked down the hill towards the front of the army. Banners marked the positions of the warrior bands of great jarls and hersirs.

'Olaf and Sigrod are making sure they're well enough away from the front,' Bodvar said, pointing his spear at the position more than halfway up the slope where the banners of the kings fluttered in the wind.

'I see Onund is looking after himself as well,' Kari said. 'That's his banner right over on the far right. What's he protecting us from? The forest?'

Einar squinted and saw a red banner with a white bird on it waving in the wind before the wall of dark pines that edged the battlefield. Before them many men had already fanned out to form a line across the bottom of the field. They stood, shoulder to shoulder, shields locked. Before them, Eirik's men from the ships began to stretch along the top of the shore to form a line opposite. Einar, Affreca, Surt and Ulrich's crew found the space that had been allotted to them. It was indeed right at the centre of the front rank of Olaf and Sigrod's army.

'Take your positions,' Skar said. He spoke in a loud, commanding tone. 'Join the shield wall. Bodvar take the centre.'

Bodvar stepped into the line. The others filled the space on either side of him. Sigurd was on his right and Starkad on his left. Kari stood beside Starkad and Surt stood beside Sigurd. Einar stood beside Kari. Their shields clacked together, each overlapping the next left to right.

Skar stood just behind them. He had an axe over his shoulder and the standard pole in his hands. Ulrich and Affreca were beside them. Olaf's archers were halfway up the hill but Ulrich had told Affreca to come with them to the front.

Despite his hangover and his apprehension of the coming fight, Einar felt a thrill that he realised was excitement. He was going to get the chance to put all the practice Skar had drilled into them on the ship into action. He felt confidence brimming in his chest. He knew what to do and he would soon have the chance to do it.

'Unfurl the Raven Banner,' Ulrich said.

Skar pulled a cord that unfurled the banner. It fluttered in the wind above their heads. Despite knowing it was a fake, Einar still strained his eyes for any sign of movement of the embroidered raven's wings.

For what seemed like an age the men from the ships filed onto the field and spread out to create their own battle lines.

'Looks like we'll have a wait for a bit,' Skar said. 'Stand easy. Shields down.'

Einar felt the relief in his left shoulder as he dropped his shield to his side. Another band of men arrived and took up positions beside the úlfhéðnar. It was Edwin and his West Saxons. Their war gear was as stunning as their feasting clothes the night before had been impressive. Their mail was polished to gleaming, their helmets were inlaid with silver and gold, the fitments of their equipment glittered with red garnets and other precious stones. Each man had a helmet with crests of horse or wolf hair. Behind the fastened helmet cheek pieces however, Einar could see faces as grey and hungover as his own. The banner they unfurled was red with what looked like a fire-breathing wyrm on it. Their shields were all painted red with a stark white cross.

Wulfhelm had now joined them. Einar noticed that, true to his name, he wore a helmet with a long, grey fur tail attached as a crest that could only be the tail of a wolf. The Saxon saw Einar and winked at him as he drew together the cheek pieces of his helmet and fastened them with a leather thong.

'We taught these Danes to drink last night,' Wulfhelm said in a loud voice. 'Now we'll show them how to fight.'

Ulrich let out a loud tut.

'So now we fight beside Aenglish Christians,' he said. 'How much lower will we sink?'

As he continued to stand, Einar became more and more aware of the weight of the helmet pushing down on his head, its iron rim digging into the back of his neck. Sweat trickled down from the padded interior and he wondered how many other men had worn it and how much sweat was soaked into it. His scalp itched at the thought. The iron rings of the brynja pushed down on his shoulders and he felt as though breathing was becoming more of an effort. His throat was dry and his head felt like it was still full of ale fumes. His stomach churned like the crayfish from last night were still alive and fighting each other in there.

'Come on, come on,' he said to himself through gritted teeth. 'Get on with it.'

He looked up at the cloud-sheeted sky. Up there, unseen by the eyes of men, were the Valkyries circling? Were they waiting to swoop down and take the souls of the bravest men to Odin's Valour Hall? Could they see him?

After what seemed like an age the other army had all got off the ships and formed up at the bottom of the slope. Their shield wall was perhaps a hundred paces from the one Einar and the others formed.

Then came a blasting of horns. The banners of Eirik's army were raised. Not far from the centre, Einar saw a large flag with a red axe displayed on it.

'Here comes Eirik himself,' Ulrich said.

The tall, wide shouldered figure of the king pushed his way through the shield wall to stand before his army. His shoulders were wrapped in a great bear pelt and his gilded helmet shone in the morning sun. He looked up and down the line of the men facing him, as if trying to look every one of them in the eye. When he saw the Raven Banner, even at a distance Einar could see a smile break out amid the king's black beard.

'Ulrich,' Eirik said, calling in a loud voice so as to he heard across the field. 'So the rumours are true. You're still alive. Olaf and Sigrod send my own treacherous úlfhéðnar to face me on the battlefield.'

'Fuck you, Eirik,' Ulrich said. 'You betrayed us.'

'Your crew seems a little short,' Eirik said.

'We've still enough to defeat you, Eirik,' Ulrich said.

King Eirik motioned to others within his ranks and their shield wall parted again to let another warrior come forward.

It was Atli.

Eighteen

'At least one of your men has some sense of loyalty, Ulrich,' Eirik said. He was still grinning.

Einar glanced over his shoulder. Ulrich was just staring, wide-eyed and open-mouthed.

'You treacherous bastard!' Skar shouted. 'When this battle starts I'll gut you myself.'

'You can try,' Atli shouted back. 'But you're getting old Skar. Today you fight your last fight. Stop your foolish threats and perhaps I'll give you a merciful death.'

'You're the fool to trust Bloody Axe,' Skar said. 'Didn't you learn anything from him leaving you to drown at the witches' skerry at Avaldsnes?'

'The king has explained that. It was just you and Ulrich who were supposed to die there,' Atli said. 'He didn't want any of our company left to take vengeance so we were chained up too. We were just caught up in it. Now I've proved my loyalty to him, he's taken me back into his service.'

'And you believe him?' Skar said.

Ulrich still had not spoken. Einar looked around again and saw the little man was still standing stock still, as if struck by lightning.

Eirik had been generous. Beneath his wolfskin cloak, the brynja Atli now wore gleamed like silver and his head was covered in a solid iron helm with embossed decoration. A large new sword, its hilt glittering with embedded garnets, rested in a scabbard at his side. His shield was newly painted with Eirik's symbol, the red axe. It was all a far cry from the rusty old borrowed war gear his former companions wore.

'I will make a new Wolf Coat pack,' Eirik said. 'Atli has been through all your training. He knows all your war secrets. He will build a new company from my finest berserkers. After we defeat Olaf and Sigrod today we will sweep north and annihilate Hakon and the rebel jarls there.'

'Are you worried I can hit you from here Atli?' Skar said. 'Is that why you lurk behind your shield?'

'I'm not stupid,' Atli shouted back. 'I know Guthfrithsdottir is somewhere behind you with that bow of hers. Bodvar, Sigurd!'

He called out.

'Eirik will take you back too. You will be the core of my new wolf pack.'

'No thanks,' Bodvar said. 'I need to trust my leader.'

'Die with him then,' Atli said and spat.

Skar lowered his head.

'Affreca are you there?' he said out of the corner of his mouth.

'I am,' Affreca said in a quiet voice. She stood directly behind him.

'It's a long shot, but do you think you could hit the king from here?' Skar said.

'I already have an arrow notched,' Affreca said.

'On three then,' Skar said. 'One. Two. Three!'

The big man ducked sideways and Affreca rose with her bow. She aimed and loosed her arrow in an instant. It soared in a high arc on a path that took it directly to Eirik.

At that distance there was enough time to see it coming. Atli, his shield already raised, leapt in front of Eirik to cover him. Affreca's arrow thudded into the linden wood, right at the centre of the red axe.

The king made an exasperated grunt. He turned on his heel, his cloak swirling around him as he retired behind his shield wall. Atli ran after them.

Horns started blowing. The battle was about to begin.

'Shields up,' Skar said.

Einar grasped his shield in his left hand, gripping the handle in his fist behind the boss in the centre. He raised it. All along the battle line the crisp thump of wood on wood came as each man joined his shield with the men on either side of him.

There came a double blast of horns, a loud swooping sound and a dark wave rose into the sky from behind King Eirik's shield wall.

'Arrows,' Skar shouted.

As one, the men in the shield wall with Einar dropped to one knee. They raised their shields to an incline over their heads and crouched in their shelter. Einar waited in the semi-darkness, his nerves itching. He heard a mighty roar and knew King Eirik's men had started their advance.

Then his ears were filled by thundering. As the arrows landed his shield bucked and rattled above him like a madman was drumming on it.

'Up,' Skar bellowed as the thunder stopped.

Einar and the men beside him rose as a dark wave of

arrows from their own archers swept overhead. His shield was prickled with arrows as were those of the men beside him and the ground all around them.

Eirik's men had advanced perhaps twenty paces while Einar was crouching. Now it was their turn to take cover behind their shields as the deadly hail of arrows rained down on them. Einar saw several of the enemy who were not fast enough with their shields fall. He felt a fierce glee and a taunting cheer escaped his lips.

Now all the waiting was over he longed for Eirik's warriors to come so the fighting could commence.

Another rising volley darkened the sky above Eirik's army.

'Arrows,' Skar shouted again.

Again Einar and those around him dropped to a crouch under their shields. Once more came the banging of the missiles striking his shield and in the cool semi-darkness he heard the battle-mad roaring of Eirik's warriors coming closer.

This time there was no need for commands from Skar. All sprang to their feet the moment the cascade of arrows stopped. Eirik's men had closed the gap further but their headlong charge had slowed already. They were running uphill and the slope got steeper the closer they got to Olaf and Sigrod's front line. They were too close for either side's archers to risk hitting their own men and Einar knew they did not have to worry about any more arrows for the time being. The fight he now longed for was coming to him.

All the men along the shield wall were screaming curses and taunts at those struggling up the hill towards them. They swelled the cacophony by beating spear shafts and sword hilts against their shields.

'Our luck has run out.'

Amid the noise, Einar heard Ulrich talking behind him.

'We're *eingongu men*,' he said. 'The Norns who rule our fate now wish us nothing but harm.'

'What talk is this, Ulrich?' Skar said.

'We're cursed by that witch, Gunnhild,' Ulrich said. His voice was obsessive, like a man with a fever. 'We fight beside Christians against the man who was our king. Odin no longer favours us. He has turned his eye away. He watches someone else now.'

'Well let's get his attention back then,' Skar said. 'We'll do deeds in this fight that Odin can't fail to take notice of.'

'When Odin looks away he never looks back,' Ulrich said.

Einar felt his heart sink. They were on the verge of battle and the crew was falling apart. It could not come at a worse time. He could not believe Ulrich of all people, the most cynical, ruthless killer of them all, was losing it. This could be the end of the Wolf Coat company. It could be the end of them all.

There was a thump. Einar snatched a glance away from the advancing warriors and saw Ulrich staggering sideways, one hand to his face. From Skar's extended arm and balled fist he surmised that Ulrich was reeling from a punch.

'Why are you looking back?' Skar spotted Einar, his lips curled into a snarl. 'The enemy is in front of you.'

Einar looked away then felt a blow across the side of his own head. He knew the big man had not used his full strength but it was still hard enough to hurt. There came the sound of a few more slaps and Einar realised Skar was hitting the others as well.

The anger within Einar blazed higher and hotter and he did not know now who he was more worried about; the approaching enemy before him or the huge, angry violent man behind him.

'Your enemy is coming,' Skar bellowed in their ears. 'I don't want to see any of you move one step backwards. Any man who goes backwards will answer to me. Stand strong, kill the enemy and we will win.'

As one, and without need of an order, the Wolf Coats around Einar drew up their cloaks so the head of the beasts came up like a hood over their helmets, the pointed ears sticking up, the maw of the creature hanging down to their visors. They looked like half-men half-beasts, wolves walking upright and armed to the teeth. The sight was both chilling and exhilarating. Einar saw Bodvar, eyes glaring, teeth bared, screaming incoherent threats at King Eirik's men. Surt stood like a rock, huge shoulder muscles bulging under his rusted old brynja. Sigurd and Starkad roared their defiance. Behind them all Skarphedin brandished the Raven Banner in one hand. Einar felt a rush of pride that he was standing with such dangerous men in the battle lines.

The noise became overwhelming. Eirik's men were about ten paces away. Javelins and light spears flew. Einar gripped the broken-shafted spear and braced himself.

Then with a deafening crash the two shield walls met.

The battle began.

Nineteen

Einar felt the impact that rattled along the shield wall. His left shoulder bucked under the concussion. His back foot slipped a bit but their wall held.

Another shield was pressed against his. Its owner was a man with a grizzled face and iron helmet. His mouth was wide open, he was screaming and Einar could see his front teeth were missing. The man jabbed a spear over the top of Einar's shield, probing to find flesh. Einar struck back with his own spear, holding it overhand, trying to hit his opponent in the face. The spear blade skidded across his helmet instead. Einar pulled his spear back, then he saw an axe come from behind his own shoulder. The blade sheared down into his opponent's helmet, smashing it in two and cleaving the skull beneath. Blood gushed from the visor of his helmet and he collapsed like a rag doll.

Glancing sideways Einar saw Skarphedin withdrawing his axe and realised it was the big man who had killed the man before him. He could not see where the body fell but for a moment there was no pressure on his shield. Then another man charged in to fill the gap. He had stopped behind his own front rank so this time the impact was not as great. He shoved his spear over the tops of the shields, its shaft grating over the rims. Einar saw it coming and ducked his head sideways. The blade punched through nothing but air mere finger breadths from Einar's left eye.

For a moment Einar thought about trying to strike his opponent under the shield but realised he was jammed between Kari on his right and a Saxon on his left. There was no room to move his arm down. The other man struck again. This time his spear point hit Einar on the brow of the helmet. Einar's head bucked backwards under the blow and he felt a rush of fear mixed with anger. Gnashing his teeth he stabbed blindly with his spear. It checked as it drove into the man's outstretched forearm. There was a rattle of metal as the blade parted the rings of his mail shirt and tore the leather jerkin under it. The man cried out as Einar's spear sliced into the skin and muscle beneath.

With a curse the man on the other side of the shields dropped his spear. He wrenched his injured arm back and tried to push himself away. The press of his own men coming behind meant he could go nowhere. Einar struck at him again and this time caught him on the chin. The spear opened up a red streak but the man jerked his head away before serious damage could be done.

He looked at Einar. Einar could see wild eyes behind the helmet visor. There was terror in them and Einar wondered if he was seeing the effect of the mythical Helm of Awe that was supposed to shine from heroes brows in the heat of battle. The man was mouthing words and with a jolt Einar realised he was pleading with him. He felt a nauseous lurch in his stomach as he pictured what must be going through the man's mind. It was a nightmare for him. He was crushed in the front rank of battle, unarmed, injured and unable to get away.

Einar gritted his teeth and gripped the shaft of his spear, trying to steel himself to strike.

'No!' the man cried. He thrashed his head from side to side, trying to dodge Einar's aim.

'I have three children,' the man sobbed.

Then something streaked past Einar's head. His opponent blinked, eyes bulging, and his cries ceased. The feathered end of an arrow protruded from his throat. His hands grasped for it then he fell forward. The men behind him pushed forward and though he was now dead, he stayed upright in the crush, wedged against Einar's shield.

Einar glanced around, half to get away from the sight of the white, dead face glaring at him over the top of his shield and half to see where the arrow had come from. Affreca stood a little behind his left shoulder. It was she who had fired the arrow and was already readying another.

'What were you waiting for lad?' Skar screamed in his other ear. 'Next time you have one of them at your mercy don't have a woman kill him for you!'

As unpleasant as having a corpse on the other side of his shield was, it also gave Einar's frayed nerves a moment's respite as no one could get at him to attack him. Then a terrible smell rose and Einar felt a warm liquid running over the top of his boots. He realised that the dead man's bowels were emptying.

The corpse's weight finally dragged it down and he disappeared from view. Almost immediately another man stepped into the gap. This one had blond hair spilling from his helmet and an axe in one hand. His shield slammed into Einar's and he hacked at Einar's head. Einar countered with his spear. It checked the axe but the shortened shaft shattered in his grip and the head dropped into the mire below.

Now it was Einar who was stuck with no weapon in the crush of battle. With panic rising in his chest, his hand grasped for the sword hanging from his wrist. He felt the leather of the hilt and grabbed it. He had no time to lift it to strike above the shields, so instead stabbed forwards underneath. A look of utter surprise seized his opponent's face as Einar's blade tore up the length of his thigh. Einar again felt warm liquid splashing under his shield but this time he could smell blood. His opponent raised his axe to strike again. Einar drove the sword further, the point going under the man's belt and up into his belly. Screaming, Einar kept pulling the sword up, dragging it through his opponent's guts until it checked on something, the bottom of his ribcage perhaps, and would go no further.

The man cried to the heavens above and the axe dropped from his hand. There was an awful slobbering sound as his innards unspooled and tumbled out through the rent Einar had opened in his stomach. Then he too dropped before Einar's feet.

The noise was incredible. All around men were screaming in rage, pain or terror. Blades rang out as they clashed against blades and mail. The wood of the shields battered off each other in a constant, rolling thunder. Through it all came a melodic chant and for a moment he thought he was dreaming. Then he realised that the Saxons who stood to his left were all singing in unison as they hacked and slashed at the enemy. Close inside his helmet, Einar could hear his own breathing, loud and rasping under his visor. Sweat was running again down his cheeks, neck and back. The air was filled with the unmistakable smell of ale, coming from the breath and sweat of the men fighting around him. It mixed with the stench of shit from spilled entrails and the emptied bowels of the dying and dead and the metallic tang of blood.

Einar braced himself for another attack but it did not come straight away. Three dead men lay heaped before him. Combined with the slope it meant the men coming behind now had to reach forward to strike him.

'Come on,' Kari screamed from his right, 'Kill the bastards!'

Einar saw the Wolf Coat, battle rage flowing in his veins, was about to charge forward, down to meet the enemy.

'Hold position!' Skar shouted. 'Hold!'

It was enough to check Kari and instead he contented himself with jabbing down at the man coming up to attack him. Einar felt the savage joy he had felt before returning. He now understood how Skar had been so confident about their chances. Eirik's men were struggling to fight uphill while Olaf and Sigrod's shield wall held firm. Now with their dead piling up against it they could not even get close enough to strike before men from the front two ranks of Olaf and Sigrod's army had struck them from above. They really could win this battle.

Bodvar stood like a tree in the line, his shield, helmet and forearms splattered with blood. A pile of dead men lay before him. Sigurd and Starkad were screaming and stabbing. Skar prowled behind them all, shoving them forward or reaching over to strike one of Eirik's attacking warriors. Affreca shot arrow after arrow into the enemy. The range so close she could not miss.

'Fight me you cowards, fight me,' Surt was shouting. Two dead men lay before him but three were pulling away, their faces terrified at the very sight of him.

The distant sound of many horns blowing rose through the cacophony of battle. It seemed to be coming from the right. Then Einar felt the whole shield wall shudder. He staggered sideways to the left as the others beside him stumbled into him. It was as if the whole army had been hit by a giant blow from the right-hand side.

Then everything started to fall apart.

Twenty

'The trees! They're coming from the forest!' Affreca shouted.

Einar looked round and saw men and banners were indeed streaming from the forest. They were many different colours, but even at a distance Einar could see the red axes painted on their shields. The cascade of warriors rushed into Sigrod and Olaf's army from the side, smashing into the men who were still fixed on trying to fight Eirik's men who were coming up the hill. As he watched he saw banners of his own side toppling as their bearers were cut down.

'That sneaky bastard Eirik. He must have sent men ashore to outflank us,' Ulrich's voice rose from behind Einar for the first time since Skar had hit him. To Einar's relief he sounded like his old self. He was equally amazed that the little Wolf Coat leader's tone of voice sounded as though he were chatting about a ball game instead of a life and death struggle.

Straight away all fell to confusion as some men in the shield wall turned to meet the new threat, but others were still engaged in fighting Eirik's men down the hill. Einar felt a cold sensation in his stomach as he realised their shield wall, which moments before had seemed impenetrable, was falling apart as he watched.

Then more horns started blowing, this time closer. Einar looked back down the slope to see some sort of shuffling going on in the opposing front rank of Eirik's army. For a moment he thought they were retreating. Then he saw some were indeed pulling back but most were moving sideways. A gap opened up in the enemy shield wall and behind it Einar saw that a large band of men had formed up into a wedge formation, their point aimed straight up the hill at the shield wall he stood in.

Shouts of *swine formation* rose along the shield wall. Einar had seen the Wolf Coats execute the move in Dublin and knew how effective it was for cleaving through shield walls. With a roar of battle cries the swine formation came charging up the hill and Einar knew he was now going to experience what it was like to be on the wrong end of one.

The flying wedge powered up the slope, its tip colliding with the shield wall a little further along to the right of Einar and the Wolf Coats. Einar felt another ripple roll through the men crushed around him as the swine formation, its front men propelled by those running behind, and its force concentrated through two men at the very front, punched a hole through Olaf and Sigrod's shield wall, sending men sprawling left and right. The charging warriors hacked and stabbed at the men as they ran over them.

'Wheel right!' Skar said. 'Hit them from the side. It's the best way to beat a swine array.'

Those around the big man rushed to reposition themselves and some semblance of a shield wall, now centred on Bodvar, rotated to the right. Einar could see the logic in Skar's plan. Their shield wall now faced the side of the wedge formation, in which all the warriors were facing forwards, their shields and weapons to the fore, leaving their flank exposed. With a chill he realised that their own flank was now exposed in the same way to Eirik's men down the slope if they were to renew their assault.

The Saxons were no longer singing.

'Atli,' Kari shouted. 'Atli is with them.'

Near the front of the swine formation was a warrior with an animal pelt around his shoulders, the body of the wolf hanging down his back, the head pulled up over his helmet like the other Wolf Coats.

Skar ordered the charge. As one, they surged forwards, shields locked together, folding in on the swine formation to hit it from the side. Einar knew he was screaming at the top of his lungs. It was not a conscious decision and where the sound was coming from he had no idea. As he ran he saw the startled faces of some of the men in the wedge formation as they realised their unprotected flank was now under attack.

It was too late for them to do anything about it. The shield wall ploughed into them as they were still trying to turn their own shields to face the new threat. Einar hacked with his sword, catching a man across the back of the neck. He fell sideways into his own men. Many others fell too and the whole wedge formation lurched sideways, pushed by the sudden pressure from the side.

The Wolf Coats and those around them pressed on, cutting down more men. In moments though, the rest of the warrior men in the swine array had turned to face them and

Einar found himself shield-to-shield with the enemy once more. The press of men became thick as both sides shoved against each other, each one trying to push their opponents backwards. Einar could feel men behind him driving him forwards and for a moment he thought he was going to lose his footing and go down. To fall under all those trampling feet, where men did not heed what they stood on as they battled for their own survival, would be certain death.

Einar gritted his teeth, set his feet as best he could and drove his shoulder into his shield with all his might. The pressure was so great none in the front ranks were able to strike effective blows. With no room to swing they just prodded and stabbed at each other. Their main effort now went into pushing, each trying to drive the other back.

Einar kept his head behind his shield and concentrated on trying to shove his enemy backwards. It was hot. The stench of bad breath, sweat, stale ale and blood was overwhelming. The press became so great Einar started finding it hard to breathe.

More of Eirik's men were pushing up the hill, surging to fill the gap that the swine array had breached in Olaf and Sigrod's shield wall. They joined their companions and soon their combined weight and muscle started to tell. Einar felt his feet start to slide backwards. He was still shoving with all his might and he was not being crushed into the men behind him; the whole shield wall was being pushed backwards.

The feet of many men and the unleashed blood had churned the ground to mud and it was getting hard to find any purchase to resist. A little further down the line a great cry arose as someone lost their footing and fell, pulling those around him down with him. Eirik's men surged forward at that point, spilling over the men, stabbing and trampling them into the mud as the shield wall began to dissolve before Einar's disbelieving eyes.

'You. Saxons: Wheel left,' Skar shouted. 'Form a new shield wall to protect our left flank.'

'It's a lost cause,' one of the Saxons in their second rank yelled back. His helmet was particularly impressive. Its crown covered by embossed scenes of warriors and the visor formed in the shape of a flying dragon. 'The rest of the shield wall is gone. Olaf is beaten. We must surrender.'

'We must fight on or die!' Skar said.

The Saxon who had spoken ripped off his helmet, revealing the sweating, pale face of Edwin.

'Peace! We surrender!' Edwin shouted, waving his helmet above his head, trying to catch the attention of someone on the other side of the shield walls.

Einar strained with all his might to hold back the tide of Eirik's men but he could feel his feet slipping backwards little by little. He peeked above his shield rim. The wolf's head of Atli stood up above his helmet perhaps four ranks back from the front of Eirik's men. Atli was on his tiptoes, straining to see who was shouting.

'You idiots,' Ulrich said with a snarl. 'They'll slaughter you as soon as you drop your shields.'

The curled lips and disconcerted grunts that came from Edwin's warriors showed they agreed with Ulrich.

'I am Edwin, Aetheling of Wessex,' Edwin called. 'I pledge myself to King Eirik. I am Aethelstan's brother.'

Atli was pointing at Edwin through the throng, shouting at others in Eirik's army and directing them towards them.

Eirik's shield wall parted before the Saxons. Warriors reached forward and began hauling Edwin's men forwards into their own ranks. Edwin sheathed his glittering sword and scrambled like a goat over the corpses piled on the ground. He pushed past his own men and disappeared into the throng of bodies beyond. Then Eirik's shield wall closed behind them like a gate.

'You cowardly bastards,' Einar heard Skar roaring like a frustrated bull above the general racket. The big man barged into the shield wall beside Bodvar. His axe was slung across his back and he wielded the long standard pole, the Raven Banner still waving at the top, in both hands like a huge spear.

Einar risked a glance over his shield and saw Skar bring the standard down. Then he realised Skar's target was Atli.

Einar felt a brief moment of satisfied joy as he saw the expression on Atli's face change to one of panic. In the press of men he could not move as the heavy pole smashed down on him. The blow was such Einar saw Atli's shining new helmet come apart, the pieces falling from under the wolf's head of his fur cloak. Atli dropped, disappearing in the crush.

Men from further down the shield wall ran to try to close the gap left by the Saxons but already Eirik's men were pouring forward again, rushing in to force the breach wider.

Panic boiled in Einar's guts. Eirik's men were now on their left and the shield wall no longer extended much further to their right. Men were fighting hand to hand. All around was confusion of death. This was the chaos Skar had warned of. There was no way they could continue to hold. They were all going to die.

'On my word, break and run,' Skar shouted. 'Now!'

Einar switched position and sprinted away from the shield wall. The resistance against them gone, Eirik's men stumbled forwards, spilling over each other like a river bursting its banks. To his relief Einar saw the men behind him had already turned and fled so they were not there to push him back onto the enemy's blades. Before him Affreca was sprinting hard, her bow grasped in one hand. Ulrich was running too and so was Skar. The other Wolf Coats and Surt pounded through the mud beside him, their feet splashing and skidding.

Einar ran for all he was worth, legs pumping, his skin crawling, expecting to feel the hot slice of a blade entering his back at any moment. The battlefield had become utter confusion. People ran this way and that. Men were fighting to the death, hacking and cutting at each other, kicking and biting or trying to drown others in the muck. Muddy pools were stained to mauve with blood. There were butchered corpses lying everywhere and severed limbs lay scattered across the ground.

The people running before him slowed. Einar just managed to avoid colliding with Ulrich as he slowed and stopped too. Before them a horde of men were pouring across the field. Their shields were battered and streaked but the red axes painted on many of them were still visible. They must have broken through further up the line and now were crossing the battlefield, cutting down everyone in their way and cutting off the Wolf Coats route of escape.

Behind them, on the left and right, Eirik's army were sweeping up the slope and over the remnants of Olaf and Sigrod's shield wall.

They were surrounded.

'Shield Fort,' Skar said. 'Circle.'

The Wolf Coats gathered around Ulrich, Skar and Affreca, standing side by side, shield to shield, in a ring facing outwards towards the enemy who were now approaching from all sides. There were hundreds of them. They were hopelessly outnumbered.

Einar swallowed, trying to regain some breath. Sweat stung his eyes. He raised his shield and gripped his sword but it seemed now that the strange energy that had filled him until now had all drained away leaving him cold and very tired. His shoulders ached and his legs felt like lead.

Einar looked across the field. Further off, up the slope, he saw the banners of Olaf and Sigrod topple and fall. He looked up at the clouds above. Were the Valkyries up there now, watching?

The position of their little group had gained the attention of a lot of Eirik's warriors. They gathered in a huge ring of shields and spears around them, ready to attack but for some reason holding off. Perhaps it was the wild appearance and frightening reputation of the wolf-coated warriors that made them hesitate. Or perhaps there was still some remnant of magic conjured by the sight of the Raven Banner fluttering above them.

Atli pushed his way to the front of the shields. His new helmet was gone and there was blood running down his face. He leaned one hand on a burly warrior beside him to steady himself and he was pointing and shouting something to the men around him but the air was filled with the groans of the wounded, the screams of the dying and the roars of their killers so his words were lost to Einar.

'Odin you one-eyed old bastard, I hope you're watching again,' Ulrich shouted to the air. 'All right you sons of whores and slaves. Come and die!'

Einar breathed in through his nose. Ulrich was back to his old self. His very presence seemed to re-evoke the fire that had previously burned within him.

As one, Eirik's men charged forwards in an overwhelming wall of steel and muscle.

Einar raised his sword and screamed his defiance into the face of the death that was hurtling to meet him.

The ring of shields closed. Einar swung his sword. It hit the first man to reach him but an instant later he was overrun by a wave of onrushing warriors. Four shields smashed him into the ground and he felt his face pressing into the mud. Someone fell on top of him and the world went dark.

Twenty-One

'Why aren't we dead?'

It was Ulrich who asked the question.

Einar opened his eyes. He was lying on his back. The leather of a tent was above him. His nose felt numb and his jaw ached and he raised his hands to his face. For some reason it was hard to see properly out of his right eye. There appeared to be something pale pink in the way of its vision. It was very close to his eye so all he could make out was a blur. As his hands came up into his line of sight he saw beyond the obstruction that they were chained together at the wrists by iron fetters. There was a faint ringing in his ears. It felt like every muscle in his body hurt.

Einar touched tentative fingers to his face. He sucked in breath through his teeth at the sharp pain that shot through his head and moved his hands away again as fast as if he had stuck them in boiling water.

He wondered how bad the damage was.

He lay for a moment more, trying to recount what had happened. He could recall nothing of the final moments of the battle save the cloying taste of the mud that filled his mouth and the impact of dozens of blows raining down on him. There was darkness, then another memory surfaced of angry faces glaring down at him and more punches. Then he was swaying up and down, possibly being carried somewhere. Then nothing until that moment when he had awoken.

With a groan he sat up.

'So our poet is still alive,' Bodvar said.

They were all there: Ulrich, Skar, Affreca, Surt, Bodvar, Sigurd, Starkad and Kari. All still alive but all looking rather battered with blackened eyes, cut cheeks and split lips encrusted with blood. They had been stripped of their rusted, hole-ridden old brynjas and all weapons were gone. Like him, all had their hands bound before them. He saw that they also had iron fetters around their ankles joined by a chain. A rattle of chain as he moved his own leg alerted him to the fact he was also fettered. They were caked with mud from head to toe and sat in a large tent with nothing in it but an oil lamp that provided some light to the gloom.

The Wolf Coats' wolf pelts were gone.

From the disgusted expressions around him, and the sharp intakes of breath, he could tell that his own face must be a bit of a mess.

'I never thought you handsome, lad,' Sigurd said. 'But you won't break too many hearts now.'

'Is it bad?' Einar said. The simple relief of not being dead was being replaced by a sense of dread that he might be horribly disfigured.

'It's not good,' Affreca said, her face twisted like she was smelling off milk.

'What did they do to me?' Einar said, his voice rising in panic. He touched his hands to his face again, once more exciting jabs of pain. 'Is it my right eye? I can't see properly from it. It's like there's something in it.'

'There is,' Ulrich said, a smile on his lips. 'Your nose.'

Einar almost turned cross-eyed, trying to look at the foreign pink blob that obscured his vision. This explained why he could not breathe through his nose and why his face was so sore to touch. Growing up, he had seen many broken noses from fights and falls during knattleikr games. He knew how they could make young, fresh faced men suddenly look like criminals or trolls. If his nose was so smashed that he could see it from his eye he must be hideous. His heart sank. What would Halgerd make of him now?

'I don't think I could look at that much longer,' Kari said. He too was grinning. Einar did not appreciate the way the others seemed to find his disfigurement so funny.

'Me neither,' Skar said. 'Lie down again lad and I'll see what I can do about it.'

'What do you mean?' Einar said. His tone was suspicious but he let Skar push him back down onto his back anyway. Once prone he found it was very hard to breathe. Was this now his life? Never to sleep on his back again.

The big man loomed over him.

'It's a while since I've done this,' Skar said. 'Now. How does that old poem go? You know the one about Haki and Hagbard that you used to have such trouble with remembering when we were on the ship?'

'What's that got to do with my nose?' Einar said, taking a gulp of air through his mouth.

'Can you recite it now?' Skar said.

Einar frowned but the words came to him and he started

to chant. He had just started the second line when his eyes widened. Skar was bearing down on him. The big man planted one thumb on either side of Einar's smashed nose and began to push.

There was a horrible grating crack that seemed to echo inside Einar's skull. His vision disappeared in a white sheet of pain. For a few moments the world dissolved in blissful darkness then everything came swimming back.

Air was flowing in through his nose again. The foreign pink object no longer obscured the vision in his right eye.

'You can stop chanting now,' Skar said. 'That was only to distract you.'

Realising he was still mumbling the *drápa* of Haki, Einar stopped and sat up. Skar was looking at him with a self-satisfied look on his face.

'Not a bad job, even if I say so myself,' he said. 'It's not completely straight but at least you look more human again.'

Einar carefully touched his tender nose, feeling the sides, relief flooding his stomach as he found they were back where they should be.

'It's safe to say they beat the shit out of us then?' he said.

'Aye,' Kari said and spat.

'But they didn't kill us?' Einar said.

'Not yet,' Ulrich said. 'I don't doubt that's coming though. Eirik probably has some sort of nasty end in mind for us.'

'And they took your Wolf Coats?' Einar said, realising that this was possibly the first time he had ever seen the úlfhéðnar without them. They wore them everywhere. They even slept in them.

'They did, the bastards,' Skar said with a heavy sigh. 'Atli made sure of that.'

Einar recalled Skar's words when they had been shipwrecked in Scotland – *My wolfskin is dearer to me than my life. It is my life.*

Without their wolfskins they looked like any other sorry band of defeated warriors.

'Eirik must mean not just to kill us but to humiliate us too,' he said.

'If he meant to kill us why not do it on the battlefield?' Bodvar said with a grunt. 'At least we could have died like men, with swords in our hands. At least Odin would have seen that and given us our reward. We'd be drinking with the *Einherjar* by now.'

'Speak for yourself,' Affreca said. 'I'd rather not die like a man if that's possible. I'd rather not die at all.'

From outside the tent there came the sound of singing, shouting and laughing. There were also occasional screams.

'The bastards are celebrating their victory,' Ulrich said.

'They have the right to,' Skar said. 'It was our bad luck we were on the wrong side.'

Ulrich hung his head. His smile was gone. Einar feared his previous dark mood from just before the battle was returning.

'Our bad luck indeed,' the little Wolf Coat said. 'We seem to be dogged by bad luck these days. The Norns hate us for some reason. I don't understand it. I thought it was that Odin had deserted us but now I know that is not true.'

'How?' Einar said.

'Because the All Father would not do that to me. To us,'

Ulrich said. He spoke through gritted teeth. 'I *know* this in my heart.'

Einar did not reply. The strength of the Wolf Coat's faith always amazed him.

'The other thing I know is that even the Gods cannot fight with Fate,' Ulrich said. 'The Norns rule the fates of all, even Odin and the Aesir. It is they who have turned against us. Not even Odin can help us if the Norns who govern our fates are against us. I've always prayed to them. Sacrificed to them. Why have they deserted me just when I need them most?'

'Those cursing poles,' Surt spoke for the first time. 'The horse's head on the stick we saw. You said there were spells carved on it.'

Affreca nodded.

'They called on our Norns to turn against us,' she said.

'That bitch Gunnhild!' Ulrich's eyes lit up. 'It's her accursed magic!'

'But if they want us dead why did the Norns not have us killed on the battlefield?' Einar said.

'Because of what Bodvar said,' Ulrich said. 'If we died a glorious death in battle Odin would have sent the Valkyries to sweep us up to his Valour Hall. They must want us to suffer more. They must have some sort of other, ignoble, shameful death in mind for us.'

'Could the Norns be so vindictive?' Einar said.

'They're women, aren't they?' Skar said.

Affreca glared at him.

'We really are in the shit. We can't fight magic any more than we can fight fate,' Kari said.

'The old man,' Einar said. 'Grimnir. Last night at the

feast. He had just started saying that he knew how to lift a witch's curse, then Olaf started speaking. I didn't pay any attention at the time.'

For a few moments there was silence in the tent.

'Well he can't help us now,' Affreca said.

At that moment the tent flap opened. Ten warriors filed in. They wore blood-splattered mail, visored helmets and their swords were drawn.

'Up on your feet,' the lead one said. 'We're taking you to King Eirik.'

'Now we'll see just what nasty fate the Norns have set aside for us,' Ulrich said.

Twenty-Two

King Olaf stood beneath the spreading branches of a big ash tree. It was at the edge of the forest beside the field where the battle had been fought.

He was a sorry sight. His hands were bound before him. His war gear was gone. His once grand clothes were torn and smeared with mud. His white hair was tousled and here and there splashed with blood. He had one boot on and one bare foot. His left eye was closed over and blackened. His jaw hung slack and his open mouth showed the bloody holes were a couple of his front teeth had been knocked out. He swayed as if barely able to stay on his feet. Indeed, it seemed as though the only thing keeping him upright was the noose around his neck, the rope from which was looped up over a sturdy branch of the ash above.

The tree had been turned into a gallows. Seven corpses dangled from other branches at various heights. Einar recognised several of them as jarls and other nobles who the night before had been seated at the top table at Olaf and Sigrod's feast.

A ring of jeering warriors, Eirik's victorious *hirðmenn*, stood around Olaf. They still wore their blood-splattered mail and most were swigging from skins full of wine or ale.

Einar, Affreca and the others, still bound and shackled, stood near the edge of the crowd. Einar saw that Atli stood near to the king. He was surrounded by eleven fearsome-looking warriors with black and brown bear pelts wrapped around their shoulders. Edwin and his Saxons were there too.

The gale that had been blowing for days had at last calmed. Darkness was falling to cover the butchery scattered across the battlefield. A large fire blazed near the ash tree, casting an eerie light on the morbid proceedings. Looking round, Einar saw that lots of other fires burned across the battlefield and camp which Eirik's army had taken possession of. Further off, smoke also rose from within the walls of Tunsberg. The town was paying the price for being on the losing side of this war.

A long-haired Galdr maðr moved around Olaf, muttering spells and shaking the branch of a birch tree to sprinkle the king with blessed water. A little way off two of his helpers were beating goatskin drums.

King Eirik stood before Olaf. He had a thick-shafted spear with a long feather-shaped blade in his hands.

'Did you ever learn any Latin, Olaf?' Eirik said.

Olaf looked at Eirik with his good eye. The expression on his face conveyed his confusion at the question.

'The Romans had a saying,' Eirik said. '*Vae victis*. It means *woe to the defeated*. I think you understand what that means now.'

'You really would kill me, Eirik?' Olaf said. His voice was hoarse. 'I am your brother.'

'I've already killed two of our other brothers,' Eirik said. 'And if the position was reversed, would you not do the same to me?'

'This is a shameful death for a king,' Olaf said. The noose was tight and he struggled to speak. 'To be sacrificed like a thrall. Am I not to be granted a warrior's death?'

'You could have had that if you didn't surrender,' Eirik said. 'Sigrod at least had the guts to fight on until he was killed. Odin granted me victory today. How else can I repay him than with a sacrifice in the way he requires? And what higher offering can I give him than a king?'

'You won by guile,' Olaf grunted. 'How did you get those men into the forest?'

'My son Rognvald led them,' Eirik said. 'We stopped three days ago further along the coast and put them ashore. Then we completed the voyage here a little slower than we would normally have with the gales to give them time to cross country on foot. That way we both arrived together.'

Ulrich inclined his head towards Skar.

'So that's what they were doing when we saw Eirik's ships at anchor the day before yesterday,' he said out of the corner of his mouth. 'He tricked us all.'

'Treacherous bastard,' Skar muttered.

Ulrich shrugged. 'Odin would be pleased with it. Is not one of his names *Ginnarr*, the Deceiver?'

'From now on the people of Norway will have a much easier life. They no longer have to choose who is their king,' Eirik said. He spoke in a loud, booming voice so all around the tree could hear. 'There is just me.'

'Our father has one more son who still lives,' Olaf said.

'Hakon?' Eirik said, raising one eyebrow. 'The little Christian will never get enough support to challenge me. You and Sigrod were my biggest threat. Now you're out of the way I can deal with him with ease.'

'He has pledged to give the poor their Odal rights back,' Olaf said. 'Many flock to support him.'

'That just shows what a fool he is,' Eirik said. 'Poor farmers with shovels and rakes will never beat wealthy noblemen in brynjas and shields.'

'I have a son. He will make you pay in blood for this,' Olaf said.

'Ah yes, Trygve,' Eirik said. 'My new Saxon friends tell me you sent him away to safety last night. I hear he is in the Gandvik district under the protection of a dead freeman's daughter and some old wise man of the district. I'll be sending Rognvald back there with enough men to find my nephew and make sure he never grows old enough to become a threat. My son, Rognvald, is just as keen to make sure there are no other rivals to the throne.'

'No,' Olaf said.

Einar flashed a glare at Wulfhelm who stood near Edwin. Even in the firelight he saw that the Saxon blushed as he looked away, avoiding Einar's eyes.

'Yes, Olaf,' Eirik said.

Olaf seemed to sag further as if whatever fight might have been left in him had finally drained away.

'Goodbye, Olaf,' Eirik said.

Eirik nodded to the Galdr maðr who in turn signalled to his helpers and three warriors who held the other end of the rope that ended in the noose around Olaf's neck. The drumming became frenzied as the warriors braced and hauled on the rope. The noose tightened and Olaf rose into the air. His right eye bulged and his damaged left one cracked open. Einar saw them both fill with blood as the king was hauled higher into the air. His face went dark puce and his tongue protruded from his mouth like a purple slug.

The warriors stopped pulling and Olaf hung suspended, his legs kicking and thrashing in thin air, making him swing from side to side. For a time Eirik stood below him, watching, then, as Olaf's movements began to slow he raised the spear.

'Odin owns you now,' Eirik shouted as he struck upwards with the spear, driving the blade deep into Olaf's right side. A torrent of blood dribbled down the shaft. Eirik let go and stepped away so he was not splashed with it. Above him Olaf stiffened, then went limp. His body twisted in ever slower, ever smaller circles as a stream of piss dribbled down his leg and off his bare foot.

'Now,' Eirik turned away from the dangling corpse of his half-brother. 'Where is Ulrich and where are my new úlfhéðnar?'

The warriors around Ulrich and the others shoved them forwards towards the king.

'Well isn't this a fine pit of snakes?' Ulrich said. 'All the traitors together.'

Eirik smiled, but there was no warmth in his expression.

'Here we are again, Ulrich,' the king said. 'Why aren't you dead?'

'Until recently I led a charmed life, lord,' Ulrich said.

'Well, that's about to end,' Eirik said. 'Atli?'

Atli approached. He had washed and changed out of the mail and muddied clothes he had worn in the battle but he still wore his wolfskin cloak around his neck. The crown of his head was now swathed in a clean bandage. He was a lot steadier on his feet than the last time Einar had seem him and now strode over to the king with a confident swagger. He had a large bag with him. Atli smiled at Ulrich and Skar in a manner that could only be described as provoking.

'How dare you still wear that wolfskin?' Ulrich said. 'You no longer deserve it.'

'My days of seeking your permission or approval for anything are over, Ulrich,' Atli said. 'I now command the king's Úlfhéðnar.'

'And who are they?' Ulrich said. 'All the Wolf Coats I know of are still with me. Perhaps it's just you? Playing with yourself was always something you were good at.'

Eirik chuckled.

'I'd forgotten what an entertaining tongue you have, Ulrich. I will miss that. But you can thank Atli that you are still alive – for now,' Eirik said. 'He has some plan for what he wants to do with you. I've made it clear this should not involve any of you continuing to live so don't get your hopes up.'

'What happened, Atli?' Skar said, pointing to the bandage. 'Did you bump your head?'

Atli's expression turned sour.

'You hit me a lucky blow,' he said. 'I couldn't move out of the way in the crush. But no matter. Do you know what I have in here?'

He held up the wool bag.

'The breeches you were wearing when you shit yourself?' Skar said.

Atli shook his head.

'Your wolf-pelt cloaks,' he said. 'King Eirik has given me some of his finest men. Berserkers and heroes. Each man who proves worthy of it will get one of these wolf pelts and join my new úlfhéðnar pack. They will replace you. In every way.'

Ulrich narrowed his eyes.

'That is not the custom,' he said. 'To become an Úlfhéðinn a man must first prove he is worthy by passing the ritual of initiation. If he manages that he must hunt and kill a wolf and take its pelt. That becomes the cloak he wears until the day he dies. So it has been since Odin founded the Úlfhéðnar in the youth of the world.'

'The world is changing, Ulrich,' Atli said. 'This will be *my* úlfhéðnar pack and I will run it as I think best. But don't worry, each man chosen will still have to prove he is worthy. We are going to have a series of *holmgang* duels. Each of you will fight one of the new men. If he kills you it will be your wolfskin he takes as his own.'

Skar shrugged.

'And what will you do when you run out of challengers for us to kill?' he said.

Atli's grin returned.

'Don't get too cocky,' he said. 'I'm not stupid enough to let you go on living when the king has ordered you dead. I was lucky enough to persuade him to let me have this bit of enjoyment, believe me. The duels won't be fair. My new men will have weapons. You won't.'

Twenty-Three

The Wolf Coats, Einar, Affreca and Surt were manhandled by Eirik's warriors across the former battlefield back towards the campsite. As they passed the walls of Tunsberg, Einar could see the glow of many fires radiating into the darkness. He heard the screams and wails of townspeople and the cheering, drunken singing and heartless laughter of Eirik's victorious warriors as they took revenge on the town for its disloyalty. If Skar had been worried about the damage a friendly army might have done once inside the walls among women and ale, then what must be going on in there now would make that seem like a children's game.

A wide river snaked around the edge of the camp before flowing into the town. Einar and the others had washed themselves in it the night before in preparation for the feast. At the time he had noted the small island about halfway across it and Skar had commented that it would be perfect for duel fighting.

Einar had fought a duel once before, against his half-brother Hrolf, and he had won it. He knew that the name *Holmgang* meant 'going to an island'. In former days two people in dispute went out to an actual island armed with weapons and shields. The confines of the island's surface provided a limited area in which they fought each other. Neither could retreat too far from the other, which ensured that the dispute got resolved, one way or another.

Duels were legal ways to resolve arguments but these days the 'island' was symbolic: A small area marked out by sticks or cloaks on the ground so the combatants did not have to get their feet wet.

It seemed that Atli meant to revive the traditional format.

Two torches were lit and set in brackets, one at either end of the island in the river and a large bonfire blazed on the bank so there was plenty of light. Many of Eirik's finest warriors and his berserkers, clad in their bulky bearskin cloaks, sat on the sloping riverbank. They were in fine spirits, laughing and celebrating their victory with ale and wine pillaged from the town. Edwin and his Saxons had followed the procession the Wolf Coats were in and they took seats on the ground among the others.

'At last! Here comes the entertainment,' someone shouted as Einar and the others were shoved and prodded down to the riverside. The watching crowd cheered.

Einar glared at Wulfhelm as he staggered past Edwin's men but the Saxon refused to meet his eye. Einar spat as if ridding his mouth of a disgusting taste.

Atli stood before them. He had a sword in one hand and the wool bag in the other. He upended the bag and the wolfskin cloaks of the úlfhéðnar spilled out into a heap on the ground.

'Tonight you men have the chance that most only dream of,' Atli said. 'You can try to become an Úlfhéðinn.'

More cheers came from the crowd.

'You must prove yourself worthy by defeating one of the

old úlfhéðnar,' Atli said as the cheering subsided. He looked around at Ulrich and the others. 'These men of yesterday. The Norns will decide which one you fight and when you kill your man then you will join my new company of úlfhéðnar.'

Atli glanced around again and this time his eye fell on Affreca. He reached out, grabbed her by the upper arm and hauled her in front of the mob on the riverbank. There were a few appreciative whistles and calls from them.

'If that wasn't enough of a prize, this is the daughter of the King of Dublin,' Atli said. 'Whoever fights the best tonight will also get her as their tent companion. So make each contest as enjoyable to watch as you can. No quick kills. Make it last.'

More excited cheering erupted from the onlookers.

'Let her go, you bastard,' Einar said.

'What are you going to do about it, farmer boy?' Atli said over his shoulder. 'Chant poetry at me?'

He shoved Affreca back towards the others and turned back to the waiting crowd.

'All right. Who's first?' Atli said as the cheering died down.

Several men all stood at once, then one of the berserkers threw down a skin of ale and strode forward ahead of the others. He stopped and turned.

'This is my right,' he said, shouting in the faces of the others. 'Mine! I'll fight you all just to get the chance to fight them.'

The others stopped. Some shrugged, then they all returned to their seats and their ale.

The berserker stomped over to Atli. He was almost as tall

as Skar and his chest was broad as an ale barrel. He wore a black bear pelt over a mail-ring brynja that gleamed in the firelight. He had black curly hair and his badly broken nose looked something like what Einar's would have been if Skar had not straightened it.

'We meet again, Ulrich,' the berserker said.

The look on Ulrich's face showed that he could not recall who the man was.

'Have you forgotten already?' the berserker said. 'A few months ago King Eirik gave you his best warriors to make up the numbers you lost in your úlfhéðnar crew. You and him were training us in the snow.'

He nodded at Skar.

Realisation dawned on Ulrich's face.

'Oh yes. None of you were good enough,' Ulrich said.

'I am Bragi,' the berserker said. He spoke his name in a way that suggested he was used to having his name recognised. His breath smelled of ale but he seemed to be completely in control of himself.

'Ah yes, Bragi,' Ulrich said, looking up at the big man who towered above him. 'I knocked your shit in and sent you back to the king, didn't I? You had a big mouth as I recall.'

Bragi scowled, the expression making his broken face even more unpleasant to look at.

'Tonight I will have my revenge,' he said.

Atli pointed to the pile of wolfskin cloaks.

'Pick one,' he said. 'Whoever owns it will be the man you will fight on the island. If you kill him you will prove you are worthy to be one of my úlfhéðnar and you will take his wolfskin coat.'

Bragi bent to sift through the pile. He pushed a couple aside then grabbed a brown-black fur. He straightened up and brandished it towards Ulrich.

'I hope it's yours,' Bragi said with a snarl.

'It's mine,' Bodvar said, stepping in front of Ulrich and meeting the berserker's glare with one of his own. Both men were well matched, being roughly the same height and weight. Both were fit, heavily muscled warriors. The main difference was one of them had war gear and weapons.

Bodvar raised his bound hands and prodded Bragi's mail shirt.

'That's a nice brynja,' he said. 'I thought you berserkers were so fearless you charged into battle naked except for your bear-skin cloaks. What are you scared of?'

Bragi now smiled and shook his head.

'I'm here to do a job. This is my chance to become an Úlfhéðinn,' he said. 'And I'm not stupid. You won't goad me into throwing away my advantage.'

A warrior stooped to unchain Bodvar's leg shackles while Atli unlocked the bonds around his wrists.

'I'm sorry you did not have the sense to join my new crew, Bodvar,' Atli said. 'Now go to the island. In case you think you can run take a look over there.'

He pointed up the riverbank with his sword to where three archers stood, arrows notched, ready to shoot.

Bodvar did not reply. He just curled his lip and began wading into the river.

'It seems the Norns have decided someone else will kill you,' Bragi said to Ulrich. 'But I still will have the pleasure of watching as you die.'

With surprising speed for a big man, he swung a meaty

fist at Ulrich. The little Wolf Coat tried to dodge but the shackles stopped him moving far enough. Bragi's punch smashed into Ulrich's cheek sending him sprawling backwards onto the ground.

Skar and the others lunged at Bragi but Atli stepped in front of them, brandishing the sword.

'Back! Get back,' he said, teeth bared. The Wolf Coats stopped.

Bragi spat on the prone Ulrich then turned and waded into the river after Bodvar.

The darkness and muddy colour of the water concealed the fact that the river was not deep and both Bodvar and Bragi were able to wade out to the little island without getting wet much above their thighs. Bodvar climbed onto the island, turned and waited for his opponent. While he did so he rolled his neck, swung his arms, twisted his back and generally loosened up his muscles in preparation for the coming fight.

Bragi strode up onto the island and drew his sword. His eyes were wide and his nostrilsflared and Einar had no doubt he was hovering on the edge of his berserker rage.

'Fight!' said Atli from the riverbank.

The crowd watching from the riverside erupted into excited, drunken cheering. Both men on the island dropped to a ready stance, feet far apart, knees slightly bent, ready to jump left or right. Bodvar held his hands high, palms open, while Bragi gripped his sword hilt in both hands. For a few moments they stood, watching each other. Then Bragi charged forward, yelling like a bear.

Bodvar skipped sideways and Bragi ran into the space he had been in. He skidded to a halt just before he ran out of island then twisted, lunging forward with his sword. Bodvar jumped backwards, away from the tip of the blade that should have gone right through his guts. Bragi recovered and advanced again, this time swiping his weapon from side to side. Bodvar dropped to a crouch and the blade passed by over his head. Bodvar sprang back to his feet and drove his right fist into Bragi's stomach. The movement was often practised so came to him instinctively, hence he had no time to think before his punch went into the metal rings of Bragi's brynja.

Bodvar let out a curse and staggered backwards away from Bragi, grasping his right hand with his left. Einar saw Bodvar's hand was hanging limp and he hoped he had not broken his wrist.

Seeing his advantage, Bragi ran forward again. He brought the sword up behind his head and then slashed it down in a strike aimed at the crown of Bodvar's head.

As Bragi moved, Bodvar stepped towards him then turned sideways so he was at right angles to his attacker. Bragi's sword came down but instead of cleaving Bodvar in two from the top of his head to his groin it swooped through empty air.

Bodvar, now standing beside Bragi, grabbed Bragi's right forearm. He pushed downwards but his injured right hand had no strength. Realising he would not be able to wrestle the sword from the berserker's grasp, Bodvar changed tactic and headbutted Bragi full in the face.

Bragi's head snapped back. Blood streamed from his nostrils, his already smashed nose now broken once again. The Wolf Coats on the riverbank cheered. Bragi tore himself away from Bodvar's grip and stumbled backwards. He still held his sword. He blinked several times then steadied himself.

The berserker took several deep breaths, looking at Bodvar with renewed respect. Then he stepped forward again, launching another overhead swipe at Bodvar. Anticipating this, Bodvar again danced sideways. This time, however, as Bragi's blade fell he changed its direction, bringing it down at an angle instead of straight down. He missed Bodvar's upper body but caught Bodvar's trailing leg. Bodvar cried out as the blade bit deep into his right thigh, sheering through his breeches and parting the flesh and muscle almost to the bone.

The Wolf Coats groaned. Eirik's men cheered.

Bodvar did not fall over. He hopped away out of the range of Bragi's sword, but blood was emptying from his wounded thigh. His face was already turning white. Bragi saw this and attacked again. Bodvar tried to get out of the way but as he moved, his injured leg gave way under his weight and he fell over.

Bragi bore down on him, driving his sword two-handed deep into Bodvar's chest. Bragi fell to his knees astride Bodvar, continuing to push his blade through the Wolf Coat's body.

Bodvar coughed. He reached up with both hands, trying to grab Bragi by the throat but the berserker tore his head away. Now pinned to the ground by the blade that transfixed him, Bodvar was unable to reach. With a final gasp his head dropped back. His arms went limp and his life left his body with the blood that gushed from the wounds to his thigh and chest.

For a moment there was silence, then Eirik's men exploded

into bloodthirsty cheers. Skar swore. Ulrich shook his head. Panting heavily, sweat steaming into the night air from his head, Bragi struggled to his feet and pulled his sword out of Bodvar's corpse. He waded back across to the riverbank and picked up Bodvar's wolfskin cloak. Grinning at Ulrich, he fastened it around his own throat.

More cheers filled the air. Atli joined Bragi, grabbed his hand and held it high above their heads.

'We have our first new úlfhéðinn,' Atli said to the watching crowd. 'Bragi has proved himself worthy of my wolf pack.'

Bragi winked at Affreca.

'You'll be mine later,' he said.

Atli pointed to the pile of other wolfskin cloaks with his free hand.

'Who's next?' he said.

Twenty-Four

'I will try,' a burly warrior said as he got to his feet. 'I am Njal Hrolfsson.'

His friends sitting around him cheered. Some patted his back as he swayed a little, then set his wineskin down, steadied himself, and strutted over to the wolfskins scattered on the ground. He had a long-handled axe over one shoulder whose blade was engraved with ornate swirling animal patterns but the blood splattered along its shaft and the forearms of its bearer showed it was no ornament.

'I didn't think I'd go out this way,' Kari said. 'As sport for a bunch of drunken lads.'

'That axe will cut an unarmed man in two,' Sigurd said. 'This is no sport. It's just murder.'

'The Norns are indeed cruel,' Ulrich said. 'A quick death in battle was not enough. We must be betrayed by one of our own and utterly humiliated as well.'

Einar felt as though there were a hole within him. He looked at Bodvar's bleeding corpse, trying to come to terms with the fact that he would not see him ever again. A hundred memories of the big man came flooding into his mind. His jokes. His constant jibing at all his companions. His frightening displays of aggression, like when he was roaring at the Scots as they stormed the gates of Cathair Aile or standing like a tree of battle in the shield wall against Eirik's men. The others were right. This was no way for a man like him to die. The thought that all of them would suffer the same ignoble end was galling. He could see from the dull looks in the eyes of the Wolf Coats that the same thought was in their minds.

His mind became angry. Such a company as Ulrich's did not deserve this fate. Was it really all because of a queen and her magic spells? There must be some way to escape this. Atli could not be allowed to get away with it. But what? Bound and shackled as they were, outnumbered ten to one and with archers waiting to shoot them down if they tried to run, their options were limited.

As they watched Njal Hrolfsson go through the wolf skins, trying to pick one, Einar found the words of a poem running round inside his head. He checked himself. This was no time for poetry. Then he realised that the words were from *Krákumál*, the poem that Ragnar Loðbrók composed in his last moments. He did not know how these words had come to him now but he realised how appropriate they were.

'Don't be downhearted,' he said.

The others all turned to face him, puzzled expressions on their faces.

'Did not Ragnar Loðbrók suffer a fate just like this?' Einar said. 'King Aella threw him in a pit of poisonous snakes, his death was to be entertainment for the Saxon nobles. What did Ragnar do? He asked for a harp so he could sing of his achievements. He sang in the face of death.'

Einar's heart lifted a little as he saw the expressions on

the faces around him lighten. It was as though a spark had reignited in them.

'Bodvar fought well,' Kari said. 'So should we all. If they want a show then let's give it to them. We'll go down fighting in a way men will talk about for years to come.'

The others nodded.

'Yes,' Einar said, surprised to find a smile creeping onto his face.

'That's easy for you to say,' Ulrich said to him. 'You have no wolfskin in that pile. You won't be next on the island.'

'This one,' Njal said, at last picking a light grey wolf pelt from the ground. He held it in the air for all to see.

Skar straightened up.

'That's mine,' he said.

Ulrich laid a hand on his Prow Man's shoulder.

'Well old friend,' Ulrich said. 'Die well. Make us proud. We shall meet again on the mead benches of Odin's Valour Hall.'

Skar grunted and tossed his head.

'I've no intention of dying yet,' he said.

Einar swallowed, astounded and moved by the big man's bravery in the teeth of so hopeless an outcome.

Two of Eirik's warriors unshackled Skar. The other Wolf Coats cheered as Skar turned and strode into the water, crossing to the island in several long strides. Then he climbed up onto the island, picking his way through some short rushes that grew at the edge and walked to its centre, where he turned around and waited for his opponent to arrive.

Njal Hrolfsson chuckled, hefted his axe and waded into the river. As he reached the edge of the island he too looked down to navigate the reeds in the shallows.

As he did so Skar sprang forward. The big man was back at the edge of the island in a couple of strides and swung a huge kick at Hrolfsson. His opponent, still half in the water, was much lower down and looking downward. Skar's boot caught him full in the face. Hrolfsson's head snapped up and Einar was sure he heard a crunch of bone. The force of Skar's kick propelled Hrolfsson back up to his feet. His arms flung wide and the axe flew from his now limp hand. It toppled through the air then landed with a splash in the river. Hrolfsson toppled backwards into the water after it.

Skar jumped in after him. For a moment both were obscured by the tremendous splash then they all saw Skar standing thigh deep in the river, holding Hrolfsson under with both hands. King Eirik's warrior's arms were above the surface but he was giving no resistance. The kick had either knocked him out cold or killed him outright.

For a moment there was shocked silence. Then the watchers on the riverbank were on their feet, yelling their anger.

'Let him go!' Atli shouted.

Skar ignored him, continuing to hold the unconscious warrior's head under.

'Let him go or I'll order the archers to shoot,' Atli said.

Skar looked up. For a moment he and Atli locked eyes. Atli raised an arm towards the archers. Einar knew if he brought it down they would loose their arrows and Skar would be dead. At such close range only a blind man could miss.

Skar knew this too. With a disgusted sneer he let go of Hrolfsson and stood up straight in the water. The body of his former opponent bobbed up to the surface but his now white face remained under water. He did not move as the current caught him and his body began to float away downstream.

As his companions waded into the river to haul Hrolfsson out, Skar stood, looking at the spot where the axe had hit the water. Einar knew what he was thinking but so did Atli.

'Don't even think about going for that axe,' Atli said through gritted teeth. 'Or the archers will shoot you. Now get back on that island.'

Skar shrugged and climbed back out of the water.

'I didn't say *fight*,' Atli said. 'This time wait for me to start.'

Skar laughed outright.

'Who's next to try?' Atli addressed the crowd on the riverbank.

'I'll kill him,' another of Eirik's berserkers was on his feet. 'He'll pay for what he did to Njal.'

The berserker emptied his horn of ale down his throat then tossed it aside. Einar saw him weave a bit as he walked to the river. The man was quite drunk, which might give Skar an advantage, except that he also wore a thick leather jerkin and a mail brynja over it. He drew a long, single-bladed seax knife as he waded over to the island. Unlike his predecessor, he kept his eyes firmly on Skar as he climbed up onto the island.

This time Skar waited for his opponent to come ashore.

'Fight,' Atli said, as if eager to make sure he said it in case Skar started the duel for him.

The berserker snarled and gnashed his teeth. He brandished the knife but he did not advance.

'What's the matter?' Skar said. 'Scared?'

The berserker shook his head.

'I'm not stupid,' he said. 'You attack me.'

'I'm not stupid either,' Skar said. He folded his arms. 'And I can wait here all night.'

Ulrich and the Wolf Coats laughed at the look of confusion on the berserker's face.

'What if the archers shoot him?' Einar said.

'Look where he's standing,' Ulrich said in a low voice. 'Skar's making sure the berserker is between him and them. If they shoot they'll hit their own man.'

'Finish him,' Atli shouted from the riverbank. The other warriors started shouting similar encouragement.

The berserker on the island snarled and, goaded into attacking, ran forward. A few paces from Skar he lunged with the knife, aiming it for Skar's guts. At the same time Skar lashed out with a punch. The big man's reach was much longer than his opponents and his fist smashed into the other man's face before the knife reached him. The berserker staggered sideways. Skar swept his leg around, taking the berserker's own legs from under him so he fell backwards, landing flat on his back.

Skar stepped over him and planted his left foot on the hand that held the knife. The berserker squealed and thrashed around as Skar ground his boot from side to side. The sound of cracking bone was audible above the man's shrieks. Still standing on his opponent's hand, Skar lifted his right boot and stomped it down hard on the man's face. Then he did it again. Then once more. The berserker lay still.

As if he had all the time in the world, Skar crouched down beside the prone berserker, took away his knife and sliced open the man's throat.

As blood bubbled and gushed from the wound, chaos erupted on the riverbank. The Wolf Coats cheered, punched the air and hugged each other as best they could. Atli shouted obscenities at the night sky. Eirik's warriors were on their feet too, shouting in outrage and pointing at Skar.

'I'll kill him,' another of the berserkers shouted. He got to his feet but was so drunk he staggered sideways, collapsing into his fellows.

'I will,' Bragi roared.

'No, I will,' another of the berserkers said, running towards the river.

'I said I will do it!' Bragi said, grabbing the other man as he ran past.

'Get off me,' the other said, throwing a punch at Bragi.

Both men began grappling.

'Enough!'

A new voice, speaking in a loud and commanding tone, made everyone freeze.

King Eirik had come to the riverbank. In the dark no one had seen him arrive and now he stood beside Atli and the Wolf Coats at the edge of the river. Edwin the Saxon Aetheling was beside him.

Bragi and the other berserker stopped fighting. They hung their heads like a couple of children caught being naughty. Silence fell all around.

'Atli bring an end to this,' Eirik said. He spoke low and through clenched teeth so only those nearest to him, including Einar and the others could hear.

'But we are not finished,' Atli said.

'You *are* finished,' Eirik said in a growl. 'How many more warriors are you going to get killed? These men are drunk.

I think we've had enough of this travesty. It would be funny except that Odin alone knows what it's doing to the men's spirits to see their champions killed one by one before them while my enemies laugh at us.'

He glowered at Atli. Atli closed his mouth. He went quite pale.

'I hope I have not made a mistake in my choice of a new leader for my Úlfhéðnar, Atli,' the king went on. Atli swallowed. 'Now take Ulrich and his men away. Kill them quietly later tonight.'

'Let my men kill them for you, Lord Eirik,' Edwin said. 'They'll make sure it's done right.'

Eirik shot a sour glance sideways at Edwin then looked back at Atli.

'Just make sure it's done,' he said, then turned and stalked off into the night.

Twenty-Five

With the archers aiming at him, Skar was told to throw away the seax knife and come back to the riverbank. The big man tossed the knife aside in a contemptuous gesture then waded back across the river where Atli and the others put his shackles back on. Then they were all marched back to the tent they had been in before.

After they were shoved inside, Atli poked his head in through the flap after them.

'There are warriors posted outside so you needn't think you'll escape,' he said. 'I'm going to gather together enough men to murder you all. There won't be any shortage of volunteers I can tell you that. Enjoy your last time in this world. When we're ready I'll send someone to get you.'

'For your sake, Atli, I hope this plan goes better than your last one,' Ulrich said. 'Eirik doesn't like men who make mistakes.'

Atli scowled and closed the tent flap.

'That was quite a fight, Skar,' Einar said. The others nodded.

'A lot of good it did us,' Skar said with a shrug. 'All I've done is delay when they kill us.'

'What's the point anyway?' Ulrich said. 'We are cursed.

We cannot fight fate. If we escape death now it will get us later. We're all doomed.'

'What if we got the curse lifted?' Einar said.

Everyone looked at him.

'How?' Ulrich said.

'The old man said he knew how to break it,' Einar said. 'We escape from here. We find him and get him to lift the curse.'

'Just like that?' Ulrich raised his eyebrows.

'Why not?' Einar said. 'If we really are doomed then we'd all have died at the river. Or at least Skar has shown we can fight back against whatever the Norns send at us. Our fate is not yet woven. We can break the threads and change the pattern.'

'But it's the Norns who are weaving the tapestry,' Ulrich said. 'They will get us in the end.'

'Then at least we'll die trying,' Einar said.

Ulrich looked at Skar. Skar nodded.

'But how do we get out of this?' Ulrich said, rattling the chains around his legs.

Each Wolf Coat began working on their bonds, trying to find some weakness or other way to open the shackles. Surt flexed his huge muscles, trying to break the iron fetters through sheer brute force.

Einar could see that the fetters were too strong and too well made to be broken. If they were to get out of this they needed a different plan. He got up and shuffled to the tent flap, then poked his head out. His heart sank to see that the tent was surrounded by warriors. They were not drinking and they were all armed to the teeth. A cursory count tallied maybe two dozen of them as well.

One of them spotted Einar.

'Get back inside,' he said, brandishing his sword.

Einar withdrew and closed the tent flap behind him.

'Well?' Affreca said as Einar returned.

He shook his head.

'There's too many of them outside,' he said. 'Even if Skar kills a few more of them we won't get far unless we get these shackles off.'

Ulrich sighed.

'We're getting nowhere with that,' he said. 'At least if we got them off we might be able to take our chances and run for it.'

The others continued working at their bonds until it became obvious to all of them that there was no way out of them.

'There's only one thing left to try,' Ulrich said. The others nodded and the Wolf Coat leader closed his eyes. The others closed their eyes as well and Ulrich, to Einar's surprise, began to sing. The words that came from him were strange. They sounded half familiar yet also ancient and obscure.

'What's he doing?' Einar said in a whisper to Skar.

Skar opened his eyes and gave Einar a disapproving look.

'Didn't anyone teach you religion, lad?' he said in a quiet voice. 'He's singing Odin's spell song to loosen fetters.'

The look on Einar's face betrayed the fact that he still had no idea what was going on.

'Remember the verse in *Hávamál*, the Words of Odin?' Skar said.

'A fourth song I know: if men bind
in chains the joints of my limbs,
when I sing that song that sets me free,
the fetters will spring from hands and feet.'

'He's trying a spell?' Einar said.

'He's asking for Odin's help,' Skar said. 'Now is the right time to do it. Some make the mistake of asking for help from the Gods before they try anything else. That just annoys Gods like Odin. Men should trust in their own strength first before they go bothering the Aesir with their pleas. We've tried all options within our own power and they haven't worked. Now is the time to ask for some help from the heavens.'

Einar fell silent and Ulrich finished his song. For a long time everyone in the tent was silent. Einar was unsure what to expect. Would the fetters just fall off his arms?

In the end it was Affreca who broke the silence.

'What do we do now?' she said.

Ulrich looked at his bonds and sighed. Einar wondered if he had indeed been expecting the iron fetters to just spring open. The little Wolf Coat shook his head.

The tent flap swept open. Everyone turned to see the Saxon, Wulfhelm and his big shovel-faced companion standing there. They were both clad in their magnificent war gear and their red garnet encrusted swords were drawn.

'We're here to take you to Atli,' Wulfhelm said. 'He's gathered warriors in a private place where you will be put to death. Say anything you need to now then we must leave.'

'It seems we haven't managed to get Odin's attention back yet,' Ulrich said. 'Our luck continues to run bad.'

The other warriors from outside the tent crowded in and hauled Einar, Affreca, Surt and the Wolf Coats up to their feet and shoved them outside.

'Let's go,' Wulfhelm's large companion said.

They set off across the campsite once more. Olaf and Sigrod's army were either dead, prisoners or had fled for their lives, leaving their tents and belongings behind. Eirik's men had taken all of it and were continuing to celebrate their victory. It was dark but many campfires burned all around, surrounded by men drinking, singing and laughing. As he shuffled along, Einar saw a bunch of drunken men making a prisoner dance for their entertainment. They were stabbing at his bare feet with spears so he hopped and jumped around while another man played a tune on a *fidla*. The prisoner looked drawn and exhausted and his shins and feet were already pricked and bleeding all over. He did not look like he could keep it up much longer and Einar wondered what his tormentors would do when he was no longer capable of entertaining them.

Vae victis, as Eirik had said.

'Where are we going?' Ulrich said after they had been walking for some time.

'The forest,' Wulfhelm said. 'There will be less prying eyes there.'

'I saved your life,' Einar said, his tone bitter.

Wulfhelm stiffened.

'We have to follow what our lord orders,' he said. 'And Lord Edwin has ordered us to do this. Keep going.'

They marched on until the tents thinned out and they

crossed into the former battlefield. Einar felt a chill at the thought of what lay all around, hidden by the darkness. The piles of the dead, white and naked, stripped of their belongings, clothes and weapons by the victors, all starting to bloat and rot while the ravens, the wolves, the other scavengers chewed on them. Soon he would be as dead as they were.

Einar could hear the wind blowing through trees and knew they must be getting closer to the forest. Wulfhelm signalled to them all that they had to stop.

'Aelfred and I will handle it from here,' he said to the contingent of warriors who had accompanied them from the tent. 'You men can go and join the others and have a drink. You've a lot of catching up to do.'

The warriors, who had clearly been told to stay sober while all those around them were drinking themselves stupid, cheered and grinned. As they walked off into the dark Wulfhelm's companion shot a questioning look at him.

Wulfhelm said something but his voice was muffled in his helmet. Aelfred clearly did not hear him as he shook his head and gestured to his ear.

Wulfhelm unlaced his helmet and took it off. He gestured to Aelfred's helmet and he did the same.

'I said: King Eirik said to do it quietly. Atli said we're to take them to him without bringing half the army with us,' Wulfhelm said, his voice now clear. 'Look at them. They're chained up. What are you worried about? We can handle them if they get out of hand.'

His big companion nodded slowly.

'Right you lot,' Aelfred said, turning his attention back to the Wolf Coats. 'Get moving again.'

As he spoke Wulfhelm smashed the flat of his drawn sword across the back of Aelfred's skull. Einar saw the big man's eyes widen as he staggered forwards. He did not fall however and his expression swiftly moved from shock to anger.

Affreca stepped towards Aelfred and swung her fettered hands upwards. Their heavy, trailing chain whipped up and caught Aelfred on the point of his considerable chin. At the same moment Wulfhelm hit Aelfred across the head again with the flat of his sword.

This time Aelfred's eyes rolled up into his head. He dropped to his knees, then pitched forward onto his face.

'Christ's blood but Aelfred always did have a thick skull,' Wulfhelm said, prodding his companion with his boot to make sure he was unconscious.

'You're not taking us to our death?' Einar said.

'Did you really think I've so little honour?' Wulfhelm said. They could see his white teeth even in the dark and knew he was grinning.

'What about your lord?' Einar said.

Wulfhelm shook his head.

'Now *there* is a man with no honour,' he said. 'I saw that today when he switched sides. He'd do anything to save his own hide. But we need to get moving. Atli really is coming to take you to be executed and when he finds that tent empty and the guards drunk this place will be hotter than Hell.'

'But Hell is cold,' Einar said.

'Let's not stand around discussing religion,' Skar said. 'What about him?'

He pointed at the prone Aelfred.

'I can't kill him,' Wulfhelm said. 'He's an old comrade but not that bright. He's loyal as a dog to Edwin and I suppose he'll tell him what happened here.'

'Then you can come with us,' Skar said.

Wulfhelm looked at him for a moment then said: 'All right.'

He tossed a key to Skar. 'That's for the shackles.'

'We should make for the shore,' Ulrich said. 'We need a ship if we're to get to Grimnir in Gandvik.'

'Who?' Wulfhelm said.

'The old man from the feast last night,' Einar said. 'We're cursed and he knows how to break it.'

'Well there's no chance of a ship,' Wulfhelm said. 'I was down there earlier. All the ships are guarded. If anyone tries to take one they'll be stopped.'

The sound of voices raised in alarm rose among the general shouting and singing from the camp behind them.

'It looks like they've found out we've gone,' Ulrich said. 'Very well. Into the trees. We run.'

Twenty-Six

King Eirik rubbed his eyes. He was tired. He had been in his helmet and mail all day and though he had not taken part in the actual fighting, his brynja was heavy and tended to dig into his shoulders. He would have to have that fixed. At least he was now out of it and dressed in comfortable furs and linen. He was seated in Olaf's chair in Olaf's tent, a large drinking horn decorated with silver filigree brimming with red wine in one hand. The only blemish on the day were the men who now stood before him.

'So Ulrich has escaped again?' he said. 'Atli, I was unsure if I was right letting you back into my service. Now I think I should have gone with my gut instinct and had you beheaded.'

'This was not my fault, Lord King,' Atli said, pointing at Edwin who stood beside him. 'If his men had not betrayed us, Ulrich and the others would be dead.'

Lord Edwin sent a sour glance in Atli's direction.

'It was only *one* of my men,' he said. 'And when we find him he will rue the day his mother birthed him.'

Seated on Sigrod's former seat was a young man with an abundance of flowing black hair, both from his head and beard. He too had a horn of wine and was clad in rich clothes like the king. It was Rognvald, Eirik's illegitimate son.

Aelfred also stood before the king. His chin was split open where Affreca had hit him with the chain and one of his companions had sewn the wound with large, clumsy stitches.

'Tell them what you heard,' Edwin said.

'They said they were going to someone called Grimnir,' the big man said. 'Something about a curse?'

'I thought this man was knocked out?' Eirik said.

'I was, Lord King,' Aelfred said, looking proud of himself. 'But I came round while they were still standing over me. I pretended to still be out in case they killed me.'

'Grimnir, Lord King,' Atli said, 'Is the old man who Olaf entrusted his son to.'

'I'll deal with them then, father,' Rognvald said. 'You are sending me that way anyway.'

Eirik leaned over and patted the young man's forearm.

'I know I can trust you to get the job done, Rognvald,' he said. 'I know I've not been good to you but Gunnhild is jealous for her own children by me. Perhaps now she will recognise your true worth, as I do. Concentrate first on killing those children, Trygve and Gudrod. Do that and I will reward you well.'

'I won't let you down, father,' Rognvald said. He straightened up in his chair and his chest puffed out.

'I don't think you will,' Eirik said, taking a glug of wine. 'The blood of Harald Fairhair flows in you as it does in me.'

'Give me a band of warriors and we'll hunt Ulrich down,' Atli said. 'They must have gone into the forest. They can't have got far.'

Eirik shook his head.

'Atli, even if you could find enough men who weren't so drunk they were any use,' he said. 'Do you think you'll find any prepared to go into a forest, at night, knowing Ulrich's úlfhéðnar are in there?'

Edwin snorted. 'Who are these men? Are they really that formidable?'

'They're the most fucking dangerous bunch of killers I've ever met,' Eirik said. 'Which is why I need them dead. However we need to do this properly. It's been a long day and we've been victorious. But our work here is just beginning. This realm supported my brothers against me and it must be punished for that. I intend to make an example of Viken so that all the other provinces of Norway know what will happen if they turn against me. The men can rest tonight. Let them enjoy themselves. Then from tomorrow we have towns to plunder, farms to burn, women to ravish and children to spit on the points of our spears. I will send my warriors through this land like wolves. The rivers will run red with blood and when we are done the folk here will know why I am called Eirik Bloody Axe.'

Eirik, who had seemed calm, almost bored before, now clutched his drinking horn with white knuckles while he spat his words through clenched teeth. Then he blinked as if waking from a trance and his former demeanour reappeared.

'Rognvald, you must sail for Gandvik in the morning,' the king continued. 'If you bring me the heads of my nephew and his companion then I was thinking perhaps you can have Olaf's title as King of Viken as well as Lord of Gandvik. I need someone in charge here who I can trust. You will rule under me, of course.'

'Of course, father,' Rognvald said.

'Atli,' Eirik said. 'At first light take dogs and horsemen and get after Ulrich. Don't let him get away or if you do this time I *will* have your head. Edwin, no doubt your sudden change of loyalty has something to do with you hoping I have a better chance of stopping your brother Aethelstan's puppet, my brother Hakon, becoming King of Norway.'

'Your deeds today, Lord King, show you are the mightier of your brothers,' Edwin said. 'My fortunes would be best served by serving the strongest of kings.'

'Whatever. Take your men and help Atli hunt down Ulrich and his men,' Eirik said. 'Perhaps that will give you an understanding of just how resourceful those men are. If you bring me their heads then who knows? Perhaps I'll consider sending a great army to Britain against Aethelstan. Perhaps you could be my representative on that expedition. However if you and Atli fail I know at least my son will deal with Ulrich and his company when they reach Gandvik.'

'We will not fail, Lord King,' Atli said. Edwin nodded.

'Now excuse me but it's time for me to retire,' Eirik said. 'With my wife out of the country I have a couple of slave girls waiting for me in my sleeping quarters. I'm rather tired so I doubt much will happen tonight but there is always the morning. All of you get some sleep and we shall deal with our problems tomorrow. Is that not what Odin himself tells us we should do?'

Twenty-Seven

Einar had never felt so tired. He had begun the day hungover and half slept, then fought in a battle, almost been executed and now he was spending the night hurrying through a forest. The Wolf Coats, on the other hand, were relentless. They just kept going. Einar could not understand where their energy came from.

'We need to get as far away as possible while its dark,' Ulrich had said as they set off through the trees. 'Keep silent. If you fall behind we cannot wait. No one will be coming back to look for you so everyone must keep up. Does everyone know the *kaun* step?'

Einar and Affreca had nodded. It was the foot movement the Wolf Coats had taught them when they had crossed the Irish countryside by night. Surt shook his head.

Ulrich demonstrated the step, sweeping his fore foot before him then sideways at an angle, close to the ground, before he actually planted his step.

'Running through a forest at night would just be stupid,' Ulrich said. 'In the dark, on uneven ground, with sticks and branches all about, before you know it you'll have two broken legs and all you'll be able to do is lie and wait for Eirik's men to come and pick you up. To most people the meaning of the kaun rune, is an ulcer, but its secret meaning is a torch. If you use the kaun step you can feel the ground ahead and still move swiftly but safely. You will know the ground ahead of you as if you held a burning torch in your hand.'

Surt nodded.

'This is like the night step of the secret killers of the Ismailis,' he said. 'They use it to move in the dark too.'

'Remember your night eyes,' Ulrich said. 'If you need to look at something don't look straight at it. You can see better in the dark from the sides of your eyes.'

Then they had set off through the trees.

Einar knew he was struggling to keep up, but he did not want to be the first to ask for a break. Affreca was on his right. He could hear her breathing and the sweep of her feet. Surt was just behind him. The úlfhéðnar were ahead and behind, keeping the four non-Wolf Coats in the middle as they thought they were the most likely to fall over in the dark. Einar did not fall outright but he did stumble twice. The second time he did it he swore to himself that he would not let it happen again. He was so tired that the thought of the effort required to get back to his feet if he did fall seemed daunting.

They kept moving through the night. Einar's eyes grew accustomed to the dark and he was surprised how much he could make out, even in the Stygian gloom of the forest. Ulrich was right: He could see more at the periphery of his vision than what he looked directly at.

Where they were heading or how Ulrich knew what direction they were going in Einar had no idea. The moon and stars above that could have given them a clue as to where they were heading were hidden by the tree canopy, though Einar could make out the outline of the little Wolf Coat ahead of him and noticed he often touched the trunks of trees as he passed them and sometimes changed their direction after doing so.

Einar did not like forests. There were woods in Iceland but they were limited to a few woods scattered across the country which got less and less with every year's charcoal burning. There was nothing like these dark, strange kingdoms of trees that covered whole swathes of countryside here in Norway. They were uncanny places where you could not see what lurked behind the trunks perhaps only a few paces away. The air was still in them and all sound deadened by the heaps of pine needles that covered the ground to unknown depths. Being in one at night was even worse, and he felt his skin crawl every time he thought about what creatures, natural or other, that could be waiting to pounce from the dark.

Just when Einar felt he could go on no longer Ulrich called a halt. They had come to a stream that bubbled its way through the floor of the forest.

'Drink as much as you can,' Ulrich said. 'We'll have a short rest then we'll be on our way again.'

All of them dropped to the ground beside the stream. They fell to slurping the cold, clear water to slake their parched throats. Einar was sweating all over and every part of his body felt tired. He plunged his face right into the stream then pulled it up a bit, desperate to lap water into his mouth with his tongue while sucking with his lips.

He felt a tap on his shoulder and looked up. Skar was kneeling beside him.

'Do it like this lad,' he said, cupping his hands together and dipping them into the stream. Then he raised them to his mouth. 'You get a much better mouthful.'

Einar followed his example and found he was indeed right.

'Skar,' Ulrich hissed from further along the stream. 'Over here.'

The big man got up and joined Ulrich and they fell into an earnest discussion, speaking in low whispers.

'What do you think they're talking about?' Surt said from nearby Einar. It was hard to see the black-skinned man in the dark but Einar recognised his accent.

'Probably some secret Wolf Coat business,' Einar said. 'Too secret for the likes of us to know about.'

'Or,' Affreca said from a little way off. 'They could be working out what we need to do next and where to go.'

'Well, I hope they take a long time to work it out,' Einar said. 'I'm shattered.'

He lay down flat on his back, looking up at the canopy of trees above, visible thanks to the starshine above them.

'Why are you northmen so afraid of women?' Surt said. 'Who are these Norns you're all scared of? Are they witches?'

'Did no one ever tell you about the Norns?' Einar said. 'I thought you had lived among us for many years.'

'I have,' Surt said. 'But I was a slave. A demon who was there to kill people for the king. King Eirik talked to his dogs more than he ever spoke to me. They thought I was less than human. They did not even realise I had learned their tongue just by being among them. I heard many mentions of these Norns though. And women called the dísir? Always their names were spoken with fear and respect.'

Einar gazed up into the blackness, wondering where to start.

'Deep down in the roots of the world,' he said, 'there is a well. No one knows where the water from that well springs from, but it's so holy that anything washed in it becomes as white as the skin that lies inside an eggshell. The well is called *Urðarbrunnr*, the well of fate.'

'I've heard of this place,' another voice came from the dark. Einar recognised the accent of Wulfhelm.

'My grandmother used to talk of such things,' the Saxon said. 'She called it The Well of *Wyrd*. This is heathenry though. Such beliefs are the road to Hell.'

'Isn't that the road we will all take?' Einar said, puzzled. 'Anyway, there is a hall near the well and three women live there. They are wondrously old. Older than the Gods and older even than the Jǫtnar. But they never grow old themselves. They are outside of time and the passing of the years that governs the lives of men. These women are called *Urðr*, *Verðandi*, and *Skuld*. They are the Norns.'

'What will happen, what is happening and what should happen,' Wulfhelm said.

'Wait,' Surt said. 'I've heard this tale before, but not here among you barbarians. When I was in al-Andalus the Emir of Córdoba had a great library of books that contained all the wisdom of the world. There were books there translated from the writings of the Greeks from the ancient days even before Rome ruled the world. The Greeks talked of three magic women who allotted men their destiny. They called them the Spinner, the Allotter and the Unavoidable.'

Einar sat up.

'The Spinner you say? Now that's interesting. Perhaps these Greeks knew something of the truth. The Norns weave a tapestry, like one of the ones you see in the hall of a jarl or king; very long and narrow, each panel depicting a scene that tells a story. The tapestry the Norns weave depicts the story of the world and all the other worlds. Each person is represented by a thread in it. When a thread starts, a man is born. When the Norns cut a thread, his life ends and so they govern the fate of all. Even the Gods are subject to their power.'

'And you think these supernatural beings, these women who guide the fate of the whole world, really care about this little band?' Surt said. 'You must have very high opinions of yourselves.'

'Urðr, Verðandi, and Skuld are the most important of the Norns,' Einar said. 'But there are many others. When a child is born it is visited by lesser Norns. Some are good and seek to protect the child while others are malevolent and only want to work harm. The gifts they bestow are good luck and good fortune or ill luck and misfortune. Ulrich thinks that Gunnhild's spells have empowered our evil Norns and they are working against us.'

'However our fates are handed out,' Wulfhelm said, 'I have to admit we agree on one thing: *Gæð a wyrd swa hio scel*, as we say in Wessex. Fate goes ever as it must go.'

Surt grunted.

'You don't believe in Fate?' Einar said.

'I do,' Surt said. 'We call it *Qadar* and it's one of the pillars of the faith of my people. But it is set by God, not weaving women beside a well.'

'Right, break is over.'

Their discussion was halted by Ulrich's voice coming through the dark.

'Back on your feet. We need to get moving again,' he said. 'This stream is going the right way so for the next bit we'll move up it. It will help get rid of our scent if they come after us with dogs. Remember, keep up. Eirik Bloody Axe will take whoever is left behind.'

Twenty-Eight

They continued along the stream. It was impossible to keep silent as they splashed through the shallow water but Ulrich judged it was better to make some noise than leave a trail that dogs could follow. Einar's misery was increased by the cold water that soaked his feet and at times it was tricky to navigate the uneven, slippery rocks at the bottom of the stream. They were going upstream as well which added to the effort required to keep going. It was not long before Einar could no longer feel his cold, wet feet which in a way came as a partial relief.

They kept going for some time, the stream bed getting steeper as they climbed, until it took a turn to the right. Ulrich signalled they had to get out of the stream.

'The stream is going the wrong way,' he said, speaking in a whisper. 'We need to head that way.'

He pointed in the opposite direction. To Einar's dismay they would still be going uphill. They set off again. Einar's wet feet were uncomfortable but the feeling began to return to them. With it came a strong itching sensation through his toes but there was nothing to do but keep going. Before long the effort meant that his feet were so warm he no longer felt their wetness.

The ground continued to slope upwards, getting ever more steep. They kept climbing and it was obvious they were scaling some sort of mountainside or out of a deep valley. As they walked, Einar thought the glimpses of the blackness of the night sky he caught through the trees above was changing to a dark blue. At first he thought he was so tired he was seeing things, then realised that the day was approaching. They became able to see more and more and before long the whole forest was bathed in the grey pre-dawn light.

Ulrich halted.

'If we go on much longer it will be day,' he said. 'Time to rest up until tomorrow night. Everyone will take a watch to make sure no one is sneaking up on us. I'll take the first one. Then each one of you will take a turn. Now build yourselves a shelter. One each.'

Einar was overcome with relief. He could not have gone on any further and the fear of who might be chasing them had already disappeared beneath his utter, exhaustion.

They each found hollows or holes in the forest-covered hillside deep enough to lie in. The Wolf Coats gathered ferns, fallen tree branches and swathes of moss and lichen from the forest floor and Einar, Affreca, Wulfhelm and Surt followed their example. They put half what they gathered into their hole first to provide some comfort beneath them, lay down on it, then pulled the rest in on top of themselves.

Ulrich went round each person's shelter, fixing branches or throwing more moss on top, making sure they were completely covered and out of sight.

Einar was asleep before Ulrich even reached his shelter to

check it was sufficient. His last thoughts were that he hoped his watch was as late as possible in the day so he would get as much sleep as he could.

It was not Ulrich that woke him, however.

Einar opened his eyes. His nose was filled with the smell of damp pine needles and moss. Bright daylight filtered through the branches that covered him. This told him he had been asleep for some time. He was tired and groggy and could have closed his eyes again and slept on with ease, so he had not woken naturally. Something had disturbed his sleep.

He became aware of a sound like drums heard from far off, or perhaps distant thunder. He peeked out through his cover and saw that Ulrich and Skar were out of their own shelters. They were crouching low and looking up the slope. Einar went to sit up then stopped, wincing at the stiffness and pain that seemed to come from every muscle in his body at once. With more care, he rolled sideways and clambered out of his shelter, scattering branches as he went.

Ulrich held a finger to his lips and pointed up the slope.

'Horses,' he said. His whisper was so quiet it was almost like he was just mouthing the words.

Einar realised that what had woken him up were the sound of hooves. Not just the sound either. The soft turf of the forest floor vibrated slightly in time to the thudding torrent of the horses' footfalls. The noise was coming from further up the slope. One thing was certain: There were a lot of them.

'They can't be riding like that through the forest,' Einar said.

Ulrich shushed him, an irritated look on his face.

The noise got louder, then a short time receded again and the quiet of the forest took over once more.

'We'd better take a look,' Skar said.

They started up the slope, moving with caution, crouched over and ready to drop to the forest floor at the first sign of movement from above.

After a short distance they saw a break in the treeline above, then came upon a track that cut through the forest from a corner not far off to the right to another further away to the left, going across the slope. It was wide and well used, like the one they had cut across on the day they had come upon the cursing pole. Its mud was pitted with the prints of the many horses that had passed by and the furrows of heavy cartwheels. There were also three piles of still-steaming horse shit at different points along the track.

'It seems we picked a great place to hide out for the day,' Skar said with a sardonic grunt. 'Right beside what looks very like the main road from Tunsberg.'

Ulrich touched Skar's forearm, finger to his lips again. They all froze. Through the trees Einar could hear more hooves beating on the track, coming closer.

'Down,' Ulrich said.

They all dived to the ground and crawled into some bracken that lined the roadside. Moments later horsemen rounded the corner to the right. The riders were clad in mail and helmets. They had swords strapped to their sides and carried spears in their free hands. All had shields slung across their backs, each one painted with the symbol of the red axe. There were about twenty-five of them, riding in a long column two, sometimes three, abreast. Einar watched from the bracken as they thundered past and on down the road until they disappeared around the other corner.

'Eirik's men,' Ulrich said. 'They're in a hurry somewhere.'

'Too much of a hurry to look for us, luckily,' Skar said.

There was no sign or sound of any riders approaching along the track. Einar, Ulrich and the others clambered out from the bracken and made their way back down the slope to where the others were clambering out of their shelters.

'It looks like it's about midday,' Ulrich said. 'We should get moving again.'

'We need breakfast first,' Skar said. 'Come with me, lad.'

Einar, who had just been about to crawl back into his shelter and go back to sleep, sighed and followed the big man as he wandered off into the trees.

Skar pulled his jerkin off and tied knots in the top and sleeves so it became a makeshift bag. He handed it to Einar then began looking around the forest floor, pulling leaves here or lifting some pine cones there and throwing it in the jerkin-bag Einar held. A lot of what he picked was a three-leaved plant that had white flowers bursting out over it. As he worked Einar regarded Skar's bare torso, which was covered by heavy muscle and decorated with black, tree-like tattoos. Einar had seen them before. They were runes, some of which Einar recognised and some he did not know.

It was those strange runes that made him think. He recalled Ulrich's consternation that Olaf might know what the Úlfhéðnar initiation involved and wondered just what strange rituals this warrior brotherhood had that he did not yet know of?

'That should do us,' Skar said when his jerkin was full. 'Mother Earth has been very generous to us today.'

'We can eat this?' Einar said, looking down into the stuffed jerkin.

'Of course,' Skar said. 'This is the very food of the Gods themselves. It'll do you good.'

They made their way back to the others and shared out what Skar had foraged. As Einar suspected, it tasted just like chewing grass but he was so hungry he wolfed it all down and was sorry there was no more. As he finished Ulrich came over to him.

'You're a good climber, right?' the little Wolf Coat said.

'I used to scale the cliffs at home in Iceland, yes,' Einar said.

'Well trees should be easy for you then,' Ulrich said. 'I'd like to know what's up ahead of us before we stumble across anything else we aren't expecting, like that road. Go up the slope a bit and find a good high tree. Climb up there and take a good look around before we set off.'

Einar nodded and set off back up towards the road. He found a good tall pine with so many branches it was like a ladder. Despite his stiff, sore muscles protesting it was not long before he was nearing the top and stopped when the trunk and the branches looked like they were getting too thin to support his weight.

Up the slope he saw the road and not much else but because of the slope he could see out over the forest canopy downhill. Einar took a deep breath of the cool, clear air. The sun was shining above. It was a beautiful day. He saw a sea of trees that covered the hillside as far as he could see. There was a waving cut meandering through the forest that was probably a river and he noticed a grey haze not too far away that was rising from another break in the trees. It was smoke, which signalled some sort of settlement or other.

Deciding he had seen all there was to see, Einar began clambering back down the trunk. When he was about halfway down he froze. He could hear the cracking of dead branches on the forest floor. Looking around the trunk Einar saw the undergrowth waving a little way up the slope.

Someone was coming through the forest. They were running fast and they were heading straight for where the Wolf Coats were camped.

Twenty-Nine

Einar scrambled to get down the rest of the tree. He had not gone far when his foot slipped and he just managed to avoid a long fall and who knew what broken bones. As he hung by one arm, trying to get his feet back on a branch, a clump of ferns parted below and a figure rushed out.

It was a boy, perhaps seven or eight winters old. He had tousled brown hair, was dressed in the simple woollen clothes of the lowly folk and had a stick in one hand. Oblivious to Einar dangling above him, he ran past the base of the tree and on down the slope. A short way off he disappeared from view again into the ferns and bracken.

Einar clambered on down to the ground. The direction the boy was going in would lead him right into the others. He had to try to catch him. Heedless of the noise he was making, Einar ran down the hill, sweeping aside bracken and flattening ferns with his boots. The boy was not that far ahead. He was running fast but Einar's legs were longer and he felt sure he could catch up with him.

Einar pushed through a juniper bush and just avoided running right into the boy. He had stopped and was looking ahead. Through the undergrowth ahead Einar could see the Wolf Coats and the others preparing to leave and knew that was what the boy had seen to make him stop. Einar grabbed the boy by the arm and spun him around.

'What are you up to?' he said.

The boy looked up at him, wide-eyed, frozen like a rabbit who has seen the hunter.

Einar glared back. He had no idea what to do next.

'Who are you?' he said, shaking the boy's arm.

'Let me go,' the boy cried. His initial shock disappeared and he struggled against Einar's grip. He held the stick in his free hand at arm's length, as if trying to keep it away from Einar. Einar could see now that the stick was straight, had been stripped of bark and it looked like it had runes carved on it.

'Not until you tell me what you're doing,' Einar said. 'What's that stick?'

'Get off me,' the boy said. 'I have to get to Vidarby.'

'No,' Einar said. The situation was getting ridiculous. He had to do something to resolve it but he had no idea what.

Then the boy swung his right foot and kicked Einar in the balls.

Einar gasped and let go of the child. As he doubled over, groaning at the sudden pain, he saw the boy run off. Still doubled over, Einar tried to go after him but all he could do was stagger a few steps. The boy was already well away through the ferns and bracken.

The next thing Einar knew he was surrounded by the Wolf Coats, Affreca, Surt and Wulfhelm. They stood in a circle around him.

'What's going on?' Ulrich said.

Einar straightened up, the pain in his groin thankfully receding.

'There was a child,' Einar said, panting. 'A boy. He was running with a stick.'

'Did he see us?' Ulrich said.

Einar nodded.

'I grabbed him but he got away,' he said.

'You had him?' Ulrich said, eyes wide. 'Why didn't you kill him?'

'He was just a child,' Einar said, shaking his head. His voice trailed off and he saw the look on Ulrich's face, a mixture of contempt and disappointment. Einar's cheeks reddened. He looked around at the others and saw similar expressions. When he looked at Affreca she looked away.

'We can't stand here talking,' Skar said. 'We need to get him before he tells someone about us being here.'

'Which way did he go?' Ulrich said.

Einar pointed in the direction where the boy had disappeared into the undergrowth.

'Fan out,' Ulrich said. 'Make sure he doesn't slip through. Get going!'

They formed a line, each one a few paces from the other. Then they moved off through the trees. The cautious movements of the previous night were gone and they were running. They could not go as fast as they could though as they still had to maintain their line while trying not to trip over fallen branches and other obstacles on the forest floor.

'The little bastard's fast,' Skar said.

'He must be a local,' Ulrich said. 'They probably have paths through the forest only they know about.'

Now and again Einar could hear the sound of branches breaking from the boy running ahead of them. He had not got away yet but neither were they getting any closer. Part of Einar was glad. If they caught the boy he did not relish the idea of watching Ulrich or Skar put him to death. With no weapons they would have to do it with their bare hands. Ulrich had looked so angry the thought occurred to Einar that the Wolf Coat might even make him do it.

After a time Einar did not hear any more sounds from ahead.

Ulrich held up a hand and they all stopped. For a time they stood in the quiet of the forest, listening.

'He's got away,' Ulrich said after a time.

'Or he's hiding,' Skar said.

'Look, I'm sorry—' Einar began to speak.

Ulrich held up a palm towards him.

'What about what I asked you to do,' he said. 'Did you at least manage that?'

Einar frowned, then a connection sparked in his mind.

'Yes,' he said. 'There was smoke coming from the trees. It was in the direction the boy is headed. He also said he had to get to Vidarby. That must be where he's going.'

Ulrich looked at Skar.

'Great,' he said. 'Soon a whole village will know we're here. Well done, lad. Really good work.'

Sarcasm dripped from every word. Einar hung his head.

'We should get to that village, Ulrich,' Skar said.

'I know,' Ulrich said. 'I only hope there aren't too many of them.'

They set off again, jogging down the slope through the trees, still looking for the boy but finding no sign of him. The smell of woodsmoke reached Einar's nose. It got stronger the further they went.

Ulrich held up a hand again and all the Wolf Coats and others halted.

They had come to a clearing in the forest in which sat a little village, which must have been the Vidarby the boy had talked about. A cluster of little buildings, long, low dwellings made of daub and wattle with thatched roofs that came almost to the ground, huddled together around what looked like a well. There was a pen beside one of the houses with six pigs rooting around the mud inside it. Chickens wandered around and a group of five women were sitting beside an open fire spinning wool. They wore the plain clothes of simple farmers, the lowborn free people. Two men were tending to the pigs. A tall, grey-haired man in a sheepskin jerkin was standing near the well looking down at the boy they were chasing, who was chattering in an excited way and pointing back into the trees were Einar and the others now watched from. The grey-haired man had a pitchfork in one hand and in the other he had the stick the boy had held when Einar grabbed him. He turned it over in his fingers and looked straight into the trees. Einar felt he was looking right at him.

'You must be the wolf warriors King Eirik Bloody Axe is looking for,' the man said.

'How did he know that?' Skar muttered to Ulrich. 'What should we do?'

'Let's go and find out,' Ulrich said.

Thirty

'You are welcome to Vidarby,' the grey-haired man said and the Wolf Coats filed out of the trees to join him beside the well. 'My name is Bard. I am the head man here.'

Einar noticed two of the spinning women were about his age and pretty. One smiled at him in a coy way as he walked past. He blushed but returned her look.

'How did you know who we are?' Ulrich said. Like the other Wolf Coats he was looking all around, checking the doorways, roofs and any possible place someone could surprise them from. The men tending the pigs, one younger than Einar the other a lot older, wandered over to join Bard and see what was going on. They started at the sight of Surt who just cast a contemptuous gaze back at them.

'Don't worry, this is not a trap,' Bard said with a smile. 'If that's what you're looking for. We are simple villagers. Sigvat, get the other bidding stick.'

The younger of the two pig keepers hurried off to one of the nearby buildings, went inside then came back. He now carried a stick very similar to the one the boy had given him: Straight, stripped of bark and with runes carved in it.

'This was delivered this morning,' Bard said. 'Two warriors rode here. They had shields painted with red axes.'

He handed the stick to Ulrich.

'What does it say?' Starkad said.

'It says,' Ulrich said, running his finger along the runes that were cut into it, 'Eight úlfhéðnar and a blámaðr are running from King Eirik's justice. Anyone who sees them must tell the king's men. Anyone who gives them help will feel the wrath of the king.'

'I got that stick this morning and then ten men turn up from the forest,' Bard said. 'Ten, if you don't mind me saying so, quite desperate and dangerous looking men. And one of them has black skin. Bard, I told myself, this can hardly be a coincidence.'

'Well guessed,' Ulrich said. 'The question is, what are you going to do about it, old man?'

Bard smiled, revealing many gaps in his teeth.

'What am I going to do about it? I'll tell you what I was supposed to do with it first,' he said. 'You know how the war arrow works, don't you?'

'You are supposed to make two copies and send all three to the nearest villages or towns,' Ulrich said. 'And they then do the same. That way the message travels faster and wider than it can with a messenger on a horse.'

'And you hold the original in your hand,' Bard said.

'You didn't send the message on?' Ulrich said. 'I'm grateful, but you're taking quite a chance old man. I wouldn't like to be in your shoes if the king finds out.'

'Eirik Bloody Axe is no friend of the ordinary people,' Bard said, his smile gone. 'He's a tyrant like his father, Harald. A fact that has been reinforced by the second war arrow that just arrived with this brave little lad.'

He tussled the hair of the boy.

'Tosti here brought it from his village through the forest,' he said. 'It's a warning. Eirik's men are rampaging through the countryside, burning and killing. They are punishing the whole of Viken for supporting his brothers.'

'We saw some of them earlier,' Skar said. 'There were warriors on the road through the forest. A lot of them.'

'The arrogance of the man!' Bard said. 'Olaf was the rightful king that his own father Harald set above us.'

'Olaf is dead,' Ulrich said.

'We heard of that too,' Bard said. 'News came last night about the battle. Many jarls, *lendrmaðr* and hersir are dead, as well as the common folk who fought under them. We do not know if our own lord survived. Even if he did he will be running for his life and we shall not see him again. Eirik will now set a new lord above us. We can only hope that he is fair. Such is the lot of the poor folk like us. Living out here in the forest though, we don't get bothered much by the nobility. We can only pray to our good Norns that this continues.'

'Eirik's wrong by the way,' Ulrich said, glancing at Einar. 'Only six of us are úlfhéðnar. You can tell who the blámaðr is. The others are an Icelander, a Saxon and the woman is the daughter of the King of Dublin.'

Bard started, realising who he thought was a crop-haired boy was actually quite a beautiful woman.

'What if Eirik's men come back?' Ulrich said. 'What if others come and decide your village has to pay the price too?'

Bard shrugged. 'What can we do? Run and hide in the forest and let the village burn. Houses can be rebuilt. Blood cannot be put back in bodies. Poor people like us can do nothing about the evils of those Fate has set above us.'

'You can stand up to it,' Einar said, surprised at the strength of his own feeling that prompted the words from him.

'That's easy for a warrior to say,' Bard said.

'Would you help us?' Ulrich said. 'It would be a way of giving Eirik one in the eye if we get away.'

'Of course,' Bard said. 'But what can we do? We are poor. We have nothing.'

'Have you any weapons?' Ulrich said.

Bard laughed. 'Do I look like a jarl? We have farm tools. That's it. We can give you some food. A little ale. We will give you whatever we can spare.'

'Thank you, Bard,' Ulrich said. 'What about clothes?'

'Clothes?' the grey-haired man looked puzzled.

'Can you give us any clothes?' Ulrich said. 'We'll take anything. Old work clothes, old rags, anything you can spare. You can have what we have on. If Eirik hunts us with dogs it will help put them off the scent.'

Bard looked at them, running his eyes over the clothes the Wolf Coats were clad in. They were the leather breeches and jerkins they had worn beneath their mail in the battle the day before. They were smudged with oil and torn in places but compared to what the peasants wore they were like a jarl's finest garb.

'All right,' he said. 'I'll see what I can do. Go into that house and strip off. We'll gather what we can.'

Not long after, their clothes lay in a pile on the floor of the farmhouse. Einar was wearing Bard's sheepskin jerkin and a pair of rough wool breeches. The others were dressed in similar simple garb and they even had a few hooded cloaks between them. Bard had brought skirts for Affreca but she refused them.

'How can I run through the forest in a dress?' she said.

Once they were all changed they filed outside again. The women of the village brought some cloths with boiled eggs, some cheese and a couple of loaves wrapped in them.

'You've been really generous,' Affreca said. 'Thank you.'

'Aye,' Ulrich said. 'We will not forget your generosity, old man.'

'It's the least we can do,' Bard said. 'Like you said. It's our little way of hitting back at Eirik Bloody Axe.'

'Hush!' Skar interrupted. 'Listen.'

They all stopped what they were doing and cocked an ear to the air.

It was distant, but Einar could hear the sound of dogs barking from the forest.

'They're hunting us with dogs,' Ulrich said. 'I knew it would come to this.'

'They're not that far away,' Starkad said. 'We should run.'

'We won't get far,' Ulrich said. 'Dogs are fast. Faster than men.'

'Come with me,' Bard said. 'I know a place you can hide.'

Thirty-One

'You're joking?' Einar said. 'You want us to get in there?'

Bard had led them to a place behind the pig sty where the midden pile was. The smell of the rotting household waste wrestled with their noses. The men of the village scattered the chickens away and brushed aside a pile of straw to reveal a trapdoor in the ground. They lifted it and underneath was a pit filled with composting material. Vegetable skins, old food leftovers, animal bones, straw from the chickens' and pigs' bedding and, going by the smell, a good portion of their shit as well was piled in and rotting down, converting it to a fertiliser that would help the crops grow. A wave of heat from the composting process rose from the pit along with an overpowering stench.

Bard told them to climb in.

'He's right,' Ulrich said. 'The only way to get away from dogs is to hide your scent. There's enough in there to bury ours.'

'But we've already changed our clothes,' Wulfhelm said. Einar was glad to see he was not the only one reluctant to get into the pit.

'That will work once we get further away from them,'

Skar said. 'It will help them lose our trail. Right now we're still standing a few paces away from our old clothes. The dogs will work out where we are unless we cover our scent. Get in. Hurry up.'

The Wolf Coats clambered down into the compost pit. Einar, Wulfhelm, Surt and Affreca climbed in after them. Einar gasped as the smell became overwhelming. He felt his feet sinking into the soft, rotting material. It came up around his legs and for a moment he felt panic at the thought he might sink right over his head and drown in the filth and ordure. Then his feet touched the bottom, leaving him standing waist deep.

Bard and the men above gathered handfuls of straw and tossed them down on top of the group in the pit then closed the trapdoor again. There came a loud thump as something was put on top of the trapdoor and the rustling and scratching of the straw and gravel being brushed over it to cover it up once more.

Einar found himself in darkness. The only light was a strip above where sunlight came through one of the edges of the trapdoor. They waited; the only sound was their breathing.

From outside they could hear the villagers chatting, talking about crops and livestock as if nothing unusual was happening.

The barking of the dogs came ever closer. Soon it was joined by men's voices, shouting to each other as they moved through the trees.

'We should be out there fighting like men,' Kari's voice came from the darkness. 'Not hiding in the dark, waist deep in shit.'

'Listen,' Skar said. 'There's a lot of them.'

There were now many voices outside. The barking of the dogs was louder.

'I'm betting they're warriors with mail, swords and spears like the men we saw on the road,' Skar said in a whisper. 'You think you can fight them dressed in peasant clothes with bare hands?'

The men in the pit fell silent. Outside the village was now a storm of shouts and calls, barked orders and dogs barking.

'You there!' a voice sounded over the others. 'Are you the head man here?'

'Atli,' Ulrich breathed. Einar could sense the other men in the pit tense and imagined their fists and teeth clenching.

'I am,' Bard's voice filtered down from above.

'We're looking for some enemies of the king,' Atli said. 'The dogs have their scent and they came this way. Have you seen them?'

'We don't see many people out here in the forest, lord,' Bard said. 'We're just simple folk, we make our living from charcoal burning. What did these men look like?'

'I don't care what you do,' another voice, its accent foreign, came from above. 'Didn't you get the king's war arrow? They were sent out this morning and it told everyone all about them. All villages and towns should have the orders by now.'

'Edwin,' Wulfhelm whispered in the dark. 'It didn't take him long to become Eirik's most fervent minion.'

'Shh,' Ulrich said.

'No, lord,' Bard said. 'But we are remote out here in the woods. It takes time for any news to arrive. We are usually the last to know about anything.'

As he spoke the sound of barking and scrabbling paws in the dirt got closer. Einar felt his gut lurch. Could they smell the men in the pit?

A loud snuffling came from above and Einar could see a shadow in the crack at the side of the trapdoor. He pushed himself deeper into the muck, hoping to cover as much of himself as he could in the stinking mire.

'Search the place,' Atli said. 'Start inside the houses.'

The sound of crashing followed and the dismayed voices of the villagers raised in protest told Einar that the warriors above were not being too careful in their search.

Then the yapping and yelping of the dogs rose in volume. They were excited about something but it sounded like it was a little way off and muffled as if inside. The dog at the trapdoor ran away and the crack became clear again.

'They've found our clothes,' Skar said.

As if in confirmation, another voice called out. Like the dogs it was muffled and Einar knew whoever it was would be inside the house they had got changed in.

'There are leather jerkins and breeches here. The sort men wear under mail.'

There was a brief wait, Einar surmised, while their clothes were brought out for inspection.

'Those are what Ulrich and his crew wore last night,' Atli said. 'So, you know nothing of them, eh?'

There came the sound of a fist smacking flesh and Bard let out a grunt of pain.

'Tear this place apart,' Atli shouted. 'Find them.'

The crashing and banging got louder and came from all around as Atli and Edwin's warriors began turning the village over. A woman cried out in fear. There were shouts and even some cruel laughter. The pigs, incensed by the presence of the dogs, began squealing in a wild cacophony.

After some time the racket died down.

'There is no sign of anyone else, lord,' someone above said.

'Where are they?' Einar heard Atli say.

When his demand was met with silence, he shouted, 'Bring those women over here. And the boy.'

His orders were followed by screams from the women. Einar pictured the little boy, Tosti, being dragged in front of the furious Atli.

'All right, all right,' Bard said. 'I'll tell you. Leave them alone.'

The screams subsided.

'Go on, old man,' Atli said. 'And don't lie or it will be worse for you.'

'Men did come this morning,' Bard said. 'Just after first light. They ran out of the forest. They wanted food and asked to swap clothes with us. What were we to do? We are poor folk, lord. The clothes they wore are more expensive than we could ever afford. Of course we took their offer.'

'Where are they now?' Atli said.

'They ran off into the forest again,' Bard said. 'They said they were going south.'

'And you did not ask who they were?' Atli said.

'They looked like dangerous men,' Bard said. 'The sort who only bring trouble if you know too much about them.'

'And this was this morning, you say?' Atli said.

'Yes, some time ago now,' Bard said.

Atli swore a curse.

'The bastards have changed their clothes to throw the

dogs off their scent,' he said. He was speaking in a different tone and Einar guessed he was now talking to Edwin.

'Why did you lie about them not being here?' Edwin said.

'Like I said, lord, those men looked desperate,' Bard said. 'They told us if we told anyone about them they would come back and kill us all.'

Edwin laughed. The sound was harsh and mocking.

'And you believed that?' he said.

'We know we're on the right trail at least,' Atli said. 'But they're still far ahead of us. We should get going again.'

'Atli,' Edwin said. 'King Eirik's orders were clear. Anyone found helping Ulrich and his men was to be punished in the most severe way.'

'These are just harmless peasants,' Atli said. 'They didn't know what they were doing.'

'And what about the next village of harmless peasants Ulrich and his men come to?' Edwin said. 'We will need to set an example of what happens to those who disobey their king. I'm sure King Eirik would agree.'

Atli's sigh was deep enough to be audible in the compost pit.

'Very well,' he said.

'Kill them all,' Edwin shouted. 'Burn the village down.'

Thirty-Two

The next few minutes was one of the hardest Einar ever had to endure. There was screaming, crying, more cruel laughter and angry shouting. There came crashing of things being smashed. Then crackling of flames and the air in the pit began to fill with the strong smell of smoke.

'Any last words?' he heard Edwin say.

'A curse on Eirik Bloody Axe and all tyrants and brother killers like him,' Bard's voice was raised above the noise. 'May he rot in the cold kingdom of Hel and you all with him.'

Then he was heard no more.

Einar ached to throw open the trapdoor and run out. Perhaps he could grab a weapon from one of the warriors and kill them, but he knew that was a hopeless thought. All the while, he also expected the trapdoor to be ripped open at any moment, and they would find themselves staring up at a ring of warriors glaring down at them from behind their helmet visors, spears ready, preparing to slaughter them all. In the pit, waist deep in filth and unable to move they would not stand a chance.

Smoke began to filter in through the gap above and the already hard to breathe air became even more stifling.

Einar's eyes streamed and his throat felt raw. It was all he could do to stifle a cough.

The noise of flames outside became a roar. They could feel the heat from above and their situation became even more unbearable. Einar felt a weight against him and realised Affreca had passed out. The crush was such in the pit that she could not fall down, which was fortunate as she would have suffocated beneath the mire. Feeling dizzy himself, he threw an arm around her shoulder to support her. He felt her head loll back on the crook of his arm and tapped her cheek with his other hand.

Affreca sucked in a deep breath and Einar felt her weight go from him as she came round again.

'I'm all right,' she muttered, trying to pull away from him but having nowhere to go. She brushed his arm from her shoulders but thanked him.

After a time the only sound from outside was the crackling of flames. Even then Ulrich would allow no one to leave the pit. Time passed and eventually the noise of the flames died away. Finally, when there had been no sound from outside for a very long time, Ulrich signalled it was time to get out.

Starkad climbed on Kari's shoulders and heaved the door up. It did not move. Einar felt a rush of fear that they were now trapped but then Starkad shoved again, there was a clatter as something fell off the door and it lifted. Starkad stopped for a moment, holding the trapdoor open a finger's breadth and looking out through the crack.

'They're gone,' he said and threw the trapdoor open fully.

Sweet, cold air rushed down and Einar took a deep breath. It still was full of smoke but compared to the suffocating, stinking miasma he had been enduring it tasted like the clear air of a mountaintop. Starkad scrambled out then helped the others clamber from the pit. They emerged, coughing, eyes raw and streaming, into the ruined shell of what had once been Vidarby.

The scene before them was horrible. The houses were burned-out shells. Smoke and flame still rose from the smouldering thatch of one while the roofs of the others had collapsed. The spinning wheel was smashed. White and brown chicken feathers were scattered around, as well as a couple of chicken's heads, but there was no sign of the rest of the chickens. The butchered remains of the pigs lay in their pens, stripped of meat. This was not the worst butchery, however.

The pig herders lay on the ground, their throats cut and their life blood spread around them in a dark, congealing pool. The two girls Einar had noticed earlier had been raped. They lay on their backs, skirts thrown aside, their groins a bloody mess, their throats also slashed open. Their sightless eyes stared upwards at the clouds above. A spear was set in the ground, butt first, and the boy, Tosti, hung impaled on it through his guts, the point coming out his back. Bard's severed head was set on the point of another spear driven into the ground beside the well. His eyes were turned up and his mouth wide open as if he were still shouting his defiance. His torso lay toppled nearby, his legs behind him. He had clearly died on his knees.

'He died bravely,' Skar said.

'They died for us,' Einar said, looking around at the carnage, shaking his head. 'All they had to do was tell them where we were but they didn't. They didn't even know us.'

'It wouldn't have made any difference,' Ulrich said. 'They'd have killed them anyway. And us as well. Then we'd all be dead and for what? Nothing.'

'Bard cursed all brother killers before he died,' Einar said.

'So?' Affreca said.

'I killed my brother,' Einar said. 'Hrolf was my brother.'

'Hrolf was going to kill you,' Affreca said. 'I'm sure Bard did not mean you. I told you before. You think too much.'

'Get those spears someone,' Ulrich said. 'At least we have a couple of weapons now.'

'We should bury the bodies,' Einar said. 'They deserve at least that.'

'And what if while we're doing that Atli and Edwin come back?' Ulrich said as Skar dragged Tosti's small corpse off one of the spears. 'Then the sacrifice of these people was for nothing. Come on. Let's not waste it. We need weapons, mail and helmets. We need to find that old man, Grimnir and get this curse lifted. Then we go after Eirik. We go north.'

They set off, leaving the destroyed village behind and the dead where they lay. Einar knew the memory would haunt him in the days to come but he also knew Ulrich was right. They had to get away. They had to find some way to thwart Eirik. It was the only way to fight back, to regain dignity.

They trekked through the forest, heading in the opposite direction to where Bard had sent Atli, Edwin and their men. They went back up the slope, crossing the road and heading on, keeping to the forest. The ground kept on rising and Einar realised this was no mere hillside but the lower slopes of a mountain or a steep, high-sided valley. As it was daylight the Wolf Coats picked up their pace. Soon they were slogging away again, jogging up the slope, everyone silent, intent on saving their breath for running. Einar soon felt the exhaustion of the night before return, however somehow he was now able to keep going. He did not feel he might drop to the forest floor at any moment, unable to go on, as he had felt for most of the journey the night before. Instead he felt like he was in some sort of trance, snatches of poetry tumbling around in his mind as he concentrated just on putting one foot in front of the other.

After some time they came to a clearing in the forest and the break in the tree cover revealed mountains towering above them, their outlines dark against the sky but also streaked with white where snow still lay. The company stopped for a moment to catch their breath.

'Where are we going, Ulrich?' Affreca said.

Einar hoped he would point anywhere but towards the mountains but felt a sense of inevitability when the little Wolf Coat leader did just that.

'Up there,' he said. 'The fastest way to get to anywhere in this country is to sail there. But as we can't, we need to cut across country. The roads and the lowlands are awash with Eirik's men but there is a pass that will take us into the mountains and on to Gandvik. It will be hard going but the higher we go, the less people we'll meet as well.'

Skar narrowed his eyes, looking up at the peaks that towered above.

'It looks like there is still snow on some of the mountains,' he said. 'The pass may not yet be open.'

'We'll have to take that risk,' Ulrich said.

'We'll need to find more clothes too,' Sigurd said. 'It'll be freezing up there.'

'Keep your eyes open for shepherd's huts, shielings or anyone strange enough to live high up where no one will come to help when we ask for their clothes,' Ulrich said.

The journey continued.

Thirty-Three

They climbed ever higher through the forest and signs of human habitation were scarce. Einar wondered if this was because the company was deliberate in avoiding main roads and trails but it could also have been just because the terrain had become so remote.

They did find a hut used perhaps by shepherds but there was little of use in it. Inside were a few skin pelts and a bale of hay, which the Wolf Coats tore apart.

'What are you going to do with that?' Wulfhelm said. 'Eat it?'

'It'll keep you warm,' Kari said, tossing a bundle of hay to him.

The Wolf Coats stuffed the hay inside their jerkins and down their breeches. Wulfhelm, Einar, Affreca and Surt followed suit.

'This would be a comfortable, dry place to spend the night,' Surt said.

'It's too early,' Ulrich said. 'We have a long way to go yet.'

When they went outside the Wolf Coats took off their boots and grabbed handfuls of grass that they wrapped around their feet before replacing the footwear.

'What are you doing?' Surt said.

'I don't think we're going to find anything better,' Starkad said. 'So we'll have to use what we can. This will help stop your toes freezing off if we end up in the snow.'

The climb recommenced and soon their thighs and calf muscles burned with the effort. Einar found the grass and hay supplied a surprising amount of heat and, as the weather was pleasant, combined with the effort of climbing it meant he soon had sweat dripping from his forehead and running down his neck. The cool, clear breeze was fast to dry it, however. They followed small tracks that could have been animal paths or human trails, always under the direction of Ulrich who consulted the sun to check which way to go. After some time they came upon another road that looked like it was quite well used.

'We should take the road,' Skar said, putting words to what everyone else was thinking. 'We're high enough up now that we're not likely to come across too many people.'

Ulrich did not look too happy with the idea but conceded.

Once on a proper track the pace increased and though tired, Einar saw they were making a lot more progress. The trees around them got smaller and more twisted by the harshness of the climate. Then they left the trees behind and as they continued to climb they were surrounded by steep hillsides coated in coarse grass, gorse and heather. Looking back they saw they were at the head of a wide, forest-covered valley that lined a long inlet from the sea. It was surrounded by mountains that rose like the sharp teeth of dragons around the edge. The earth itself grew thinner and dark rocks, the bones of the land, protruded through.

In several places in the valley below clumps of smoke rose above the trees. It was not the single column of a lone house fire but the smear of whole villages and farms set ablaze.

'Eirik is punishing the folk for betraying him,' Ulrich said.

At one point, as the sun was starting to slide towards the mountains, a goat appeared on a tall rock above the trail. It stood, silhouetted against the sky, looking down on the travellers below.

'If he wasn't so far away,' Skar said. 'He would make a nice supper.'

The others muttered their assent. The goat would run away as soon as they went for it. It was very far away and high above them as well.

'Give me a spear,' Wulfhelm said.

They all looked at him.

'You think you can hit it?' Kari looked surprised.

Wulfhelm just held out his hand. Skar passed him one of the spears. The Saxon looked at the goat for a moment, then cocked his arm. He looked again at the goat, which was still looking down at them, as confident they could not get him as the Wolf Coats knew it was almost too difficult.

Wulfhelm launched. The spear shot through the air, spinning as it went. The goat saw it and began to skitter backwards but it was too late. The spear hit the goat and transfixed it through the chest. The weight of the shaft pulled the animal forward and it tumbled down off the rock to land on the track about twenty paces in front of the company.

'I don't believe it!' Starkad said.

The Saxon grinned and bowed to the others. The others

cheered. Skar twisted the goat's neck to finish it off then slung the dead animal over his shoulders. The company set off again and broke into song, despite Ulrich's disapproving glances, but they all knew that the land around them was now so remote and desolate they could both see others coming from a very long way off and that they could also see them.

As it began to grow dark they came upon a mountain stream tumbling through a rocky bed and Ulrich signalled they needed to start building shelters for the night. The only cover available on the uplands was heather which would make a prickly night, but Einar was so tired he did not care. They used the spears to cut turf and dig a pit that would hide the glow of a fire from any watching eyes. After some time striking rocks off the spear blades to create sparks they managed to light some lichen that provided kindling to get the fire going. Their spirits rose higher when the goat carcass was over the fire roasting.

'Tonight we feast like Thor himself,' Skar said, as he began handing out chunks of roasted flesh.

Surt looked at his portion with a disappointed expression on his face.

'Is this some sort of ritual of your faith?' he said.

'No, it's just an old tale,' Einar said. 'Thor has two goats, Tanngrisnir and Tanngnjóstr, which pull his chariot. When he rides it over the top of the sky the rumble of the wheels is what we hear as thunder. Then when he is on his travels and he stops for the night he kills and eats the goats.'

'That's a bit hard on the goats,' Wulfhelm said. 'And short-sighted. How does he get about the next day?'

'He keeps the hides and the bones,' Einar said, 'then in

the morning he blesses them with his hammer and they rise from the dead.'

Wulfhelm snorted, unable to hide his laughter.

'And you believe that?' he said.

'You believe your Christ God rose from the dead,' Ulrich said. 'Is that any more believable?'

Wulfhelm's mirth vanished.

'That's different,' he said. 'Jesus is the son of God.'

'And Thor is the son of the God, Odin,' Ulrich said.

'Don't get into a religious argument with these idolaters, my friend,' Surt said, nudging Wulfhelm with his forearm and pointing a goat bone at Ulrich. 'Especially that one. I've been watching them. He is the most fervent in his belief. You will end up talking in circles. These are good men but when we're all dead it will be you and I who will be in Paradise.'

The smile on Surt's face showed that while his words were sincere, he was also half teasing.

'You and I?' Wulfhelm looked at the black-skinned man, eyebrows raised.

'We are People of the Book,' Surt said. '*Ahl al-kita*. I know all about the great prophets, Abraham, Moses and Jesus. The revelation which has come down to us will come down to you: Our God and your God is one.'

Wulfhelm blinked, a look of astonishment on his face.

'If you're so sure of this faith of yours,' Einar said. 'How come you were so scared when you found out about Gunnhild's curse? Her power comes from the Gods, the dísir and the Norns. If they all don't exist then what have you to fear?'

Surt's smile vanished.

'I never said they did not exist,' he said. 'These beings the pagans worship exist all right, but they are demons. Djinns and shaytans.'

'When a child is baptised in Wessex,' Wulfhelm said, 'the parents promise to forsake Thunor, Woden and Tiw and all the devils who are their followers. Thunor is what our forefathers called Thor, Woden is Odin and Tiw is who you Danes call Tyr.'

'I was cursed before by a witch in al-Andalus,' Surt said. 'I believe it was because of that I ended up a slave here. If we can lift this curse perhaps the other will be lifted too.'

'Enough of this talk,' Skar said. 'Religion should not be discussed while eating. It only leads to arguments.'

'Eat up then get as much rest as you can,' Ulrich said. 'Tomorrow we must cross the mountain pass. It will be a long, hard day and we need to be across it by nightfall.'

Einar nodded. He had heard tales back in Iceland of the creatures that lurked in the high places of the world and no one wanted to be caught outside at night on high ground. The old men also swore that the mountains of Norway were even more haunted than the ones of Iceland.

'What's wrong with being in the mountains after dark?' Wulfhelm said.

'There are things that dwell on the tops of the mountains,' Einar said, his tone serious. 'Light Elves, trolls and *bergrisi*, mountain giants. All of them have a taste for human flesh.'

'There is that,' Skar said, 'but mostly it's because the weather and the cold will kill you. Ulrich, this will be risky. We don't have the right clothes or equipment. It looks like the snow still lies up there. Is there no other way?'

Ulrich shook his head.

'You saw the fires in the valley today,' he said. 'The lowlands are crawling with Eirik's men. This is our best chance of escape.'

'Einar, give us a song then,' Skar said. 'Chant some poetry to inspire us to do great deeds in the morning.'

Thirty-Four

Despite their tiredness, the light of dawn and the uncomfortable heather meant everyone was awake and up at the break of day. There was some left-over goat for breakfast then the climb resumed.

The track they had been following got narrower and narrower until they were all walking in a single file. After a time they started to come across clumps of snow resting on top of the heather and the air became ever colder. About mid-morning the ground became saturated with meltwater as the little track came to the snowline. All above was pristine whiteness rising up to the points of two mountain peaks that towered above them. From the depth at the edge Einar judged it might be about knee-deep, at least to begin with.

Ulrich was delighted.

'This is the last snows of the year,' he said. 'It maybe fell weeks ago. Look at it. Not a footprint. No one has been this way recently. Anyone we meet will not even know Olaf and Sigrod are dead. Eirik's message won't have made it up here either.'

'Anyone we meet? Who would that be?' Einar muttered

to himself as he looked at the desolate, snow-covered slopes above.

They set off into the snow. Skar and Sigurd led the way, poking the shafts of the spears into the snow ahead of them to make sure they were not about to walk into a snow-covered hole. Einar's lower back ached from the climbing and he envied the men with the spears to lean on.

The sun shone bright and clear and it glared off the snow, making Einar squint. He became glad of the grass and moss stuffed under his clothes as his legs started to feel the damp cold that also nipped at his exposed fingers and lips. They struggled on for a time until Skar halted them for a rest.

'I feel like the sun is burning my skin,' Einar said. 'Yet we're surrounded by snow.'

'We're closer to the sun up here,' Kari said. 'Its heat is stronger.'

They started off again and the weather changed. Cloud came down, enveloping them in a misty nothingness that obscured the sun and limited the view to about ten paces all around. It became very cold. All of the jerkins they had got from the villagers in Vidarby had hoods and everyone pulled theirs up, which at least kept the cold from biting exposed ears but it was only scant comfort. Einar's fingers started to hurt. His feet became numb and a new dread crept into his heart. This was not a good sign. He remembered seeing men in Iceland whose toes had turned black and dropped off while making cross-country journeys in the winter. Einar had no desire to take his boots off only to find his toes drop out one by one.

By midday the mist cleared and the burning sun returned.

They kept their hoods up, now for protection from the sun instead of the cold.

The view was spectacular. Looking back they could see down the whole, wide valley right to the sea and beyond. Like before, there were pockets of smoke rising where Eirik's men were ravaging the land. Above, it looked like they were approaching a saddle between two high peaks, the pass Ulrich wanted to cross.

The higher they climbed the tougher the effort became. Each step was not just uphill but each foot had to be dragged out of the snow as well. Einar and those around him were breathing heavily. Sweat coated their faces and Einar knew for sure now from its stinging progress as the sweat trickled down his skin that he was indeed sunburned. At the same time the wind was cold and his lower legs, hands and nose were freezing. It was an insane mixture of feelings that he did not think he would be able to endure much longer.

'Can we rest for a bit?' Einar said, panting. He stopped, his head lolling back against his shoulders. The others did too.

Ulrich shook his head.

'We need to get over the pass during daylight,' he said. 'If we get caught up here at night we'll all freeze to death. It's already past midday and we haven't even reached the pass. Come on.'

'But the dog is not there,' Wulfhelm said.

They all turned to look at the Saxon. He was swaying a little and his eyes looked like he was staring at something far off.

'What dog?' Einar said.

Wulfhelm frowned.

'I can't find the words in your tongue,' he said. 'It's strange. I feel like I'm a little drunk.'

Skar looked at Ulrich.

'The cold and the height are getting to him,' Skar said.

'Keep an eye on him,' Ulrich said. 'Now get going. We can rest when we reach the top.'

They trudged on, ploughing a path through the snow. Wulfhelm muttered a few times and then tried to say something to Einar but the words that came out were nonsense. Seeing the look of incomprehension on Einar's face the Saxon fell silent again.

Twice Einar thought the top of the pass was just up above, only to reach it to find the slope stretched onwards even higher. The disappointment almost took his heart away and he thought he would just fall into the snow, never to rise again. He kept going though, and at long last Skar lifted the spear and pointed upwards with it.

'We're at the top,' he said.

There were no cheers or any other words said. They were all too exhausted to speak. The last few paces were agony but they made it and Einar felt relief flooding into his burning legs as the ground changed from steep upward slope to level ground.

The pass was a wide, sickle-shaped gap with mountains continuing upward to the left and right. Ahead they saw the sky above, a reasonably flat part about a couple of hundred paces across then it fell away as the slope down the other side began.

Sweat steaming from their heads into the cold air, the company collapsed onto the snow, gasping to recover their breaths. They grabbed handfuls of snow and sucked on them to slake the thirst that itched in their dry throats.

'Is he all right?' Ulrich said, pointing at Wulfhelm.

'He's not making a lot of sense,' Einar said.

'This is not good,' Skar said. 'This is the first stage of death by cold.'

Einar glanced at the sky. It was well past midday. If the descent from the pass was not faster than their ascent, they would be stuck above the snowline in the dark. The temperature would plummet and Wulfhelm would die for sure. Perhaps more than just him.

'What in Odin's hundred names is that?' Starkad said.

He was looking across the pass, one hand shading his eyes from the glare of the sunlight and the snow. They all followed his gaze. Einar noticed for the first time that on the mountain to the right, slightly up the slope from the pass, was a long, flat, snow-covered ridge. Then he noticed grey smoke drifting from a hole in it.

'That's a house,' Skar said. 'Someone lives up here.'

Now it was pointed out, it became obvious. It was a big house, longer and taller than the hall of Einar's mother's farmhouse. What Einar had thought was a ridge was the roof. This was no farmer's hut. It was the substantial dwelling of someone of consequence. And there were five other, smaller buildings gathered around it. The whole compound was half buried in snow.

'You think there is anyone there?' Starkad said. 'It would be a great place to shelter.'

'It doesn't look like there's much life about it,' Skar said.

'Someone lit that fire,' Einar said.

'Maybe it's a summer house,' Kari said. 'For when the cattle and sheep are in the high pastures.'

The sound of a horn blowing made them look higher up the slope. Three people were approaching fast, sliding over the snow on skis, a cloud of snow rising behind them. They swept past the house and on towards the Wolf Coats. All three bore bows and as they approached, like practised hunters, they notched arrows and drew them, all the while still skiing down the slope.

A door opened in the side of the house. Ten more figures emerged. They spent a moment looking in the direction of the Wolf Coats, Einar and the others, then crossed to one of the outbuildings. They re-emerged soon after and started approaching.

Einar was surprised both at how fast they were coming over the snow and how tall they were, then realised they were tramping across the top of the snow using snowshoes. They were swathed from head to toe in heavy furs, including fur hats with flaps that covered their ears. Snowshoes aside, three of them were indeed huge men, as tall and broad-shouldered as Skar or perhaps even taller. Two of these men also had bows and the others carried spears.

'This doesn't look good,' Skar said.

'No point in running,' Ulrich said. 'They'll catch us before we get halfway back to the slope. We'll have to wait and see what they want.'

The men on skis arrived first, skidding sideways to a halt a little way away, bows still levelled.

'We mean no harm,' Ulrich said.

The men did not answer. The bows remained steady and drawn, the bright blue eyes of the archers watching.

'Maybe they don't speak our tongue?' Skar said from the side of his mouth.

'Hallo, there,' the tallest of the men approaching on snowshoes hailed them.

'We want no trouble,' Ulrich called to him. 'We're just crossing the mountains.'

'That's not a problem,' the big stranger said. 'As long as you pay the toll you can go on your way.'

He spoke with the thick accent of the people of the uplands. His eyes were the same pale blue as the others.

'What do you mean, toll?' Ulrich said. 'This is a mountainside.'

'It is my lord Thorir's land,' the other said. 'And anyone who wishes to cross the pass must pay the toll.'

'And how much is this toll?' Ulrich said.

'How much have you got?' the big man said. His bushy beard split in a grin that revealed his upper front teeth were missing.

'I thought you were going to say that,' Ulrich said. 'We have nothing, friend. We've lost everything.'

'Then you cannot cross the pass,' the other said.

'We have these spears,' Skar said. 'What if we insist on going on?'

The big man shrugged.

'True,' he said. 'You have two spears. But there are thirteen of us. You can throw both spears and my bowmen will bring five of you down. It won't take long before you are all dead. But it's up to you. Feel free to try.'

Skar's knuckles whitened as his fist clenched on the shaft of his spear and for a moment Einar thought he might actually try something. Then Ulrich touched Skar's forearm and he relaxed.

'If you can't pay the toll then you're going to have to talk to my lord,' the big man shrugged again. 'Come with us.'

Thirty-Five

They were marched through the snow over to the longhouse and in through the door in the side.

Einar blinked for a few moments, unable to see anything. After the bright sun and its reflective glare from the snow, the interior of the house was dark. If it had any windows in the walls they were buried in the snow. There were whale oil lamps lit and set on the four wooden pillars that held the roof up and a fire glowed in the middle of the floor but it was not enough to dispel all of the gloom. The smell was overpowering as well. The air inside reeked of musty, unpleasantness: A mixture of old, rotting straw, stale sweat, cold grease and bad breath, the fug of many people all living in the one place, no doubt stuck inside perhaps for weeks on end by the wild mountain weather outside. There was also the unmistakable tang of cats' piss. Three of the animals rushed over to rub themselves around the legs of the newcomers. As Einar's eyes adjusted to the gloom he saw another large black and white piebald one, sitting near the fire, arch its back and hiss at him.

Affreca pushed one of the cats away. It hissed at her for her lack of attention and moved on to Skar's leg.

'Don't like cats?' Einar said.

'I don't mind them,' Affreca said. 'But for some reason whenever one is near me I start sneezing.'

'That's because you smell the evil inside them,' Surt said.

Peering around, his eyes already smarting a little from the smoke that hung in the air, Einar saw a long room with a fire in the middle of the floor and sleeping cots along the walls. The floor was strewn with old straw and there were discarded animal furs everywhere, some hanging on the walls, some across the cots, many around the floor. The inhabitants of the house clearly spent a lot of time hunting.

Two scrawny slave girls with thin hair and bare feet scuttled around, laying out tables in preparation for a meal. Their faces were dirty, their clothes ragged and threadbare. One of the girl's hair was streaked with grey but they were so thin it was hard to tell how old they really were. They hurried at their work, avoiding all eye contact.

The house was like a smaller version of the jarl's halls that Einar had been in, and like them, at the far end of the room was a high seat for the lord with two sturdy wooden pillars on either side of it. The left high seat pillar was carved with Thor's hammer and the right spinning sun-wheels.

A man sat on the high seat. He was of later middle years with black, greasy hair flecked with dandruff. His nose was round and red and he wore fur boots, expensive breeches and a richly embroidered linen shirt. Over it all he had a fur cloak that was pinned at one shoulder by a magnificent gold brooch. His forearms were circled by many gold and silver arm rings. A heavy silver chain was round his neck with a gold, jewel encrusted amulet on it that rested on the top of his considerable belly. In one hand he held a large drinking horn that was decorated with silver and gems.

'What have we here, Bjorgolf?' the man said, his thick lips wet with ale. 'Visitors?'

The big man who had brought them there had just entered, stooping to get through the doorway. He straightened up and Einar saw that he truly was a giant of a man, a good head and shoulders taller than all the others around him. His chest was like an ale barrel and he had legs like trunks of trees. He took his fur cap off to reveal his blue eyes lurked under a forehead that overhung his face like a crag of the mountain outside.

'Travellers, Lord Thorir,' the giant man said. He spoke in a deep, cracking voice. 'They want to cross the pass without paying the toll.'

'Oh they do, do they?' the man in the high seat said. He spoke in the same thick accent as the big man who had brought them there. 'If I let everyone cross the pass without payment I would be as poor as a slave. Is that what these people want?'

'My name is Ulrich and these men are my crew. But you look like you're doing all right, Lord Thorir,' Ulrich said. 'That's a very nice silver chain round your neck. And that brooch must have cost a fair bit.'

Thorir smiled. 'I'm an important man. I need to dress well. This is my land. I am in charge here. If you want to use the pass you will pay up like everyone else.'

'And what is the charge?' Ulrich said.

'Whatever you can afford,' Thorir said. 'And whatever else we think you can afford added to that.'

Ulrich laughed.

'Oh, I'm not joking, friend,' Thorir said. His smile disappeared. 'Don't think that for one moment. Everyone who passes here pays a price. In one way or another. Everyone.'

'And what do you believe the king would think,' Ulrich said, his own mirth gone, 'if he knew the man who ruled one of the passages in his kingdom was a robber who stole from travellers trying to journey across his realm?'

'King you say? And which king would that be?' Thorir said. 'Eirik? Olaf? Sigrod? Perhaps Hakon? They're all too busy fighting each other to interfere with anyone. Everyone pays, Ulrich.'

'But we have nothing, Lord Thorir,' Ulrich said. 'We have nothing to pay you with. Perhaps we could do some work for you? My men are trained killers. A man like you always has work for someone like us.'

'I'm sure we can find something,' Thorir said. 'We will discuss it over food, Ulrich. We're about to eat. My wife will have to take a look at you first.'

Skar and Sigurd looked at Ulrich. Einar could see the little Wolf Coat's eyes darting around the room and could guess what was going through their minds: Was it possible to fight their way out? It was obvious however that, outnumbered and out-weaponed as they were, they would not manage without some of them getting killed.

Ulrich shook his head. Skar sighed.

Bjorgolf had seen the silent exchange also and he too had guessed what they were thinking. He gave a booming laugh. Skar returned him a sour look.

'At least we still have the spears,' Ulrich said, muttering out of the side of his mouth so only those near could hear. 'We wait for the right moment, then take our chance.'

'Sit down, sit down,' Thorir said, waving his free hand at a couple of benches that sat beside one of the tables.

The Wolf Coats and the others sat down, filling the benches half on one side and half on the other. Skar and Sigurd laid the spears across their knees, one hand each resting on the shafts in readiness to snatch them if the opportunity arose.

'Ah! Here she comes,' Thorir said.

Through a door at the back of the hall near the high seat came a woman. Her face was wan and pinched like the slaves and her long grey hair was swept back and held in place by two bone combs on either side of her head. Her dress was long and made of dark blue material with some sort of tassels that swished around the hem and bottoms of her sleeves. Einar noticed that despite not being dressed for the cold outside, the woman nevertheless wore a pair of gloves made of fine, short fur. With a start he realised that the black and white pattern of them was the same as that of the pelt of the cat that had hissed at him. He also was not sure, but it seemed as if Thorir's men all stiffened as she entered the room.

'We have some guests, Aslaug dear,' Thorir said. 'Will you run your eye over them and see if there are any you like?'

The woman nodded and approached, making a faint clinking sound as she moved. She peered with curiosity at everyone, like a housewife examining meat on a market stall, or a horse dealer assessing a potential purchase. So much so, that Einar would not have been surprised if she had not pushed back some of their lips to examine their teeth and gums. For a long time she looked at them all, moving round the table, sometimes coming close, sometimes stepping back as if to get a view from a distance. A couple of times she seemed to be examining something invisible in the air above their heads.

'There's something uncanny about this,' Starkad said in a quiet voice. 'I don't like it. These people are strange.'

'They live at the top of a mountain,' Ulrich said. 'What do you expect?'

'What do you think, my dear?' Thorir said, after a time.

The woman stroked her chin.

'These men,' she waved a long finger at Ulrich, Skar, Kari, Starkad and Sigurd, 'have something about them. They smell of death and more. I believe they can change their skin. They are shapeshifters. Or berserkers.'

'We are úlfhéðnar,' Ulrich said.

The woman nodded and looked pleased with herself. 'I knew it was something like that.'

'He is foreign,' she said, pointing at Wulfhelm. Her tone was dismissive and the expression on her face suggested distaste.

Wulfhelm still looked confused but the warmth in the house was having enough effect that he recognised her contempt and frowned.

'How does she know all this?' Starkad said.

The woman moved her attention to Affreca. Affreca scowled at her.

'A maiden!' the woman said. She leaned in close to Affreca, pushing her face very close to hers. Einar could almost taste Affreca's discomfort. 'Do you know the *Varðlokur*? The spell songs every high-born girls should be taught?'

Affreca's expression changed. She still looked uncomfortable but now also curious.

'My nurse taught me them when I was a child,' she said. 'I haven't sung them since though. My mother did not allow it. They can be used for seiðr.'

The older woman clapped her hands.

'But you *know* them!' she said. 'We haven't had a girl here in a long time. And even the ones who did come could not sing the Varðlokur. They were useless to me. And you—'

She pointed a long forefinger at Einar and moved over to him. It was all he could do not to flinch as her breath wafted into his nostrils. It smelled like she had been eating rotted fish.

'What are you?' she said, squinting with her left eye. 'I cannot quite see your fetch. Are you a wolfman like the others?'

She fixed Einar with a stare that he felt was reaching right inside his being.

'I'm a skald,' he said.

'A poet!' the woman looked as delighted as she had been at Affreca. 'Odin loves poets. He will love you.'

To Einar's relief she moved away from him. He caught sight of Affreca who was pointing at the woman's dress and mouthing something to him. He looked and saw that the clinking noise when she moved came from hundreds of little shells sewn into the tassels and hems of her dress. The sight awoke a memory somewhere deep inside his head but he could not place where he had seen something like this before. He wondered how she had got them up here, so far from the shore.

Surt, who still had his hood up, pulled it down as the woman loomed over him. She gasped and put her hand to her mouth.

'A black-skinned man,' she said in a breathless voice. 'You will be a great gift. The spirits will be very generous in return.'

'You approve of them, dear?' Thorir said.

'I do,' his wife said, with a wide smile.

'Excellent!' Thorir said. 'Slaves. Bring ale. Not the usual stuff. The special guest ale. Let's eat as well.'

The slaves ran off. Thorir's men shrugged off their furs and took seats at the other tables. They set their weapons down but put them within easy reach.

The slaves returned with drinking horns brimming with ale.

'Guests first,' Thorir said, directing them to Einar and the others with his free hand.

The women handed horns to the Wolf Coats, Einar, Surt, Wulfhelm and Affreca. Einar smelled the aroma and his burning throat got the better of him. He took a large swig. It was not a bad beer. Perhaps a bit stale but they were on top of a mountain.

The slaves went out and got more horns for Thorir's men and his wife. When everyone had a horn in their hand, Thorir stood up. He held his own horn aloft.

'To new friends,' he said, then took a long drink.

'New friends,' everyone else repeated and drank.

'To victory in battle!' Thorir said, taking another drink. Everyone followed him.

Einar knew that, as was custom, what would follow was a series of toasts. That suited him fine. Despite the weirdness of the situation he had a drink in his hand. Perhaps all would work out for the best.

He felt a nudge and turned to see Affreca cocking her head towards Aslaug who was now beside her husband.

'She's mad, right?' Einar said, leaning close to her so he could whisper. 'It's probably living up here in the mountains away from everyone. There's something a bit odd about all of them.'

Affreca shook her head.

'Did you see her dress?' she said.

'The shells?' Einar said, absentmindedly scratching the ale horn with his thumb nail. 'What of it?'

'Don't you see?' Affreca hissed. 'That's what a *vǫlva* wears.'

Einar realised that, without thinking he'd scratched an Odal rune onto the drinking horn. He frowned. Why that? Then concluded that it must be on his mind most these days.

'You think she's a witch?' he said.

'To good harvests,' Thorir said, prompting another round of drinking. This time Einar stopped as he was lowering his horn, peering into it. The last mouthful had tasted bitter. Perhaps it was off?

As was custom, two more toasts followed, one to the glorious dead and one to peace. The ironic jeers that met the last one betrayed the attitude of all in the room to it. The slaves brought in platters of meat and bread and placed them on the tables. Einar was unsure what meat it was but he was more than happy to tuck in. With a few drinks in him Wulfhelm began to look like his old self again. Einar started to feel a warm glow of contentment. Things were going to be all right.

'Now let's eat,' Thorir said.

'Wait,' Ulrich said, rising to his feet. 'There was no toast to Odin. That should be next. Why was there no Odin drink?'

Einar frowned. Ulrich's words sounded odd, half slurred, as if he was having trouble saying them.

Then Skar and Sigurd jumped to their feet at some unseen signal between them. They had their spears in both hands and turned towards Thorir's men. For a moment silence fell on the hall.

Bjorgolf laughed his deep, booming laugh.

To Einar's confusion, Skar laughed back. As did Sigurd. Skar seemed to find the whole thing so funny he dropped to his knees, laughing uncontrollably. Sigurd looked at him with confusion as great as Einar's. He stood, rooted to the spot as if under a spell.

Einar stood up. The room tilted before his eyes. He looked at the ale horn in his hand, then at Affreca. She was looking at him but her face seemed strange and distorted.

'The ale...' he said, recalling the bitter taste. 'They've poisoned it.'

Then darkness rushed up before his eyes and overcame him.

Thirty-Six

'Well here we are again,' Skar said.

Einar awoke to hear Skar's voice. He sounded irritated.

It was dark. Einar was lying on his side. His hands were bound at the wrists behind him. His legs were bound at the ankles. Other warm bodies were pressed close on either side of him and Skar's voice did not seem that far away. From this, Einar deduced they were all lying together on the dusty, hard packed dirt floor of a room.

'It seems like every time we try to get somewhere these days we end up tied up, someone's prisoner,' Skar said.

'It's the curse,' Ulrich said. 'The Norns won't just let us change the fate they plan for us. When we fight it they fight back.'

'So we're now fighting the king and the Norns,' Skar said. 'This has to be our greatest battle yet, lads.'

'I'm not sure I like the odds on this contest,' Kari said.

'At least we're not dead,' Einar said. 'Whatever they put in the ale only sent us to sleep. I thought it was poison. When it all went black I thought that was it. I'd wake up in the Valour Hall.'

'Where do you think we are?' Affreca said. 'It's dark and

cold. Maybe this is the kingdom of Hel. Maybe we really are dead.'

Einar felt fear lurch in his gut. Perhaps she was right? In his arrogance he had assumed Odin's Valkyries would choose him when he died and he would be swept up to an after-life feasting in the golden roofed hall of Odin. But he had done shameful things. He had strayed from the path fate seemed to have laid out for him, trying to be a skald instead of a warrior. If he was dead his end had not been heroic. Had he in fact ended up in the cold, dark kingdom somewhere northwards and netherwards, where the unworthy dead go?

'My guess,' Ulrich said, 'is that we are in one of those outbuildings near the house.'

Einar hoped he was correct.

'Why do you think they've kept us alive?' he said.

'These mountain folk are strange people,' Ulrich said. 'I dread to think what they have in mind for us.'

'Someone's coming,' Starkad said.

The sound of feet crunching through snow crust came from somewhere outside. There was rattling, then a door opened and light spilled into the room. Einar looked and saw fur-clad figures in the doorway, outlined in the light from two burning torches held behind them. Their breath rose in clouds into the cold air. Above them was the darkness of the night sky.

'Get the black-skinned one, the woman and the poet,' the sound of Thorir's wife, Aslaug's voice came from outside.

A huge figure filled the doorway, shutting out the light from outside. This could only be Bjorgolf. He moved into the room and two others followed him. The room filled with light as one of the fur-wrapped men held up a torch. They grabbed Affreca, hauled her to her feet and dragged her outside. Other men came in and pulled Surt and Einar out. They struggled but bound as they were, there was little they could do to resist.

Outside in the cold night air Einar could see that Ulrich had been right. They had been held in one of the outbuildings near the main house. Thorir's men, swathed in furs, stood around, some with torches. Sitting in the snow was what looked like a farm wagon except the wheels had been replaced by sleds for travelling through the snow. Two reindeer were harnessed to the shaft of its yoke and a burning torch was set in a bracket at all four corners of the wagon. Four of Thorir's men went into another outbuilding and emerged with sets of skis and spears.

Einar, Affreca and Surt were lifted and dumped into the bed of the wagon. Aslaug placed a goatskin bag in the wagon then she and another man clambered onto the driving bench. The man took up the reins while the four with the skis strapped them to their feet. The driver of the wagon snapped the reins and cracked a riding crop and the sledge pulled off into the night. The four on skis, each with a torch in one hand and an inverted spear in the other, set off behind them.

The wagon was not tilted and Einar could tell that they were travelling across the mountainside away from the pass as opposed to climbing or descending. The sky above was clear and the stars and a crescent moon shone bright, visible even through the glow from the torches. The only sounds where the crunching footfalls of the reindeer in the snow and the swishing of the sledge and skiers following behind.

After a little way a new sound reached Einar's ears. At first he thought it was his own heartbeat, then as it got louder he realised it was the sound of drumming. Somewhere up ahead in the darkness several people were beating drums.

'Do you think we're going to some sort of party?' Einar said.

'Not the sort I want to go to,' Affreca said. 'Witches use drums when they craft seiðr.'

'Hush,' Aslaug said over her shoulder. The driver turned and cracked the riding crop in the air above Affreca to emphasise the point.

The drumming got louder the further they went through the night. Einar noticed a new orange glow begin to light up the dark as well. Then the sledge stopped.

'Up,' the driver said.

Einar sat up and saw they were now stopped at the mouth of a cave that opened like a maw in the mountainside. Fires burned inside, their heat and glow spilling into the darkness outside. The sound of drums was coming from inside the cave as well. Einar felt as though he was looking into the huge mouth of a fire-breathing rock troll.

The men on skis opened the back panel of the sledge and beckoned for the prisoners to get out. Einar squirmed and slid towards them feet first. The man at the back of the sledge pulled a knife and sliced the bonds around his feet.

'Don't think we're going to carry you over there,' he said. 'But if you're thinking about running, think again. There is nothing but mountainside from here to the valley below. Half of it is still covered in deep snow. We have skis. You won't get far on foot. Even if you do manage to get away, you'll just end up freezing to death.'

Einar jumped down from the sledge and Surt and Affreca followed him, both of them getting the bonds on their feet released as well.

'To the cave,' Aslaug said, lifting the goatskin bag. She and the driver clambered down from the driving bench and set off through the snow. The skiers removed their skis and planted them upright in the snow. Then they manhandled Einar and the others over to the mouth of the cave.

Warm air wafted out into the freezing night air like the cave was breathing out. Einar could now see that a large bonfire blazed inside, sending lurid shadows around the rock walls and roof. The smoke from it travelled across the roof and out into the night. On the far side of the fire three people were beating on goatskin drums. Two were women and one was a man and all three were stripped to the waist. Their torsos were covered with stick-like symbols painted on in black, not unlike the tattoos Einar had seen on Skar. The heat inside the cave was such that their skin was slick with sweat. Their eyes were empty and black, as if they were entranced by the rhythm they thumped out on the goatskin. The man's ribs looked like they were about to break through his skin. His hair was lank and thin and he looked like he could collapse at any moment. It was the women's naked breasts, however, that Einar could not help but stare at. The women themselves were neither young nor pretty, but there was something about the way their breasts undulated in time to the drumbeat that made it hard for him to look away.

As they moved around the fire he saw a large flat stone on the floor of the cave that looked like a wide, low table. Iron rings were driven into the rock floor of the cave at the top and bottom ends of the stone and its flat surface bore large dark brown stains that Einar did not like the look of.

Aslaug pointed at the stone. Thorir's four men and the sledge driver laid hands on Surt. They manhandled him first into a sitting position, then pushed him down flat on his back. He struggled but it was five against one and soon they had pulled his bound hands above his head and a strap secured them to one of the iron rings. Then they went to work doing the same on both legs so soon he was splayed out, tied flat to the stone. The sight reminded Einar of a trussed chicken ready to be carved in his mother's kitchen. Then they shoved Einar and Affreca into kneeling positions beside the stone.

'You cannot witness this,' Aslaug said to her husband's men. 'This is seiðr. It is secret to those who have been initiated.'

The scrawny man beating the drum stopped and went over to stand beside Einar.

'I don't want to see what you get up to,' the man who had driven the sledge said, handing his spear to the half-naked man with a look of disdain on his face. 'This sort of magic is unmanly.'

'But you'll welcome the blessings it brings to us all the same,' Aslaug said.

'We'll be outside if you need us,' Thorir's man said. He and the other men in furs left the cave. The former drummer took up a guard stance over Einar and Affreca.

'You said you know the Varðlokur,' Aslaug said to Affreca.

Affreca nodded.

'Perfect,' Aslaug said. 'It only has power when sung by a

young woman like you. The jǫtnar, dísir, risi and the spirits of the land listen to a maiden's voice. They will grant us great bounty.'

'My singing voice isn't that great,' Affreca said. 'I'm sorry to say that any spirits who might hear it won't give much in return for a song from me.'

Aslaug gave an unpleasant laugh.

'Your singing is only what will attract them here, dear,' she said, pulling a long-bladed knife from her goatskin bag. It was a broken-backed seax. The blade was sharp on one side and the blaze from the fire glinted on its rune-etched surface as she pointed it at Surt and then at Einar.

'What they will reward me for, is the sacrifice I make to those two.'

Thirty-Seven

Aslaug stripped off her furs. Underneath she wore the same long, dark blue dress with the seashells they had seen her in before. She took more items from the goatskin bag and began putting them on. Even before she had finished Einar knew what they would be: A black lambskin hood lined with white fur and a fur belt of the same colour. Her feet were clad in hairy calf-skin shoes she wore that ended in a large metal ball and her cat-skin gloves. She now wore the complete costume of a vǫlva. A witch.

He recalled the *spækona*, Heid, who had come to his mother's farmstead at the start of the last winter. She had said something to his mother about him. It was the night before the fight that had got him outlawed from Iceland and set him on this course of adventure that had led to this cave. Was this how it was to be? A tale that started and ended with a witch?

Aslaug took a metal staff with a large knob on one end from the bag. It was either brass or gold and gleamed in the firelight. With the staff in one hand and the knife in the other, she turned to Affreca.

'Sing,' she said.

Affreca opened her mouth but only a dry cough came

out. The heat from the big fire was intense. Einar could feel it through the back of his jerkin and his own throat felt parched.

'Sing,' Aslaug said again.

'I'm not comfortable here,' Affreca said. 'The rock hurts my knees. That makes it hard to sing.'

'Aw, is the poor little girl not used to hard floors?' Aslaug said, her voice brimming with mock sympathy. 'I thought you had the look of a spoiled bitch about you. A rich father's little princess, are you? Stand up if you must then sing, or I'll cut your throat first.'

Affreca, struggled to her feet, which was difficult with her hands bound before her. Then she cleared her throat and started chanting.

The women beating the drums increased their rhythm in unison as if they could somehow read each other's minds. Aslaug bent over the prone Surt and cut open his jerkin, pulling the material aside and throwing away the grass and bark he had stuffed inside to keep him warm until she had laid bare the skin of his torso. She leered down at him, taking the knife and staff in one hand and running her other over his sweat-slicked skin.

'Get off me you hag,' Surt shouted. His voice was high and filled with panic. He added something in his own tongue which Einar did not understand. The black man looked terrified. His eyes were wide and he thrashed his head this way and that, seeking any possible escape. His arms and legs bulged as he pulled on the bindings that held him on the stone but all that did was draw them tighter. Einar remembered Surt's reaction when they first saw Gunnhild's cursing pole and his words when they talked of witches and curses in the forest and he knew this must be like the worst of nightmares for him. Surt was a warrior. He feared no man in a straight fight, whether it be a fair one or one of the ring contests King Eirik had forced him to battle, but now he was tied down and at the mercy of the very thing he feared the most; a magic worker. A *seiðkona*.

In contrast to the awful scene in the cave, Affreca's song was sweet sounding. It rose above the frantic drumming and the roaring crackle of the bonfire. The words were strange and the tune haunting, ancient sounding but the way Affreca sang them was clear and beautiful. Einar was amazed at how good a voice she had, and that he had never realised this before. Even the witch was captivated. Aslaug stood up, her head slightly back, waving the knife in time to the music, entranced by the sound. A single tear escaped the corner of her right eye and ran down her cheek.

Then Aslaug seemed to come back to herself. She gripped the knife, blade downwards, in her right hand and held her metal staff up in the air with her left. She began to chant.

'Norns, Vanir, *thurs*, dísir, *völvur*, giant women, *jötnar* and *risi*, hear our prayers.'

Aslaug continued, her harsh voice a contrast to Affreca's pure song. Einar recognised in her words names of otherworldly creatures but she did not mention any of the Aesir, the Gods who most prayed to. Aslaug was calling on beings of the darkness and remote places. One word she repeated several times was *Mörnir*. Einar had not heard that name before.

The witch, still holding her staff aloft, moved to the side of the stone beside where Einar knelt and Affreca stood. She was now beside Surt's naked belly. Einar swallowed as he realised this was so she would not have to stoop over and reach out to stab him with the knife.

He felt panic rising in his guts. He could not just watch as Surt was butchered before his eyes. He had to do something. But what? His hands were bound and he was on his knees. He looked up. The scrawny man standing above him bared his teeth and prodded the spear point down into the flesh of his neck.

'Move and you're dead,' he said in a hiss.

Einar gnashed his teeth in frustration. There was nothing he could do to help but pray whatever Aslaug was about to do would give Surt a quick, painless death.

Then he would be next.

The witch's knuckles whitened on the handle of the knife.

'Mörnir, Mörnir, Mörnir,' she said. 'May you receive this gift we give you. Please be generous and reward us in return.'

Aslaug struck downwards. Affreca launched herself sideways, pushing herself off her right leg. Her shoulder barged into the witch's right. The knife dropped from her hand as Aslaug was shunted sideways, stumbling away from the stone. The witch regained her balance, then with a cry of frustrated rage, came rushing back, now brandishing her metal staff in both hands like a club.

Affreca jumped up on the stone slab, standing astride Surt and turned to face Aslaug. Before Aslaug got close enough to swing her staff Affreca lashed out with her left leg, lifting it off the ground and balancing on her right. She hit the running woman with all the combined power of the biggest muscles in her body. Aslaug went flying, falling backwards into the flames of the bonfire.

Einar saw the man with the spear standing over him was distracted by the action. Still on his knees, he threw himself sideways to the ground. The man guarding him saw his movement and stepped forward to strike at Einar with the spear. As he lifted one foot, Einar scythed his own leg in an arc that swept the skinny man's feet from under him. With a cry he fell, landing heavily on the rock floor on his side. Einar was already scrambling to his feet. In a moment he was standing over the half-naked man. The man on the ground rolled onto his back and tried to bring the spear up to stab Einar. Einar was too close now for the long-shafted weapon to be effective. He ducked out of the way of the blade then grasped the shaft with both of his still-bound hands. He wrenched upwards, pulling the spear out of the other's grasp. Without bothering to reverse it, Einar simply smashed the shaft back down, driving the butt into the right cheek of the man below. There was a crack of bone breaking. The man cried out. A tooth and splash of blood burst from his mouth. Einar struck him again, then a third time and the man stopped moving.

Aslaug, her dress ablaze, scrambled out of the fire and ran at Affreca. Affreca repeated her sideways kick, sending the witch howling back into the flames. Affreca jumped off the stone slab, grabbed the fallen knife and ran to Einar. She slid the knife between his bound wrists and in one movement sliced his bonds apart.

'The others outside,' Einar said, realising at any moment the five men outside would be rushing in to see what was happening.

Affreca nodded.

'Go,' she said, kneeling to slice Surt's hands free.

Einar, spear in hand, ran around the bonfire towards the cave entrance. Affreca freed Surt's legs and scrambled to his feet. Surt took the knife and cut Affreca's hands free. He gave her back the knife, grabbed Aslaug's metal staff and charged around the other side of the fire, following the wall until he slid to a halt beside the cave mouth.

Einar, on the other side of the entrance, ducked his head out and saw the driver of the wagon, a knife in one hand, was running towards the cave. The other four were grabbing their spears and following close behind.

Aslaug rose from the fire once more. The sight of her was terrifying. Her dress was completely ablaze, as was her hair. Her skin was blistering and cracking. Howling like one of the thurs she had summoned, the witch ran towards the mouth of the cave, desperate for the cold air and freezing snow outside. She hurtled past Einar and straight into the driver who was running in.

Einar lunged forward, driving his spear through Aslaug's back. He pushed with his thighs and shoulders, shoving the blade through her body, out of her stomach and into the guts of the man on the other side. Both engulfed in the burning witch's flames and impaled through the belly, the driver cried out in agony. Einar wrenched his spear back and the driver dropped to the ground, curled in a ball around his punctured stomach as his life blood dribbled out onto the rocks.

To Einar's amazement Aslaug did not fall. Instead, still screaming like a Valkyrie, she ran on, stumbling out of the cave and away from the entrance.

The second and third of the men outside came to the cave mouth. The first one ran in, spear ready. Oblivious to

Surt, lurking in the shadow of a slight alcove at the side of the entrance, he ran right past him. Surt leaned out and brained him with the witch's metal rod. With a crack his skull shattered and the staff bent under the impact. The man went sprawling face forward to the ground like all the bones in his body had in an instant become disconnected.

Einar stepped out and hurled his spear at the second man outside. At such close range he could neither miss nor could the running man avoid it. It took him in the chest and he fell backwards, the spear blade embedded deep in his flesh.

Looking up, Einar saw the fourth man was now charging at him, spear levelled and realised he had just thrown away his own weapon.

There came a screaming behind him. Einar glanced around to see one of the drummer women running at him. Her teeth were clenched in a grimace of hatred and her hands were outstretched, fingers clawed, going for his face. Without thinking he drove his right shoulder into her, slid his right arm around her side then, twisting at the middle, hurled her past him out of the cave. It was one of the movements that Skar had drilled into them on the ship. She flew through the air and landed, skewering herself on the weapon of the approaching spearman. Screaming, the woman died and fell to the ground, pulling the spear with her.

Einar snatched up the driver's knife and ran out of the cave entrance, driving the blade into the fur-clad spearman as he was still trying to free his weapon from the woman's corpse. Einar stabbed him again and again, feeling hot blood spurt out over his hands with every strike. Then the man grunted and collapsed into the snow.

The last of Thorir's men decided he would rather live to fight another day. He turned and ran for the skis. He was still fumbling with cold hands to attach the bindings to his feet when Surt, after running from the cave, reached him. The big man shoulder charged Thorir's man, knocking him over into the snow. Surt fell on him and grabbed his head with both hands. The muscles on his bare arms and torso bulged as Surt made one violent twist. A resounding crack echoed across the snow-covered mountainside and the man went limp.

Surt checked he was dead, then dropped him back into the snow.

Einar heard footsteps rushing behind him. He turned and saw the other drummer woman, running away from the cave mouth. Einar tensed but she just skipped past him and ran off across the snow.

Affreca joined Einar.

'Good luck to her,' Affreca said as the woman disappeared into the dark beyond the glow from the cave. 'Half naked, thigh deep in snow on a mountainside at night. I wouldn't like to be in her shoes. If she was wearing any.'

For a few moments they stood panting, trying to catch their breath. A little way away from the cave entrance a hole in the snow showed the place where Aslaug had finally fallen, face down, succumbing to the flames that still smouldered on her charred back.

'Well, you broke her spell,' Einar said to Affreca. 'I didn't know you could sing like that.'

'Her magic wouldn't have worked, anyway,' Affreca said, a lopsided smile on her lips. 'She said it only worked if the song was sung by a maiden.'

Surt walked back to join Affreca and Einar.

'At least they've left enough skis for all of us,' Einar said, pointing at the discarded wooden planks now scattered across the snow. 'Getting back should be easy.'

Surt shook his head.

'I've no idea how to do it,' he said.

Einar, who had grown up in Iceland where learning to ski or skate – anything to get across a frozen landscape – was the first thing children learned after walking, raised his eyebrows.

'I'd never seen snow until I came to these northern lands,' Surt said. 'And then I was a slave.'

'I can't either,' Affreca said.

'But you're Norse, like me,' Einar said.

'I grew up in Ireland, Einar, remember?' Affreca said. 'All it does there is rain.'

'All right,' Einar said. 'You two will have to take the sledge. I'll ski. We'll take the furs off these people and whatever weapons there are and get back to free the others. Then we need to get off this cursed mountain.'

Thirty-Eight

They stripped the dead of their furs, cladding themselves in the warm clothes and throwing the rest into the wagon. Einar strapped a set of skis to his boots then they gathered the rest and along with the weapons put them in the wagon too. Surt and Affreca climbed onto the driving bench, snapped the reins and they all set off back along the track from the cave.

Einar had not been on skis since the last winter but the track was quite flat and he had a chance to get back into the way of movement, sliding one foot then the other. At times when the track went uphill he grabbed the side of the sled and let the reindeer pull them all along. When the track sloped down he slid along, using an inverted spear for a ski pole, planting it on his left then his right like someone punting a skiff down a river.

When they were in sight of Thorir's mountain hall they stopped. All looked quiet.

'I'll go ahead on my own,' Einar said. 'I'll make a lot less noise than this wagon and we don't want to alert the people in the house.'

Einar took one of the burning torches from the sled then skied the last bit down to the house. He slid to a halt beside the outbuilding where the Wolf Coats were. For a moment he stood still, listening. There was muffled noise coming from inside the main house, laughing and some singing. Einar undid the bindings of his skis, opened the door of the outbuilding, then slipped inside.

Ulrich, Skar, Starkad, Kari, Sigurd and Wulfhelm still lay tied up on the floor. Einar shoved the fur hat up to show his face and held his finger to his lips. Then he set to work cutting the others free with the witch's knife.

'I thought we'd seen the last of you,' Skar said in a whisper. 'What about the others?'

'They're all right,' Einar said. 'We've got furs, a couple of spears, a wagon and skis. The witch is dead. Let's get out of here before the rest of the folk in the house find out.'

Skar patted him on the shoulder and Einar felt a thrill of pride.

'Well done,' Skar said. 'We're starting to fight back against those evil Norns at last. It's a pity you couldn't get more war gear though.'

'Follow me,' Einar said.

He led them outside and over to the other outhouse where earlier he had seen Thorir's men get their skis and spears. Opening the door, the light from Einar's torch showed that it was a sort of store house. There were more skis standing up against the walls and some bows, arrows, spears and four old shields as well as more fur.

The Wolf Coats worked fast, putting on the fur clothing then grabbing spears and skis. Ulrich, Skar, Starkad and Kari slung the shields over their backs by their straps. Ulrich spotted one of the bows and lifted it along with a quiver of arrows. It was shorter than a normal bow and slightly less curved. Then they went outside.

Skar looked at the main house. A wave of laughter came from inside. Thorir and his men were having a fine time.

'We should block the door and burn them all to death inside,' Skar said in a quiet voice.

'It's buried in snow. The thatch underneath will be frozen solid,' Ulrich said. 'We'd have to go inside to find anything that will burn. Unlike this place.'

He took the flaming torch from Einar and tossed it back into the store house. It tumbled across the floor and Ulrich closed the door.

The Wolf Coats and Einar carried their skis and spears up the little slope back to the waiting wagon.

Ulrich tossed the bow to Affreca. She caught it and turned it over in her hands, noticing the differences in it to a normal bow.

'That's a Finnish bow,' Ulrich said, as he threw the quiver of arrows into the back of the wagon. 'I think you'll do a lot of damage with that.'

Skar lifted the remaining torches from the corners of the wagon and threw them aside.

'Are we going to ski in the dark?' Einar said.

'Take a look around you,' Skar said.

Einar did, realising now that the firelight was away from his eyes that the clear sky, the moon and the stars and the white of the snow made the night almost as clear as day. He looked down the slope and could pick out a winding trail. It swept down the far side of the pass, sometimes moving through forest and sometimes through open slopes as it criss-crossed the mountainside like a Sun Rune on down to the valley below.

'That looks like the way we should go,' he said.

'I can't ski, I'm afraid,' Wulfhelm said. He seemed to have recovered his wits now.

'Get in the wagon with them,' Ulrich said.

Behind them, smoke was starting to filter out from the cracks around the door of the outbuilding they had left.

'Let's go,' Ulrich said.

Surt cracked the reins and the reindeer set off along the track to the valley. In summer it was probably a road or other well-used path but now it was just a visible depression in the snow. The wagon slid along and the Wolf Coats skied behind it. They went a little way down the slope then round a sharp bend and continued their descent, now going in the opposite direction. The going was easy and Einar found his skis slid easily over the snow. The furs he wore, including a large cap and big gloves, kept him warm. It was a beautiful night. If it had not been for the imminent danger it might even have been pleasant.

The sound of shouting came from above. Einar looked up. They had by then doubled back on themselves and were now directly below Thorir's hall, but further down the mountainside. Above them was a steep slope the track had gone around. Einar could see figures at the top of the slope, outlined against the snow on the mountain behind them. They were shouting and pointing in his direction.

'They've found out we're gone,' he said.

Surt cracked the reins, driving the reindeer into a trot. Einar looked up again and saw three people on skis launching themselves over the edge of the slope above. They came straight down, reaching a speed that would cut down Einar and the Wolf Coats' head start in moments.

The track entered a clump of forest before the skiers caught up with them. They came flying over the bank from the slope onto the track and skidded in tight turns after the wagon. Einar heard a thump to his left. He looked and saw an arrow embedded in the back panel of the wagon an arm's length away from him.

He looked over his shoulder and saw the men chasing them were aiming bows. The skill of these men was impressive that they could ski so fast and shoot a bow at the same time. Einar had heard tell of practised hunters who could do this but he had never seen it done. It was no doubt a common skill for those who lived in the high mountains, which was unfortunate for Einar and his company.

Affreca clambered off the driving bench into the back of the wagon. She notched an arrow to her new bow and let it fly. The arrow missed the skier behind and Einar could see the look of surprise on Affreca's face. The new bow was different to what she was used to.

The pursuers shot another arrow. Starkad wobbled on his skis as the missile thumped into the shield slung over his back. Affreca aimed again, this time taking longer. Then she shot. This time the arrow just missed the skier she was aiming at. He swerved sideways as the arrow flew past him. Affreca had another arrow notched already and let it fly. The skier she aimed at saw her do it and swerved again in the same direction to avoid her shot. Then, intent on watching Affreca, he ran out of track and skied straight into a tree. There was a loud thump as he hit the trunk and rebounded into the snow, arms and legs flailing like a rag doll.

Another arrow flew from the second chaser. Affreca ducked. It passed over her head and into the trees. Then she was back up again, taking aim at the man who shot it. She loosed her own arrow and this time hit the skier dead centre of his chest. The force was such he fell backwards then went tumbling through the snow, sending up clouds of it as he spun to a halt.

'This has great power,' Affreca said, eyes wide as she looked at the bow as if in disbelief.

Einar could hear more shouting behind them and saw glimpses of torchlight through the trees. There were others coming down the slope in pursuit.

They came out of the trees again and came to another sharp corner. The reindeers pulled the wagon around it as the Wolf Coats and Einar dug their skis in to take the turn. The turn was tight and they were going fast. Einar saw the right sled of the wagon lift off the snow.

'It's going over,' he shouted a warning.

Affreca and Wulfhelm, already realising what was happening, sprung to their feet and jumped off the wagon. They landed in the snow at the side of the track, thumping large holes into it and sending up a wave of white into the air. As the wagon tilted higher Surt, on the driving bench, became aware of the looming accident but it was too late for him to get off. He threw himself into the bed of the wagon as it overturned.

The vehicle crashed onto its side. The reindeer made gruff honks as they were pulled over with it. They fell on top of each other in a tangled heap of thrashing legs and twisting necks. The wagon, now sideways across the track and on its side, slid a little further then came to a halt.

The Wolf Coats skidded to a stop beside it. Affreca and Wulfhelm were already pulling themselves out of the snow. They came jogging down the track to catch up with the others. Wulfhelm was limping.

'Hit my knee on something,' he said, gritting his teeth. 'I'm all right.'

Surt clambered from the back of the overturned wagon. He was holding his head and swayed a little as he got to his feet.

Affreca picked up the bow where it had spilled from the wagon.

'You all go on,' she said. 'We'll try and hold them off from behind the wagon.'

Ulrich unslung the shield from his back.

'Skar, Kari,' he said. 'Give them your shields.'

'You're going to leave them behind?' Einar said. 'In that case I will stay with them.'

'Very heroic of you, I'm sure,' Ulrich said. 'But unnecessary. We'll all get off the track and go straight down the slope. These three can sit on the shields and use them as sleighs. It'll be slower than skiing but a lot faster than that wagon.'

They all went to the edge of the track. The slope fell away beneath them in a wide, steep snowfield that ended in forest far below. The trackway turned back and snaked across the slope about halfway down it.

'You see where the slope divides in two around those trees beneath the track down there?' Ulrich said. 'You three on the shields go left, we'll try and lead that lot behind us to the right.'

Einar looked down and felt his stomach lurch.

'It's like a cliff,' he said. 'We're going to ski down that?'

'What's the matter, farmer boy?' Kari said. 'Do they not have mountains in Iceland? What are you scared of? A bit of speed? I haven't had this much fun since I was a young lad.'

Affreca balanced the shield on the edge of the precipice. Then she jumped on as it tipped over the edge. In a moment she was away, scrambling into a sitting position on the back of the shield as it picked up speed. Surt went after her. Wulfhelm threw his shield down then dived on top of it, speeding off down the mountain head-first.

Something buzzed past Einar's head and thumped into the snow. It was an arrow.

'They're coming,' he said.

'Right, let's go,' Ulrich said. 'Stay behind them on those shields and remember to break to the right when we get to the trees.'

Then he hopped over the edge and was gone.

Skar followed him, then Kari and Sigurd. Einar took a deep breath, trying to steal himself for what was coming.

'Don't worry lad, it's easy enough,' Starkad said. 'Just point your skis straight down the hill and you're away.'

Then he too disappeared over the edge.

Einar looked over his shoulder and saw the dark figures coming down the slope above him. He clenched his teeth, tightened his knuckles around the spear shaft he was using as a pole, dug it in and pushed himself forward over the edge.

Thirty-Nine

In a moment, the wind went from being a mere whisper to a deafening roar in Einar's ears as he plummeted down the slope.

He had never travelled so fast. Not on a galloping horse, a ship speeding over the waves or on his skates across the ice in a game of knattleikr. He felt like a hawk, diving from high in the sky to snatch prey on the ground below. The cold rushing air made his eyes stream and he had to blink so he could still see.

At first he tried to jump from side to side to try to control the speed of his descent but soon realised it was futile and in fact more dangerous. He had no choice but to go with it. His skis pointed straight down the mountain and all he could do was concentrate on keeping his feet in position and staying upright. The pole was useless. He was in a crouch with it held across his body. The snow shot past beneath his skis. His feet shuddered up and down. Before long his thighs felt like they were on fire but he knew if he changed position at this speed he would fall. The thought of the bone-shattering impact that would result made him grit his teeth and endure the pain.

The others were already far ahead, streaking straight down. He could hear their delighted shouts, scarcely able to believe the whoops of joy that reached his ears. He had no idea what was going on behind him, so intent was he on watching his path ahead.

Wulfhelm, lying flat on his front, shot ahead of the others. He was first to reach the track below. The Saxon shot off the bank at the bottom of the slope, bounced once on the track then was across it and flying down the next slope. Affreca came next. When she hit the track the shield spun out of control. Hanging onto the leather straps for grim death, she rotated through three turns across the track then was off down the next slope, now facing backwards. Surt, who was a lot heavier, was behind them. He bumped across the track then was on down the next slope.

Einar realised he would have to slow down if he did not want to smash straight into the track and most likely fall as the terrain changed from slope to flat in an instant. The Wolf Coats ahead of him, however, showed no signs of slowing. Ulrich, the first of the skiers, swerved to the right. The others followed. Einar did not know what he was doing but followed anyway. Then he saw Ulrich was heading for a ridge of snow running up to the track like a ramp. He hit the ramp, tucked himself down on his haunches then sprang up as he reached the end. Ulrich flew through the air, crossing the track without hitting the ground, then was on his way down the next part of the slope.

The others jumped the track in the same way then it was Einar's turn. He hit the ramp. The rumbling hiss of his skis in the snow ceased as he was in the air. He crossed the track and over the edge of the slope on the other side.

The ground fell away and there was a moment of fear as Einar kept falling with it. A little way below the track he reconnected with the snow. Einar dipped, absorbing the impact with his knees and then he was on his way down the second slope.

The incline of the second slope was slightly less than the first and the speed of their descent was a little less wild. At the bottom, the ground began to level out as it went into forest. The thought occurred to Einar that they were descending in moments the heights that it had taken them most of the previous day to climb.

An arrow shot past his head and he was reminded of the men chasing them. He did not dare chance a look over his shoulder. He was still going so fast all his attention was captured by the slope ahead. The slightest mistake would mean a bone-shattering fall. If that did not kill him then he would be at the mercy of the men behind him. He had to keep going. Though what they would do when they ran out of slope he had no idea.

Einar began making sweeping turns as he descended. If he could not get away from them at least he could make it harder for them to hit him. Ahead down the slope, Wulfhelm, Surt and Affreca, who had recovered from her spin, reached the point where it split on either side of a line of trees that reached up the mountainside like a black finger. They leaned over, hauling on the straps of the shields like reins, turning onto the slope on the left of the trees while the Wolf Coats continued to the right.

As Einar reached the point of turning, a movement at the edge of his vision caught his attention. He risked a glance to the left again and saw two men on skis, one with a bow, hurtling down the left-hand slope after Affreca and the other two. Ulrich's plan to lead the men chasing them to the right had only partially worked.

A little further down the slope he spotted a small track, white through the dark of the trees, leading from the right slope to the left. Einar dug in his right leg, turning himself towards the track. At the same time, a rumbling sound from above reached his ears. He had to look and glanced over his shoulder. There was a pursuer right behind him, perhaps a couple of ski lengths away. Einar hoped he did not have a bow. At that distance, the chaser could not miss.

Einar headed for the track. There was nothing he could do now but try to get to the other side and see if he could shake off the man on the other slope. The little path through the trees was narrow, wide enough for just one person. It weaved through trees and there was a dip into a small gulley in the middle. At the speed he was going at there was no room for error. Any small mistake and he would hit a tree and that would be the end of him.

He shot into the trees, turning right then left to avoid trunks, dipping to avoid branches, then into the gulley. As he went down the side of it the swift changes in position left him unbalanced. His left leg wobbled and for an instant he thought he was going to fall. Then he regained his balance. Einar felt the way he did in the heart of the battle. It was like his body reacted with the correct movement before his mind had time to instruct it what to do.

He hit the bottom of the gulley hard. He crouched to absorb the impact but it still nearly drove his knees into his chin. Then he was heading up the other side, momentum propelling him out of the gulley. He was nearly out of the trees already.

Einar's eyes widened. There was a low hanging branch right across the track ahead about shoulder height. He went to duck then stopped himself. Willing himself to stay upright until the very last moment possible.

The moment arrived and he dropped to crouch. Einar shot under the branch and out of the trees. He glanced over his shoulder. Obscured by Einar's body, the man chasing him did not see the branch until it was too late for him. He slammed into it at full speed. The branch broke under the impact but it had already smacked him backwards off his skis and back into the gulley.

Einar came out of the trees and turned down the slope. Down the slope from him he saw Affreca, Surt and Wulfhelm speeding on their shields, nearly at the bottom. Between them and him two men on skis hurtled after them. One of the pursuers was aiming a bow.

Einar pointed his skis straight down the slope. He crouched into a tucked position to go as fast as he could. The wind roared in his ears once more as he sped down the hill. Catching up with the man who was upright and about to shoot an arrow, Einar aimed his skis just to the left of him. At the moment he drew alongside he sprang up, shoving his shoulder sideways. He barged into the archer, knocking him to the right. His arrow shot off into the sky as the man fell, crashing into the snow and flying into an uncontrolled tumble.

The movement put Einar off balance too. For an instant he almost fell backwards, managed to straighten but knew he had to slow himself or he would fall. He planted the pole in the snow and jumped around it, aiming himself across the slope instead of straight down it. He dug in hard with his right leg. His thigh muscle felt like it was pulling apart as he decelerated fast, sending a broad wave of snow in an arc down the slope.

Then he was stopped. He stood, panting, his body exhausted, sweat streaming down his face from under the fur cap. He savoured the relief as the fire in his leg muscles dissolved as they were released from the effort they had been under.

The other skier he had seen was further down the slope, chasing after the three on the shields. He had no bow but like the others was using a spear as a ski pole.

Affreca had reached the bottom of the slope. She shot across the level ground for a little way then, judging that her speed had diminished enough for it to be safe, tossed her bow away then threw herself off the shield after it. She tumbled through the snow over and over. The moment she stopped she scrambled to her feet and started wading to where her bow had fallen. Moments later she reached it, snatched it up and notched an arrow.

Kneeling in the snow, Affreca drew the bow, aimed it up the slope and shot. The other skier was perhaps still forty paces uphill. Her arrow struck him in the chest and he crashed backwards. Momentum carried his body a little way on down the hill, leaving a red smear across the snow behind him.

Einar looked up the slope. No one else was coming, which meant the other pursuers had gone after the Wolf Coats.

Through the long finger of trees he could see Ulrich and the others had also got to the bottom of the slope on the other side. They had turned around and now stood just in front of the edge of the forest, facing back uphill. They had formed a line and stood, spears ready. About halfway back up the slope he could see their pursuers had also stopped for some reason. One of them had a bow.

'Get those shields over to the others,' Einar shouted to Affreca, Surt and Wulfhelm, the latter two now stopped at the bottom of the slope as well. Surt and Wulfhelm grabbed their shields and started to wade through the snow across the bottom of the slope but to Einar's consternation Affreca instead began scrambling up the slope instead.

He had no time to wonder what she was doing. Einar dug his pole in and set off downhill again, traversing the slope from left to right until he too reached the bottom, stopping beside the long finger of trees that parted the slopes.

Ripping off a glove he fumbled with the bindings of his skis then jumped out of them. Spear in hand, he struggled through the snow into the trees and across to the other slope to join the Wolf Coats. Surt was just behind him and Wulfhelm, still limping a bit, was a little further away.

The Wolf Coats had all taken off their skis and stood, waiting, watching their enemies up the slope as sweat from their bodies steamed off into the night air. Einar joined their line.

'What are they waiting for?' Wulfhelm said.

Einar counted the men above. There was ten of them. In the middle of them was a giant figure much taller than the others who could only be Bjorgolf. With a thrill he realised the odds were nearly even. That was what had made the others pause. Reluctant to just ski straight onto the spear points of the úlfhéðnar, they were trying to work out how best to attack.

The archer loosed an arrow. It hurtled down the slope but Skar had time to duck. It passed into the trees and out of harm's way.

Then the bowman himself cried out. He doubled over and dropped his bow as he clutched at an arrow shaft that protruded from his left shoulder.

All eyes shot to the right. Affreca was further up the slope, in the trees, about halfway to where Thorir's men were. It was her arrow that had shot the archer. She notched another and sent it flying at them.

Thorir's men avoided it but it sent panic through them. The next moment they were scrambling to undo their skis then scrabbling back up the slope, desperate to get out of range of Affreca's bow. She let them go, conscious that her supply of arrows was finite.

'Go on, run away you cowardly bastards,' Skar shouted up the slope.

The Wolf Coats did not relax. They kept their defensive stance until Thorir's men were back up the track as far as it traversed the mountainside above.

Affreca came out of the trees and climbed up to where the skis of Thorir's men lay abandoned. She grabbed each one and sent them sliding down the slope then slid down after them on her bottom.

'You have won this one,' the booming voice of Bjorgolf drifted down from above. 'But we will gather more men and come after you. This is our land. We'll track you down. You won't get away.'

'Well that's just about everyone in the entire country chasing us now,' Ulrich said. 'Come on. We've still a long way to go.'

Forty

Ulrich was convinced they would not be followed until daylight at the earliest.

'They're too scared,' he said, the contempt in his voice clear. 'But let's put as much distance as we can between them and us before the sun comes up.'

They found a small track leading away into the forest. Each man who had them smashed his skis against a tree to stop them being used by Thorir's men. They were of no use now as they trekked downhill. The snow was ever scarcer under the trees and before long they had descended below the snowline completely. The ground became very soft and saturated with meltwater. The trees hid the moon and without the reflective glare of the snow it became hard to see where they were going. They struggled on in the dark but eventually, despite Ulrich's misgivings, he ordered them to build shelters and get some sleep until daylight. They arranged a watch rota then got some rest.

Einar was not sure if he slept much or not. He was dog tired and nodded off but discomfort woke him often. The sound of dripping, running water was all around. It was cold and damp and at any moment he half expected to see the giant shape of Bjorgolf looming over him, an axe raised to strike off his head.

After some time the dark of night changed to the blue before dawn then grey as the sun crept up over the horizon. Cold, wet and miserable, they dragged themselves from their shelters and set off down the hillside once more.

After a little way they found a stream, swollen with melted snow, gushing down over rocks through a valley in the trees.

'All we have to do now is follow this,' Ulrich said. 'And eventually we'll end up at the sea.'

'Why the sea?' Einar said.

'Because that's where ships are,' Ulrich said. 'We're still heading the right way but sailing is still our fastest way to get back to Gandvik.'

They trekked on, following the course of the mountain stream as it got wider and fuller. As the sun rose higher they came to a wide clearing in the forest, caused most likely by a fire the previous summer. They stopped for a break. Skar went hunting for edible plants while the rest of them flopped down into the ferns on the forest floor for a rest.

The vista before the company was impressive. They were on a mountainside and ahead of them stretched a long, wide valley, not unlike the one they had left on the far side of the mountain pass. The forest stretched onwards and covered a lot of the valley floor. It petered out into meadowland then in the far distance there was what looked like a wide estuary that opened into the sea. It looked like there was a settlement at the edge of the sea near the mouth of the river, big enough to be seen even at this distance.

'There's no smoke or fires anywhere in this valley,' Sigurd said. 'Eirik's men must not have got here yet.'

'It's more likely that the people here were loyal to him,' Sigurd said. 'They have no need for punishment.'

'That's just great,' Starkad said. 'That will make it even harder for us to get through this country. Even if his warriors have not arrived he'll have sent a war arrow. Everyone here will be on the lookout for us.'

Ulrich rose to his feet. He muttered something to himself. Einar was not sure but he thought he heard him say *this is perfect*. He walked off a little bit, his lips moving in silence. Einar had noticed Ulrich often did this when thinking. It was like he was having a conversation with himself, or debating pros and cons with an unseen companion.

'What is this war arrow you keep talking about?' Surt said.

'It's a way to send a message fast across a district,' Kari said. 'The person wanting to send it, the king, say, takes an arrow or a stick and breaks it in half. He carves the message in runes on both halves. Something like *all men with weapons come to me at Tunsberg*. He gives each half to two riders. They ride in different directions. At the first settlement each comes to they pass on the message. The head man there copies the message onto another two arrows and sends those off in three different directions. And so on.'

'They call it the war arrow,' Sigurd said. 'But the message flies faster, further and wider than any arrow. It's more like a wildfire.'

Surt nodded.

'This is clever,' he said. 'Perhaps you're not the complete barbarians I thought you were.'

Skar returned with their breakfast of herbs and handed them round. Ulrich rejoined them.

'I've been thinking,' he said.

Everyone turned to look at him.

'From here on we must part our company,' Ulrich said. 'If this valley is full of people loyal to Eirik then we stand a better chance if we split up. Eirik is searching for a company of nine. We will split into three groups. We Wolf Coats are well known. We look like what we are – a warband. If anyone sees us they will ask questions, so we must hide as we run. You others, though. You won't stand out.'

Surt raised an eyebrow.

'You can travel the roads,' Ulrich said. 'You can talk to people. Find out what is going on. Find out what Eirik is up to. Find out where we can get a ship. We could do with helmets, brynjas and more shields too. Anything you can get.'

He pointed at Einar and Affreca.

'You two will go together,' he said.

'Why us?' Einar said. His eyes slid sideways towards Affreca. 'Why would we be any less suspicious?'

'You're both about the same age,' Ulrich said. 'You could pass as a newly married couple, travelling home for a blessing, perhaps.'

This time both Affreca and Einar started.

'Now wait one moment—' Affreca said.

Ulrich held up his hands.

'You only have to pretend,' he said. 'I'm not asking you to actually like each other.'

Skar snorted.

'Like you actually do,' he said.

'What?' Einar said.

'Locals will know we aren't from here,' Affreca said.

'If anyone challenges you, say your mother was from here but you were born overseas. You've returned to the family homeland to have your marriage blessed.'

'Why would I do that?' Affreca said.

'They have weird, ancient beliefs in this country,' Ulrich said. Einar recalled the odd Gods Aslaug had prayed to the night before. 'You can say you're travelling as a religious obligation.'

Einar opened his mouth to object further but the scowl on Ulrich's face made him stop.

'Must I work it all out for you?' Ulrich said. 'Use whatever wits you have. Don't get caught. Find us some war gear and where we can find a ship to get us out of here. You two do the same.'

He turned to Wulfhelm and Surt.

'We can hardly say we're a married couple,' Wulfhelm said.

'Tell people he is your thrall. You're on your way to fight for King Eirik. Think of something.'

Einar, Affreca, Wulfhelm and Surt all looked at each other. No one looked too happy with the situation.

'Make your way to that settlement,' Ulrich said, pointing to the town in the distance at the edge of the estuary. 'We'll meet you there in two days' time.'

'How will we find you?' Affreca said.

'We'll find you,' Ulrich said. 'Don't worry about that. As you travel remember the advice of Odin: "Those who travel must use their wits. Check every entrance and check it again before you go in, lest an enemy lurks beyond."'

'How will we know which way to travel when we're in the forest?' Einar said. 'We don't know whatever magic you were using to get through the woods in the dark the other night.'

Ulrich laughed.

'Moss is thicker on the north side of a trunk,' he said. 'I just felt the trees to see which side that was. Now go. And try not to get yourselves killed.'

Forty-One

'Ulrich just wanted rid of us,' Einar said as they trudged along. 'He thinks we'll slow him down or make mistakes and get them caught.'

'He might have a point,' Affreca said.

'We saved his life up there on the mountain,' Einar said. 'Him and his precious Wolf Coats.'

Since parting company with the Wolf Coats, Surt and Wulfhelm, Einar and Affreca had been walking for most of the morning, following the river down from the high mountainside into the valley below. The pine forest around them became no less dense but the river got ever wider. Swollen by the melting snows above, the waters roared as they gushed down the valley. The track they travelled on also got wider as they got lower in the valley and the way became more used. Around midday they came to a fork. The left-hand branch led away from the river but using Ulrich's moss trick they judged it to be heading more in the direction they needed to go. A little way on it became a well-used track pitted by horse hooves and rutted from cartwheels. It looked like a main thoroughfare.

Affreca had her bow slung over her shoulder. A hunting bow was normal for a traveller in the forest but a battle spear would attract unwanted attention. Einar had used the witch's knife to prise the rivets from his spear so he could take off the head. He was now using the shaft as a walking staff while the blade jangled along with the rivets in Affreca's arrow bag.

They met no one else, however, and the strange quiet of the forest around them remained unbroken except for their conversation. The longer they went without meeting anyone the more confident they became and tramped along the road, wrapped in their argument.

'I don't think Ulrich would do that to us,' Affreca said.

Einar grunted.

'I wish I was as sure as you,' he said.

'Why would you doubt him?' Affreca said. 'Why would he want rid of us?'

'Because we're not one of his precious Wolf Coats,' Einar said. 'We're not inside their ring of secrecy. We haven't been through their secret rituals. Maybe that's why he wants us away from them: They plan to practise some weird custom only Wolf Coats are allowed to know about. Did you notice he got rid of Surt and Wulfhelm too? Coincidence?'

'So what are you suggesting?' Affreca said. 'Should we forget about them? Just strike out for ourselves and escape alone? Is that what you think?'

'Why not?' Einar said.

Affreca shook her head.

'We have to stick with Ulrich,' she said. 'What about revenge? Have you no honour? You let Eirik and Atli betray us all and don't seek retaliation? What about your father too? What sort of man are you?'

'Revenge?' Einar let out an exasperated gasp. 'I grew up

in Iceland, Affreca. Revenge is the bane of our country. Men kill men and the sons of the dead men kill the killers. The sons of the dead killers then kill the revengers and so it goes on, generation after generation. There is no end to it and no way out of it.'

Affreca shot a sharp glance in his direction. She was about to say something when Einar stopped dead.

They had just rounded a bend. Ahead the track led to a bridge over the fast-flowing waters of what could only be the river they had followed earlier. The track must have doubled back to the river again.

A group of men stood on the track before the bridge. The first thing Einar noticed was the glint of metal. They were warriors, wearing mail brynjas and visored helmets. They had shields slung across their backs and swords at their hips. Einar counted fifteen of them.

'Who do you think they are?' Einar said.

'Armed men are never good news,' Affreca said. 'What do we do?'

As she spoke they saw several of the men glance around. They had been spotted.

'There's not much we can do now,' Einar said. 'Just keep walking or we'll look suspicious. For all they know we have every right to be here. Remember our story.'

'Where's the head of your spear?' Affreca said.

'Still in your arrow bag,' Einar said.

The loudness of the *tutt* that came from her discouraged him from looking at her. Instead he concentrated on the men ahead as they walked closer, trying to look as nonchalant as he could. He could see now that there was a large runestone beside the bridge. Like the one he had seen in Gandvik, someone had daubed a large Odal rune over the rune-carved memorial in red paint.

One of the warriors had filled his helmet with water from the river, while another couple of them had dipped cloths in it and were trying to wash the scrawled rune off.

As Einar and Affreca got closer four of the warriors began watching them and finally fanned out across the track. It was clear they would not be able to just stroll past.

Einar did his best to avoid too much eye contact as they approached, but as they closed the final paces between them, he saw scarred forearms, gold and silver arm rings and cold, appraising gazes. These men were practised warriors.

Einar nodded to them as he stepped sideways to walk around them. As he passed a particularly tall man with blond hair that flowed around his shoulders from beneath his helmet, he reached out a meaty fist and caught Einar's upper arm.

'Where do you two think you're going?' he said.

'We're on our way home,' Einar said, doing his best at a disarming smile. He pointed to the defaced stone. 'You don't like the decoration?'

The blond-haired warrior let go of Einar's arm and grunted.

'Rebels,' he said, shaking his head. 'They don't know when they're beaten. The battle at Tunsberg should leave them with little doubt.'

'You are men of King Eirik?' Einar said.

'Aye,' the warrior said. 'The king summoned all able-bodied to fight for him at Tunsberg. A fit lad like you should be in the king's army. Who is your lord?'

Einar hesitated for a moment, then said the first name to come into his head.

'Bodvar.'

'Bodvar? Never heard of him.'

Einar saw the blond-haired warrior's eyes narrow behind his helmet visor. His four companions stiffened.

'He's...' Einar's mind searched for an answer. 'Not from around here.'

'Not from around here?' the blond-haired man repeated. 'What's that supposed to mean? And who's this?'

He stepped forward and prodded a finger at Affreca, who had been keeping her head down to avoid eye contact.

'Is this your slave? Look at me boy!'

Affreca raised her head and met the warrior's gaze with a cool stare. The man's jaw dropped open slightly as he realised the assumption he had made based on her short-cropped hair was very wrong.

'I'm not his slave,' she said. 'I'm his wife.'

'Same thing, isn't it?' the blond-haired man said. Several of the warriors laughed. 'But tell me, lady, why would a woman as beautiful as you shave her head?'

'I got the head lice on our voyage,' Affreca said. 'I grew up here but now I live in Ireland. He is Irish, as is his lord, Bodvar of Limerick. I'm surprised you haven't heard of him? He's a Viking of great renown. We came here to have our marriage blessed according to my forefathers' customs.'

'Why do you carry a bow?' the warrior said, pointing at the weapon that was slung across Affreca's body.

'For hunting,' she said. 'We have to eat on our journey.'

The warrior looked at her for a moment without replying.

'We really need to be on our way...' Einar said.

'Well you're not going this way,' the blond-haired man said. 'We have orders to guard this bridge and not let anyone cross it. Especially anyone coming from the direction you came from. And don't think that living in Ireland excuses you, lad. If your parents lived here then you owe King Eirik spear service.'

'As soon as we have our marriage blessed I'll join the army, don't worry,' Einar said. 'How could I refuse the chance to fight for Eirik Bloody Axe?'

The big warrior just grunted and flicked his head in the direction they had come from to signal they should move on.

Affreca and Einar turned and began walking again. Now their pace was a lot faster than when they approached the warriors. As they went, Einar could almost feel the heat of the warriors' gazes as they watched them go.

'Do you think they believed us?' Affreca muttered out of the side of her mouth when she thought they were far enough away.

'You two! Wait!' The voice of the blond-haired warrior came from behind them.

'There's your answer,' Einar said. 'Run! Into the trees.'

Forty-Two

Einar and Affreca jumped over the ditch that ran along the side of the track and scrambled into the forest beyond. Behind them came the shouts of the warriors as they ran up the track towards them.

They kept going, charging through the ferns and bracken that grew at the base of the trees, their feet pounding on the carpet of pine needles beneath. Affreca unslung her bow as she ran. Once she had it in her grasp she stopped, swung around and notched an arrow. Einar skidded to a halt beside her.

They waited, panting, for the first of the warriors to come.

'I'll drop a couple of them,' Affreca said. 'That should make the rest slow down.'

'Wait,' Einar said, holding a hand up. 'I don't think they're coming after us.'

He dropped to the forest floor and put his ear to the ground. Then he looked up at her and nodded. They crouched, looking back towards the track. No one came through the forest behind them.

Affreca relaxed her bow. They crept back towards the track. After a short distance they began to approach the track.

Through the undergrowth and tree trunks they could see the trackway. Five of the warriors from the bridge stood on the road, looking into the trees.

Einar and Affreca dropped to the ground. Affreca held her bow ready.

'It might be a trap,' one of the warriors on the track said.

'I don't think so,' another said. 'They looked harmless. They probably just shit themselves when we shouted and ran away.'

Affreca scowled.

'Some of the men we're supposed to keep a look out for are úlfhéðnar,' the first man said. Einar could hear the unease in his voice. 'They're dangerous bastards.'

'One of those two was a woman,' the second warrior said. He sounded exasperated. 'How likely is it that she's a Wolf Coat? Not very. The Irish lad looked like a half-wit.'

'They could be trying to draw us away from the bridge,' a third said. 'So there's less men guarding it.'

'Come on lads,' the first one said. 'We should get back to the others. We've done our job. They didn't get across.'

The warriors left, walking back the way they had come.

'What now?' Einar said.

'We need to get across that river. It cuts through our path,' Affreca said. 'Maybe we can find another way across somewhere.'

'It has to be a bridge,' Einar said. 'The river's so swollen with meltwater we'll be swept away if we try to swim it. We could follow the river until we find another one. Maybe it won't be guarded.'

'If that one was guarded then the next will be too,' Affreca said. 'I wonder how they knew we were coming this way?'

'They maybe didn't,' Einar said.

'But they said they were told to watch for úlfhéðnar,' Affreca said.

'Among others,' Einar said. 'There is a war on. Eirik will have sent war arrows to those loyal to him. He'll want to stop survivors fleeing from Tunsberg and the only people he will want moving freely are his own men. We'll just be part of a list of people to look out for.'

Affreca did not reply and there was a moment of silence.

'Perhaps Ulrich was right after all,' Einar said with a sigh. 'We've a better chance of travelling through this country if we're separate from the Wolf Coats.'

'We should warn them,' Affreca said.

'I think they'll be well aware,' Einar said. 'And without us they can travel fast and hidden. They won't run into any traps.'

Affreca looked him in the eyes.

'Maybe you were right too, then,' she said.

'Let's not sit around arguing about it,' Einar said. 'You said I think too much. Let's get moving instead of thinking.'

They tracked back through the trees, back around the corner they had come around before so they were out of sight once again from the men at the bridge. They scuttled across the track and back into the forest on the other side. Tracking down the slope, they headed in a diagonal until they once more reached the river, now downstream of the bridge.

The waters of the river gushed by, roaring over the rocks of a short waterfall. Both of them could see there was no chance of crossing.

There was an animal track along the riverbank and they

followed it downstream. They talked little. At one point Affreca saw a rabbit in the trees and shot it with an arrow. It was well past midday when they rounded a bend in the river and found another bridge. Ducking behind some rocks, they surveyed the crossing. Like the last bridge, there were warriors on this one.

'We can't cross here either,' Einar said.

Affreca held up the rabbit she had killed.

'Time to eat,' she said. 'Let's find somewhere safe to cook this.'

They trekked back into the forest until out of sight of the bridge. On a ridge above the track to the bridge Einar got a fire going by striking sparks from the blade of the witch's knife with a stone and it was not long before they were drooling at the aroma of roasting meat.

'If you don't want revenge for what's been done against you then what do you want, Einar?' Affreca said as they pulled apart the rabbit meat to start eating.

Einar sighed as he thought for a moment.

'You know, when I was growing up in Iceland I used to sit on the beach and look at the sun rising or setting over that broad, open ocean,' he said. 'My spirit would cry for leaving. All I thought about was getting away. To go to Norway, to Britain, to Orkney, to Miklagard! Anywhere but that freezing, backward island at the edge of the world with its small-minded farmers and their interminable bickering over who owns what patch of bog. Now it seems like all I want—'

Affreca started as she heard his voice catch in his throat.

'All I want,' Einar continued, 'is to go home.'

'Home? Iceland you mean?' Affreca said.

Einar nodded.

'I want to play knattleikr again,' he said. 'I want to see how the crops are coming on. I want to know my mother is all right.'

He blushed and lowered his eyes.

Affreca made no attempt to conceal her sneer.

'Well you can't,' she said. 'You're still an outlaw there for the next year and a half, in case you've forgotten. Right now you're stuck here in this mess with the rest of us. So you may as well accept whatever fate the Norns are weaving for you.'

'We're trying to change that fate in case you've forgotten,' Einar said. 'And who says our fates are what we think they are? I could still become a great poet. Perhaps that is what the Norns have planned for me.'

The smile returned to Affreca's lips.

'So the son of Thorfinn the Skull Cleaver, heir to the Jarldom of Orkney, still just wants to be a lowly bard?' she said.

'It was always my mother's hope, I suppose,' Einar said. 'She said bards were honoured among the Irish. She gave up so much for me. It was for my sake she ran from Thorfinn. Then she brought me up on her own, with no help in a strange land. She paid for me to have lessons from a skald when she could barely afford to eat herself. I feel I owe it to her.'

Affreca pursed her lips and did not reply. Then she reached out and touched the back of his right hand. Einar looked up and their eyes met.

'That smells delicious.'

A new voice made them both start. Affreca dived for her

bow. Einar dropped the rabbit leg he held and grabbed the witch's knife. He looked round and saw a stranger standing a little way away in the trees. He was a man. He was either completely bald or had shaved his head that way. He wore a long, hooded cloak over a white tunic and very wide breeches that were woven in a checked pattern. He had a long beard that was braided and hung down his chest and his eyes were rimmed by dark paint.

'Who are you?' Einar said.

'I could ask the same of you,' the stranger said. 'I smelled your meal and came to see who was cooking up here.'

Einar sighed. Ulrich had indeed been right. The Wolf Coats would never have made as stupid a mistake as this.

'Please don't be alarmed,' the man said. 'My name is Arinbjorn. I mean you no harm. These are dangerous times. The king's warriors are everywhere and they're not always a force for good. It's best to find out who is travelling these forests as well as us.'

'I am Affreca and he is Einar. We ran into some of those warriors at the last bridge,' Affreca said. 'They stopped us going where we need to. These are bad days when we can't travel our own roads.'

'You're from here?' Arinbjorn said.

'My mother was,' Affreca said and repeated the story Ulrich had suggested.

A look of delight lit up the stranger's face.

'That is wonderful,' he said. 'It's so good to find people of faith who remember their roots. A rootless tree will fall when the winds come.'

Affreca held up a scrap of meat attached to one of the rabbit's thigh bones.

'It's all we have, I'm afraid,' she said. 'We were very hungry.'

'Well if you're still hungry,' the bald man said, 'we would be honoured if you join us for something to eat instead. We have plenty.'

Affreca looked at Einar. He shrugged.

'Why not?' he said. 'I'm still starving.'

'Excellent,' Arinbjorn said. 'Follow me.'

Forty-Three

The stranger led them through the trees, along the top of the ridge then down off it. As they walked, the sound of voices came from up ahead. At the bottom of the slope they came to a clearing beside the track. It was filled with people.

Einar and Affreca looked around. In the centre of the clearing was a large covered wagon. It was the same design as a farm cart but the decorations carved into its dark, polished and oiled wood showed this was no mere cart for moving dung. It was covered top to bottom by intricate carvings of beasts, jötunns, heroes and Gods twisting and turning around each other in eternal frozen conflict. The posts and the end of the yoke shaft were sculpted into dragon's heads. The top of the wagon was covered with a tent made of material that was embroidered with scenes of dragons and horned wizards dancing with crossed spears.

The wagon was surrounded by people; men and women of all ages but no children. A quick reckoning told Einar there was twenty-four of them. They were dressed in odd clothes, baggy trousers, loose tunics and cloaks with long hoods. The skin of their faces and forearms was covered with strange paintings that looked like swirling tree branches or as if a bird had walked through paint then over their skin. They all stared at Einar and Affreca with wide eyes. All of them, that was, except for eight scrawny wretches in ragged clothes who had the look of thralls about them. There were four men and four women. They were of different years but all had the resigned expressions of the enslaved. They stood at the side of the clearing, looking bored and showing little interest in what was going on.

'Who are these people?' Einar muttered out of the side of his mouth.

'I think this is a god wagon,' Affreca said, keeping her voice as low.

Einar had heard tales of this sort of thing. It was a very old custom that still lingered in the wilder parts of the northern realms. Before men knew of the Aesir, the Gods of *Asgard*, they worshipped the Vanir, the Gods of Vannaheim. These elder gods had power over the fertility of the land. Holy people would put the gods in wagons and wheel them throughout the land for some reason. There had been a war between the Aesir and the Vanir and now the race of men knew that Odin and Thor were the most powerful Gods. When people settled Iceland they had left such beliefs behind in the old countries. The only remaining Vanir anyone paid heed to where he grew up were Frey and his sister Freya, The Lord and The Lady.

He remembered Ulrich's words – *The folk here have strange beliefs and odd notions about the gods.*

'You are very perceptive,' Arinbjorn said. Einar realised he had overheard them. 'This is the holy wagon of our God, Lytir. This is the appointed time of year that we pull him through the district so the land is blessed and the crops will grow.'

Einar had heard of Tyr, but never of a God called Lytir, however he judged it best not to say anything.

'Of course, Lytir,' Affreca said, as if she knew what he was talking about. 'My mother brought me up in the traditions of holy Lytir.'

'She did?' Arinbjorn said.

'She did?' Einar said, giving Affreca a questioning look. She hit Einar a surreptitious kick on the shin to keep him quiet.

'How wonderful,' Arinbjorn said. 'And now a daughter of faith has returned to the home of her ancestors.'

He turned to face the rest of the crowd in the clearing.

'These young folk need our help,' he said in a loud voice. 'They have travelled here to the home of this lady's folk, to have their marriage blessed in the customs of our faith.'

Approving murmurs circled around the folk in the clearing.

'But with the war on the king's men are stopping them from getting to where they need to go to.'

This was met with frowns, tuts and shaking heads.

'We must help them,' a man said.

There was general agreement and Einar and Affreca found themselves at the centre of attention. The people in the clearing gathered round, offering words of reassurance.

'They seem all right?' Affreca said, when she and Einar had the chance to speak.

'Slightly odd,' Einar said, 'but yes. Let's go along with them and see what happens.'

Arinbjorn, who from the way the others treated him

seemed to be some sort of leader, joined them. He clapped a hand on Einar's shoulder.

'The Norns are looking after you two,' he said. 'We are the very folk who can get you where you need to go.'

'How come?' Affreca said.

'The wagon of Lytir can go anywhere,' Arinbjorn said. 'No one questions us or tries to stop us. We pay no tolls on any road. If you come with us, you will be able to do the same. Everyone welcomes us because if we are stopped the land will be barren and the crops will not grow. I thought you would know that? Your mother must have told you?'

'Of course she did,' Affreca said. Einar could see her smile was strained. 'I am just surprised you would risk the wrath of King Eirik by travelling at this time.'

'The king's men follow their orders. They do not know why or what they do,' Arinbjorn said. 'Lytir does not care about the wars of today or who sits on the throne. Our task is sacred and you are of our faith, so we will help you.'

'Thank you,' Affreca said.

'And as for your marriage blessing,' Arinbjorn said. 'We can do that too. We will do it tonight, in fact. Now, we need to make you look like one of us.'

The others swarmed around, pulling garments from the back of the wagon. Affreca had a long white cloak thrown over her shoulders and a shining bronze helmet with long, curved horns and a bronze face mask plonked on her head. Einar found himself being put into a strange costume. It was made from the actual skin of a bear, the head of the animal creating a headdress that stood high above his own shoulders and made him a towering size.

The worshippers of Lytir brought food. They had a lot.

Bread, meat, salted fish, berries: There seemed to be no shortage of anything. When they were full they got ready to travel.

The others donned costumes every bit outlandish as the ones they had put Einar and Affreca in. Some of the women had tall headdresses made of straw that trailed around their shoulders. Most had checked cloaks wrapped around their shoulders. Arinbjorn donned a helmet with curved horns that looked like a crescent moon. He wore a fur belt and held two spears. Einar put the bear head on. Inside his vision was limited to a viewing slit. His nose was filled with the smell of musty old fur.

Arinbjorn pointed to the thralls. Without enthusiasm, they got to their feet and took up the draft pole, four on one side and four on the other. Einar realised that the wagon was not pulled by horses, which explained why he could not see any in the clearing. Instead it was hauled by the slaves. They strained forward, turning the wagon in the clearing and dragging it out onto the track that ran through the forest.

'It's indeed lucky for us we met you,' Affreca said.

'Luck has nothing to do with it,' Arinbjorn said. 'We bear the God Lytir himself in this wagon. It is his holy presence that aligns fate.'

Einar glanced at the covered wagon. The expression on his face betrayed his inner thoughts.

The long bearded, bald man chuckled.

'You look sceptical, young man,' Arinbjorn said. 'But your wife here is one of us. She knows what I mean.'

Affreca nodded though Einar could tell she was struggling to look as sincere as she could.

'Let us begin the procession of Lytir,' Arinbjorn said.

Everyone started chanting and dancing. Einar heard someone banging drums behind him while others were playing pipes and he could hear at least one fidla.

They moved out of the clearing onto the track. The slaves pulling the wagon along while everyone else danced around it, chanting and singing. Einar was glad he wore the bear's head. It meant they could not see that he had no idea what the words of their songs were.

A little further down the track they were back at the bridge Einar and Affreca had seen earlier. The warriors guarding it blocked the way across and the procession stopped.

'This is the holy procession of Lytir,' Arinbjorn said. 'We must pass. It is our sacred duty.'

'Have you seen anyone else on your travels?' one of the warriors said. 'Any men who look like they might be fleeing from the battle in Tunsberg?'

'We saw a woman and a man running,' Arinbjorn said. 'They went off into the trees that way.'

He pointed back down the track.

'Very rude they were,' Arinbjorn continued. 'They demanded to know where the river was then pushed some of us out of the way on their way past.'

'Very well,' the lead warrior said. 'On your way.'

The other warriors looked to their leader, surprise on their faces.

'We've already a problem with these Odal rebels,' the lead warrior said. 'If we stop the Lytir wagon the whole country will be up in arms. Let them through.'

The warriors stood aside and the procession set off again, crossing the bridge. As Einar passed by the lead warrior he heard him mutter 'fucking religious fanatics' to his companion. 'The sooner they're away from here the better. They make my skin crawl.'

Then they were over the bridge and heading down the track.

Einar's heart lifted. They had past the first obstacle with ease and were on their way. A nagging voice at the back of his mind, however, agreed with the lead warrior guarding the bridge.

Forty-Four

The procession moved across the countryside for the rest of the day. In places the forest had been cleared to grow crops and the slaves hauled the wagon from farmstead to farmstead. In between they visited forest villages and lonely woodland dwellers. Everywhere they went the people ran out to meet them. Children threw flowers, women danced in circles around them and the farmers gave them bread, meat and vegetables. In return the wagon of the God was hauled over their newly planted fields.

Einar began to enjoy being so popular. His costume in particular seemed to entice the children who laughed and sang as they danced around him.

There were no signs of violence or oppression anywhere in this valley but there were plenty of examples of the district's loyalty to Eirik. His red axe symbol was painted on house sides and farmers who toasted Lytir with ale made sure to also toast the king. Three times they came across companies of Eirik's warriors who stopped them but every time they let the wagon pass.

'Do you think there really is a god in there?' Einar said to Affreca as they watched the slaves toiling to drag the wagon across the furrows of a ploughed field. 'And if there is, do you think it makes the crops grow?'

They had a moment to themselves, apart from the others. Einar had removed the bear's head.

'I don't know,' Affreca said. 'But this lot seem to be doing very well from the idea.'

She cocked her head in the direction of a farmer who was approaching with yet more armfuls of gifts in appreciation of Lytir's future bounty.

'But who cares?' she continued. 'They're taking us right through this country without any problems.'

'You should watch out,' Einar said. 'You've convinced Arinbjorn you're a true believer. What if he asks you to take part in some Lytir ritual?'

'I'll deal with that if it happens,' she said.

Some of the others came over and they had to stop their talk.

They continued their journey for the rest of the day, all the while travelling further down the valley. The air became softer and the birches and pines of the forest became mixed with spruces and other trees of the lower lands. Grasslands became more frequent. As it drew towards evening they arrived at a wide meadow surrounded by trees at the bottom of a wooded slope. Arinbjorn ordered the procession to stop for the night. The followers of Lytir began pitching tents and lighting fires. A very large bonfire was lit right in the middle of the meadow.

The thralls set the pole of the wagon down and flopped down beside it, exhausted from hauling it around all day. It had not been all dancing and gifts for them.

Darkness fell and an air of celebration took over. By the light of the fires the many casks of ale and skins of wine donated by faithful residents of the valley were broken open and the plentiful loaves of bread, salted meats and fermented fish from the same source were shared around. People were singing and those with instruments began playing jigs. The religious folk also brewed another drink in a large pot over one of the fires. This was distributed around all but Affreca, Einar and the thralls.

'It's quite a party,' Affreca said.

'They don't seem too happy,' Einar said, nodding towards the exhausted slaves who were already asleep on the ground under the wagon.

Einar and Affreca sat a little way off from the main group who had gathered around the large fire in the middle of the clearing. They had stripped off their weird costumes and reclined on the ground. They had a wineskin but were sipping it with restraint. It was not the time to let their guard down. Even so, after the stress and effort of the previous days, the warm feeling the drink and the fire induced created welcome relaxation to them both.

'The slaves will be happy soon.'

The voice of Arinbjorn came from the dark nearby, making both Einar and Affreca jump. The bald man seemed to be an expert in appearing when least expected. Einar made a resolution to be careful what he and Affreca discussed even when they thought they were alone.

'How so?' Affreca said.

'The wagon of the God is kept in a secret place, up in the mountains. It's a beautiful place beside a high lake,' Arinbjorn said. His eyes had a faraway look in them as if he were gazing on that mountain lake instead of Einar and Affreca. 'At this time when the earth begins to awaken from winter, we choose eight slaves and bring them to the high place. They take the wagon from the secret place and wash it in the sacred lake. Then they spend the next weeks hauling the wagon through the valley, bringing Lytir's fertility to the land with us. When our sacred work is done they will haul the wagon back up the mountain, wash it in the lake again and it will go to its secret place until next year.'

'So the thralls can get a rest then?' Einar said.

'They will get a rest from all their cares and toil,' Arinbjorn said. His eyes glittered in the firelight. 'No one but the truly faithful must know where the wagon of Lytir is stored. When they finish washing it we drown them in the holy lake. We give them that blessing and the location of where Lytir's wagon is remains secret.'

Einar glanced at the thralls. He doubted that they would see their fate as much of a blessing.

'But we should not be talking about slaves,' Arinbjorn said. 'Tonight is time for celebration. This is your night. Come. We will have your marriage blessing.'

Einar, who was taking a sip of wine at the time, spluttered.

'Thanks, but there's no need to rush,' he said when he had wiped his chin.

'Yes,' Affreca said. 'Tonight is your celebration. We can do the blessing any time.'

'The blessing will form the centre of our celebration,' Arinbjorn said. 'What could be more joyful than having one of our faith return to our homeland. Lytir's wagon will only be travelling through this region for a few more days anyway, so the time is right tonight.'

Einar exchanged glances with Affreca. She shrugged. They did not have much choice. Einar reasoned to himself that it should cause no harm. They had to continue the pretence. What could be the consequences of a couple who were not really married receiving a blessing from a god neither of them had heard of?

The nagging, uneasy voice at the back of his mind that had troubled him all day was still muttering away, however.

Arinbjorn led them to the centre of the clearing, beside the main bonfire. Their arrival was greeted by an approving murmur that went around the people gathered at the fire. Einar saw them turn pleasant, welcoming faces at him and Affreca. Despite their warmth, Einar noticed that their eyes looked glassy which he put down to the wine and beer they had drunk. Their smiles seemed stretched across their bony faces though as if they were making the expression for outward show, while the hearts that lay behind them were empty. This was no doubt a trick of the flickering firelight but it still made them look a little uncanny.

'Let us begin the blessing ceremony,' Arinbjorn said in a loud voice.

The crowd let out squeals that were almost childlike in their delight. Some of them began to beat drums, thankfully in a much more relaxed rhythm than Einar and Affreca had been subjected to in the witch's cave the night before.

'Wait while I get ready,' Arinbjorn said and he disappeared into the darkness leaving Einar and Affreca to smile in an awkward manner at the crowd around them.

'Lytir's blessings be upon you,' one of the watchers said.

'Let the God rain down his favour on the happy couple,' another said.

'May he make your union fruitful as he makes the land fruitful,' a third added.

Einar sent a sharp look in the direction of the speaker. The nagging voice in his head got louder.

Arinbjorn leapt back into the firelight. Affreca started. Einar's heart sank. The bald man was wearing the horned helmet and fur belt he had worn in the procession earlier, but apart from that he was now completely naked. He bore his two spears in one hand. The worshippers of Lytir let out a little cheer.

'Beloved faithful, children of Lytir,' Arinbjorn said, 'we gather tonight under the holy moon to witness the joining of the bodies of two young people. One already is of your people, the other we welcome into your family. From these seeds will grow a whole new tree of your faithful.'

Einar looked at Affreca. He could tell that like him, she was torn between trying not to antagonise the people around them but desperate to escape from whatever strange ritual they were now going to be subjected to. He looked around and saw Lytir's faithful had formed a tight circle around the fire. To leave they would have to push through them. If they did that the crowd would not react well.

The eyes which Einar had thought glassy before now looked full of glee along with something else he could not quite place. Expectation perhaps? They had the look of hungry people about to tuck into a feast.

Arinbjorn was calling out to the night sky, invoking Lytir to come and join them.

'I thought he was in the wagon?' Einar said in a mutter.

'Never mind where he is,' Affreca said. 'I don't like where

this is going. If we don't find a way out we might actually end up married. Or worse.'

Einar was unsure whether or not he was offended by her words, but he shared her desire to get away. He could not think of a way out, however. Not without causing great offence.

'Look, maybe it will all be over quickly,' he said out of the corner of his mouth. 'We'll have to go along with it or we'll annoy them. We need to get to that town by tomorrow night, remember?'

'Lytir bless this couple,' Arinbjorn said. 'Now we will proceed to the fulfilment of their bond.'

To Einar's consternation some of the people watching were starting to take off their clothes as well. To his further consternation the state of excitement some of the men were in was clear.

'All right I was wrong,' he said to Affreca, grasping her arm. 'We need to get out of here.'

Arinbjorn was looking at them, an expression of expectation on his face.

'What?' Affreca said.

'You must undress,' Arinbjorn said, his expression changing to a puzzled smile. 'Surely you do not expect to join your bodies in sacred union with your clothes on?'

'Now wait a moment,' Einar said, holding up his hands.

'There is no need for shyness,' Arinbjorn said. 'We will all be naked.'

'We're leaving,' Affreca said, now speaking loud enough for all to hear.

A collective gasp rose from the watching crowd.

Arinbjorn's eyes widened. Sudden anger blazed in them.

'No you are not,' he thundered, levelling his two spears in their direction. 'We are in the presence of the God. We have summoned him here to witness and bless your union. Lytir will not be disappointed!'

'More like you won't be disappointed,' Affreca said.

Three men in the crowd now had knives in their hands. The blades glittered in the firelight as they held them up so Einar and Affreca could see them. Einar cursed himself for leaving his own weapons on the ground at the edge of the clearing with their wineskin and Affreca's bow.

'Now get undressed,' Arinbjorn said, prodding Einar with the points of his spears. He spoke through gritted teeth, saliva bubbling across his lips.

Einar looked at Affreca. It seemed there was little they could do. Outnumbered, surrounded and with no weapons, they could try to run but would not even get past the bonfire.

Affreca began unlacing the britches she wore.

'Troll!'

A new voice came from the darkness. The sound of crashing footsteps came from the trees beyond the clearing. Everyone turned around. A man came running out of the forest into the firelight.

'There's a troll chasing me,' he shouted. His accent was a little strange. 'An *ettin*! Run for your lives.'

The people in the clearing all looked bemused. Then in unison they flinched as a feral roar came from the trees. Another figure came out of the forest. It was man shaped but bigger than most men, its limbs packed with heavy muscle. Like Arinbjorn, the newcomer was nearly naked but unlike him, the firelight showed that the skin that covered its body was black like the night.

Frightened screams rose from the people in the clearing. Total chaos erupted. The ring around the bonfire dissolved and the people started running this way and that, all trying to flee the terrifying sight. Seeing Arinbjorn was distracted, Einar stepped close to him, moving inside the points of his spears. Arinbjorn caught the movement out of the corner of his eye and was just turning back when Einar slammed his fist into his jaw. The naked man toppled backwards, unconscious.

'Let's go,' Einar said, turning to Affreca only to see she was already running towards where they had left their belongings. He went after her.

Behind him, Surt, who Einar had already recognised as the 'troll', threw back his head and let out an appalling screech. This evoked even more panic in the followers of Lytir who began fleeing into the trees.

As he ran by the parked wagon, Einar saw the thralls, roused from their sleep by the noise, looking around in bewilderment.

'If I were you I'd start running,' he said to them. 'And I would not stop until I was well away from here. Get away from these people if you value your lives.'

Then he and Affreca gathered their belongings and ran off into the trees.

Forty-Five

Einar thought Wulfhelm would never stop laughing.
The Saxon held his ribs and rocked from side to side, tears running down his cheeks into his long moustache.

'It's not that funny,' Einar said.

'The look on your face,' Wulfhelm said, his words came as squeaks amid his giggling. 'I only wish we could have waited longer. He wouldn't let me though.'

He gestured to Surt, who was now wearing his jerkin and breeches again. They sat around a campfire they had made in the forest far enough away from the track that the light would not be seen. The fire was in a pit and its smoke drawn off through a trench so it dissipated through turf, providing some disguise. Wulfhelm had picked up a couple of wineskins dropped by the fleeing faithful of Lytir and they shared them as they talked.

'I would not let the lady be shamed,' Surt said, wiping his mouth. At first he had said he could not drink the wine, then had reneged and now supped with the others.

'Were you going to take your breeches off?' Wulfhelm said.

'She started to,' Einar nodded towards Affreca.

'Perhaps we were too hasty,' Wulfhelm said. 'I'd have liked to have seen that.'

'If you *had* seen that,' Affreca said, 'I'd now be taking your eyes out with my new knife.'

Wulfhelm's grin faded a bit.

'I can't believe they all fell for your trick though,' Einar said. 'They really thought you were a troll, Surt.'

'People like them,' Surt said, 'they are easily fooled. They are already too quick to believe. They believe in a God who is wheeled around in a farm cart. Their minds are weak and lack knowledge of the world. People like them have never seen anyone who does not look like them. When they see someone who does, they look on them with suspicion. It's the same the world over.'

'I see. And when they see someone with black skin,' Einar said. 'To them it's like seeing someone from one of the other Nine Worlds. They are ready to believe they see a troll.'

'How long were you following us?' Affreca said.

'Since late afternoon,' Surt said. 'Despite what Ulrich said, we came to our own conclusion that we would not go far without raising suspicions. We stuck to the woods and crossed the countryside instead of the tracks. Then we heard this terrible racket; the drums and singing of those Lytir folk. You were at a farm. We went to spy on what was happening and saw a marvel! A dancing bear. Then to our amazement the bear took its head off and underneath was Einar. It wasn't long until we spotted you, Affreca, too. From then on we just followed you from the woods.'

'It was a good thing we did,' Wulfhelm said. 'Or else you'd be man and wife now. You weren't the only old friends we saw today either.'

'You saw the Wolf Coats?' Affreca said. Her face lit up in a smile.

Wulfhelm shook his head. Affreca's smile died.

'He thinks they've got rid of us so they can travel faster,' she said, nodding towards Einar.

'Maybe he's right. We saw nothing of them,' Wulfhelm said. 'But we did see Thorir from the mountain and his big friend Bjorgolf. They had eight men with weapons with them and they were on horses. They were riding down one of the forest tracks. That bastard Thorir had my helmet, the one with the wolf tail crest, on.'

'I have six arrows left,' Affreca said, peering into her arrow bag. 'Not enough for all of them.'

'They didn't see you?' Einar said.

'I don't think we'd be telling you this if they did,' Surt said. 'They're looking for us though. Why else would they have come down from their mountain?'

'We did kill his wife, I suppose,' Affreca said.

'Thorir will want revenge for that,' Wulfhelm said.

For a few moments they sat in silence, each thinking about the situation they were in.

'How did you get across the river?' Einar said after a time. 'The bridges were all guarded. The river was like a torrent.'

'We crossed it almost as soon as we left the Wolf Coats,' Surt said. 'When it was still just a big stream. We got wet but it was still manageable. It is only further down the stream that it becomes the convergence of many waters and the snows melting on the mountain.'

'So you were on the other side of the river from the start?' Einar shook his head. 'We wouldn't have had half the trouble we did if we'd thought of that.'

Maybe Ulrich was right to abandon us, he thought.

Einar handed the witch's knife to Affreca. He had been looking at it, trying to read the runes etched onto its blade.

'So what does it say?' she said.

'I don't know,' Einar said. 'I've not seen runes like these before. They're maybe some sort of secret seiðr tongue. Perhaps Ulrich would know. The Wolf Coats are keen on secret things.'

'That's quite an impressive weapon,' Wulfhelm said. 'You should give it a name.'

'I was thinking of calling it *seiðkonar feikinstafir*,' Affreca said, watching how the firelight danced on the blade.

'Witch's curse?' Einar said. 'I wouldn't call it that in front of Ulrich. Not with Gunnhild's curse hanging over us.'

'All right then,' Affreca said. 'I'll call it *seiðkonar heita*. Witch's Promise.'

'So what do we do now?' Wulfhelm said. Einar realised he was asking him.

'What do you mean?' he said.

'What's our next move?' the Saxon said. 'If you think Ulrich has got rid of us then what do we do?'

'Ulrich has not done that,' Affreca said.

'First thing, we should get some sleep,' Einar said. 'I'm exhausted. Then tomorrow we should carry on towards the sea. Even if Ulrich has left us…'

He glanced at Affreca.

'… I don't see what else we can do. Finding a ship and sailing away is as good a plan as any. We keep going 'til we reach that town, we find a ship that can get us out of here and if Ulrich is there to meet us then all the better.'

'Most of this realm are hunting for us,' Wulfhelm said.

'More people will live on the coast than in these woods. It'll get more and more dangerous the further down the valley we go.'

'Do you want to live out the rest of your days in a forest?' Einar said. 'We still have to get to Grimnir so he can tell us how to break the queen's curse, remember? And there is Halgerd. What about her farm?'

Wulfhelm chuckled once more.

'Ah yes. The beautiful young maiden with the inheritance problem,' he said. 'I do believe the boy is in love.'

Einar scowled. He was getting tired of the Saxon's jokes.

'I'm off to sleep,' he said. 'With all this laughing you'll find it too hard to get to sleep, Wulfhelm, so you take the first watch.'

Affreca raised a hand.

'I'll do the second one,' she said.

'You do third and I'll do last then,' Einar said to Surt. Then he left the campfire and crawled into the shelter he had built a little way away. Moments later he was asleep.

He was not sure how long he slept but when he woke it was still the dark of night.

Someone was leaning over him.

It was Affreca. There was enough light from the stars and moon for him to recognise the shape of her head. He could almost sense her presence too. He knew her smell. Her face was very close to his. He felt her hot breath on his cheek.

Reacting on instinct, Einar reached up with his left hand, running it around the back of her shorn head and pulling her closer as he raised his lips to meet hers. As their mouths met he moved his right hand up the side of her chest, feeling its way towards her breast.

She put her hands on either side of his face. Einar felt sharp, intense pain as she twisted both his ears. He pulled his head back from her at the same time she did the same.

'Get off me, you idiot,' Affreca hissed in a whisper. 'Someone's coming!'

'I thought... because of earlier,' Einar began.

'Like I told you before,' she said, 'you think too much. Get your spear ready.'

She handed him the head of his spear and Einar fumbled in the dark for the shaft. When he found it he slotted the blade onto the top. He did his best to make it secure but he had neither the time or the tools to hammer in the rivets. Then he crept after Affreca, remembering to keep the top end of the spear raised so the blade would not fall off.

Affreca stopped near the now smouldering campfire. Einar could see little more than an outline of her in the dark. She was pointing. Using the trick Ulrich had taught them for seeing in the dark, Einar looked to the right of where Affreca was indicating. His peripheral sight saw a shape flit between two trees. It was low and swift. Was it a man, running at a crouch?

Affreca drew her bow. She stood still as a stone, waiting. Einar grasped the spear shaft. He placed his feet apart, right behind left, knees bent, ready if someone came charging.

There was a rustle in the undergrowth to their right. Affreca spun and let her arrow fly. The missile shot through the trees but as far as they could tell hit nothing. There was no cry, no thump of a body falling.

Einar caught another movement from the corner of his eye, this time to his left. He turned holding the spear before him.

There was a rustle from the undergrowth. Something rushed at him. It was black and low to the ground. Einar just had time to drop to a crouch. There was a snarl then it was on him. He felt something crash into him. It seemed like a frenzied ball of fur and claws that tore at his clothes.

'Wolves!' he shouted.

The creature on him drove its snout at his throat. He felt its hot breath and a spray of drool splattered his face.

Spear now in his right hand, with a roar he grabbed a handful of the beast's fur and pulled it away from him. He kicked at it with his left foot. The creature twisted fast and sunk its teeth into his ankle. Einar cried out as he felt the sharp teeth sink into his flesh. He shoved the spear down at the wolf. He felt it sink into the beast's flesh. Its snarls turned to a high whimper and it twisted away.

Whining, the wolf ran off into the dark. Einar realised his spear felt lighter than before. He swore as he felt the top of the shaft and realised the head had come off. The wolf had run off with the blade still embedded in its body.

He saw another black shape streaking toward him in the dark. Something shot past him in the opposite direction. The wolf stopped its charge, stumbled, let out a snuffling grunt then fell over. Affreca stepped past him, bow in hand.

'Got it,' she said.

'What's going on?' Wulfhelm's voice came out of the dark.

'Wolves,' Einar called over his shoulder. 'Get that fire going again. It'll keep them away.'

Surt was up now too and he and Wulfhelm set to work on the fire. Einar and Affreca stood ready, waiting for anything that could come from the dark. Einar, realising that the spear shaft was now little more than a long stick, hoped that if another wolf came at them Affreca could shoot it before it got to him.

'Are you all right?' Affreca said.

'It bit my ankle but I think it's fine,' Einar said.

Before long, the fire was blazing again and the wolves had not returned. They started to relax again and gathered around the warmth of the flames and the light that kept the wild creatures of the night at bay. Einar knew there would be no more sleep that night.

Affreca dragged the dead wolf she had shot over to the fire and began working on it with the witch's knife.

'I'm taking its pelt,' she said, catching sight of Einar's questioning look. 'The Wolf Coats lost all theirs. This will be the first replacement for them. I'll give it to them when we meet them again.'

Einar looked into the dark, wondering what was out there, watching from the dark.

'I only hope they're there to meet us,' he said.

Forty-Six

At first light they set off. They moved through the forest until they found the river again, then followed it onwards as it got wider and twisted and turned its way to the sea. The forest gave way to open meadowland.

Einar became more nervous the further they travelled. They stayed off the main tracks but the wooded areas got more sparse and farmsteads, villages and settlements were more frequent. By mid-morning the ground was almost level and they knew if they were to keep going they would have to risk moving onto the track that followed the river's course. It would be risky but they would be more likely to attract attention running across someone's newly planted crops than walking down the road like normal folk.

The river had widened into a broad waterway. It was still full to the brim but its width meant the water was more of a swift, full flow than the narrow torrent it had been higher up the valley.

Surt kept his hood up as they joined the main track. Their progress increased but so did the number of people they met. A farmer's cart rumbled past, then a group of women came walking the other way. All of them smiled and walked on but a couple of them cast second glances at the spears carried by Wulfhelm and Surt.

'I wish there was some other way to cross this valley,' Einar said.

Wulfhelm stopped.

'Maybe there is,' he said, pointing ahead.

A little way ahead was a long building that might have been an inn beside the river. A wooden jetty stood near it on the riverbank. On the other side of the river was another, identical jetty. A rope crossed the river between the two, suspended not far above the water. A rectangular, flat skiff bobbed in the water, tied to the near jetty and a thin, grey-haired old man crouched on it, a long pole for propelling the boat held against his shoulder. He looked like he was dozing in the morning sun.

'You think we should take that ferry to the other side?' Affreca said, screwing up her face in puzzlement.

'Let's see,' Wulfhelm said.

A man came out of the longhouse and they waited for a moment as he went to an outbuilding then came back struggling under the weight of a large wooden barrel. Once he had gone inside again the little company approached the old man on his boat.

Wulfhelm clambered straight onto the skiff and gestured to the others to do the same. Their footfalls and the rocking they caused started the boatman awake.

'You want to cross?' he said, getting slowly to his feet. 'Well the fee is extra this time of year. All the meltwater means the river is swift and the current is strong. It's hard work to get across. Especially for an old man like me.'

'We want to get downstream, old man,' Wulfhelm said.

'How much do you want to take us right to the big town down by the sea?'

The old man frowned.

'Town?' he said. 'You mean Lundr?'

'If that's the large town on the estuary, then yes,' Wulfhelm said. 'We saw it from the top of the valley. We need to find a sea-going ship.'

'That can only be Lundr,' the boatman said. 'I won't take you there. I only ferry across the river. If I take you downstream how will I get my boat back up here? Upstream? Against the flow? No. I don't care what you pay me.'

He folded his arms.

'Very well,' Wulfhelm said. 'Take us across.'

'The fee is—' the boatman began but Wulfhelm cut him off.

'We'll pay you whatever you ask,' he said. 'In fact I'll give you extra silver if you go as fast as you can.'

The old man smiled, revealing toothless gums. He untied the skiff and pushed the boat away from the jetty with the pole. Then he set the pole down and began hauling on the rope. The knotted muscles on his scrawny arms tightened as he moved the boat across the river.

'If you want a ship that's the right place to go,' he said. 'There are always ships there. Everyone who sails the seas past this realm must stop there and pay Viking tax.'

'Viking tax?' Einar said. 'What's that?'

'The seas around the coast here are dangerous,' the boatman said. 'There are many Vikings lurking in the creeks and bays, waiting to rob ships voyaging from Tunsberg up to Erindalr. If skippers dock their ships in Lundr and pay the Viking tax to the lendrmaðr of this district, Finn

Thorsteinsson, he makes sure that they're not attacked by Vikings.'

'And what if they don't?' Affreca said.

'Then Lord Finn makes sure they *are* attacked by Vikings,' the old man said, his smile returning. 'It would be a brave man who tries to sail past without paying the fee.'

'Christ's bones! Is every nobleman in this country a robber?' Wulfhelm said.

'Careful what you say, stranger.' The old man said with a sniff. 'Lord Finn only takes tribute from outlanders. And the king in turn demands payments from him. Where is he to get that silver from?'

There was a moment of silence. They were approaching the middle of the river. The rope was bowed downstream between the two jetties and Einar could tell that the pull the river current was putting on the boat was strong. He also noticed the suspicious glances the boatman cast in the direction of his passengers every time he moved his hands along the rope.

'How come you don't know of the Lord Finn or what Lundr is called?' he said. 'Who are you people with your strange accents and talk of foreign Gods? Who carry spears and a bow? Why does that one not take his hood down, even though it's a beautiful morning?'

He nodded at Surt.

'We are simple travellers, friend,' Wulfhelm said. 'That is all you need to know. You must meet many travellers in your work. We're no different to any others.'

'I meet many travellers, true,' the old man said. 'But these are dangerous times. The kingdom is at war with itself. A company of the king's men rode past early this morning.

They warned everyone to be on the lookout for strangers. People like you. A company of desperate men are running from the king's justice. They have committed many murders. There is even a rumour this morning that a troll is loose in the upper valley and it's eating people.'

'We're not man-eating trolls, friend,' Wulfhelm said, with a nervous laugh. 'Surely you can see that?'

'No, I don't believe in such things,' the boatman said. 'But you *might* be desperate men. I need to be careful who I am ferrying across this river. This crossing is hard enough with the swollen river. If the king's men found out I was helping outlaws I would pay dearly for it. I must consider if the price of ferrying you across is worth the risk.'

He shot a sly glance at Wulfhelm.

'I understand, friend,' Wulfhelm said. 'Desperate men must expect to pay dearly too if they need to get across this river. Don't worry. We have plenty of silver to make this trip worth your while.'

Einar gave Wulfhelm a questioning look but the Saxon ignored him.

The boatman licked his lips, then let go of the rope. The boat started to drift downstream, tightening the rope across his body but that in turn stopped it drifting further with the current. The old man held out his hand towards Wulfhelm.

'I will go no further until you give me what I'm owed,' he said. 'If this work puts me in danger then I want paid now.'

'I understand. I would too,' Wulfhelm said, stepping towards the old man. He planted his right hand in the centre of the boatman's chest and shoved, adding momentum to the drag from the rope.

The old man's eyes widened as he shot backwards, arms

rotating like windmills, off the boat. He landed in the water, sending up a splash that was surprising in its size for a person so slight.

Released from the rope, the strong current dragged the boat downstream straight away. Wulfhelm grabbed the boatman's pole and began punting it along as well. In moments they had left the crossing point behind. By the time the boatman resurfaced they were already too far away to make out the words of the curses he shouted after them.

'He'll tell the king's men about us,' Affreca said.

'If they were here this morning they won't be back for some time, I'd say,' Wulfhelm said. 'And by then we'll be well down river.'

It was not long, however, before they heard the sound of hooves beating on the track that followed the river. From the direction they had come, a horse with two men on it came galloping after them. Einar squinted and saw what looked like the man they had seen with the barrel earlier and the dripping-wet boatman clinging on behind him.

Forty-Seven

'Do you think they're chasing us?' Surt said.
'Either that or riding for help,' Einar said.
'I hadn't thought of that,' Wulfhelm looked. 'Lady do you think you could do anything to discourage them with your bow? It's a hard shot, I know.'

Affreca took an arrow from her dwindling supply and made a face. Then she notched an arrow and drew her bow. For several moments she tracked the riders as they galloped closer. Einar wondered if she could really hit them. She stood on a moving platform and she was trying to hit a target that was maybe sixty paces away and also moving but at a different speed.

Affreca loosed her shot. The bowstring twanged and the arrow sailed in an arc, back towards the riders on the track. Then it dropped, thumping into the thick flesh of the horse's left flank.

The wounded creature let out a whinny. It reared up on its hind legs, throwing the two men on its back to the ground, then took off back the way it had come, though moving with an injured limp.

'An amazing shot,' Wulfhelm said, clapping her on the

shoulder. 'Even if you did miss them that should slow them down a bit.'

'I didn't miss,' Affreca said. 'I was aiming for the horse. They're just simple country people. We're not murderers, despite what Eirik's men are telling folk.'

The boat slid on down the river, leaving the men on the bank far behind. Einar, Surt and Affreca sat down while Wulfhelm stood, steering the boat with pushes on the long pole and keeping it midstream. Surt opened a leather bag the boatman had left on the skiff and found to their collective delight that there was bread and a lump of cheese inside. As they drifted along in the sunshine, chewing on the bread, Einar reflected that were it not for the lurking danger all around, the experience would have been most agreeable. He also thought about the boatman's words about how murderers were at large and wondered just where Ulrich and the Wolf Coats were, and what they were up to.

As they drifted downstream, carried along by the fast current, they passed by farmsteads and several little villages that nestled beside the river. Wulfhelm waved at children playing on the riverbank, farmers passing by, anyone who they passed.

'Should you really be drawing attention to us like that?' Einar said.

'What I'm doing,' Wulfhelm said, as he nodded and smiled at a young woman gathering rushes at the water's edge, 'is acting like I belong here. Like I have nothing to hide. You should do the same.'

Einar saw he had a point and from then on he did. They made good progress and by afternoon Einar judged they must be well on their way to Lundr.

They were travelling along a straight stretch of the river with woods on either side when the peace was broken once again by the sound of beating hooves approaching. This time it was more than one.

Einar stood up. Looking back he saw horsemen rounding the corner behind them. The sun glinted on metal and he made out helmets and spears. They had shields across their backs. There was six of them and they were riding hard along the track beside the river. A seventh horseman rounded the corner a little way behind them.

'It's the ferryman,' Einar said, recognising the scrawny figure on the last horse. 'He must have found some of Eirik's warriors to tell about us.'

'He's a persistent old bastard, I'll give him that,' Wulfhelm said.

'I don't have enough arrows for all of them,' Affreca said.

'We'll have to run for it,' Einar said.

'Head for the opposite bank, ditch the boat and run,' Wulfhelm said. 'By the time they find a bridge to get across we'll be well away.'

He shoved the pole into the river and propelled the skiff towards the far side of the river as the horsemen galloped closer. Einar, Affreca and Surt dipped their arms in the river to lend their efforts to moving the boat. Wulfhelm drove with the pole again and the skiff went into the reeds at the water's edge where it halted, half grounded on the muddy river bottom.

They leapt off the boat into the reeds and began scrambling up the bank. Einar glanced over his shoulder and saw that they had misjudged the horsemen. Instead of heading on down the other side in search of a bridge they simply rode their horses straight into the river. The horses started swimming and despite the current that dragged at them Einar could see it would not be long before they were across and on him and the others. They could not outrun horses.

He stopped and turned, jumping back onto the boat.

'What are you doing?' Affreca called from up the bank. She had turned too.

Einar grabbed the end of the long punting pole from where Wulfhelm had dropped it. He jumped back onto the riverbank again, dragging the pole behind him.

The first horseman was almost across. Einar crouched, kneeling on one knee, the pole lying on the ground in the grass before him. The first horseman struggled out of the water onto the riverbank beside the boat. He levelled his spear, kicked his heels on his mount's flanks and rode straight at Einar.

The other five horsemen were coming out of the river behind him. At the last moment, Einar raised the pole, aiming the far end at the first rider's chest. The horseman rode straight onto it. It was so long it outreached his spear. It struck the rider and propelled him off the back of his mount. He tumbled head over heels, landed heavily on the riverbank and went straight under the hooves of the horse and rider coming after him. There was a sickening crunch of bones.

Einar dropped the pole, turned and ran. Affreca was standing behind him, an arrow notched in her bow. She let it fly. It streaked over Einar's head and hit the second horseman in the face, just below where his visor stopped.

Intent on chasing Einar, the rider had never even seen it coming. He toppled off his mount.

Seeing what had happened to their fellows, the remaining four riders stopped. They started to unsling the shields from their backs so as to be able to protect themselves. Each shield had a red axe painted on it, which removed any doubt that these were warriors of King Eirik.

Einar ran as fast as he could up the bank. Wulfhelm came running back towards him. He hurled his spear at the clump of horsemen who were still struggling to get their shields into a position where they could protect themselves. The Saxon used the whole strength of his body: Arm, shoulder, hips and thigh all combined to launch the spear. The force of his throw was such he sent himself off balance, right arm outstretched before him, hopping for a few steps as he tried not to fall. The weapon hurtled through the air. It struck one of the riders in the right thigh. The blade went right through and into the side of the horse he was on. The creature cried out and reared up. The warrior riding it screamed in pain as the horse twisted and fell sideways. Horse and rider, impaled together, crashed into their companions, sending the other horses staggering and wheeling in different directions. The wounded horse and rider collapsed onto the grounded boat, the weight of the animal smashing the end of the skiff to splinters.

The remaining three riders fought to get control of their animals. With a blood-chilling howl, Surt came charging back down the riverbank, his spear grasped in both hands. Einar ran after him, dipping to pick up the fallen spear of the first fallen rider on the way past. The sight of Surt rushing towards them, combined with the swift loss of their three companions, drove panic into the riders. One of them dropped his shield, turned his horse and began to gallop away along the riverbank. Affreca shot him in the back, her arrow drilling through his mail shirt and his chest beneath. The man threw his arms in the air as if in some sort of protest then fell off the horse.

'Don't let them get away,' Affreca shouted. 'Or they'll be back after us with more men.'

The last two horsemen turned their steeds to ride back into the river. Surt was just behind them and launched himself sideways, driving his shoulder into the flank of the nearest horse. Though heavier than Surt, his shove was enough to knock the back end of the animal sideways. The unexpected movement toppled the rider from its back and Einar drove his spear into him as he fell into the water.

Surt dropped his spear and with a huge leap, reached up and threw his arms around the shoulders of the last rider. He fell back again, his weight pulling the horseman off his mount. Both men landed in the water with a tremendous splash. Einar waded into the water. The fallen horseman, spear still in one hand, was struggling to rise. Einar kicked him back down. Surt rose from the water and fell on him. He straddled the fallen man, ripped the helmet off his head, tearing its leather thongs asunder with sheer brute strength, then tossed it aside.

The warrior tried to bring his spear up at Surt but the black-skinned man was too close to him and he could not stab him. Surt smashed a big fist into the warrior's now unprotected face. He hit him again, then a third time. The fallen rider went limp and Surt let go of him, letting him sink backwards into the water.

Panting, Surt and Einar staggered back to the riverbank. Wulfhelm, now armed with the witch's knife, finished off the wounded rider he had speared by cutting his throat. Then he went round the other three fallen riders on the riverbank and made sure they were dead too.

Quiet returned to the river. The four unwounded horses, now with no riders, stomped about, unsure where to go. Blood draining from the dead men formed a long slick that trailed out into the river. Surt, Einar and Wulfhelm walked up the bank to rejoin Affreca.

The boatman, still sitting on his horse on the other side of the river was watching them, a look of astonished dismay on his face.

'Here's your second chance to shoot him,' Wulfhelm said.

Affreca took her last arrow and notched her bow. She drew the string back to her ear and levelled it at the boatman.

'Old man,' she said in a loud voice so that he could hear her from the other side. 'You have seen me shoot. You know I can hit you from here with ease.'

Einar saw the boatman go pale and swallow.

'But I will let you go,' Affreca said. 'If you swear you will not bring any more of the king's men after us.'

The boatman's jaw fell open. He began to nod vigorously.

'I swear it, lady,' he said. 'I swear it. Thank you.'

'Very well,' Affreca said. 'Now go. Your boat is here for you when you find another way across the river.'

The old man turned his horse and rode away in the direction he had come from.

'You let him go?' Wulfhelm said.

'I've one arrow left,' Affreca said. 'And I won't waste one on him. And like I said before, we aren't murderers.'

Looking at the carnage on the riverbank, Einar nearly laughed out loud at her words.

'You think he'll keep his word? I don't. That old bastard will find more of the king's men,' Wulfhelm said. 'They'll be after us again soon. Things will be even more dangerous for us now and we've no boat any more.'

He pointed at the shattered remains of the boat.

'You should have killed him,' he said.

Affreca just scowled.

Einar looked at one of the dropped shields with its red painted axe. He looked at the helmet Surt had torn from the last warrior's head.

'Round up those horses,' he said. 'I have an idea.'

Forty-Eight

The sun was sinking as they arrived at Lundr.

It was a large town, though not as big as Tunsberg. It was surrounded on three sides by an earth rampart topped with a wooden palisade, and on one side by the sea. The settlement sat at the mouth of the river Einar, Affreca, Surt and Wulfhelm had followed all the way from the mountains to here where it sprawled wide, emptying into the sea. As they approached along the track, they could see a forest of masts rising from the town's harbour.

'It looks like we are coming to the right place to find a ship,' Wulfhelm said.

He and Einar were now wearing the helmets and mail they had stripped from the dead warriors on the riverbank. Their broad, round shields, each painted with the red axe of King Eirik, were slung across their backs. They rode on their horses, a spear in one hand and reins in the other.

Affreca and Surt rode in front of them on the other two horses. In contrast to Einar and Wulfhelm they still wore the old peasant clothes and furs they had come down from the mountain in. Surt in particular must have been very uncomfortable. He was swathed in furs and had his fur hood up so the colour of his skin was hidden. They had no weapons and rode with their hands together, as if they were bound.

'A couple of rebel prisoners,' Einar said to the warriors who guarded the gate in the ramparts of Lundr. 'We caught them painting Odal runes on runestones up the valley.'

The lead guard shook his head.

'Idiots,' he said. 'Folk should stay in the place the Gods put them in. He's a big lad.'

He nodded at Surt.

'Must have been hard to capture?'

'Not big enough,' Einar said, grinning.

'There's no horses allowed inside the walls so leave them in the corral,' the gate guard said, pointing to a fenced off area outside the ramparts where other horses were penned. 'And then take these two to Lord Finn's hall. He'll see that they're hung.'

They took the horses to the corral and left them there.

'What have they got against horses?' Surt said.

'It's not that unusual,' Wulfhelm said. 'The town is probably crowded enough without horses and other animals as well.'

They walked back towards the gate, Einar and Wulfhelm walking Surt and Affreca before them at spear point. The guards stood aside to let them in. As they passed by, the sound of many dogs barking made them look back. A large group of riders were approaching along the road. They were surrounded by a pack of dogs.

Einar narrowed his eyes, peering towards the approaching group.

'It's Atli and Edwin,' he said, recognising the lead riders.

'Carry on as before,' Wulfhelm said, speaking in a

low voice. 'If we start running they'll know something is wrong.'

They walked on through the gate, though with quicker steps than before.

'You there.'

Einar heard Atli's voice from behind him.

'We're on a special task for King Eirik. We got a message that Lord Finn has captured one of the fugitives we're chasing,' he said. 'We came as soon as we heard.'

'We've got him,' the gate guard said. 'Lord Finn will hand him over to you. You'll have to leave the horses outside at the corral. Those dogs too. Can't you control them a bit better? They seem very excited.'

The dogs were yelping and barking.

Einar and the others, in no doubt that it was their scent that was agitating the dogs, kept walking. Inside the rampart they found themselves at the top of a street made by a long wooden walkway that kept the feet of the denizens of the town out of the filth and muck that flowed beneath. The walkway was lined on either side with longhouses that opened onto it. Some had stalls displaying merchants' wares and men and women hawking them. The street was crowded, busy and very straight. Einar realised at once if they kept going when Atli and Edwin followed through the gate they would be walking directly in front of them. They were bound to see them.

The heavy wooden gates of the town stood opened inwards. Einar shoved the others sideways then behind the gate on the right.

'How did they know we were here?' Affreca said, talking in a hoarse whisper.

'They can't know,' Einar said. 'This Lord Finn must have caught someone else.'

'What now?' Surt said.

'We need to find out who they've got,' Einar said. 'But as Wulfhelm said, we need to carry on as before. You two go to the harbour and see if you can find a ship we can take. Wulfhelm and I will go to Finn's hall and see if we can find out what is going on.'

'What are you going to do?' Affreca said. 'Just walk straight in?'

Einar tapped the rim of his shield with the red axe painted on it against the visored helmet he wore and smiled.

'Yes,' he said.

They waited as Atli, Edwin and the contingent of warriors with them trooped into the town and down the street, oblivious to the group watching them from behind the gate. Einar could sense Wulfhelm stiffen beside him as he saw his former brother warriors, Edwin's bodyguard, stomp past. Behind them came around twenty of Eirik's men. The company was splashed with mud and covered by dust. They carried packs and leather sleeping bags over their shoulders as well as their shields, each one of which was painted with the bloody red axe. They walked with the tread of weary men who had spent the last day or so living off the land.

Atli also carried a wool bag. Einar remembered that he had the wolf pelts of Ulrich and the others inside it. His lip curled at the sight of Bragi with Bodvar's wolfskin around his shoulders. The berserker strutted down the walkway, glaring at everyone who he past.

'Let's go,' Einar said when they had all gone by. He handed Surt his spear and gave Affreca back her bow and her arrow bag with the lone arrow rattling inside. Affreca gave him the witch's knife.

'Take Witch's Promise,' she said. 'May she bring you luck.'

Einar and Wulfhelm ducked out of the alley and walked down the street, keeping a respectful distance behind Atli and Edwin's company but not staying too far back to lose them.

As he always did when first entering a town, Einar felt a little overwhelmed by the noise of folk talking, laughing, arguing over the price of goods, the number of people hurrying here and there and the stench of shit mixed with the aroma of beer malt and woodsmoke. Amid the merchants, the other normal town folk and children playing, he also noticed a lot of men with weapons and war gear; men of violence. Either this was an unsettled time or Lundr was a dangerous place.

After walking along several streets they arrived at a very big hall surrounded by a wooden fence that could only be the residence of Lord Finn. The gate in the fence was open and there were a lot of people going in and out. This made sense as the hall of the lord would be the centre of life in Lundr. To Einar's relief he saw that as well as those with Atli there were many others of Eirik's men there, each bearing shields marked like his. He and Wulfhelm were just another two among many. They would not stand out.

There were other warriors as well, their shields bore a blue fish as well as the red axe. Einar guessed that the fish was the sign of Finn, which made sense for a sea lord. The axe was added to show his loyalty to King Eirik.

Atli, Edwin and their men, who had arrived a little ahead

of Einar and Wulfhelm were now standing in a semicircle around the door of the hall. It appeared they were waiting for something. Wulfhelm and Einar sidled in behind them and took up a stance beside the inside of the fence, trying to look as nonchalant as they could.

A man came out of the hall. He was of middle years with long black hair tied in a braid. His blue tunic was embroidered with many coloured threads and looked expensive. There was no sign of an ale-swollen belly so common in men as they got older. His skin was the colour of dark wood that came from a lifetime in the blistering sun or the biting wind.

Einar judged that if this was Finn, he was not the sort of lord who spent his days sitting on the high seat in his hall.

'Lord Finn,' Atli spoke, confirming Einar's assumption. 'I am Atli Bjarnarson. I am a hirðmaðr of King Eirik. We heard you caught one of the men we're searching for.'

'And I am Edwin of Wessex,' Edwin added. 'I also serve King Eirik.'

Atli shot a glance at Edwin that suggested to Einar that Atli's tolerance of Edwin's presence was wearing thin.

Finn looked at the company gathered outside his hall.

'You are an Úlfhéðinn?' he said to Atli, noticing the pelt around Atli's shoulders.

'I am too,' Bragi said, pointing to Bodvar's wolf pelt around his own shoulders.

'I'm honoured to have warriors with such a fearsome reputation come to my hall,' Finn said. 'Helgi, get the prisoner.'

Forty-Nine

One of his men hurried off towards the back of the hall where there were outbuildings between the hall and the fence.

'King Eirik is sending many men my way these days,' Finn said.

'He values your loyalty,' Atli said. 'Most especially at this time when others are not.'

'I sent men to fight for him at Tunsberg,' Finn said. 'I'm only sorry that was not the end of this trouble. Yesterday, the king's son Rognvald was here. He was sailing north to deal with more problems in Gandvik.'

'You took Viking tax from the king's son?' Atli looked surprised.

Finn shook his head, a smile on his face.

'Please, I'm not that stupid,' he said. 'Rognvald knew this was a safe harbour for him to stop at for the night. I gave him hospitality and provisions for his voyage. He left this morning.'

'We may have to follow him to Gandvik if this prisoner of yours doesn't tell us where to find his friends,' Atli said. 'How did you catch him? In fact, how did you know we were looking for him? Did you get the war arrow?'

'We didn't,' Finn said. 'He tried to sail up the coast without paying my Viking tax. My ships caught him and brought him back here. As he claimed to have no silver I took his ship, a rather fine snekkja, as payment instead.'

Helgi returned. He was dragging a slight man whose skin was tanned every bit as brown as Finn's. Both his eyes were black and swollen, and there were scabbed scratch marks on his right cheek. The prisoner's hands were bound behind his back and Helgi held him by his upper arm.

Einar recognised Roan straight away. He looked at the ground in case the skipper saw him and his reaction gave them away. Then he remembered his helmet visor masked his face and raised his head again.

'When Rognvald sailed into my harbour he recognised his ship,' Finn continued. 'It was stolen from him in Gandvik a week ago by a band of renegade úlfhéðnar, the men you are searching for. Rognvald sent messengers to his father's camp at Tunsberg straight away.'

Atli walked over to Roan. For a moment they looked at each other. The skipper nodded at Atli. His eyes flickered to the Saxons and the warriors of Eirik. Einar knew he must be confused as to what was going on but Roan remained as impassive as always.

'Well, old man?' Atli said. 'What were you up to? Where is Ulrich?'

'Are you a prisoner too?' Roan asked.

'Where is Ulrich?' Atli said again.

'Isn't he dead?' the skipper said. 'I thought you were all dead. I was in the town when Eirik's fleet arrived. I went back to the ship and hid under the strakes. Eirik's army went right past me and up the hill. I saw Olaf and Sigrod's banners fall and knew the battle was lost. I had to get away so set sail straight away. I was sailing north when these Viking bastards caught me. How did they get you?'

Atli cursed and looked at the ground for a moment. He shook his head then looked up again.

'They didn't,' he said. 'I saw the error of Ulrich's ways.'

Roan's face fell as he finally understood the situation.

Atli turned to Finn.

'This man is no use to us,' he said. 'He knows nothing. He was just the skipper of the ship the others sailed in.'

Finn blew out his cheeks.

'Then I am sorry you were dragged here for no reason,' he said. 'Let me make it up to you. Accept my hospitality tonight. I will feast you and give you enough ale to get Thor himself full.'

'This chase is getting nowhere,' Edwin said to Atli.

Atli shot an annoyed look at him.

'Do you want to go back and tell King Eirik that?' he said.

'I think that would be foolish,' Edwin said with a strained smile. 'But I think we should change course. We know where Ulrich is going; this Gandvik place. We should go straight there and lay a trap for them.'

'I can give you ships to take you there,' Finn said. 'In fact you can take the snekkja the prisoner was on. It belongs to Rognvald anyway. You can take it back to him at Gandvik.'

'Very generous of you,' Atli said.

'Anything to help the king,' Finn said with a grin.

'It's getting dark,' Edwin said. 'We may as well stay here for the night and enjoy ourselves. It's been a long couple of days. We missed the celebrations after the battle. Let us drink to victory tonight instead.'

'Very well,' Atli said. 'We stay.'

The men around him cheered.

'But we leave at first light in the morning,' Atli added. 'Don't drink too much.'

'What about this prisoner?' Helgi said.

Finn looked at Roan for a moment.

'There's a trader leaving for the slave markets in Dublin tomorrow,' he said. 'Sell him to him.'

Helgi nodded and dragged Roan back to the outbuildings behind the hall.

'Now, enter my hall. I bid you welcome,' Finn said, spreading his arms towards Atli, Edwin and their men.

The others filed forwards. Einar and Wulfhelm joined the end of the column.

Finn held one hand up.

'No offence but please respect normal rules of any lord's house,' he said in a loud voice so all could hear. 'No weapons, helmets or shields are allowed in my hall.'

Atli and Edwin nodded. They and their men began to unstrap swords, unsling shields and take their helmets off.

Wulfhelm pulled Einar's arm.

'We can't go in,' he said in a low voice. 'If we take our helmets off someone will recognise us. It's bad enough already even with this on. I'm sure Aelfred looked at me twice, like he maybe recognised me but could not place from where. Lucky he's as thick as pig shit and couldn't work it out.'

Einar thought for a moment.

'You shouldn't take any more chances,' he said. 'Find the others at the harbour and make sure we have a ship ready to sail.'

'What are you going to do?' Wulfhelm said.

'I can't leave Roan here to be sold as a slave,' Einar said. 'I just hope that lot drink themselves stupid. I'll wait here. Hopefully later when it's dark an opportunity to get him out of here will arise.'

Wulfhelm glanced around the enclosure about Finn's hall.

'What are you going to do until then?' he said.

'I'll find somewhere to hide,' Einar said. 'Go. I'll meet you at the harbour.'

Wulfhelm nodded and walked out the gate of the fence back into the street. The last of Atli and Edwin's company were going into the hall, leaving a pile of shields, helmets and weapons stacked at the door. Einar sloped off, heading down the side of the hall towards the outbuildings Roan had been brought from.

The enclosure was busy. There was a strong smell of roasting meat coming from one of the buildings that must have been the kitchen. There were lots of thralls and other members of Finn's household hurrying around with annoyed expressions on their faces and Einar surmised that their lord's sudden decision to invite an extra thirty guests for dinner had been a source of some consternation. There were many other warriors as well and Einar was glad to see they were armed and wearing their helmets, as they were guarding their lord's hall.

'Are you lost, friend?'

A voice made him turn around. He saw Finn's man Helgi looking at him.

'The rest of Eirik's men are all in the hall, now,' he said.

Einar realised all the other warriors in the enclosure

around him had the fish and axe on their shields. Now Atli and Edwin's company were inside he was the only one with just an axe on his.

'I need a piss,' he said, the first thing that came into his mind. 'We've been riding all afternoon. That bastard Atli is a hard taskmaster. He wouldn't let us stop.'

'The *garðhús* is that one,' Helgi said, pointing to a long, low hut set up against the fence. 'Make sure you leave your war gear outside when you go into the hall afterwards.'

Einar nodded and walked towards the outhouse. Nervous as he was, it was the last thing he needed to do but he had to follow through with the pretence now. He opened the door and blinked, the stench that wafted out to meet him was so intense it almost made his eyes water. Taking one last breath of mostly fresh air, he went inside and closed the door. A tallow candle provided some light and he saw a standard latrine with two benches, one on either side facing each other. Six round holes were cut at equal intervals into each of the benches for the people of Finn's household to empty their bowels through. From the smell arising from the foul pits beneath they must have been doing a lot of it but then a *gardr* like Finn's was home to a lot of people, and it was near the end of the day, so they were most likely full and would not be emptied until morning.

When he had stayed as long as he could stand the smell, Einar opened the door again and peeked out. Helgi was gone. Einar slipped out of the outhouse. He went to the next building along but found it was a store, filled with barrels and sacks. Legs of dried ham hung from the ceiling and big wheels of cheese were stacked in one corner.

The noise and activity around it, combined with the

woodsmoke and steam rising from a hole in its thatch, told Einar that the next outbuilding was the kitchen. At the back of the hall he came upon a stone building with no windows. A warrior stood outside the door, the fish and axe painted on his shield. This looked like the sort of place to keep prisoners. Einar walked past, trying to take as much in as he could. The main thing he noted was that the door of the stone building was secured by a simple iron bolt on the outside. This was good. At least he would not have to mess about trying to find a way to break locks.

Just to be sure, Einar continued around the hall, checking the other outbuildings but none of them were prisons. Then he went back to the store. He looked around and saw that everyone else was too busy making preparations for the unexpected feast to pay any attention to him.

Sure no one was watching, Einar slipped into the store house and closed the door behind him. Using the witch's knife, he cut himself a bit of cheese, hacked off a hunk of ham from one of the legs, then crawled over to the back corner furthest from the door. He sat on the floor and pulled some big flour sacks in front of him so anyone coming in could not see him.

There was nothing to do now but wait.

Fifty

It got dark. As time wore on and the excitement of his situation faded, Einar found his biggest problem was dealing with the boredom. He knew he had to wait as long as he could, however, or risk getting caught.

The sound of the feast in the hall got ever louder. A sort of rumble of conversation broken often with laughter and good-natured shouts. He ate the cheese and ham but the smell of whatever was being roasted, boiled or baked in the kitchen almost drove him mad.

The storeroom was now pitch dark. At one point the door of the storeroom opened and a thrall came in, the candle in her hand casting light across the room. Einar froze but the slave just rummaged around near the door, lifted something he could not see and left again.

Then the noise from the hall died away. There were several moments when he could hear nothing, then everyone said something at once. This was repeated and Einar guessed the pre-feast toasts were being drunk. The eating and drinking would begin in earnest soon.

Einar stayed put in the dark as the noise level in the hall rose yet again. After some time the noise was considerable.

Voices raised in drunken conversation competed with raucous laughter, chanting and singing.

Judging that by now the feast must be in full swing, Einar pulled himself out of his hiding place. He had been sitting so long he was stiff. He stretched himself and rubbed his backside which was numb from sitting on the hard floor. Then he went to the door.

Standing behind the door, he opened it a crack and looked outside. The enclosure was dark. There was no one outside. Einar opened the door wider and crept outside. He looked around. Here and there around the enclosure, torches stood in brackets to provide light in the night. The gates to the street were now shut and two warriors stood guard behind them. He would have to find another way out.

With the eating part of the feast over, the kitchen was not as busy as before. From the lighthearted conversation he heard flowing from it he guessed the cooks were now enjoying the ale also being served in the hall. A couple of thrall women hurried out of the kitchen carrying trenchers of food. Einar stepped back into the shadows, waited until they had gone past, then continued on his way.

He hurried past the kitchen to the stone building at the back of the hall. The lone warrior still stood guard at the door but there was no one else around. Everyone was at the feast in the hall. Even though it was dark, Einar slung his shield across his back in case the guard could spot that there was only a red axe on it.

'All right friend, your watch is over. I'm the poor bastard who has to take over now,' he said to the guard. 'You can go and enjoy yourself. My turn.'

'You're early,' the guard said. Einar heard suspicion in his tone.

'Helgi says you can go early,' he said. 'You've been working hard.'

'Helgi?' the guard said. 'That bastard's not usually so decent.'

'I know,' Einar said. 'I think he's had too much ale. All the more reason to take advantage of this. Go on. It's quite a feast in there.'

The guard hesitated for a moment more. Then he licked his lips.

'That food smelled great,' he said.

'And the ale's even better,' Einar said. 'Off you go. At least one of us can have a good time tonight.'

The guard nodded, then hurried off towards the front of the hall.

As soon as he had gone Einar slid the bolt back on the door and opened it.

'Roan?' Einar said, whispering into the darkness inside.

There was a moment of silence, then the Frisian skipper's voice floated out.

'Who's that?'

'It's Einar,' Einar said. 'I'm here to get you out.'

Roan loomed out of the dark. He was peering at Einar as if not sure what was going on.

'Atli betrayed us all,' Einar said. 'He's fighting for Eirik Bloody Axe again. There's a feast in the hall. They won't notice you're gone until tomorrow. This is your only chance. Come with me. We're going to meet Ulrich and the others and get to Gandvik. We're all cursed by Queen Gunnhild.'

'Well at least that's better than going to Dublin,' Roan said. 'I'm too old to be a slave.'

He came out and they hurried across the enclosure, back past the kitchen.

'The gate's guarded so we'll have to climb out over the fence,' Einar said in a low voice. 'I think if we climb on the outhouse roof we should be able to reach the top of the fence.'

'If there's a feast on,' Roan said. 'Won't the outhouse be busy?'

Einar stopped. He had not thought of this.

As if to confirm Roan's words a door opened in the side of the hall, letting out a blast of light, heat and noise. A figure was outlined against the light from inside. It swayed for a moment as the person announced, 'I'm going for a piss.'

Einar recognised Bragi's voice. He grabbed Roan's wrist and pulled him to the side. They both ducked into the shadow of the roof against the wall of the hall.

Bragi staggered out of the hall and threw the door shut behind him. He lurched towards the outhouse.

At that moment a slave girl came hurrying from the kitchen. She had a jug of ale in one hand and a trencher of breads balanced in the other. She saw Bragi and changed her course so as to go round him. There was a water trough to their left however so she had to stop and go back the way she had originally been going. Bragi, clearly very drunk, went to do the same but instead stepped into her. They collided and the girl dropped the trencher and jug.

'Watch where you're going you stupid bitch,' Bragi said, his voice slurred.

The girl dropped to her hands and knees and started gathering what she had dropped as Bragi stumbled off to the outhouse and went in. She was still trying to clean up the mess when the outhouse door banged open and Bragi lurched back out, still lacing up his breeches.

He stopped and stood for a moment, glaring at the slave girl's shapely backside, then went over to her. Grabbing her by the arm he hauled her to her feet.

'Come here,' he said.

'Get off me,' the thrall said.

'No,' Bragi said, wrapping his arms around her. 'You and me are going to have some fun.'

'I don't want to,' the girl said. Einar could hear the panic and fear in her voice.

'It doesn't matter what you want,' the berserker said. 'It's about what I want.'

Holding her with his left arm, Bragi grabbed the front of the girl's dress and tore it open, exposing her breasts. He grabbed her right breast in his hand and squeezed it like someone trying to wring water from wet clothes. The girl gasped.

'No,' she shouted. She swung her right hand, hitting Bragi across the side of his face.

He cursed, then grabbed her by the shoulders and forced her to turn around. Holding her by the back of the neck he forced the girl to bend over the water trough. With his other hand he lifted her dress. Einar, watching from the shadows, could see her white buttocks in the moonlight as Bragi fumbled with his breeches again.

The girl cried out as Bragi forced himself into her.

'Shut up,' he said through clenched teeth. 'Pretend to enjoy it or it'll be worse for you.'

Einar's hand dropped to the hilt of Witch's Promise. Bragi had his back to him. He had no idea Einar was there.

We're not murderers, Affreca's words came back to him.

'No,' the girl said again. Her voice was just a broken sob now.

Einar crossed the space between them in moments. He clamped his left hand over Bragi's mouth and punched the blade of Witch's Promise into his back. Bragi's back arched. Hot blood gushed down over Einar's hand. He pulled the knife out and drew it across Bragi's throat, sawing at the flesh with a viciousness that was more than required to ensure he was dead.

More blood erupted from the berserker's opened throat, raining down on the slave girl's white backside. She looked around, her face a mask of terror.

Bragi dropped to his knees. Einar kicked him over and then crouched over the dying man.

'That's for Bodvar you bastard,' Einar said. He drove the knife into Bragi again. The berserker tried to say something, then went limp.

Roan ran over to join them. He threw an arm around the sobbing slave girl.

'He won't bother you again, girl,' the skipper said. The girl nodded.

'We can't leave him lying here, though,' Roan added. 'The next person who comes out to piss will see him and raise the alarm.'

Einar nodded.

'I know just where to hide the body,' he said.

He grabbed a handful of Bragi's clothing and dragged him to the door of the outhouse. Pulling the door open he heaved the corpse inside. With some effort Einar manhandled the dead body up onto the right-hand bench.

By the light of the candle that still burned in the outhouse Einar saw that Bragi was still wearing Bodvar's wolf pelt. He pulled it off the dead berserker then shoved his head into the middle hole in the bench. Pulling and hauling, Einar managed to push the dead man down into the hole until his weight took over and he fell on in, landing with a wet splat in the pile of shit below.

Einar blew out the candle to make it harder to see then left the outhouse.

'We can get you out of here or you can stay,' he said to the thrall.

The girl thought for a moment.

'Where would I go?' she said.

'Come with us,' Einar said. 'We're sailing out of this town tonight. Then you'll be free, no longer a slave.'

She nodded.

'I'll come,' she said.

They all clambered up onto the roof of the outhouse. Einar had been right and from up there they were able to reach the top of the fence that surrounded Lord Finn's hall. Outside was an alleyway running between the fence and the next longhouse in the street.

Roan put his hands on the top of the fence, preparing to climb over. Einar looked at the wolf pelt he had in one hand. He remembered the bag Atli had.

'You two go on,' Einar said, speaking in a forced whisper. He could see the look of confusion on Roan's face.

'Find the harbour,' Einar said. 'Affreca, Surt and one of the Saxons are there. They should have a ship. Wait for me there. I need to get something else.'

'How long should we wait?' he said.

'It will be some time,' Einar said. 'But if there's any sign of trouble, any noise at all, then set sail without me. Understand?'

Roan nodded. Then he clambered over the fence and dropped down into the dark on the other side. The slave girl followed him.

Einar lay down on the outhouse roof and waited.

Fifty-One

The noise of the feasting went on into the night. Below him, people came and went from the hall to the outhouse, unaware they were pissing on the body of Bragi in the pit underneath. Above him the moon and the stars revolved across the sky. As the night wore on the noise in the hall diminished and the traffic to and from the outhouse dwindled then stopped. At length all was silent.

Einar continued to wait until he was sure the feast was well and truly over and everyone had gone to sleep. Leaving the shield and helmet on the roof he slid down to the ground and crept over to the door in the side of the hall.

With caution he opened it and slipped inside. The hall was gloomy but far from quiet. Drunken snoring filled the air from all around. Finn, Atli and Edwin's men were all sprawled around the edge of the floor, either in straw cots or in their sleeping bags. Einar picked his way through the bodies on the ground, stepping over them and checking who was below him in the glow of the dying embers from the fires in the middle of the hall floor.

Eventually he found Atli. He was asleep, flat on his back. The wool bag was under his head. Eirik drew Witch's

Promise. He crouched over the sleeping man. The smell of ale wafted up from Atli's mouth. Einar put the knife between his teeth and put his left hand under the Wolf Coat's head. He drew the bag away with his right. Then he gently set Atli's head back onto the ground.

Einar stood up. He took Witch's Promise out of his mouth and looked down at the sleeping Atli. He knew he should kill him but many memories came back to him of the time they had spent together; on the ship, in battles, in danger over the last year. The rage that had driven him to kill Bragi was gone.

We're not murderers, Affreca's words came back to him once again.

Einar left.

He climbed the outhouse again and slipped over the fence into the alley below. He had seen Roan leave to the left so did the same. At the end of the alley he came upon a street with its wooden-planked walkway in the middle. It was now the dead of night and the town was dark and deserted. Einar turned right and hurried down the sloping walkway, reasoning that, as with the valley they had descended, if he kept going downhill he would eventually get to the sea. He knew he would find the harbour though. Lundr was a large settlement but it was nowhere near as big as Jorvik where he had previously lived, with perhaps forty or more streets. He could not get lost. The main thing would be to find the harbour before those back at the hall discovered something was amiss.

After turning onto two more streets he spotted ship masts rising up against the moonlit sky above the rooftops ahead and knew he was going in the right direction. Arriving at the harbour, the moonlight revealed a natural semicircle inlet with a narrow entrance. It was filled with ships of all sizes and several wooden jetties jutted out into the water. There was no sign of anyone around and it was dark, except for a large brazier that burned on the quay at the mouth of the harbour, a guiding beacon for any sailors trying to find safe haven in the night.

Einar jogged up and down the first jetty, conscious of how loud his boots must sound on the wood. He found no one however. Starting down the second jetty, he spotted the snekkja they had stolen from Rognvald, the one which Roan had been caught with. It was rigged and ready to sail. Five figures were crouched in it.

'You took your time,' Wulfhelm said, by way of welcome. 'We were starting to think about leaving without you.'

'We didn't though,' Affreca said.

'Isn't this ship a bit obvious?' Einar said, climbing down from the jetty into the snekkja.

'Finn said he was going to give it to Atli and Edwin,' Wulfhelm said. 'If we steal it back it will slow them down a bit.'

Einar grinned.

'You're right,' he said. 'Let's set sail.'

They untied the ship and shoved it away from the jetty. Wulfhelm and Surt took oars on one side and Einar, Affreca and the slave girl took to the oars on the other, while Roan took up his place at the steering board. With some effort they turned the ship in the packed harbour and headed for the harbour mouth. As they reached the narrow entrance Roan pulled the ship close to the right-hand harbour wall.

'What are you doing?' Einar said. 'We'll break the oars.'

'We've prepared something else to keep them off our backs,' Wulfhelm said.

Wulfhelm and Surt pulled their oars into the ship as the side bumped into the stone harbour wall beneath the burning brazier. Surt scrambled up out of the ship and up the wall. The snekkja drifted on out of the harbour. Einar and the others watched as Surt disappeared from sight, then appeared again. Now he had a rope over his broad shoulders and was straining forward, dragging something behind him. Then Einar saw he was pulling a *karfa*, a fast, six-man ship. Using the rope he hauled it into the harbour mouth. Then Surt dropped the rope and pulled off the fur jerkin he wore. Using it to protect his hands, Surt shoved the burning iron brazier off the harbour wall. It tumbled down into the karfa below, spilling charcoal and blazing wood into the belly of the boat.

Surt jumped off the harbour wall. He landed with a splash in the sea, surfaced and swam over to the snekkja.

'With any luck the karfa will lodge in the harbour mouth and sink,' Wulfhelm said as they helped Surt aboard.

They went back to the oars as the wind filled the sail and the ship surged into the night. There was a good wind behind them and soon rowing was no longer needed.

They had not sailed far when Affreca said, 'What's that?'

She was standing at the prow of the ship, pointing at what looked like a large fire burning in the sea ahead. The others joined her.

'It wasn't there before,' Affreca said. 'It's like someone just lit it.'

'There must be land ahead. Are we headed the wrong way?' Wulfhelm said over his shoulder.

Roan looked up at the stars above and shook his head.

'There are islands all over the mouth of this fjord,' Einar said. 'We saw that from the mountaintop, remember. There must be someone on one up ahead.'

'But who?' Surt said.

'It's Ulrich,' Affreca said. 'Who else could it be?'

'It could be Lord Finn's men, luring us into a trap,' Wulfhelm said.

'No. It's him. I know it,' Affreca said. 'I knew he wouldn't abandon us. Sail for the fire.'

As the snekkja got closer, the light of the big bonfire picked out five figures on the shore of the little island. They were waving their arms above their heads. Seeing the snekkja turn towards the island, they ran to a karfa like the one Surt had left burning in the harbour behind them. They shoved it into the sea, jumped in and started rowing towards the approaching longship.

Affreca was right.

'Hallo,' Skar called from the approaching karfa. 'Glad to see you finally made it.'

They brought the karfa alongside and Einar, Surt and Wulfhelm helped the five remaining Wolf Coats onboard.

'I told you we'd find you,' Ulrich said. The moonlight showed a smile on his face.

Starkad pried a silver ring off his arm and handed it to Skar.

'I bet him that you'd get yourselves killed,' he said.

Skar grinned and slid the ring onto his own forearm.

'We've been waiting all day,' he said. 'We were starting to think Starkad was right and we were going to have to go and steal a ship ourselves. Then we saw that fire in the harbour mouth so we knew it could only mean you'd got here at last.'

'Stealing Rognvald's snekkja for a second time is a nice touch,' Ulrich said. 'You've done well.'

He looked at Einar.

'When you didn't kill that boy in the forest I thought you didn't have what it takes,' Ulrich said. 'But you proved me wrong.'

'I've something for you,' Einar said.

He upended Atli's wool sack and the wolf pelts tumbled out onto the deck.

For a few moments there was silence. Everyone looked at the pile of furs as the ship rolled up and down over the waves.

'I can add another,' Affreca said, tossing the wolf pelt she had taken from the wolf in the forest.

'And one more,' Einar said. 'Bodvar's'

He threw the pelt he had taken from Bragi onto the pile.

The úlfhéðnar cheered. Each man retrieved his own wolf pelt and wrapped it around his shoulders. Skar, Starkad, Sigurd and Kari swarmed around Einar, pulling him, Affreca, Wulfhelm and Surt into a group hug.

'Well done,' Skar said. 'Very well done.'

They broke apart. Einar saw Ulrich had remained separate. He had not yet picked up his wolf pelt. He looked Einar straight in the eyes. The little man's chest heaved as if he was having trouble breathing. Einar thought he saw the moonlight glinting on tears in the little Wolf Coat's eyes.

Then Ulrich's normal demeanour returned. A smirk crept onto his lips.

'Good work,' he said, bending down to pick up his own wolf pelt, Bodvar's and the new one Affreca had added. 'Now at last we can go and get this blasted curse broken. We sail for Gandvik.'

Fifty-Two

The horse's head had been picked clean by carrion birds. Now only the skull, a few brown scraps of flesh stuck to it, rested on the top of the rune-carved cursing pole.

Skar raised his boot and kicked the níðstang over.

'That's what we should have done in the first place,' he said.

They were back in the little island in the fjord at Gandvik. The sailing up from Lundr had been every bit as hard as their original voyage south. They knew Atli, Edwin and their men were chasing them so Ulrich had insisted on sailing without stopping. The days were filled with riding the waves of the open whale road. There was no stopping for a good night's sleep on land. Instead they spent the night taking turns on lonely watches, fear of the ever-present chance of hitting rocks lurking in the dark sea gnawing at their nerves while Roan and Ulrich took turns at the steering board.

They had sailed into the fjord at Gandvik in the night. Luck was finally with them as in the dark they spotted a large fleet of ships anchored near the shore. Some were beached on the banks of the fjord. Beyond them a village was ablaze, the flames roiling up into the night sky. The outlines of houses, their burning roofs collapsing in on themselves, stood out against the flames.

'Who do you think that is?' Skar said.

'It can't be Atli and Edwin,' Ulrich said. 'There's no way they could've got here before us.'

'Whoever it is, they aren't very friendly,' Starkad said, looking at the fire from the burning settlement.

They sailed on until they found a wooded island big enough they could beach and hide the snekkja, then Ulrich finally allowed some rest. Straight away, everyone dropped into a deep, exhausted sleep.

It was mid-morning when Ulrich woke them all up again, announcing that they were now near where the níðstang had been placed. They sailed the snekkja to it and now stood on it.

'So what now?' Einar said.

'We met the old man in the woods over there,' Ulrich said, pointing to the near shore with its tree-covered slopes. 'He must live around here somewhere. The girl at the feast said he was some sort of important man around here so the locals will know where to find him.'

'Is that wise?' Affreca said. 'It seems like we've spent most of our time lately running and hiding from people.'

'We know the people of this district hate Eirik as much as we do,' Ulrich said. 'They'll help us.'

'That looks like some sort of settlement,' Skar said, pointing further along the shore where, in the distance, some boats sat at the water's edge. There were buildings as well.

'Let's start there, then,' Ulrich said.

They refloated the snekkja and sailed on up the fjord.

The settlement Skar had seen turned out to be a large village. It had a wooden jetty that reached into the fjord. The boats moored at it were small fishing vessels. Fishing nets were draped over poles. Rows of gutted and skinned fish hung on lines of rope, being air-dried in the morning sun to preserve them. There were a couple of huts on the river's edge and a track led up to the village, which was a cluster of long, thatched houses ringed with animal pens.

There was no sign of any people.

Roan beached the snekkja and he, the Wolf Coats, Einar, Affreca, Surt, Wulfhelm and the slave girl, who had since revealed her name was Rekon, went ashore.

They walked up the track that led into the village, still without meeting anyone.

'It's very quiet,' Skar said.

In the centre of the cluster of buildings that made up the village they came upon a large herd of horses that had been penned in a makeshift wattle-fenced corral. Three bored-looking young boys were minding the animals.

'Where is everyone?' Ulrich asked them.

'They're all at the Thing,' one of the boys said.

'What Thing?' Ulrich said.

'Isn't that what you're here for?' the boy said. 'Everyone in the district was summoned.'

Ulrich smiled in an effort to stop any suspicion arising in the boys.

'Of course,' he said. 'I meant *where* is the Thing?'

'Where it always is,' the boy said. 'On the Thing Mound beside the old *borg* on the far side of the village.'

Ulrich nodded and they trekked on through the deserted village. Einar noticed that the boy followed them. They needed no more directions as the sound of many voices raised in what sounded like strong disagreement came from ahead. On the far side of the village was a small meadow and beyond that a crowd was gathered. There were men, women and children there. Their simple homespun clothes marked them out as farmers, bondsmen and carls, the lowliest of the free folk in the kingdom.

'That's quite a gathering of commoners,' Ulrich said. 'There must be a couple of hundred of them.'

'The boy did say everyone in the district has been summoned,' Skar said.

'Let's see what's going on,' Ulrich said.

The people were gathered around a low, grassy mound, which Einar guessed was the Thing Mound. Just like at home in Iceland, every place in Norway had a mound or other natural platform where the people of the district gathered at the appointed times of the year to discuss important matters on the running of the district and hear legal cases.

Beside the mound was another structure. A deep ditch surrounded a round, grass covered rampart that was about forty paces across. The rampart was topped by a wooden palisade that looked very old. In places some of the stakes that made it up had rotted and fallen down, the gaps being patched with wattle fencing. There was a gap in the rampart where a large wooden gate stood open. Inside Einar could see stacks of hay.

'Is that a fort?' he said.

'It's a borg, yes,' Skar said. 'It's seen better days, though. It looks like they use it to store animal fodder these days.'

Einar and the others walked up and stood at the back

of the crowd. The assembled folk were occupied in a lively debate. People were pointing at each other and shouting. On the top of the mound a man in his later middle years stood, a staff in one hand and a stick in the other, waving his arms and trying to be heard over the row.

'Please, let's not fight each other,' he shouted. 'We have enough other people to fight as it is.'

'We cannot fight Rognvald,' a man near the bottom of the mound in a blue tunic said. 'We should give him what he wants.'

'But no one knows where those boys are, Thorketil,' another man said. 'How can we give him what he wants?'

The man on the mound spotted the Wolf Coats at the back of the crowd.

'Strangers!' he cried, pointing at Einar and the others. 'There are strangers among us.'

All the arguments and shouting died away as everyone turned to look at the newcomers.

'I hope you're right about people here, Ulrich,' Affreca said. 'They don't look too friendly.'

The expressions on the faces of the folk at the mound ranged from suspicion to outright hostility. The crowd swarmed around the Wolf Coats, surrounding them on all sides.

'Get ready. We'll have to fight our way out,' Skar said to the others.

'Wait!'

A woman's voice came from the middle of the crowd. There was some jostling as she pushed her way to the front. Einar recognised her nimble figure as she wove through the mob the same way she had danced around Olaf's warriors at the feast in Tunsberg. Free of the others, she stumbled ahead of them then turned to face the throng, arms spread wide.

'These men are friends,' she said. 'They fought for King Olaf and King Sigrod at Tunsberg. They're not Eirik's men.'

The mob stopped advancing.

Einar felt his heart flood with relief. It was Halgerd.

'That's right. You went to Tunsberg with Grimnir,' the man called Thorketil said in a tone that suggested he had just remembered something. He was looking at Halgerd with narrowed eyes. 'You came back very quickly, late at night.'

The hostility on the faces of the folk gathered around the Wolf Coats was gone but they still did not seem very welcoming.

The older man they had seen standing on the mound pushed his way through the folk to the front.

'My name is Berg,' he said. 'I'm the head man here. You are warriors?'

'We are Úlfhéðnar,' Ulrich said.

A murmur ran through the gathered throng.

'Well maybe you can be of help,' Berg said. 'We got this war arrow this morning.'

He held up the stick in his right hand. Einar saw that there were runes carved on it.

'It says Rognvald Eiriksson is now the lord of Gandvik,' Berg continued. 'And he now rules us. Rognvald seeks two boys, the sons of Olaf and Bjorn the champion. If they are not handed over to his men he will punish the whole district.'

'The bastard already burned Eikby,' a man behind him

374

in the crowd said. 'They killed everyone. Men, women and children. He didn't need to do that.'

'Rognvald will not be a good lord,' another man on the mound said. 'We should not accept this. He's harsh and cruel. We have no chance of getting our Odal rights back now.'

'Why don't you fight him?' Einar said.

Some in the crowd nodded and made noises of agreement. Others shouted their opposition.

'Rognvald is the son of King Eirik,' Thorketil said. 'He has maybe two hundred men with him. All hardened warriors. We're simple farmers. Rognvald will slaughter us then take revenge on our families.'

'If everyone in the district stands against him you would have more men, I'm sure,' Einar said.

'Rognvald has four *Drakkar* longships. His men have swords, mail and war gear,' Thorketil said. 'We have a few old spears, our farm tools and that old fort over there.'

A muttering went around the crowd.

'Frodisborg,' Einar heard someone say. 'This would not have happened in King Frodi's day.'

'Frodi is long dead,' Thorketil said. 'He can't help us now.'

'He's not dead,' the boy from the corral said. 'He and his men just sleep in their mounds. They will return at the time when we need them most.'

'Isn't that time right now?' another man said, his arms spread wide. 'Where is he?'

'We should help these people,' Einar said to Ulrich. He spoke so only they could hear him.

'All nine of us?' Ulrich said, raising his eyebrows. 'Maybe the slave girl and Roan could help too?'

'You know how to fight,' Einar said. 'You can organise them. Lead them. We could give them a chance against Rognvald.'

'No,' Ulrich said. 'We're just here to find the old man, remember? We need to find him before Rognvald arrives and kills everyone.'

Ulrich held his hands up to try to get the attention of the crowd.

'Does anyone know where we can find the one called Grimnir?' he said. 'We have urgent business with him.'

People in the crowd around them shook their heads.

'That old wizard?' someone said. 'No one has seen him since he went to see King Olaf at Tunsberg.'

'What use is a Wise Man if he is not around to advise us?' Thorketil said. Many made sounds of agreement.

Ulrich leaned close to Halgerd.

'You must know where Grimnir is,' he said from the corner of his mouth. 'You left Tunsberg with him and the two boys Rognvald is looking for.'

Halgerd shot a sharp glance around her. She looked fearful that anyone had heard his words.

'Come with me,' she said.

Fifty-Three

Halgerd's farm was not far from the village. It was a large enough holding, comparable to Einar's mother's farm in Iceland. There was a large main building, a barn and several outbuildings. A river flowed past the farmstead. She led Einar and the others there along a path that went through some woods near the village.

'Someone in the crowd said Grimnir is a wizard,' Einar said. 'Is that true?'

'He's very wise, that is true,' Halgerd said. 'He knows many things, some that help folk, others that good folk should not know. People go to him for advice but he does not practise seiðr, if that is what you are asking.'

'How did he learn these things?' Einar said.

'When he was young he travelled far,' Halgerd said. 'They say he went to Svartalfheim and learned dark, secret knowledge from the dwarfs there.'

She stopped and pointed to a path winding its way up the riverside.

'He lives in a house on the uplands above the valley,' she said. 'If you follow the river all the way up you'll come to it.'

'How will we know it's his house?' Ulrich said.

'No one else lives up there,' Halgerd said. 'You'll know it when you come to it.'

'Has he got the boys up there with him?' Einar said. 'We saw Gorm hand them over to you in the tavern in Tunsberg, if you're wondering how we knew.'

'Grimnir asked me to promise not to tell anyone in Gandvik where they are,' Halgerd said. 'He knows word will get back to Rognvald somehow, no matter how much folk here hate him and his father Bloody Axe.'

'He is indeed a wise man,' Ulrich said. 'Thank you for your help. We will be on our way.'

'Perhaps we can come back later and see you again,' Einar said. 'I mean, me, maybe.'

He blushed and looked down.

'That would be nice,' Halgerd said.

A big grin broke out across Einar's face.

From over his shoulder he heard Affreca tut.

They trekked off, following the river. Like the one they had followed down to Lundr, it was swollen with meltwater from the uplands and fast flowing. The path went on uphill and twisted and turned along with the course of the river.

'Hiking up and down river valleys seems to be becoming a habit of ours,' Wulfhelm said. 'This country is all mountains and valleys. When I get back to Wessex I'm never going to climb another hill. At least I won't need to there.'

'I'm starving,' Einar said.

'Me too,' Surt said.

'Save your breath for walking, lads,' Skar said.

They climbed on. The path, already steep, became narrow and they had to hike single file. The sun was well past its mid-peak when a house came into view. The river had cut a deep cleft in the hillside and up ahead was a particularly steep part where the water tumbled and cascaded over rocks, through deep pools and over waterfalls. Perched right beside the river was a building that looked like it was half dug into the hillside and half hanging over the water. The walls were made of overlapping wooden planks almost in the manner of a ship. It was a strange looking house built with multiple storeys on top of each other. It rested on the steep, higgledy-piggledy, rock strewn slope and Einar wondered how the builder had found ground flat enough to build it on. Then he saw that the house stood on thick wooden pillars, each of different heights but level at the top, resulting in a flat platform the house was constructed on.

Beyond it looked like there was a plateau or perhaps a summer pasture and further away mountains marched ever higher, snow still on their peaks.

The barking of dogs came from above. Two great, shaggy hounds came loping down the path towards them.

The Wolf Coats tensed, preparing to have to fend the beasts off. Those with spears readied them. Then a figure appeared on a platform that was built on the roof of the building above. It was Grimnir. Einar recognised his wide-brimmed hat.

'Hop! Ho!' the old man called to the dogs. 'It's all right boys. They're friends.'

The dogs began to wag their tails. They waited until the Wolf Coats passed then came along behind them, sniffing at their heels like hounds herding sheep.

Grimnir disappeared from the roof, then a few moments later appeared at a door at the lowest level of the house.

'Welcome, Ulrich,' he said. 'I'm glad to see that you and

your company of wolves survived the battle. Come in, come in.'

They filed inside. The interior of the house was dark and gloomy and the first thing they found was a ladder leading up to the next level. They followed Grimnir up to the next level to find themselves in a long room that must have been the length of the house. There were no windows but several tallow candles burned to give light. The room was filled with all manner of curious items. There were tables and chests everywhere. They were piled high with jars and pots, metal canisters and carved stone blocks. There were several rectangular boxes, covered in leather. Strange glass jars, full of either powder or liquids, blackened underneath as if they had stood over a flame, sat here and there. All manner of dead animals, stuffed and mounted in a variety of positions, were around the walls or set on the floor. An eagle, wings raised, was at one end of the room. A stag's head with wide spreading antlers was mounted on the wall.

On one of the tables Einar spotted a creature with four curved claws, a long snout filled with sharp, pointed teeth and a long, curling tail the same length as its body, which was covered in big, dark green scales.

'Is that a baby dragon?' he said.

'Some might think so,' Grimnir said. 'It's a sort of lizard that lives in rivers to the south of Serkland.'

'It's a crocodile,' Surt said.

Grimnir looked at Surt.

'I see by the colour of your skin, my friend, that you are from that country,' the old man said. 'Perhaps you've seen one alive?'

Surt nodded.

'I apologise for the mess,' Grimnir said. 'Living here on my own I don't have much reason to tidy up.'

'It makes it easier to hide those boys, no doubt,' Ulrich said. 'Where are they?'

Grimnir screwed up his face.

'Boys? What boys?' he said.

'Trygve and Gudrod,' Ulrich said. 'We know you took then from Tunsberg. You can stop feigning.'

The old man sighed. He turned to Ulrich.

'Did you come here to kill me?' Grimnir said. 'If so, it is time for you to stop feigning.'

'No. We came because we are cursed by Queen Gunnhild,' Ulrich said. 'You said you knew how to lift it.'

Grimnir gave a little laugh.

'The country is torn apart by war. Olaf and Sigrod are dead. King Eirik's son is ravaging Gandvik. He marches this way with a small army and you say you came here because of a *witch's curse*?' Grimnir said in a tone that suggested he was struggling to believe it.

'It's caused us great suffering,' Ulrich said. 'Gunnhild has great magical power. She turned our Norns against us. Our good luck has vanished. One of my company, Bodvar, is dead. Another deserted me.'

The old man looked at Ulrich for what seemed an age. Ulrich returned his gaze.

'We are not Eirik's men,' Ulrich said at length. 'He betrayed us.'

Grimnir pursed his lips.

'Very well,' he said. 'Follow me.'

They climbed up two more ladders, Grimnir leading the way. The old man came to a trapdoor in the ceiling at the top of the second ladder and pushed it open. He climbed through into daylight above.

They found themselves on the roof platform Grimnir had been on when they first saw him. Einar looked around. From this vantage point he could look right down the narrow river valley they had climbed up. Beyond he could see the village and the fjord beyond. Uphill he could see the uplands the river valley opened into. It was a wide, level meadow covered with many low mounds surrounded by forest. Beyond that the great mountains, their peaks still covered with snow, rose like the saw teeth of the strange stuffed lizard in the room below.

'This is quite a house, old man,' Skar said. He too was gazing around at the view.

'I built it myself,' Grimnir said, with evident pride.

'You chose the place well,' Skar said. 'Apart from the view, if anyone was going to attack you, you'll be able to see them coming from well before they get here.'

'That path up the river will make them come one at a time as well,' Starkad said.

Grimnir nodded and smiled. His pleasure at the compliments was obvious.

'The only thing is,' Ulrich said, 'if someone did manage to catch you in here you would be stuck. There's no way out.'

'Ah.' The old man raised a finger. 'Don't worry. I've a means of escape if that ever happens.'

Ulrich frowned, looking down at the steep valley, the narrow path and the river gushing down over the rocks and pools.

'How?' he said.

'If I went around telling people about it then it won't

work,' Grimnir said. 'Let me show you a different secret instead.'

He pointed to the field of low mounds above the house.

He took a piece of metal from a purse attached to his belt. It was polished to shining and as the old man turned it around in his hands Einar caught a clear glimpse of his own face reflected in it. Grimnir took it in both hands and turned towards the mounds. He held the metal at an angle to the sun that was now sinking towards the mountains and moved it back and forth.

The sunlight glinted on the metal. Einar noticed Grimnir's movements were deliberate, as if he were creating a pattern with the light.

Then two small figures seemed to rise up from the far side of one of the mounds. They stood up, looking in the direction of the house. Grimnir waved and the two figures started to run towards them.

'Trygve and Gudrod,' Ulrich said.

'It is. Folk think that the war arrow is the fastest way to send a message,' Grimnir said, tapping the piece of metal. 'But what is faster than light itself? Now come. It will be getting dark soon. You must stay until morning. Let's eat. Tonight your meal will be served by the son of a king.'

Fifty-Four

The sour expressions on their faces as they brought trenchers of bread and horns of ale, combined with the careless way they slapped pots of food onto the table told Einar that neither Trygve nor Gudrod seemed too happy in their new work as table servants.

Grimnir had his own dining hall on the second floor of his house. It was long and narrow with a similar table set in the middle of it, benches on either side and a high seat for Grimnir at the end. A fire blazed in a hearth at the far end of the room, its smoke pulled out of the room through a channel in the wall.

The old man had prepared a stew of boiled fish and instructed the boys to serve the men seated at the table. Only then would they be allowed to eat their own supper.

Grimnir made a face as Trygve dumped a bowl in front of him, the contents sloshing around and some spilling over the rim. The old man shook his head.

'Olaf has spoiled that boy,' he said. 'I'm trying to instil some sense of humility in him while he is here but I fear I'm too late. A king without humility quickly becomes a tyrant. Nothing more than a spoiled little boy in charge of a land. Olaf's and Eirik's own father Harald understood that, even if he did take away our Odal rights. That's why he fostered Olaf with a humble man like Vifil. So he would understand what life is like for ordinary people.'

Trygve scowled and went to join the other boy at the far end of the room to eat their own food.

'Does he know about the battle at Tunsberg yet?' Ulrich said, chewing a mouthful of fish.

Grimnir shook his head.

'If Rognvald finds him and his friend then your lessons will be in vain old man,' Ulrich said. 'And he will. What is your plan? Surely you're not going to wait up here until he finds you?'

'I have my plans, don't worry,' Grimnir said, dipping his spoon into his stew.

It was clear he would say nothing more on the subject.

'Those mounds the boys were hiding in,' Skar said. 'They look like *haugan*. Whose graves are they?'

'Those are the *Kunungar Haugan*,' the old man said. 'They are the burial mounds of the ancient kings of this part of Norway. The men who ruled here many generations ago, in the days before Harald Fairhair when Norway was many kingdoms with many kings.'

'They're buried in these uplands?' Starkad said.

'What better place to be buried than somewhere where you can look out over your whole realm?' Grimnir said.

'This King Frodi everyone keeps talking about,' Einar said. 'Is he buried there?'

Grimnir pursed his lips, an expression that Einar now realised was a habit of his.

'Perhaps,' he said. 'If Frodi ever existed, that is, then his grave would be one of those mounds.'

'You don't believe in the legend, then?' Einar said.

'I believe very much in what it means,' the old man said. 'Whether it is true or not, it gives the people of Gandvik hope: Hope that when times are darkest someone will come to help them.'

'And what about when that someone does not arrive,' Ulrich said. 'And instead Rognvald comes. I would say they are about to face the darkest of times. Rognvald will show no mercy.'

'Rognvald is not the real danger,' Grimnir said. 'That is his father, Eirik. Until he is no longer king no one in this land will live in peace.'

'Olaf and Sigrod are dead. Who will stand against Eirik now?' Ulrich said, his upper lip curled in his habitual sneer. 'That bunch of farmers in the valley below?'

Grimnir laid his spoon on the table.

'There is only one man in Norway strong enough to stand up to Eirik now,' he said.

Ulrich looked puzzled for a moment, then Einar saw his expression change as realisation dawned on him.

'Hakon!?' Ulrich said. 'He's just a boy.'

'He is sixteen winters old,' Grimnir said. 'He is no longer a boy.'

'He's a *Christian*,' Ulrich said.

'He's a son of Harald Fairhair, just like Eirik,' Grimnir said. 'He's our only hope now. He is Trygve and Gudrod's only hope too.'

'Some hope,' Ulrich said and grunted. 'You think he will care about Gandvik? Why would he come here? Maybe to build one of his churches, yes, but to fight Eirik? How would he even know about this place?'

'He will come,' the old man said.

Ulrich shook his head, slumped in his seat and folded his arms.

'They say in the village that you are a wizard,' Einar said to Grimnir. 'That you learned black arts in Svartalfheim. Is it true? How did you travel there?'

Grimnir laughed.

'No that is not true,' he said. 'Unless the realm of the Dark Elves is really located in the great city of Paris. I learned many things there, the wisdom of ancient people. The Romans, the Greeks. To some, that knowledge would seem like it came from the dwarfs.'

'Aristotle, Ptolemy, Euclid,' Surt said, nodding. Einar frowned at the strange words. 'Algebra, geometry, alchemy. I read all this in al-Andalus.'

'So you are an educated man, my friend?' Grimnir said. 'I look forward to many intelligent conversations with you. All this is not witchcraft. It is knowledge. Men see things they don't understand and think it is magic.'

'But you *do* know how to break the curse that is on us, don't you?' Ulrich said. He was leaning forward, elbows on the table, now.

'To my knowledge there are three ways to break a witch's curse,' Grimnir said, holding up the pointer, index and middle fingers of his left hand. 'First.'

He pointed to his left pointer finger with the thumb of his right hand.

'You kill the witch.'

'Well right now Gunnhild is under the protection of Einar here's father,' Ulrich said, 'the Jarl Thorfinn of Orkney. He has fortresses, many ships and hundreds of warriors against which we have the nine of us here. Killing her does not look like an option any time soon. Next?'

Grimnir pointed to his middle finger.

'You do a deed so selfless, so full of reckless courage that it grabs the attention of the Gods themselves,' he said. 'Something of such suicidal bravery it is not certain you will survive or not. But if you do, then Odin will be impressed. He will intercede with the spirits that have been turned against you and your luck will be returned.'

'I don't like the sound of suicidal bravery, old man,' Ulrich said. 'What's the third option?'

Grimnir closed his fist.

'I will not tell you,' he said. 'Yet.'

'What?' Ulrich said.

'I will tell you the third way to break the witch's curse,' Grimnir said. 'Only if you swear to do something for me first.'

Starkad drove his knife into the wood of the table.

'What if we *make* you tell us how to break the curse, old man?' he said.

'You can try,' Grimnir said. 'But I'm a very stubborn man. I will go to my grave without telling you anything. I promise you that.'

He gave Starkad a look that was hard as steel.

Ulrich sighed.

'Look, we'll do whatever you want,' Ulrich said. 'Name your price.'

'Help the villagers,' Grimnir said. 'They're farmers, not fighters. If Rognvald comes he will slaughter them but if someone teaches them how to fight a battle they stand a chance. You could do that. You could work out how to beat Rognvald and teach them how to do it.'

Ulrich hung his head and blew out his cheeks.

'I knew it would come to this,' he said. 'I knew it. We have a few spears and knives. Little mail. We've as much war gear as the peasants. What do we teach them with? Sticks and stones?'

'If you swear to help them then I will give you war gear fit for kings,' Grimnir said. 'Those people need you. You must do this if you want to know how to break Gunnhild's curse. It is part of the thing that you will have to do to break it.'

Ulrich sat for a moment, looking down at the table. His lips were moving but no sound could be heard. Finally he looked up.

'All right. We'll do it,' he said. 'I swear to help those farmers. I won't swear to die for them, though. Mark that.'

The old man smiled.

'Excellent,' he said. 'Now, let me show you some real magic. Trygve, get my special flask and the cups.'

The tow-haired boy got up and slouched over to a side table.

'This is a secret I learned on my travels,' Grimnir said. 'If you boil wine and collect the steam it turns back into liquid that is a drink worthy of the Gods themselves.'

Trygve returned and handed a glass jar and a stack of horn cups to Grimnir, who poured a little of what looked like water out of the flask into each cup. Then he handed them to the people at the table.

'Let us drink to seal our pact,' the old man said, drinking the contents of his cup in one go.

Einar looked down at the clear liquid in his, finding the whole thing a bit odd. Pacts were sealed with ale, not water.

Then he and the others all drank.

Einar's eyes widened. It felt like fire was blazing down his throat. Coughs and splutters exploded from him and the others. He felt a moment of panic as the thought came to him that Grimnir had poisoned them all, then the fire in his throat subsided and he felt as though his whole chest was filled with a warm, pleasant sensation.

'Good stuff, yes?' Grimnir said.

'Aye it is,' Ulrich said, a grin spreading over his face.

'You were at Tunsberg.'

Trygve's voice made everyone turn around. He was still standing beside the table and was looking at Ulrich.

'I think I heard you say something a moment ago,' he said. 'About my father. You fought for him in the battle, didn't you? Have you any news?'

Ulrich wiped water from his eyes. His grin faded. He straightened up and looked directly at the boy.

'Your father is dead, lad,' he said. 'Eirik's men killed him.'

The boy's face fell. He looked unsteady on his feet. Grimnir reached a hand up and placed it on Trygve's shoulder, guiding him down onto the bench.

'Take a seat, lad,' he said, his voice gentle. He poured a mouthful of the fire liquid into a cup and pushed it towards him. 'Drink this. It will help.'

The boy looked at the table. Einar could see he was struggling to come to terms with the news. It was like he was fighting back tears but at the same time longing to let them flow. 'Did he die well?' Trygve said, still looking at the table.

'He did,' Ulrich said. 'He was brave. The Valkyries will have seen how he died and chosen his spirit. Odin will have welcomed him into his Valour Hall.'

The boy nodded. He clenched his fists so the knuckle bones showed white through his skin.

'I will avenge him,' Trygve said through clenched teeth.

'Good lad,' Skar said, patting Trygve on the back. 'That's the best thing for it.'

Einar thought how he had no idea what the boy must be feeling as his own father and his mother still lived. Even though he was perhaps eleven winters older than the boy, this was a part of life he was yet to experience.

Grimnir held up the flask.

'Shall we have another?' he said.

Ulrich placed a hand over his cup.

'Thank you, but no,' he said. 'There is something very important we úlfhéðnar have to do tonight.'

He looked round at Einar, Affreca, Wulfhelm and Surt.

'You wait here,' Ulrich said to Einar and the others, then the Wolf Coats left Grimnir's house.

Fifty-Five

'What do you think they're up to?' Affreca asked.
Einar shook his head.

'Some secret Úlfhéðnar work no doubt,' he said, his voice heavy with sarcasm. 'So secret it is only for their eyes. You know what I think?'

'Tell us,' Affreca said.

'I think they're worried that we might laugh at them,' Einar said. 'I think whatever secret rituals they get up to is really so silly or so embarrassing, that they just don't want anyone else seeing it. Laugh and they'll lose some of their dreaded reputation.'

'I've told you over and over,' Affreca said. 'You think too much.'

They waited in silence. After a while the door opened once more. Had he not been sitting at the same table as him, Einar would have thought it was Surt standing at the threshold. It was in fact Starkad. He was stripped to the waist though still wore his wolf pelt around his shoulders. His body was painted all over with a black paste, the sort Einar had seen Skar made in the past by mixing soot from the fire with grease. The Wolf Coats smeared it over the blades of their weapons and their bodies when they needed stealth at night,

lest any glimmer of moonlight on metal or pale flesh gave
them away.

'You four come with me,' Starkad said.

Einar looked at Affreca. Affreca just shrugged.

Einar, Affreca, Wulfhelm and Surt followed him out into
the night, leaving Roan, Rekon, Grimnir and the two boys
behind.

'What's happening?' Einar said. 'You look ready for
night fighting.'

Starkad did not reply. Instead he led them up the path
from Grimnir's house to the barrow field.

The moon shone down from a clear sky. It cast an eerie
silver light over the meadow with its rising and falling
grave mounds. In the centre of the meadow, surrounded
by barrows, was a new construction. A slim arch had been
raised and four dark figures stood beneath it. Two burning
torches were stuck into the ground to provide light. As they
got closer Einar saw by the torchlight that the four people
were Sigurd, Kari, Skar and Ulrich. Like Starkad they were
stripped to the waist and their bodies and faces painted
black, making the whites of their eyes stand out. They too
wore their wolf pelts around their shoulders. Skar bore a
spear.

It looked like the arch had been made by scoring out three
long strips in the turf side by side. The ends had been left
attached to the ground, while the middles had been raised
up above head height. Three spears had been driven into
the ground, one under each strip, the butts holding the turf
arches up.

Starkad went and joined the other Wolf Coats. Ulrich
stood in front of the others, at the entrance to the arch.

He had his hands behind his back and was looking at the ground. A sword stood before him, its tip plunged into the earth.

For a few moments, there was no sound but the guttering of the torches and the buffeting of the slight wind. Then Ulrich spoke.

'Since the time when Odin came from the east to these lands and taught the craft of war to those who would listen, Odin's warriors have met like this, in the dark, their weapons blackened, their skin painted black. This is how our ancestors terrified and slaughtered the Legions of Rome in the night-shrouded forests of Germania. Their descendants, our warrior brethren, fought Attila then joined with him. When King Adils fought King Áli at the battle on the frozen lake our brothers were with him, as they were with Hrolf Kraki and his warband of mighty heroes. Those men all met as we do now and passed on their secrets to each other.'

He looked up.

'If a man wants to become an Úlfhéðinn, he must pass the initiation ritual,' he said. Affreca gave a cough. 'That ritual takes the form of a test. He must move across a hostile realm where everyone is a danger to his life. He must live off the land like a wolf, killing to eat, stealing what he needs. If he survives, he proves himself worthy of becoming one of the Úlfhéðnar, a warrior of Odin. A few days ago I set you four that test.'

'Wait. Are you saying that splitting up on the way to Lundr was a test?' Einar said.

'And you passed it,' Ulrich said with a smile. 'You all did. I stand here tonight to offer you a place in my company. To become an Úlfhéðinn. *If* you want it.'

Affreca took a deep breath. She straightened up and pushed her shoulders back.

'I want it,' she said.

Ulrich nodded. 'What about the rest of you?'

Wulfhelm looked at Surt. Surt shrugged.

'I'm honoured by the offer,' Wulfhelm said. 'But I'm worried what this may do for my eternal soul.'

'If you die well then Odin will reward you with endless ale after death in his Valour Hall,' Ulrich said.

'That's what I'm worried about,' Wulfhelm said. 'Thank you, but no.'

'The same goes for me,' Surt said. 'My God would not like it.'

Ulrich nodded.

'Very well,' he said. 'But I still would offer you a place in my company. We need good men like you and I need to get twelve people. Otherwise Odin will not favour us. Will you still become our blood brothers?'

Surt and Wulfhelm nodded.

'And what of you, Einar Thorfinnsson?' Ulrich said. 'Do you want to be an Úlfhéðinn?'

Einar looked up at the stars above. Was this really what his fate was to be? Was he about to take a step onto a path that would have no return? Would it mean he could never change his course in the future?

The endless black of the sky made the stars look like tiny points of light hanging in infinite depths of emptiness, the *ginnungagap*, the yawning void. Perhaps there was nothing else. Maybe there were no Norns. Nothing and no one was spinning his fate and he was making it up himself day by day.

A shooting star streaked across the black above.

'Yes,' Einar said.

Ulrich pulled the sword from the ground and ran it across his left hand. Blood welled up from the sliced flesh. Then he turned and did the same to the other Wolf Coats behind him.

Ulrich pointed the sword at Einar. He walked forward to the arch.

'Your right hand,' Ulrich said.

Einar held his hand out, palm upwards, and Ulrich slit it with the sword blade. As blood surged up from the wound Ulrich held his own bleeding palm up and clasped it against Einar's.

'Do you swear to follow the ancient Viking laws?' Ulrich said. 'To never back away from a fight unless outnumbered and there is no way to win? To not rob from poor farmers or lone women unless you absolutely need to. To never eat raw meat or rape women?'

'These are the Viking laws?' Einar said.

'Do you swear?' Ulrich said, his gaze boring into Einar's.

'I swear,' Einar said.

'Do you swear to follow the will of Odin?' Ulrich said. 'The Lord of storm and frenzy? The wanderer, the warrior, the lord of the dead and of the Einherjar? The master of secret knowledge, the magician and the god of ale and of poets?'

'I swear,' Einar said.

Ulrich nodded.

'From now on you will be a wolf among men,' he said. 'Your fetch, your spirit *fylgja*, will be the wolf. You will be a wolf in holy places. Now enter the sacred arch.'

Einar ducked to pass through the arch. As he did so he felt the icy touch of cold metal on the back of his neck. Looking up he saw Skar had brought the blade of his spear down on him. The weapon was sharp and the edge nicked Einar's skin.

'This blow represents the end of your old life,' Skar said. 'From now on you must act as though the person you have been up until now is dead. Now you are one of Odin's wolves. Odin owns you.'

Einar passed on through the arch, clasping bloodied hands with Skar, Starkad, Kari and Sigurd in turn, then he continued out the other side.

Affreca did the same. Wulfhelm and Surt mixed their blood with the others but did not swear anything to Odin.

As Surt left the arch the Wolf Coats threw back their heads and half sang, half shouted their galdr, the holy chant of their tradition. When it was done, they cheered and slapped their new companions on the back.

'Welcome lad,' Skar said. 'I always knew you would become one of us.'

'I had my doubts,' Ulrich said. 'But you proved me wrong. The next stage for a new úlfhéðinn is to go into the forest and kill his...' he glanced at Affreca, '... or her, wolf. The pelt of the animal becomes his wolf coat.'

He handed Affreca the pelt of the wolf she had killed in the forest.

'You have already killed your wolf,' he said. 'As have you, Einar.'

Ulrich handed Bodvar's wolf pelt to him.

Einar took the fur in both hands. He did not know what to say.

'Put it on, lad,' Skar said, clapping a hand on his shoulder.

Einar drew the wolf pelt around his shoulders and fastened the catch at his neck. He pulled the wolf's head up over his own. As it settled over him he felt a strange sensation. His heart beat faster. He felt strength pulsing through his blood. The stars above seemed brighter and the night warmer.

He thought of the path that had brought him here. He had been his mother's son, a farm boy, a lad who played knattleikr, a poet. Now he was a Viking. A wanderer on the whale roads. A killer of men. He was an Úlfhéðinn.

Fifty-Six

The farm dog was barking. Halgerd woke. It was dark but a shaft of grey dawn light filtered down from the Wind's Eye, the hole in the gable wall of the farmhouse near the apex of the roof that let smoke from the fires out.

What had disturbed the dog at this early hour? There had been a fox nosing around lately and perhaps it was back. She would have to take a look. The fox knew that the dog's bark was worse than its bite and if she did not go herself they would risk losing another chicken.

Halgerd rubbed her eyes and dragged herself from the warm straw of her bed. Her two brothers, Regin and Ottir snored in their own beds along the wall.

The sound of hooves reached her ears from outside. Horses were approaching the farm. This was no fox. Halgerd could not think who it could be. Whoever it was, if they were abroad at dawn there must be good reason.

She went over to her brothers' beds and shook them awake. Bleary-eyed, the three of them walked to the door, picking their way across the dark farmstead floor. Halgerd had just laid her hand on the door handle when the dog's barking abruptly ceased. There was a short whimper, then silence. Halgerd froze and she and Regin, her eldest brother, exchanged looks.

'I'll get the spear,' Regin said.

He hurried off to the back of the farmhouse, then returned, now carrying the rusty old weapon that had once been their father's.

Halgerd opened the door and they filed out.

In the yard outside stood a company of around thirty horsemen. The breath of the horses rose in clouds in the dawn air. They all wore helmets, the visors covering the top half of their faces. Some had unslung their shields which were all painted with the bloody red axe of King Eirik. Three horsemen stood before the others, clearly their leaders. One was a big man in a fine, fur-trimmed cloak whose long black beard flowed from beneath his visor. The man beside him had long, thin blond hair, a clean-shaven chin but long moustache. He looked a bit foreign. The third wore the pelt of an animal as a cloak.

The poor dog lay in a pool of its own blood, a spear skewered through its guts.

'Good morning,' the rider with the animal pelt said. 'Halgerd isn't it? We meet again.'

'Are you one of Ulrich's men?' Halgerd said, unsure where she had seen him before.

'I am Atli,' the man said. 'I was one of Ulrich's pack but now I'm more of a lone wolf.'

'What do you want?' Regin said. 'Why did you kill our dog?'

The black-bearded man pushed his horse forward.

'I am Rognvald Eiriksson,' he said. 'I am your new lord. I

want to know where the old man called Grimnir is. He has something that belongs to me.'

'We don't know where he is,' Halgerd said.

Rognvald chuckled.

'Lord Edwin, bring the prisoner forward,' he said.

The blond-haired rider trotted forwards. He was pulling a rope behind him. At the other end of it a man staggered. The rope was tied around his torso, keeping his hands to his sides. His blue tunic was torn and there were rips in his breeches. His face was bruised and blood dripped from his smashed lips. When the horseman stopped his horse the man dropped to his knees, head bowed.

Halgerd saw it was Thorketil.

'This man tells us different,' Rognvald said. He swung himself down from his horse and all the others followed suit. 'He says you went to Tunsberg with Grimnir, before the battle against the rebels Olaf and Sigrod, but you returned very quickly. The old man has not been seen since. I think you may have brought something back. Maybe two things? I think the old man is hiding them from me somewhere.'

Thorketil sobbed. He raised his head and looked at Halgerd.

'I'm sorry,' he said. 'I thought they would spare the village if I told them.'

'I don't know what he's talking about,' Halgerd said, trying to force a smile.

Rognvald drew his sword. The movement was so swift all Halgerd saw was the flash of the blade in the dawn sun. An instant later it sliced through the shaft of the spear in Regin's hands, cutting the blade off so it tumbled to the ground.

Regin was still looking at his decapitated spear shaft when Rognvald swept his blade back down and across. This time it was Regin's head that tumbled to the ground. Blood shot upwards from his severed neck as his legs folded under him and his corpse collapsed to the ground.

Halgerd gave a startled cry of horror, her hands going to her mouth.

Rognvald grabbed Ottir with one hand and put the point of his sword at the bottom of the young lad's throat.

'Now,' Rognvald said. 'You've lost one brother. Do you want to lose the other one as well? Tell me where Grimnir is hiding those boys.'

'No,' Halgerd snarled. Tears ran down her face. 'Never. I'll tell you nothing you bastard. You bastard son of a bastard! You have no right to rule here. Kill him. Kill me. You'll kill us anyway. But I will tell you nothing.'

'Please,' Ottir said to her. His eyes were wide with terror as he looked at his sister. 'I don't want to die.'

'Lord Rognvald, I think she's telling the truth,' Atli said. 'I believe her when she says she will not tell us.'

Rognvald lowered his sword.

'Then we do it the hard way,' he said. 'We get the others, come back and tear this village and its people apart, piece by piece, limb from limb. Someone will know something. Someone will talk.'

'No,' Halgerd said again.

'My Lord Rognvald,' Lord Edwin said. 'If I may make a suggestion? I don't think she will respond to threats but I know other ways of persuasion. I know a few tricks to make her tell us what we need to know.'

'Really, Lord Edwin?' Rognvald said. 'I had no idea you

had such talents. It's not that I don't have faith in you but just in case whatever it is you have in mind doesn't work, I will take some of the men and ride back to get the rest of my warband. We'll come back and put the village to the sword.'

'Very good,' Edwin said. 'But I won't let you down. She will talk I promise you.'

Rognvald chose five riders, got back on his horse and they galloped off.

The rest of the warriors grabbed Halgerd and her brother and tied their hands behind their backs.

'Take them all to the barn,' Edwin said. 'Bring the rope, get me a knife and if there are any blacksmith's tongs around I want those too.'

'I'll tell you nothing,' Halgerd said, spitting at Edwin's face.

'Oh you will, I can assure you of that,' Edwin said, wiping her spittle from his cheek with the back of his hand. 'The only question in my mind is how long you'll manage to hold out.'

Fifty-Seven

Einar woke to the smell of salted pork frying. Grimnir had prepared a hearty breakfast for them all. They had slept on the floor of his dining hall, warm inside leather sleeping bags he had provided.

It was still early morning and the sun was low on the horizon. After eating, Grimnir got two wooden chests and three shovels from his cluttered room on the first floor of his house. They carried them back up to the high meadow where the burial mounds stood. A low morning mist lay on the field, flowing around the mounds so they looked like islands in a grey sea. They walked to the centre of the meadow and set down the chests. The arch cut from the ground was gone, the strips of turf pressed back to the ground as if it had never stood.

'I've watched over these grave mounds for years,' Grimnir said. 'I've made sure they were never robbed. Before me, generations of other guardians did the same. I know each one like the back of my hand. I taught these boys here to run and hide in them if I thought danger was coming. Now Trygve, you've been in and out of these graves over the time you've been here. You've seen what I have seen and you will be a king one day. Choose a mound you think would suit each of these warriors.'

'You're asking him to pick our graves?' Ulrich said.

'No,' Grimnir said. 'I'm asking him to pick your war gear.'

Trygve, who had been sullen and silent all morning, raised his head. Einar saw his eyes were red-rimmed and raw and remembered it was less than a day since the young boy had learned of his father's death.

The boy regarded each one of the Wolf Coats in turn. He raised his right finger and pointed at Einar. Then he pointed to a mound to the right. They crossed to it and climbed up the side. Grimnir crouched and felt the ground with his fingers until he felt what he was looking for. Then he stood up and pointed at the turf. Skar and Starkad dug the shovels in to find that a crack opened up in the ground straight away. It was an entrance.

They lifted a stone cap, revealing a shaft going into the heart of the mound. Grimnir lit a torch and handed it to Einar.

'Go,' he said. 'Take what you need.'

'But you say you've guarded these mounds from robbers for years,' Einar said. 'Now you tell me to take their treasures?'

'Not their treasure,' Grimnir said. 'Take the war gear of the king who lies buried here. This is the time of our greatest need in Gandvik and I think you can do more good with it than he can right now.'

Einar descended into the mound with tentative steps. He had heard it said that some of the dead did not pass on to the otherworlds. Instead they became *draugr* or *aptrganga*, after-walkers who lived on inside their burial mounds. For that reason the inside of great men's graves were built like a room and packed with everything he needed in life, from food to weapons. Sometimes his horse was killed and put in there too and maybe a slave girl or two as well. His nerves ached, half expecting some pallid undead thing to come lurching out of the dark, skeletal hands reaching out for him.

He held the torch up high, casting light into the interior of the mound. He caught his breath at the gleam of silver and gold the light danced across. The firelight showed a square room, the walls made of tree trunks stacked one above the other. Furs hung on the walls as well as a long embroidered tapestry. The many colours of its threads were faded by time and dust. Barrels, jars and chests were stacked around the edges of the floor. There was a pile of bones in one corner. The air was still and smelled of dust, stale air and the aroma of earth.

In the middle of the underground room a human skeleton lay on its back on a fur-covered bed. Its torso was clad in a brynja, its iron rings dull grey in the torchlight. The empty eyes of the skull looked out from inside a magnificent helm. Its cap was iron and embossed with images of twisting beasts and dancing warriors. A ridge ran over the top, from front to back, to protect against a cut to the top of the head. It was cast in the shape of a boar. Long, narrow strips of iron hung down from the cap at the sides and back to protect the wearer's neck but each one was hinged so not to restrict his movement. The lower face was protected by a single piece of iron that resembled a metal beard. The nose guard was in the shape of an inverted raven. Its beak pointed downward to where the skull's lips would have been, its wings protecting where the nose once was. Above the raven two dragons, *orms*, went left and right, their worm-like bodies forming the brow guard over each eye.

A broad-bladed sword sat on the corpse's chest. The hilt was set with white bone, perhaps walrus ivory. Into that were set many red and blue garnets, cut into triangle shapes so they reflected the light.

Set against the bier was a large round shield. Its blue paint was still clear. The metal boss was engraved with the image of a one-eyed man.

The treasures of the mound did not just include war gear. The bony fingers that clasped the sword hilt still bore gold and silver rings which, now the flesh was gone, hung loose, like the thick bands of gold and silver that encircled the skeleton's forearms. A big gold chain with a silver amulet was round the neck of the dead man.

Einar set the torch down and began to gather the weapons and war gear. He worked as respectfully as he could, trying not to disturb the bones. This proved impossible when taking off the brynja but once he had it off he did his best to rearrange the ribcage and backbone as they would have been before. When he finished he looked down at the bones, all that remained of a once mighty king, now stripped even of the war gear that would have made him so fearsome in life. All that now remained of his former glory was his treasure. The rings were still on the arms and fingers, the chain and amulet rested on the cage of his ribs.

Einar looked at the gold and silver for a moment. It was

more wealth than he had seen in his lifetime. It could make him a rich man.

Then he shook his head and left the mound.

Outside, the others crowded around to see what he had found. Einar enjoyed the smell of the fresh air for a moment as Affreca picked up the mail shirt. It was supple and flowed over her arm without any stiffness or grating.

'It's incredible,' she said. 'It looks as good as the day it went into the earth.'

'Mail rusts when it's in the air and the rain,' Grimnir said. 'These mounds were built well. No water has got in and when the tombs are sealed there is little air down there.'

Skar picked up the helmet and slid it over Einar's head.

'Trygve chose well,' Skar said. 'It's about your size. You look like one of the old heroes you sing about, lad.'

'This is a very fine sword,' Starkad said, turning it over in his hands. 'You should give it a name.'

'I will call it Grave Giver,' Einar said, staring fascinated by the waving pattern the sunlight had uncovered on its blade. 'Because a grave gave it to me.'

'And you will put many men in their graves with it,' Affreca said.

'Now, Trygve,' Grimnir said as he laid a hand on Affreca's shoulder. 'Do you know which of these mounds holds the body of the king known in life as *körtr*, "the short"?'

They continued to visit the barrows, entering each one to retrieve the war gear inside, until all the Wolf Coats, Surt and Wulfhelm were equipped with the most magnificent weapons and war gear. Grand as it was, it was still old and needed some repairs. Buckles had rotted, rivets were loose. Weapon grips needed to be tightened. They packed everything in the chests and carried these back to Grimnir's house where they got to work. Trygve and Gudrod polished the brynjas in sand and soon they shone like silver. Einar fixed a broken strap on his new shield. The others did their own repairs, using supplies from Grimnir's strange, cluttered room that seemed to have something of everything lurking somewhere.

It was approaching midday when Einar heard Grimnir's dogs, Hop and Ho, barking outside.

The old man frowned. He went up the ladder to the platform on the roof. Einar and Ulrich went up after him. Below them the dogs stood on rocks beside the river, barking at something downstream.

Clambering up the path by the river was a warband.

Working fast, Einar counted twenty-four men. They moved in single file because of the narrow, twisting path. They had spears and their helmets glinted in the sun. Most had their shields on their backs but the men at the front carried theirs ready in case of attack. The red axe of Eirik was painted on them.

'It seems that you're going to find out what my escape plan is after all,' Grimnir said. 'Come. We must move fast.'

Fifty-Eight

'Should we run and hide in the barrows?' Trygve said.
'It's too late for that, lad,' Grimnir said. 'These men do not have the look of simple nosey passers-by.'

'We should go that way anyway, though,' Skar said. 'It's the only way out.'

'It's an uphill run,' Ulrich said. 'They'll catch us.'

'There's too many of them to fight,' Skar said. 'Not without losing someone ourselves.'

'There will be no need for that,' Grimnir said. 'Get the war gear and come with me.'

He hurried down the ladder. They followed him to the dining hall and threw the brynjas and weapons into the chests. Then they grabbed the shields and those with helmets put them on. They went down the next ladder to the room full of curiosities. Grimnir kept going to the narrow hall at the very bottom floor of the house. He pushed the side wall and a door opened in it. They hurried inside and Grimnir closed the door behind them. Einar found himself in a wide room with a ceiling so low they all had to bend almost double. It looked like it ran under the whole house. There was daylight coming in from slats at the top of the walls.

Grimnir led the way to the far end where they came upon two boats. They were small karfas, long and narrow with three rows of benches for rowers.

'We go down the river,' Grimnir said.

'Good idea, old man,' Ulrich said, 'but by the time we carry those out of here Eirik's warriors will be standing outside the door waiting on us.'

Grimnir went to the front of the first boat and crouched down. He pulled up a trapdoor in the floor and daylight flooded up from below. Looking down, they saw that it opened into the space under the house created by the wooden columns that held the ground floor level over the uneven rocky riverbank. Directly under the trapdoor a ditch had been dug in the ground. It sloped from ground level, through the riverbank and into the river.

'It's like a slipway for a ship,' Einar said.

'He's a clever one,' Grimnir said. Einar was unsure if there was sarcasm in the old man's voice. 'Choose a boat.'

They put the chests into the karfas and divided themselves between them.

'Now we wait for the right moment,' Grimnir said.

'How will we know when that is?' Sigurd said.

The sound of splintering wood came from the other side of the wall. Eirik's warriors were breaking their way through Grimnir's door.

'That time is now,' the old man said.

He pulled the nose of the karfa to the edge of the trapdoor and lined it up with the makeshift slipway below, then climbed in. Sigurd, Kari, Starkad and the two boys clambered in behind him. Skar went to the stern and shoved while the others shuffled their bottoms to help the boat on its way. Skar jumped in as the boat tipped up. It dropped through the hole in the floor into the slipway and slid down into the river.

The rest hauled the other boat to the trapdoor then Einar, Ulrich, Wulfhelm, Affreca, Rekon and Roan clambered into it. Surt heaved it from behind then jumped in. The boat tipped up and dropped through the hole just as Eirik's warriors smashed through the door behind them.

The karfa slid down the steep slope, picking up speed as it went. At the bottom it shot into one of the deep pools in the river, sending up a huge splash in all directions. The prow dipped under the surface of the water but it popped straight up again.

There were paddles in the bottom of the boat. Everyone grabbed one. The strong flow of the swollen river took the boat straight away and it shot sideways. Wiping water from his eyes, Einar looked around and saw that the first boat had turned around and was heading for the edge of the pool, those in it using their paddles to drive it forwards as well as the current.

Cries of alarm came from the riverbank and they knew Eirik's warband had spotted them.

Everyone in Einar's boat dug their paddles in on the right side, turning the boat so it pointed downstream. The first boat had already disappeared from sight over the edge of the pool. The powerful flow of the river shoved the karfa forwards. They came to the edge of the pool. Einar had only a moment to see they were at the top of a series of steep drops, the river falling across cascades, rocks and pools at an incline that was both dizzying and terrifying.

Then the gushing water shoved them over the edge and

they were rushing downwards, sliding over the rocks, their momentum aided by the green slime that coated the river bottom, gaining ever more speed as they went.

Eirik's men rushed towards the riverside. Some threw their spears but the boats were going too fast to hit. Einar just had time to recognise Atli standing on the riverbank, his mouth open, roaring in dismay as the karfa shot past.

In moments they were on down the river and out of sight. The paddles were of no use now. Everyone in the boats dropped them and held onto the sides for all they were worth as the karfas bounced and bucked, shooting down the rapids and over the waterfalls. Several times there came a teeth-rattling bang as the bottom of the boat smashed hard into a rock beneath. Each time Einar was sure the boat would split apart and spill them all into the running water. Then they really would be in trouble. Tumbling over the rocks unprotected by the hull of the boat their bones would be ground to pieces in moments. The karfa survived, however.

The two boats carried on down the river, leaving Grimnir's house and Eirik's warriors well behind them. As they got further down the valley their descent became less steep and they were able to gain some control over the karfas again.

When Einar judged they were about halfway down the river between Grimnir's house and Halgerd's farm they rounded a bend and below saw the river flowing into a wide pool. Beside it was a herd of tethered horses. Three of Eirik's warriors stood guard over them. They could only be the horses of the warband they had just escaped from, left when the climb up the riverside became too steep to safely ride up.

Skar and the others in the first boat were already in the pool and digging their paddles into the river, driving themselves towards the water's edge. In moments Einar's boat splashed into the pool as well and they paddled for the riverbank as well.

The boats had arrived so fast the men guarding the horses were still grabbing their weapons and shields when Skar was jumping out of the lead karfa. He had on his helmet from the mound, a shield in one hand and sword in the other. As the boat ground into the shale at the edge of the river Sigurd, Kari and Starkad were already armed and right behind him. As the second boat headed after them, Einar scrabbled for his own shield and sword.

Eirik's men raised their shields and crouched into a defensive stance. Skar barrelled straight into them. In one fluid movement he swept his shield sideways, knocking two of their spears out of the way, then pulled his shield back before him, dipped his shoulder and did a sort of skip step the way Einar had seen him go at Affreca in the arming tent in Tunsberg.

The big man smashed into the man in the middle of their shield line. His weight and power sent the man sprawling backwards. He had not had time to lace his helmet and it slewed round over his eyes as he fell over. Skar stepped into the gap he had opened in the shield line. He slashed his sword down at an angle. The blade caught the man on his right behind the calf muscle of his right leg. It sheared through flesh, muscle and bone, severing the man's lower leg. As he toppled over Skar was already twisting toward the man on his left, who was also turning to try to put his shield between the two of them.

Skar pulled his sword back up and drove it into the warrior's now exposed back. The man cried out, his back arching as the point of Skar's blade erupted from his chest. Kari stepped over the man who had lost his foot and finished him off with a cut to the neck. Sigurd and Starkad killed the third man while he was still lying on his back, struggling to fix his helmet so he could see again.

Einar's boat scrunched into the gravel at the riverside. They all jumped out but there was no need for their help.

'You didn't leave much for us to do,' Kari said to Skar.

'I didn't need you to do much,' Skar said. 'The one in the middle was too small to be in a shield line. They were all dead men as soon as they tried to form one.'

He shot a glance at Affreca from the shadows of his helmet visor. She looked away.

Einar looked down and saw the helmet of the warrior Skar had knocked over had rolled away from his face now. His dead eyes stared up into the sky. The terror of his final moments was still etched on his face. He was a slight lad, perhaps only fifteen or sixteen winters old. The other two were not much older. They were not much more than boys. That was probably why they had been left to look after the horses.

'We'll ride from here,' Grimnir said. 'Take a horse each and scatter the rest. The others will be coming back down the path soon.'

The Wolf Coats, Surt and Wulfhelm pulled the war gear from the chests. They donned the shining brynjas and buckled sword belts over them. They slung their shields over their backs. Then they fastened their wolf pelts around their shoulders.

As they prepared, a column of black smoke began rising into the sky from up the river.

'It looks like Atli is burning your house, Grimnir,' Ulrich said.

Grimnir sighed. 'Well, at least they're not burning us. Keep your wolf heads down, please. Let the folk see your helmets. It will inspire them.'

Einar looked around. They were indeed a sight to behold. Their brynjas gleamed in the sunlight. Skar's helmet encased his head, the visor covered the top half of his face and the bottom was sheathed in a scarf of chainmail that flowed from the edge of the helmet to his shoulders all around his neck. The nose guard of Ulrich's helmet came right down to his chin. The helmets of the others were equally as magnificent and shone in the sun like silver. None of their faces could be seen.

'You look like the heroes of old,' Grimnir said. 'Like our great ancestors returned to life. Let's ride.'

Fifty-Nine

Once mounted, Grimnir led them away from the riverside to a sidetrack that headed perpendicular to the flow of the stream. They rode on as it joined a wider track then into the middle of a small village. As their horses turned and wheeled amid the square of buildings, Grimnir called out to the folk who lived there.

'Folk of Hringby,' he said in a loud voice. 'Follow us. Rognvald Eiriksson is coming with his warriors. We must make our stand against him.'

The villagers gathered around, amazement on their faces at the sight of the mounted men in their gleaming war gear.

'Grab whatever weapons you have,' Grimnir said. 'If you have no spear bring a spade. If you have no sword bring a pitchfork. Make for the village at Frodisborg. We will fight there for the return of our rights. We will make our stand for our freedom from tyrants like Eirik Bloody Axe.'

A few cheers rose from the gathered people.

Grimnir kicked his heels into the flanks of his horse and galloped back out of the village. The others followed. The old man led them on down the track, passing through several more villages and repeating his call for action. At each one Einar could see the upturned faces of the people, their expressions of admiration at his shining war gear and the looks of something else that crept into them. It was a combination of hope and expectation.

At last they rode back into Halgerd's farm on the edge of the village at Frodisborg. As they passed by the farmstead Einar noticed there were a group of people gathered in the yard. He called to the others and they rode into the farm. As they dismounted, Einar saw the people were gathered around the decapitated body of a man. His severed head lay on the ground a few paces away.

Einar pulled off his helmet and approached the crowd. They were a mixture of farm workers and folk from the nearby village at Frodisborg.

'There has been murder here,' a woman said. 'Rognvald is to blame.'

'Who is it?' Einar said, nodding at the corpse.

'It's Regin Vifilsson,' one of the farmhands said.

'Where is Halgerd?' Einar said. He felt a sinking feeling in his stomach.

Several of them glanced towards one of the farm outbuildings.

'She's in the barn,' the woman said. 'But I wouldn't go in there—'

Einar pushed his way through the knot of people and hurried over to the barn. The door was open and even before he entered he could smell the iron-like stench of blood. Gritting his teeth, he took a deep breath and went in.

Halgerd was naked. Her body was hung upside down by a rope thrown over one of the rafters of the barn above. Her skin was white as milk. Her throat was cut across by a wide gash and all the blood in her body had emptied into a dark brown pool beneath her. Flies buzzed above it. Some was splashed across the walls. Another man, Einar presumed it was her other brother, hung beside her. Like her he was naked and like her he was dead. Both their dead eyes were wide open and staring, their faces frozen in twisted masks of anguish.

A man was sitting on the barn floor against the wall. His clothes were torn and he had been beaten up. His shoulders were slumped and he hung his head.

'I am sorry,' he said, looking up. 'This is all my fault. I thought if I told them what they wanted they would let us all live in peace.'

Einar recognised Thorketil, the one who had been so against fighting Rognvald at the Thing the previous day. He walked over to the hanging bodies. Looking up, Einar saw that the backs of both their heels had been sliced on either side. The ropes that suspended them had been fed through the wounds, behind the Achilles tendons and out the other side. The agony as they hung, their body weight slowly pulling the tendon away from the bone, must have been appalling.

'This is Edwin's work.'

Einar turned and saw Wulfhelm had entered the barn behind him.

'I've seen him do it once before,' the Saxon said. 'It's how he makes people give him information they don't want to tell him. The pain is indescribable. Even the strongest of men cannot hold out. Edwin often talked about how one day he will do it to his brother, Aethelstan.'

Einar looked at the once-beautiful face of Halgerd, now ravaged by pain and frozen by death. He felt a swirling turmoil of emotion within him. He did not know whether to cry or scream. Instead he clenched his teeth together, sucking heavy breaths in through his nose.

'I see now that Rognvald is not someone we can trust,' Thorketil said. 'We cannot bargain with him. We cannot reason with him. We must fight him. It is our only choice.'

Einar looked at him. His upper lip curled into a snarl.

'It's a pity it took this to happen for you to see that,' he said.

A small cry of dismay made them turn to the door again. Grimnir had entered. He was looking up at the corpse of Halgerd. Einar could see the shock and sadness etched on the old man's face.

'The poor child,' Grimnir said, his voice cracking. Einar saw tears sparkle in his eyes.

Then he swallowed and looked at Wulfhelm, then at Einar.

'She wanted her Odal rights back,' he said. His tone had changed. Now it had a hardness. 'It's too late for her now but not for the other people of Gandvik. Not for the rest of the free folk of Norway. Let this terrible deed put fire in our bellies, determination in our minds and take the pity from our hearts.'

He turned and left the barn. Einar took one last look at Halgerd then he and Wulfhelm followed. They joined the others, mounted their horses and rode to the Thing Mound and dismounted.

A group of men were working on the old fort. Berg the head man was one of them. The animal fodder had been taken out. The holes in the palisade of the borg had been replaced with newly felled and sharpened timbers.

'Preparing for battle, Berg?' Grimnir said.

'So you've returned to us, Grimnir?' Berg said, walking

over to join them. 'And who are these men with you who look like great warriors from the olden times? For a moment I thought you had come back to us accompanied by Sigurd the Volsung and his nephew Sinfjotli or perhaps even King Frodi.'

'These men are Odin's own warriors,' Grimnir said. 'They are here to help us.'

'Help us to do what?' Berg said.

'To fight Rognvald,' Grimnir said.

Berg scowled.

'We held a Thing here yesterday, Grimnir,' he said. 'Folk are too scared. Rognvald is a tyrant but there are not enough folk willing to stand up to him.'

'Yet you repair the fort?' Ulrich said.

'We might need somewhere to take refuge when Rognvald comes,' Berg said. 'I've been trying to organise some of the men to put up some sort of fight but we just don't have enough people.'

Grimnir pulled a horn from his leather shoulder bag.

'Let's see if we can't change a few minds,' he said and led the way to the top of the Thing Mound. Once at the top he began to blow the horn.

Before long, summoned by the horn and by the news of the arrival of the strangers, the villagers had gathered around the mound.

'Is this about fighting Rognvald?' a man in the crowd said. 'We talked about this yesterday. Like Thorketil said, we can't fight him.'

'I was wrong,' the voice of Thorketil came from below. He now stood at the foot of the mound too. 'I now understand what Rognvald is really like. We must stand up to him.'

'And what of your talk yesterday?' Berg said. 'You said Rognvald's warriors would slaughter us all.'

'All the more reason to fight, then,' Thorketil said. 'If we're going to die anyway I'd rather go down fighting than on my knees pleading to be spared.'

'I'm with you,' another man in the crowd beside him said.

'And me,' another said. 'Look what the bastards did to Halgerd and Ottir.'

Others joined in and the noise swelled through the crowd. Unlike the day before, all were now on the same side. As the cries died away Berg turned back to Grimnir.

'So we will fight then, Grimnir,' he said. 'But how? We're just farmers. We know nothing of how battles are fought.'

The old man laid a hand on Ulrich's shoulder.

'This man will teach you,' he said. 'He knows the craft of war. With him and his men on our side we will soon give Rognvald a bloody nose.'

Einar could not see Ulrich's face beneath his helmet but he had no doubt the little Wolf Coat was scowling or rolling his eyes.

'I'd like to give him more than a bloody nose,' Ulrich said.

'Then tell us what we must do,' Berg said. 'Please. We need your knowledge.'

Ulrich nodded.

'Let's take a walk round this village of yours,' he said. 'Lesson one is that it's always best to survey the ground before going into battle on it. Tell me what you were planning and I'll see if we can't make it as effective as we can.'

As the sun travelled across the sky the Wolf Coats organised the village folk. They split them into companies.

They instructed them how they should form lines of spearmen and taught them how they could make up for their lack of shields by using sticks to parry blows. They drew up plans for what they should do if Rognvald's men attacked from the fjord or from the land.

All the while other men from other villages and outlying farms kept on arriving to add to their forces.

Einar could see how the locals, many of them men a lot older than him, looked on him and the other Wolf Coats with expressions of admiration. Their every word commanded the men's attention. With a swell of pride he knew these men who he hardly knew would follow him to the gates of the kingdom of Hel if he asked them to.

He also saw how poorly they were equipped. Some had rusty old swords, more had spears but many had just brought the tools from their barns; hoes, billhooks and shovels. None had mail or helmets. Only a few had shields. He wondered how they would fare against Rognvald's men; practised warriors with well-used weapons clad in the best of war gear.

Some had brought their hunting bows.

'Can any of you hit a rabbit at about forty paces?' Ulrich said.

Ten men and three young lads raised their hands.

'Then you'll find hitting a man at that distance a lot easier,' he said. 'Affreca, form these men into our band of archers.'

They worked on well into the evening until darkness fell. Then, long into the night, around campfires, they talked on, repeating the details of their plans of what to do if Rognvald attacked from the fjord, from the woods or from the mountain.

At dawn they were all up and back to work again, preparing for the coming battle.

In the mid-afternoon they took a break. Everyone sat on the ground before the Thing Mound as their wives and daughters brought out ale and hunks of bread and cheese.

'You know what?' Skar said, looking around at folk gathered in the meadow around them. 'There's enough of them now to give Rognvald a fight.'

Ulrich grunted.

'They'll still lose,' he said. 'Farmers against trained warriors? They'll be slaughtered.'

As they munched on their food a boy came running up from the jetty and through the village. Einar recognised him as the boy who had been minding the horses the day before.

'Ships!' the boy cried. 'There are many ships in the fjord. They're sailing this way.'

Skar turned to Ulrich.

'Rognvald is coming,' he said.

'Shit,' Ulrich said. 'I'd planned to be well away from here before he got here.'

'But what about your oath to help these people?' Einar said.

'I just pledged to teach them what to do in battle,' he said. 'I was quite clear I was not prepared to die with them.'

'It looks like we don't have much choice now,' Skar said.

He got to his feet.

'To your positions,' he shouted.

Sixty

Rognvald's four Drakkar surged up the fjord toward Frodisborg. Each one had a ravenous, snarling beast carved on its prow. Their sails were full and their oars undulated like the wings of dragons.

The longships' shallow drafts allowed them to ground on the banks of the fjord. As the boats stopped moving the ranks of warriors clad in war gear on the rowing benches got up, lifted their red-axe painted shields, their spears, swords and axes and swarmed over the sides.

Their visored helmets glittered in the afternoon sun and their burnished mail coats shone. With the discipline of trained warriors, Rognvald's men formed close ranks, locked their shields and advanced towards the village.

Moving into the houses they fanned out. They were ready for battle, alert for any movement or sign of attack.

None came. The longhouses around them were silent. Ducks and chickens wandered around but it seemed these were the only living things in the village.

Rognvald, his long black hair and beard flowing around his shoulders and chest from beneath his helmet, stepped off the last ship and stalked into the village. In his right hand he bore an unsheathed, broad-bladed, ivory and gold hilted sword. He glared around at the surrounding silent houses with eyes that blazed with anger, a sneer of undisguised contempt curling his lips.

'They've run away,' he said. 'The cowards.'

Rognvald spat. His chest heaved and his breath hissed through his teeth as he tried to contain the rage that boiled within him.

'I wanted a fight,' he shouted at the empty houses. 'Or even just a slaughtering.'

His men that were nearest him took surreptitious steps further away.

'Cowards,' Rognvald said again, swiping his sword at the air, then sliding it back into its scabbard. He folded his arms and looked around once more. His gaze fell on the Thing Mound and the crumbling fortification beside it that stood beyond the village.

'That old borg,' he said, pointing at the fort. 'They're probably hiding in there. Come on.'

The warband advanced through the quiet village. The track from the fjord continued on out of the village towards the mound and the fort. Another track that ran perpendicular to it met it in the clear space in the centre of the village.

The war party had just passed where the tracks met when shouts of pain and surprise came from behind them.

Rognvald turned and saw five of his men at the very rear falling to their knees. A bunch of villagers stood behind them, bloodied pitchforks in their hands. They must have been lurking in one of the empty houses then run out when his men had passed by to stab them in the back.

He howled an incomprehensible roar and ripped his

sword back out of its sheath, pointing it towards the rear. His warriors turned around and saw what had happened.

'Kill them,' Rognvald yelled.

The villagers turned tail and began sprinting away as fast as they could back towards the fjord. Rognvald's men at the back, roaring and shouting, ran after them.

Perhaps he caught a glimmer of movement from the side of his eye, but some sort of warrior's sixth sense made Rognvald look skyward. A group of men were on the thatched roof of the longhouse to his right. Before he could react, they flung one end of a large fishing net across to another band of men standing on the roof of the house opposite.

The other men caught the net. For an instant it was stretched above, crossing the span between the rows of houses. There was no time to shout a warning before they dropped it.

Shouts of consternation erupted as the warriors around him found themselves enveloped in the tangling folds. More villagers poured out of the houses presumed empty on both sides. They grabbed the ropes of the net and swept it closer around the contingent of warriors caught in it. Others hauled one end of the rope as though they were trying to drag a huge shoal of fish ashore.

The captured warriors roared in fury as they were compressed together. Shields collided and weapons tangled in the ropes of the net as the men found themselves crushed. More men rushed from the houses, brandishing weapons. Not swords and spears but shovels, pitchforks, knives and lumps of wood. They laid into the entangled warriors, stabbing, slashing and beating through the webbing.

The warriors around Rognvald struggled to retaliate but every movement drew the net tighter. They could neither swing their weapons nor raise their shields to defend themselves. A couple of them stumbled and their combined weight dragged the others down too. In a jumble of men and clatter of weapons they collapsed to the ground.

The villagers fell on them with enthusiasm, raining down blows, stabs and kicks at their prone foes. Shouts of pain and frustration came from the fallen warriors amid the rattling of mail and the crack of breaking bones.

Trapped in the middle of it all, Rognvald screamed with rage. He thrashed and kicked in all directions, heedless of the damage he was doing to his own men around him. In moments he cleared enough room for himself to move. He released his magnificent sword hilt, drew a knife from his belt and began sawing at the tough, thick ropes that made up the net. After several moments frenzied cutting, it parted. Despite the blows that rained down on him he kept cutting until there was a hole big enough for him to get out.

Rognvald took up his sword and struggled to his feet through the gap in the net. He drove his weapon upwards into the nearest villager, gutting the man from navel to chest. As he fell, Rognvald withdrew his blade and hacked sideways at the villager beside him, connecting with his neck and taking his head clean off his shoulders. A fountain of crimson blood erupted from the severed neck as the man's body collapsed to its knees.

Rognvald inhaled deeply through his nose, relishing the stench of hot, freshly-spilt blood. Others of his men were cutting themselves from the net. In a matter of moments they would all be free.

His warband was split in two. Half of them were still chasing the first three villagers, oblivious to what had happened behind him. The rest had frozen, taken by surprise by the trap that had snared their leader. Seeing Rognvald out of the net, these men now ran towards him.

The villagers attacking the net turned and fled, running in all directions. The incensed warriors who had been in the net ran after them.

Rognvald was about to do the same when there came a whooshing noise followed by thuds and a chorus of shouts of surprise and pain. Four of Rognvald's men collapsed to the ground, pierced all over by arrows.

Another volley of arrows rained down, wounding two more men. Everyone looked around, desperate to see where the archers were.

A third wave of arrows came. This time Rognvald saw they were coming over the houses to the left. Someone was on the other side, shooting arrows up into the air so they fell in an arc into the middle of the village.

'They're behind those houses,' Rognvald said.

His men put their shields above their heads to protect themselves from any more falling arrows. Almost as soon as they did so five archers ran out from behind a building near the meadow. They unleashed their bows, sending five arrows straight down the track at waist height. The five warriors nearest, their shields over their heads, could not protect themselves. The arrows drilled into their stomachs and thighs, tearing through their leather breeches and bursting the mail rings of their brynjas.

The archers turned and scrambled back behind the building.

Rognvald whirled around, gnashing his teeth. Moments before he had led a disciplined force, advancing in step, shield to shield. Now his men were in chaos. They were running in all directions, chasing villagers who scattered this way and that.

This was no accident.

'Stop,' he shouted. 'It's a trap.'

Intent on blood, his men were too incensed to pay heed. Rognvald's warband dissolved around him into a disorderly mob.

More villagers attacked. They seemed to be coming from everywhere at once. They ran out of the houses, came from the trees outside the village and ran from the meadow where the mound and fort were. Some had swords, some had spears but most had farming tools, hammers or woodcutting axes. They charged straight into Rognvald's men and then everyone was fighting.

Rognvald's fury boiled over. He cut down villagers to his right and left, venting his frustration. His men had good war gear but their real strength came when they worked together. If they formed a shield wall then they would advance as one and mow down all these peasants like reapers harvesting wheat but this was more like a mass brawl than a battle. Men struggled with each other hand to hand, some wrestled each other on the ground. A warrior beside Rognvald arched his back and cried out as a villager stabbed him in the back with a billhook, then ran away.

Rognvald pulled a horn from his belt and blew on it. Some of his men disengaged to rally around him but most were too caught up fighting man-on-man struggles to be able to.

On the other side of the village centre Rognvald saw another band of eight men in war gear like his own, except theirs was like something from ancient times. Their helmets were full faced and shone with gold and silver. They fought together in formation, shields side by side, advancing along the track in step, cutting a bloody swathe through his own men. He saw the wolf pelts around their shoulders and realised these must be the úlfhéðnar everyone, including himself, had been hunting. As he saw his men falling before them Rognvald felt a chill as for the first time that day doubt that he would win this fight crept into his heart.

Then another horn was blowing. At the far end of the sidetrack into the village a new line of warriors was advancing. They too marched with shields locked. Nineteen of them were painted with the red axe of Rognvald's father and the other six each had a white cross. The warrior in the middle too wore a wolf pelt around his shoulders. It was Atli, Edwin and the rest of the warriors he had left them with that morning.

As they advanced, they cut down the villagers in the same way the Wolf Coats were killing Rognvald's warriors. They freed Rognvald's men from their personal battles as they went and his warriors joined their line, strengthening their numbers every time.

'Form a shield wall,' Rognvald said to the men around him. They came together and joined their shields. Then they too began to advance.

With Atli and the others advancing from one end of the village and Rognvald, his own shield wall swelling with every villager they killed, advancing from the other, it was not long before they commanded the whole middle of the village. They met in the space in the centre, catching a few unfortunate locals between them and cutting them to pieces. Then they joined forces and turned to face towards the track that led to the fort where the Wolf Coats and the remaining villagers stood.

Rognvald's previous doubts faded. His forces had been bloodied but they had much better war gear than the locals, were better fighters and now they had regrouped it would not be long before they finished the villagers off.

A third horn sounded, this time coming from one of the Wolf Coats, a little man who could only be Ulrich Rognisson. He blew three short blasts followed by a long one, then repeated it. It was clearly a pre-arranged signal.

'Run,' someone shouted. 'Get to the fort.'

The locals turned and sprinted out of the village. The Wolf Coats broke formation and followed.

'After them,' Rognvald shouted to his men. 'Kill every last one of them.'

Sixty-One

Einar slung his shield over his back and ran for the fort. His mail and helmet were heavy but the thought of the enemy coming behind him made him go as hard as he could. The others were doing the same. All around him men were screaming and yelling.

They were perhaps a hundred paces away from the gates of the borg. Einar glanced over his shoulder. He saw Rognvald's men were right behind them.

Looking forward again he saw Affreca and her group of archers standing in a line in front of the gates of the fort. Their bows were drawn. He and the others ran around them. As soon as they passed, the archers unleashed a volley of arrows straight into Rognvald's men coming behind. Those in the centre of their line took the brunt of the attack. Seven of them went down, pierced by arrows. Some of their fellows, charging behind them, tripped over the bodies and went sprawling face first towards the ground.

Affreca shouted an order and the archers swung their bows right. They sent another flight of arrows at Rognvald's men on that side of the line then another at those on the left.

Men fell at both ends of the line. It was enough to make the others halt their headlong charge. Rognvald's warband regrouped, closing the gaps the casualties caused by the arrows had opened in their lines. With clacks of wood they joined their shields to create a defensive wall.

While they did this the last of the villagers and the Wolf Coats ran into the fort. Affreca and her archers turned and followed them. With a screech of rusted old iron hinges, they slammed the wooden gates of the fort shut.

Einar, panting to recover his breath, looked around. Apart from the Wolf Coats, Surt and Wulfhelm had made it back as well. Grimnir and the two boys, Trygve and Gudrod had been in the fort all the time, waiting to slam the gate when the others came back. Berg the head man stood, clutching a notched old sword. Thorketil was there too but not all the village men and farmers had made it. A quick count told him that there were perhaps forty of them inside the fort. The others must have been either dead or, unable to make it to the fort, had fled into the surrounding countryside. It was still enough to defend the little borg, though.

'To the ramparts,' Ulrich said.

The defenders streamed up to the top of the ramparts and took up positions behind the newly repaired palisade. As Einar reached the wall of wooden stakes the first of Rognvald's warriors were arriving outside. The first to rush into the ditch screamed out in pain, falling this way and that as their feet were impaled by sharpened sticks planted in the ground and covered by straw by the villagers earlier in the day at Ulrich's direction.

Alerted to the danger, the warriors coming behind leapt over the bottom of the ditch and scrambled up the rampart. They hurled themselves at the palisade, jabbing spears and swiping swords at the defenders above. The men behind the wall of wooden stakes slashed and stabbed back.

One of Rognvald's men shoved his spear at Einar. Einar ducked backwards to avoid it. This was what the attacker intended as it gave the man beside him, shield on his back, time to jump up and get his hands on the top of the palisade. He began to haul himself up.

Einar slashed the spear point aside, cleaving the shaft with his blade, then hacked down at the man climbing. His sword embedded itself in the top of the wooden stakes as the severed fingers of the warrior's right hand fell into the fort. He cried out, fell off the palisade and tumbled back down the rampart.

The other warrior dropped his now useless spear shaft and went to draw his sword. Einar yanked his sword back out of the wood. He leaned over the top of the palisade, hacking down at the man below. His sword caught the warrior across the top of his head, knocking his helmet sideways and making him stagger. A villager standing to Einar's left stabbed his pitchfork at him, the second and third prongs catching the warrior at the base of his neck in the gap between his helmet and mail shirt. The farmer, teeth clenched and eyes wide, drove the fork deep down into the man's body. He dropped to his knees then fell back down the rampart. The pitchfork, still embedded in the dying warrior, was wrenched from the grasp of the farmer.

Another warrior coming up the rampart hurled his spear. The farmer was still looking at his empty hands when the spear hit him and went right through his neck. Choking, he fell backwards off the rampart and into the fort.

The man who had killed him drew his sword and charged up the rest of the rampart. Einar swung at him but he ducked under his shield and Einar's blade hit that. The attacker came out from his shield's cover and swiped up at Einar, who dodged his blow. Einar stabbed at him but the warrior parried his blow.

Another of Rognvald's men sprinted up the rampart and jumped up to grasp the top of the palisade. With the defender beside Einar dead and the next man along also busy fending off attackers there was no one there to stop him. In another moment he had scrambled up and was pulling himself over the top of the palisade. Einar turned, intending to strike him. As soon as he did the attacker beneath him lunged upwards and he had to turn back. He just managed to parry the blow that would have gouged into his chin.

The other attacker sprawled over the palisade, rose to his feet and drew his sword. Einar felt panic. He could not fight both attackers at once. As soon as he turned his attention away from either the other one would kill him.

There were two dull, wet thumps in quick succession. The warrior who had crossed the palisade cried out and toppled back out of the fort, two arrows transfixing his chest. He dropped backwards, landing on his fellow who had been engaging Einar from below. Both tumbled down the rampart into the ditch.

Einar glanced over his shoulder and saw that Affreca had marshalled the archers in a circle in the middle of the fort, facing outwards.

On the opposite rampart, one of the defenders fell backwards, tumbling down into the fort, his face opened from chin to forehead in a massive wound. At the gap on the rampart he left, one of Rognvald's warriors clambered onto the top of the palisade. One of Affreca's archers shot him and he fell back off.

The scene was repeated all around the rampart. As soon as an attacker appeared on the palisade he was shot down again by arrows.

Einar stepped sideways, trying to cover both his own position and the gap left by the fallen farmer. Another attacker hurled himself at the palisade and dragged himself up. As his head appeared at the top of the line of sharpened stakes, Einar stabbed him in the face, forcing the point of his sword through the eyehole of his helmet visor. The man screamed as a sheet of blood gushed from under his visor then he dropped back off the palisade.

'There's too many of them,' Berg yelled. He was panting and his tarnished old sword now had more notches in the blade.

'Keep killing them and you'll even things up,' Skar said.

Einar looked around again. All around the rampart men were fighting. The farmers drove their long-shafted pitchforks down at Rognvald's warriors below, stabbing and piercing their mail or swinging shovels that cleaved helmets and skulls or smashed bones under mail. The Wolf Coats stabbed and hacked with practised, deadly blows. As soon as any attacker did manage to get on top of the palisade he was shot by Affreca or one of her archers. The ditch at the bottom of the rampart outside was filling up with corpses, as others of Rognvald's men dragged unconscious injured friends away from the fort and out of harm's way.

Einar counted the bodies of five defenders lying at the bottom of the rampart inside the fort where they had rolled down from the palisade, but they were holding the attack. He felt a thrill in his heart. Perhaps they could hold out. Perhaps they would prevail after all.

Excited shouting came from further along the rampart. Einar turned and saw a group of men coming from the direction of the village. They were Rognvald's warriors and they were pushing a heavy farm wagon they must have taken from either Halgerd's farm or somewhere in the village. Atli was directing them.

As they got closer, other men joined them and soon the cart was trundling across the grass, heading for the fort at an ever increasing speed.

'Affreca,' Ulrich shouted. 'Get some of those archers up here.'

Affreca and two of the bowmen scrambled up onto the rampart. They began sending arrows at the men pushing the wagon. They managed to drop two of them before the wagon crossed the meadow. Then the warriors shoving it from behind heaved and let it go. The wagon trundled on, its own weight and momentum carrying it forward to smash into the gate of the fort.

The heavy gate rattled and bucked under the impact, but it held. Rognvald's warriors rushed forward to pull it back again. Seeing what was happening, many of the others attacking the ramparts turned away and ran to help their comrades with the wagon. The archers shot three more of them down as they pulled the wagon away from the gate and back a distance across the meadow.

Then they all shoved it again. The wagon rolled forwards once more. It crashed into the gate again. The front of the wagon bed shattered into splinters. Again the gate did not open but the impact of the wagon was met by an ominous, loud crack, heard by both the defenders inside the fort and the attackers outside.

Rognvald's men rushed forward to pull the wagon back again. They drew it away and more of them joined the effort, abandoning their attempts to attack the ramparts. This time they did not let go but kept pushing, pumping their legs and heaving with their shoulders, driving the wagon right into the gate of the fort.

The wagon disintegrated into a tangled mass of splintered wood but it had done its work. With a tremendous crash, the rotted old wood of the gate gave way. It tore away from its rusted hinges and toppled backwards into the fort.

Skar leapt down from the rampart and ran to the broken gate. Starkad followed him. Rognvald's men were scrambling over the wreckage of the wagon to get to the now open entrance. Skar chopped down the first man through with a mighty stroke of his sword. Starkad impaled the next man on his spear. As fast as they fell, however, others rushed to replace them.

Einar was going to run to help them when the rest of Rognvald's men attacking the rampart renewed their assault. He and the rest of the men defending the rampart had to stay where they were or be stabbed in the back by men coming over the palisade.

Affreca ran back down to join the rest of the archers in the middle of the fort.

'Form a line,' she shouted. 'Face the gate.'

Big as he was, Einar knew Skar could not hold the gate alone. Many of Rognvald's men were now abandoning their attack on the ramparts and swarming towards the breached entrance. Einar shoved a man who was climbing the palisade off and turned around to check what was going on.

Skar gutted another man coming through.

'Skarphedin,' Affreca shouted. 'Get out of the way.'

Skar looked over his shoulder then threw himself to the ground.

The line of archers let fly a volley of arrows. The nearest men struggling through the debris at the gate were all mown down.

'Again,' Affreca commanded.

Another storm of arrows shot into the men trying to get to the broken gate. Another line of them fell.

'Forward,' Affreca said. The archers rushed a few steps closer to the gates and unleashed another shower of arrows. The second line of men trying to breach the gate went down. Now no attacker in the breached gate was on his feet.

'Forward,' Affreca said again. The bowmen moved forwards again and let fly more arrows. This time warriors just reaching the back of the smashed wagon went down.

The attackers now saw the danger. Their frantic charge towards the gate stopped in its tracks and Rognvald's warriors crouched behind the cover of their shields.

A horn began blowing from the direction of the village.

The man attacking the section of the palisade Einar defended dropped back down and ran from the rampart. Einar leaned over the wooden stakes and saw the same thing was happening all around the ramparts. At the far end of the meadow, a group of warriors were gathered around the red-axe standard. It could only be Rognvald and his bodyguard. The horn sounding the retreat was coming from there.

'Rognvald takes after his father I see,' Ulrich said, looking at the same bunch of men at the end of the meadow. 'Eirik also likes to stand well back while his men do the dying for him.'

Seeing their enemies retreating, the defenders of the little fort cheered. Their cry spoke of exhaustion as much as exultation.

Einar looked around and saw their victory was just temporary. He counted only twenty defenders still on their feet and capable of fighting.

Affreca threw her bow on the ground and looked up at Ulrich.

'We've no arrows left,' she said.

Rognvald's men had pulled back about fifty paces. They stopped and turned around, joining their shields together again. There was still enough of them to completely surround the fort.

The defenders were now hopelessly outnumbered. The gate was breached. They could not hope to hold out against the next attack.

Sixty-Two

The defenders looked out over the palisade.

'What are they waiting for?' Einar said.

'Come on you bastards,' Skar was on his feet again. He shouted from the broken gate. 'Get on with it. Attack.'

Einar saw behind the ring of shields Rognvald and Atli were talking and pointing at the fort.

Then a new figure joined them. Einar had not noticed him before. He was stick thin and wore the long white robe of a religious man. His head was bald apart from a ring of long white hair that reached to his shoulders.

He looked familiar. Einar frowned, trying to remember where he had seen this man before.

Affreca walked up onto the rampart to see what was going on.

'That was an impressive movement you did with the archers at the gate,' Einar said. 'It saved us.'

'It's how my father's men sometimes had to fight the Irish,' she said. 'They were often outnumbered. I fear all we did was delay them getting in, though.'

Rognvald pushed his way through his men. Holding his shield up before him, the red axe of Eirik emblazoned on it, he walked a little way forward. When no arrows or spears came at him from the fort he lowered his shield so he could look over the top.

'You in the borg,' he said.

Berg looked at Grimnir. The old man nodded.

'What do you want?' Berg shouted back.

'You must see your position is hopeless,' Rognvald called to them. 'When I give the order my men will attack once more. Your borg will be overrun. You will all die.'

He paused for a moment to let his words sink in.

'But you don't all have to,' Rognvald went on. 'Give me what I want. Hand over Trygve and Gudrod and I'll let the rest of you walk away. They're my nephews, after all. I will take care of them.'

'We all know how you will take care of them, Rognvald,' Grimnir shouted. He now stood beside Berg at the palisade. 'You'll cut their throats. Isn't that what you're here for? Do you expect us to believe Eirik Bloody Axe, your father, has changed and will let Olaf's son grow to one day become a threat to him?'

'And I will be a threat!'

Trygve had pushed his way through the men in the fort to join the others at the palisade. 'I will kill you. I will kill King Eirik. I will take revenge for my father's death.'

Einar looked at the little boy standing on his tiptoes to see over the palisade of a doomed fort, shouting threats at the son of the king in his full war gear. He could not help but see the scene as pathetic.

Rognvald was equally unimpressed.

'Good luck with that,' he said. 'But I'm not here to talk

to children. What about the rest of you? The question you must all ask yourselves is, *am I really willing to die for this brat?*'

A murmur went around the folk huddled in the fort.

'Are we, Grimnir?' Berg said.

'What are we doing here, Ulrich?' Kari said. He spoke in a low voice so the others around would not overhear. 'We should take his offer and walk away. What do we care about Olaf's son?'

'Do you think Rognvald will keep his word?' Ulrich said. 'And Atli is out there with him, don't forget. He knows we'll kill him first chance we get. Do you think he'll let us just walk away? Do you think Eirik will just forget about us any more than he will forget about Trygve?'

Kari sighed.

'I suppose we're stuck here then,' he said.

'It's not just about the boys,' Grimnir said. 'It's about what Trygve represents. He is our hope for the future. He should rule us, not Rognvald. If we want our rights back we must fight on. Hakon will reward us.'

'Hakon? Hakon Haraldsson?' Berg looked at him like he was mad. 'Where does he come into all this?'

'Think about this,' Grimnir said. He raised his voice to make sure the rest of the people in the fort could hear him. 'Think about it all of you. Rognvald's only trying to deal with us because he's lost too many men. He's worried. We've given him a bloody nose after all.'

'But Rognvald is also right,' one of the men at the palisade said. 'If he attacks now he'll kill us all.'

'Not without losing even more men in the process,' Grimnir said.

'What difference does that make?' Berg said. 'We'll all still be dead. I am head man, Grimnir. I'm responsible for the lives of all these people. What's left of them anyway. If Rognvald will let them live then I must consider the offer.'

'No,' Thorketil said. 'Rognvald lies. He'll kill us all anyway. We can't trust him. We have to fight on.'

The others in the fort looked on Thorketil with surprise on their faces. Then they looked at each other, nodding and murmuring their agreement.

'Fight on,' one said.

'Aye,' another said.

Soon they were all shouting their assent.

Berg nodded. He held up a hand for silence and the cries died away again.

'Very well,' he said.

He turned to address Rognvald outside.

'I am Berg, the head man at Frodisborg, Rognvald,' Berg said. 'Our answer is *no.*'

Rognvald stood for a moment, then said: 'Die, then. I will show no mercy. You will be killed. Your wives and children will be killed. We will burn this village to ashes and all the villages around it. In your final moments think on how this was what you chose.'

He turned and walked back behind his warriors' shield line.

As he did so another man came out past him. It was the thin man Einar had seen before. His lank white hair blew in the breeze. He carried a small chest before him in both hands.

'I have something for Einar Thorfinnsson,' the man said. 'Can I approach in safety?'

All eyes turned to Einar.

'Isn't that your father's Galdr maðr?' Affreca said. 'He was at Avaldsnes with Eirik when we were there last.'

'Vakir,' Einar said, now recalling how he knew the man. 'Thorfinn's seiðr-worker you mean? I wonder what he wants.'

'Only one way to find out,' Grimnir said.

'Very well,' Einar shouted over the palisade. 'Approach. You won't be harmed. You have my word.'

Vakir walked over to the edge of the ditch below the rampart. He looked up. Seeing Einar at the palisade above he smiled.

'Your father, the Jarl Thorfinn sends his greetings,' Vakir said, laying one hand on the lid of the chest he carried, supporting it with his other beneath. 'I came here to tell King Eirik that his wife and family are now safe in the protection of Jarl Thorfinn in Orkney. However I sailed by the long way round. I visited Iceland on my way. I was in the company of Sigtryggr snarfari and Hallvard harðfari.'

'Those two old murderers of King Harald?' Einar heard Ulrich say. 'I thought they were dead.'

He felt his heart sink.

'Your father sends you this,' Vakir said. 'He thought if I bring you this gift from him then perhaps it would encourage you to come and visit him. He wishes to deal with you in person. It looks like there will be no need for that now as you won't escape here alive. However it's important that you see it before you die.'

He lifted the lid of the chest.

Einar froze. He felt as though time was slowing down. He could hear his own breathing but felt as though a fiery bolt of Thor had come from the heavens and struck him through the chest. He could see what lay inside the chest but his mind did not want to recognise it, to realise what it was and what it meant. His mouth dropped open then snapped shut again, the muscles at the top of his jaw clenched into tight balls.

The chest was packed with salt. Sitting in the midst of it was the severed head of his mother. Salt was matted in her grey hair, crusted on her cheeks and clogged around the butchered stump of her neck. It was a mercy that her eyes were closed.

Einar's mouth opened again but all that came out was a whine. He shook his head and blinked but when he opened his eyes again the awful sight was still there.

'She did not die quickly,' Vakir said. 'We made her pay dearly for every moment of the years she betrayed my Lord Thorfinn.'

He snapped the chest shut, then turned and walked back to Rognvald's shield line.

Einar turned away and slumped to the ground, his back to the palisade, his elbows on his knees, head hung low. The sight of his mother's severed head seemed burned into his mind. Her cold, unmoving skin that had once been so warm and filled with life. Her eyes that had twinkled with laughter, now closed and still. The lips that had kissed him so many times, now stiff and crusted with salt, never to move again.

He felt a hand on his shoulder and looked up. Affreca crouched beside him.

'That was Unn's head, wasn't it?' she said. 'I'm sorry.'

Einar opened his mouth but still no words would come.

His eyes slid past her and he saw Trygve who was also looking at him. The boy's dismay at Einar's reaction was clear.

Einar felt light-headed, as if his feet were no longer on the ground. He could hear his heart pounding. He looked upwards at the sky. Was anyone watching or were the Gods just laughing?

A strange, prickling feeling ran down his back. It felt like a cold liquid was rushing through his body instead of blood. He felt like his gums were itching. Grasping his shield he clamped his teeth on the iron rim to try to dispel the sensation. The metallic taste of the metal rim in his mouth was like that of blood.

Einar took a deep breath and clambered to his feet. He pulled the wolf's head of Bodvar's wolfskin cloak up over his helmet. A weird sensation coursed through him. The tension of battle that had fettered all his senses in a vice-like grip, the anxiety of where the next blade may strike him, the fear of defeat and death dissolved and left his heart. He looked up. The world around him seemed to be bathed in a strange ochre hue.

As his doubts and fears slid away a deep, cold rage replaced them. He no longer cared if he lived or died, but he lusted to maim, destroy and kill. To stab, to slash, to bite, to blind. To bring red slaughter on Rognvald and all his men.

Wrapping his fingers around the hilt of his sword Einar threw back his head and roared his anger at the heavens above. He jumped down off the rampart and ran out of the shattered gate of the fort.

Sixty-Three

'What are you doing?' Affreca shouted after Einar as he disappeared through the smashed entrance.

'He's throwing away his life,' Berg said.

'Maybe,' Skar said. 'But if this really is the end for us all then if I were him I'd want to take as many of those bastards with me as I could. And I'm going to do the same. Who's with us?'

The defenders of the fort hesitated, looking at each other.

'I am,' Affreca said.

'Then I have to go too,' Wulfhelm said with a sigh, though he was smiling. 'I owe you and Einar my life, so I suppose I really should.'

'I'll go too,' Thorketil said.

'The lad's right,' Grimnir said, speaking to the rest of the men in the fort.

Ulrich shot a questioning glance at Skar.

'This is a battlefield, Ulrich,' Skar said. 'I give the orders. Atli is out there. I almost got him at Tunsberg. At least today we might be able to make him pay for his betrayal.'

'Very well,' Ulrich said. 'We've given Rognvald that bloody nose. Now let's see if we can't take his whole fucking head off.'

449

The others all cheered. They all rushed down from the ramparts to the gate.

'Stay in here, old man,' Ulrich said to Grimnir. 'You and the boys wait. Get away if you can while they're busy fighting us. At least if we all die it won't be for nothing. Rognvald and Eirik still won't get what they want.'

Grimnir nodded.

'Let's go,' Skar said.

The defenders rushed out of the fort.

As he ran Einar could see many of the jaws of Rognvald's men before him drop open in surprise under the bottom of their visors. Then their training took over and they tensed, legs braced. There was a loud clack of wood and the shield wall reset.

'Form the *svinfylking*,' Skar shouted above the noise of pounding feet and clinking of mail. 'Go for Rognvald.'

The Wolf Coats fanned out into an arrowhead formation with Einar at the centre. Each man had his shield to the fore. What was left of the farmers and villagers filled in behind them.

The encircling ring of shields tightened. Those surrounding the fort came running forwards to narrow the circle around the running men instead of the borg.

As the ring tightened Einar ran harder, pounding towards the part of the shield wall in front of where Rognvald and his standard stood. He was twenty paces from the enemy. Then fifteen. Then ten. He felt like he was flying over the ground.

He looked over the rim of his shield. One of the men before him in Rognvald's shield wall was smaller than the others. He had his spear held above his head. Einar aimed at him and put his head down.

He aligned himself behind his own shield the way Skar had taught him. Left hand in the handle behind the boss, shield pulled close to his left shoulder, body half turned sideways behind the shield. Grave Giver was in his right hand, his knuckles white around the hilt. There was a loud noise in his ears that he realised was his own screaming.

At the last moment he did the swift dip-and-step movement he had seen Skar execute twice now, thrusting himself forwards with the muscles of his trailing right thigh.

Einar smashed into the shield wall. His teeth rattled together. He felt like a wave of force rippled through his left shoulder, into his spine and down his back. There was a cry and the resistance before him vanished. The man on the other side of his shield was reeling backwards, driven out of his position by Einar's impact.

It was as if everything around him slowed down. Einar saw the man fall before him, landing sprawling on his back. He adjusted his stance and stepped forward, planting his right foot on the fallen man's chest, then standing on him and driving his sword blade down into his neck.

To his left and right, Skar and Starkad powered into the hole in the shield wall Einar had made. They drove the men on either side back and sideways, using their shields first, then as the men stumbled out of position driving their swords into their bodies.

The others came behind, slashing in both directions, tearing the shield wall open and driving on through to the other side. In moments it was clear the wall could not be recovered. Rognvald's men on either side pulled away, knowing if they did not regroup themselves they would be cut down.

Einar looked up. About twenty paces further was another, smaller shield line. Most shields were painted with the red axe of Eirik but some also had the cross of the Saxons on them. Behind this line was Rognvald. Einar was close enough to see the grin fixed on the king's son's face. Whether it was glee, anger or fear he could not tell. Rognvald stood next to his merkismaðr, who bore the standard of King Eirik, the flag fluttering in the breeze above their heads. Lord Edwin stood next to them.

Seeing Einar and the Wolf Coats break through the first line, the men guarding Rognvald hurried to change positions so they now stood two deep. To get to Rognvald the Wolf Coats would have to fight through two lines of warriors.

Einar halted. The rage that boiled within him still simmered but he felt like he could think again. Charging straight into the second shield wall would just result in a quick death.

Behind him the rest of Rognvald's war party were also fast to reorganise. Those who had been on the other side of the fort rushed around the ramparts. The men on either side of the breach Einar and the Wolf Coats had torn in the first shield wall retreated to join up with the men standing before Rognvald. In moments another ring of shields was formed, this time encircling the Wolf Coats and farmers instead of the fort.

'Skjaldborg,' Skar shouted.

The Wolf Coats moved into a circle to form their own shield wall facing outwards towards the encircling shield wall. Only nine of them had shields however and they could not complete the circle. The gaps were filled by some of the farmers, ready with old spears or axes.

Einar looked around. They were completely surrounded and outnumbered perhaps five to one, maybe more.

Beyond the encircling line of shields, Einar saw Grimnir and the two boys sneaking out of the gate of the fort, unnoticed by the warriors of Rognvald. He consoled himself that if nothing else, Rognvald would still not get what he came here for.

It was cold comfort, however. The situation was hopeless. Rognvald's grin was one of glee. He had won. Einar could not even see where Vakir was. He would not get the chance to avenge his mother.

Horns were blowing. Rognvald was signalling the last attack that would end it all.

Then Einar saw that it was not Rognvald. The king's son and his men were also looking around as well to see who was blowing the horns.

At the other side of the meadow, men were streaming out of the village. They were clad in good war gear. Their helmets gleamed in the sun. Many had brynjas. Their shields were painted with many different colours. They filed out across the meadow, forming a long shield line. More and more men kept on arriving behind them.

'Who is this?' Skar said.

A standard flew above the new shield line. It was green with the white head of a stag emblazoned in white on it.

'That's the banner of Jarl Sigurd of Hlader,' Ulrich said. 'He's a long way from home. What's he doing so far south?'

As they watched, another standard was raised beside the white stag. This one was red and triangular in shape. Embroidered in black on it was the image of a bird, claws curled, beak ready to strike. As the wind caught the flag, making it flutter, it seemed to Einar as though the outstretched wings of the bird were flapping.

'The Raven Banner,' Affreca said. 'The *real* Raven Banner. It can only be Hakon.'

'Hakon has come,' Berg said. He was grinning, as if scarcely able to believe what he was seeing. 'Grimnir was right!'

'I don't know why or how he is here,' Ulrich said. 'But I have to admit that for the first time in my life I'm actually glad to see that Christ child.'

Already there were more of Hakon and Sigurd's forces than Rognvald's and behind them more men were still arriving.

Ulrich looked around at the men surrounding the Wolf Coats and the farmers. He did a full circle, sweeping his gaze across as many of them as he could.

'It seems things have changed. The question you must all now ask yourselves is,' Ulrich said, pointing his sword at Rognvald, '*am I really willing to die for this bastard*?'

Einar could see the dismay on the faces of the warriors surrounding them. He could almost smell their sudden uncertainty, confusion and fear.

Then one dropped his shield and broke from his position. He began sprinting as fast as he could away from the shield line towards the trees at the edge of the meadow. Two more followed him. A fourth went to do the same but this time the men on either side of him grabbed him to stop him running. He turned and struck one of the men holding him with his sword.

The horns blew again. A great shout went up as Hakon and Sigurd's warriors started to charge across the meadow.

Mayhem ensued. Rognvald's ring of shields disintegrated.

The meadow was full of men either running or trying to stop others from running. Those warriors who were determined to fight on were only in pockets. They stood, looking around them, bewildered.

The double line of shields guarding the king's son had collapsed like the rest of his forces but some men still stood to protect their lord.

'Go for Rognvald,' Einar yelled.

The Wolf Coats ran forwards.

'Protect your Lord,' Edwin shouted to his Saxons. 'Remember your oaths of loyalty to me.'

His men banded together in front of him. Like the disciplined warriors they were, they joined their shields again, blocking the way to Rognvald and Edwin. Aelfred stood in the middle of their line like a huge oak tree, an axe in one hand, snarling over the top rim of his shield.

Behind them, Edwin turned and ran. One of the Saxons glanced round and saw him go. He shouted a warning and the others turned and ran as well.

Aelfred stayed. It was as if he had not even noticed the others were gone.

'You,' he shouted, pointing his axe at Wulfhelm. 'I see it's you, Wulfhelm, under all that fancy foreign war gear. Come and die. Come and get the payment you deserve for betraying your lord, your God and the rest of us.'

Wulfhelm approached the big man, sword in one hand, shield in the other. For a few moments they faced each other, each one ready to strike.

Then Wulfhelm looked up into the sky.

'Good Lord!' he said, a look of surprise on his face.

Aelfred looked up.

Wulfhelm drove the point of his sword into the big man's exposed throat. He wrenched it back, unleashing a torrent of blood that sheeted the front of Aelfred's mail shirt. The big man dropped his axe and shield, both hands going to the wound as he dropped to his knees. His face was a mask of confusion.

'You always were an idiot, Aelfred,' Wulfhelm said and the big Saxon toppled sideways, dead. 'I can't believe you fell for that.'

Thorketil dodged around Rognvald's remaining men. He sprinted towards Rognvald, screaming, a spear grasped in both hands.

With little effort, Rognvald stepped out of the way of the spear point and struck Thorketil across the back of his neck. His sword blade separated the bones of Thorketil's spine and almost took his head right off. Thorketil's body fell to the ground like a stone dropped in a lake.

All across the meadow men were fighting hand to hand. Hakon and Sigurd's men were now in among the remnants of Rognvald's who struggled for their own survival.

Rognvald screamed in rage. He and the five warriors still with him charged towards the Wolf Coats.

'Shield wall,' Skar shouted once again.

They locked shields. Einar had Skar on his right and realised that the warrior to his left was Affreca. On the other side of her was Surt.

Rognvald saw the small, slight body of Affreca too. He changed the course of his charge and headed straight at her, barrelling forwards with his shield held in front of him.

Affreca just had time to brace herself before Rognvald

crashed into her shield. The impact sent her reeling backwards, falling to the ground.

Rognvald stepped into the gap she left in the shield wall. He raised his sword to strike across Einar's now exposed back.

On the ground beneath him, Affreca ripped Witch's Promise out of its sheath and drove it upwards. The blade opened the inside of Rognvald's right thigh from the midpoint right up to the top. Affreca grasped the hilt in both hands and shoved it further, driving the point right up into Rognvald's groin.

The king's son froze, howling in pain as his blood rained down, showering Affreca in gore. Einar drove his own sword into Rognvald's stomach, splitting the rings of mail and sliding into his guts beneath.

Surt swung his sword, hitting Rognvald on the neck just beneath the helmet. His head came off. Still wearing its helmet, it tumbled through the air, hit the ground, bounced once then rolled to a halt.

As Rognvald's body fell, Einar scrambled after his severed head. He sliced the laces of the helmet and ripped it off the head. Grabbing Rognvald's mane of black hair Einar held the head high in the air.

'Rognvald is dead,' he shouted. 'Rognvald is dead.'

Seeing their leader's severed head, the last of Rognvald's warriors gave up. Some ran for the trees. Others dropped their weapons and shields and raised their hands to show they would no longer fight.

It was over.

Sixty-Four

Hakon stood on the top of the Thing Mound. The sun was going down behind it, casting long shadows of him, Jarl Sigurd, Grimnir, Trygve and Gudrod, who stood alongside him.

Einar and the Wolf Coats watched from the large crowd gathered at the bottom of the mound. In the meadow behind them the work of stacking the bodies from the battle was complete. Soon bale fires would be lit and those with no one to take away their corpse for burial would be cremated.

Hakon was no longer the bored fifteen-year-old Einar had seen slouched in a chair listening to nuns singing in Jorvik. His frame had filled out in the way that often happens to those travelling between fifteen and sixteen winters of age. His long hair blew in the wind. The wispy moustache he used to have had disappeared beneath what was becoming a full blond beard. He stood tall, shoulders back, hands on hips. He wore the brynja of a warrior. At the shoulder and the left hip he was splattered with dried blood.

'I'll say this for the Christ's child,' Ulrich said. 'I never saw his brother Eirik after a battle with blood on his brynja.'

Jarl Sigurd held up his hands for quiet. An expectant

hush fell on the crowd. He was a squat, barrel-chested man with long blond hair tied behind his head.

'Folk of Gandvik,' he said. 'You have endured much at the hands of King Eirik. He treated you cruelly. He imposed his son Rognvald on you. But you have shown them both what you thought of that.'

A cheer rose from the people at the bottom of the mound.

'But a people cannot live without a king,' Sigurd said.

'We do in Iceland,' Einar said in a mutter.

Hakon stood, head bowed, hands behind his back.

'This young man is Hakon Haraldsson,' Sigurd said, sweeping a hand towards Hakon. 'Like Eirik he is a son of the great Harald Fairhair, the man who first brought all of Norway under one king. And look at him, now. If any of you are as old as I am you will remember Harald. Is this young man not the very image of the great king? Is he not like Harald returned to life?'

There were many nods and murmurs of agreement from those standing around Einar and the Wolf Coats.

'Who better to be your king than this son of Harald?' Sigurd said. 'But this son has none of the cruelty or the bad humour that runs through Eirik. What do you say? Will you support him? Will you have him as your king instead of Eirik?'

'Harald took away our rights,' a farmer in the crowd said.

'We got rid of Rognvald,' another man said. 'How do we know we're not just switching one tyrant for another?'

Sigurd looked at a loss and a little annoyed.

'I'm with them,' Einar said to Affreca, nodding in the

direction of the men who had spoken. Others in the crowd also nodded their agreement.

Hakon unclasped his hands and held them up for quiet.

'Folk of Gandvik,' he said. 'You have every right to be suspicious. You have done a great deed here today and I will show you how much I value your support. I have been talking to Grimnir here—'

He gestured to the old man standing beside him.

'I know the hardships you have been living under,' Hakon said. 'And for that reason if you support me, if you name me as your king and help us drive my brother Eirik from this land...'

He paused. Einar realised every person in the crowd was hanging on his every word.

'He's got his father's silver tongue, I'll give him that too,' Ulrich said out of the corner of his mouth.

'Then I will return the Odal rights my father took away to every freeborn person in Norway,' Hakon said.

The crowd erupted in cheering. People grinned and hugged each other. Chants of *Hakon, Hakon, Hakon,* began.

'Clever bastard,' Ulrich said. 'They'll support him now. No question about it.'

As the cheering started to die down Hakon once again held his hands up for quiet.

'You have earned this,' he said. 'Through your blood and determination. Through your courage.'

Grimnir looked down at the Wolf Coats.

Ulrich dropped his head.

'Don't mention our names,' the little Wolf Coat leader muttered. 'Please don't mention us.'

'Lord Hakon,' Grimnir said. 'We could not have resisted Rognvald without the help of these men.'

He pointed at the Wolf Coats.

Ulrich swore.

Hakon looked down, a bemused smile on his face.

'I was wondering who these men dressed in war gear like the heroes of ancient times were,' he said, gesturing for them to approach. 'Come up here and take that war gear off. The fighting is over. Now is the time to celebrate. Come on.'

Ulrich did not move.

'What's he going to do?' Skar said to him. 'Kill us in front of all these people he's trying to win over? We're they're heroes. Let's take their gratitude. There might be silver in it.'

Ulrich sighed. He nodded and the Wolf Coats, Wulfhelm and Surt clambered up the mound.

'So who are you then,' Hakon said. 'Let me guess? This is Hrolf Kraki and his band of heroes, yes? You are Bodvar Bjarki and you are Svipdagr?'

The Wolf Coats pulled off their helmets and wiped their sweat-soaked hair away from their faces.

Hakon's smile died on his lips.

'Ah,' he said. 'It's you. We meet again. I must say I'm surprised to see you here.'

'I am just as surprised to see you here too, Lord Hakon,' Ulrich said, looking sideways at Grimnir. 'How did you know the people here needed your help?'

'Kings are not the only ones who can send a war arrow,' Grimnir said, with a wink. The smile on his face was broad. 'I sent word to the north as soon as I left Tunsberg.'

'I sent my skald, Ayvind, to Norway with you,' Hakon said. He was grinning at the crowd below but Einar could tell the expression was strained. 'I don't see him. Where is he?'

'He went for a swim,' Ulrich said. 'We haven't seen him since.'

Einar recalled the poet, his previous teacher's cries as their ship had left him to drown in the northern sea.

Hakon and Ulrich looked each other in the eyes for a long moment.

'So you no longer serve Eirik?' Hakon said, after a time.

'We do not,' Ulrich said. 'But that does not mean we serve you.'

Ulrich looked right and left, then stepped closer to Hakon. He spoke in a low voice so only those around them could hear. They fixed false smiles to their lips, aware of the crowd watching them.

'I know you're a Christian,' Ulrich said. 'Does Jarl Sigurd know?'

Hakon did not reply. Ulrich raised an eyebrow.

'You *are* a Christian?' Ulrich said. 'Aethelstan would allow nothing else.'

'But he flew the Raven Banner?' Affreca said. 'The flag of Odin. And it brought victory today. Why would Odin grant victory to one who didn't believe in him?'

Ulrich folded his arms. Hakon still said nothing.

A sea of expectant faces looked up at them from the bottom of the mound.

'Jarl Sigurd is a man renowned for his support of the customs of our faith,' Ulrich said, as he smiled and waved at the crowd below. 'I wonder what he would say if he knew you followed the Christ God?'

'You dare to threaten me?' Hakon said from the corner of his mouth. His face was also fixed in a grin.

'You sent us to Eirik with a fake Raven Banner, knowing he would most likely kill us when he found out,' Ulrich said. '*After* we had won a battle for you in Scotland.'

Hakon pursed his lips.

'Fair enough,' he said. 'It seems we all have common cause here anyway.'

Ulrich shook his head.

'I'm just here because of a curse,' he said. 'Speaking of which—'

He turned to Grimnir.

'The third way of breaking a witch's curse,' Ulrich said. 'You can tell it to me now. I've done what you asked.'

The old man smiled as if he had just completed a winning move in a game of tafl.

'There is no third way,' he said. 'I made that up so you would help the folk of Gandvik.'

Ulrich's jaw dropped open.

'So we can't break the curse?' he said.

Grimnir held up his forefinger.

'If you remember,' he said. 'I said the way to break the curse, apart from killing the witch who made it, is to do a deed so selfless, so full of reckless courage that it grabs the attention of the Gods themselves. I believe you did that when you ran out of the fort today. Odin could not have failed to see that.'

Skar nodded.

'I would have been highly entertained by that fight,' he said. 'I'm sure Old One-Eye would have been too.'

'Atli got away though,' Ulrich said. 'He must pay for his treachery. Edwin got away too.'

Hakon nodded.

'I know you think we are like two horses running in different directions, Ulrich,' he said. 'But it seems to me that our goals could align. Lord Edwin has already tried to kill Aethelstan once. I doubt he will now just give up. I'd hate to think someone so dangerous to my foster father would be left to do more mischief.'

Ulrich smiled. This time the expression looked genuine.

'We úlfhéðnar wear the pelts of wolves, Lord Hakon,' he said. 'I have heard your God likes to say he and his followers are lambs. You, however, appear to me like a wolf who wears the pelt of a lamb.'

Sixty-Five

With its sail full of wind and oars beating, the snekkja sliced through the waves. It was gaining on the karfa.

The sight of land had long since slipped below the horizon. All that could be seen in every direction were the grey, choppy waters of the northern sea. For anyone to try to cross this whale road in such a little vessel as the karfa was dangerous to the point of self-slaughter. It was a clear sign of just how desperate to get away from Norway its crew were.

The seven men in the karfa bent their backs at the oars to lend more speed but it was of limited effect. With its bigger sail and many more oars the snekkja closed the distance between the two vessels with ease.

When the ships were close enough for the crews to see each other, an arrow came sailing through the air from the snekkja. It landed with a thump on the deck of the karfa, just behind the mast.

Closing the rest of the distance, the snekkja slid alongside the karfa. Its left side smashed through the oars on the right. The men at them, Edwin's Saxons, dropped the splintered oar shafts and scrambled for their weapons. Edwin himself grabbed a sword and ran to the stern.

On the snekkja, Skar hurled a grappling iron attached to a rope. It snagged the prow of the smaller boat. Surt and Skar hauled on the rope, drawing the snekkja and the karfa together.

One of Edwin's men ran towards the rope, knife drawn. Affreca rose above the side of the snekkja, bow drawn, an arrow aimed at the Saxon. He stopped, dropped his knife and stood, hands raised. Affreca smiled. None of the other five went to cut the rope. Instead they gathered in front of Edwin, forming a protective line before their lord, swords ready.

Surt and Skar held onto the rope, keeping the karfa and snekkja together.

Sigurd, Kari, Starkad, Ulrich, Wulfhelm and Einar scrambled down into the karfa. Einar, Wulfhelm and Ulrich stood, spears raised, facing Edwin and his line of bodyguards. The others began working their way from the prow, tossing everything they found over the side. Broken and complete oars, bags of food, skins of wine, ale and water, all splashed into the sea.

'You,' Edwin said to Wulfhelm through clenched teeth. 'You traitor! You were one of my men. But you killed Aelfred. You swore an oath of loyalty to me. The same one as these men who stand before me. Yet now you would kill me? Have you no honour?'

Wulfhelm looked at his former lord.

'You're right, Edwin,' he said. Behind him, Starkad and Kari were cutting the ropes used to attach the sail to the sides. 'I did swear an oath to you. And unlike you I'm a man of my word. I will not kill you, Edwin. None of us will.'

Edwin looked as equally surprised as he was delighted.

Kari and Sigurd cut the sail of the karfa down. They climbed back up into the snekkja, pulling the sail with them. The karfa had now been stripped of everything. There was no longer anything on its deck. There was no sail, no oars, no food, no water.

'Are you going to tow us back to Norway?' Edwin said. 'Does Hakon want me to join his army?'

Ulrich grunted.

'No,' he said.

'So what will happen now?' Edwin said.

'We're getting back on our ship and sail back to Norway,' Ulrich said. 'You are free to do what you want.'

Edwin screwed his face up.

'What can we do?' he said, his face a mask of confusion. 'We have no sail. No oars. No food. We'll just drift on the sea.'

'That's about it, yes,' Ulrich said. 'The currents will carry you south from here, away from the coast. There's no hope of making landfall anytime soon. You're in an open boat. The sun and the wind will burn your skin during the day. It will be freezing at night. The rain and hail may come down. With no food and no water it should take you a few days to die.'

'Which will give you plenty of time,' Einar said, 'to think about how you tortured and killed Halgerd Vifilsdottir. And the poor folk of Vidarby you slaughtered.'

'Who?' Edwin looked just as confused. 'Where?'

One of the Saxons rushed forward. Affreca loosed her bow. The arrow took him in the throat and he went over the side, landing with a splash among the other flotsam thrown from the boat by the Wolf Coats.

Affreca notched another arrow. The others got her message. No one else moved.

Covered by her bow, Ulrich, Einar, Wulfhelm and Starkad climbed back into the snekkja.

Skar cut the rope to the grappling iron and they shoved the karfa away from their own ship. Roan turned the steering oar. The wind filled the sail and they pulled away, leaving those in the little boat to their fate.

'You may as well have killed him,' Affreca said to Wulfhelm.

'Like I said, I'm a man of my word,' the Saxon said. 'I swore an oath to protect him, not to harm him.'

'And yet you've just abandoned him to a long and very certain death?' Affreca said.

'What God decides to do with Edwin is up to Him. It will be His wind and sun that brings vengeance,' Wulfhelm said, holding his hands up, palms outwards. 'Not these hands.'

Einar walked away to the prow. He gazed out at the endless, undulating waves of the ocean before him. Behind the snekkja the cries of Edwin, pleading for them to come back, were fading into the distance.

The memory of his dead mother's face surfaced in his mind again. Einar sighed and rubbed his eyes, as if trying to rub away the memory.

A hand touched his shoulder. He looked up. It was Affreca.

'Are you all right?' she said.

Einar did not reply for a moment.

'So you finally got what you wanted,' he said after a while. 'You're now one of Ulrich's úlfhéðnar.'

'And so are you,' Affreca said with a smile. 'And have you worked out yet what it is you really want?'

'Oh yes,' Einar said, looking back out to sea. 'I want to pay my father Thorfinn that visit he requested.'

About the Author

TIM HODKINSON grew up in Northern Ireland where the rugged coast and call of the Atlantic ocean led to a lifelong fascination with vikings and a degree in Medieval English and Old Norse Literature. Apart from Old Norse sagas, Tim's more recent writing heroes include Ben Kane, Giles Kristian, Bernard Cornwell, George RR Martin and Lee Child. After several years New Hampshire, USA, Tim has returned to Northern Ireland, where he lives with his wife and children.

@TimHodkinson

www.timhodkinson.blogspot.com